LAND
DIVIDED
HOUSE OF ISRAEL VOL. 2

OTHER BOOKS AND BOOKS ON CASSETTE
BY ROBERT MARCUM:

House of Israel: The Return

HOUSE OF ISRAEL

VOL. 2

LAND DIVIDED

ROBERT MARCUM

Covenant Communications, Inc.

Covenant.

Cover image © David Rubinger/Corbis

Cover design copyrighted 2003 by Covenant Communications, Inc.

Published by Covenant Communications, Inc.
American Fork, Utah

Printed in the United States of America
First Printing: September 2003

10 09 08 07 06 05 04 03   10 9 8 7 6 5 4 3 2 1

ISBN 1-59156-307-0

FOREWORD

This is a work of fiction based on historical events. I hope the reader will have a greater understanding of those events, peoples, and places, along with the effect that the return of the Jews to Palestine has had on both Arab and Jew. But, once more, that is not my main function as a writer. I wish only to entertain with a good story. For further understanding of the actual events and characters of history, please refer to the chapter notes.

LIST OF CHARACTERS

Fictional characters

Daniels family
Ephraim, *American, married to Hannah*
Hannah, *Polish émigré, married to Ephraim*
David Schwartz, *German émigré, adopted*
Elizabeth Schneider, *German émigré, adopted*
Jacob, *Sabra*
Joseph, *Sabra*
Naomi Stavsky, *Hungarian émigré*
Aaron Schwartz, *German émigré, David's older brother*
Rachel Steinman, *German émigré, living on a kibbutz in the Negev*
Zohar Mendelsohn, *German émigré, interred on Cyprus*

Rabbi Mordechai Salomon, *Sabra, Hasidic Jew*
Dr. Yehuda Messerman, *Sabra, friend of Amos Aref*
Abraham Marshak, *Sabra, rabbi's son, archaeologist*
Mithra Birkelau, *Hungarian émigré, Daniels' neighbor*

Colonel Jack Willis, *former commander of Highland Light Infantry*

Aref family
Amos, *medical doctor*
Izaat, *Amos's eldest son*
Rhoui, *Amos's second son*
Mary, *Amos's daughter*
Raoul Khatib, *Rhoui's friend*

Nonfictional characters to whom reference is made or who play a minor role, interacting with the fictional characters

Jewish
Isser Be'eri, *German émigré, replaced Sheal'tiel as leader of SHAI*
David Ben-Gurion, *Russian émigré, Head of Jewish Agency*
Shalom Dror, *German émigré, leader of the Michmash battalion*

Yis'rael Funt, *Jewish Quarter Haganah commander, replaced Holtzberg*

Avraham Halperin, *Sabra, first Jewish Quarter Haganah leader to effectively use tunnels for defense*

Binyamin Holtzberg, *Austrian émigré, Jewish Quarter Haganah commander*

David Sheal'tiel, *German émigré, leader of SHAI*

Eleazar Sukenik, *Sabra, archaeologist, discovered Dead Sea Scrolls*

Arab

Ibrahim Abou Dayieh, *commander of Jerusalem under Khader*

Tal Abu Falal, *commander in the Old City*

Abdul Khader Husseini, *commander of Haj Amin's Holy Strugglers*

Haj Amin el Husseini, *Grand Mufti of Jerusalem*

Fawzi el Kaukji, *former Ottoman officer given leadership of ALA*

Note: A Sabra is a native-born Israeli.

GLOSSARY OF TERMS AND CHARACTERS

Arab Liberation Army or ALA—Arab military force led by Fawzi el Kaukji but funded and directed by the Arab League. Because it had commanders and fighters from all the League nations it was fragmented and ineffective; each commander was more loyal to his own country than to Kaukji.

Arab League—Founded in 1945 by seven countries that surrounded Palestine. The League put the weight behind the basic demands of Palestine's Arab nationalists but arrogated to themselves the right to select who would represent the Palestinians in their councils, so long as their country was not independent. This, coupled with the deadlock within Palestine, meant that "the initiative in Palestine Arab politics . . . passed to the heads of the Arab states" and "major political decisions on the organization of Arab resistance to Zionism were thereafter taken not at Jerusalem but at Cairo." It is this body that put the Husseini clan back in charge of the Arab Higher Committee in 1947, with Haj Amin el Husseini as its leader. He quickly removed all opposition leaders, and the AHC became his method of governing from exile.

Arab Higher Committee—Established in 1936, disbanded by the British in 1938, it was the Arab Nationalist Movement's governing body in Palestine. It was reinstituted by the Arab League and Haj Amin, though an enemy of the British and an advocate of the Nazi solution to the "the question of the Jews." When given control, Haj Amin quickly removed all opposition and used the AHC for purposes of destroying the Zionist movement. Because of this control, and the elimination and exile of most of the opposition, the Palestinian people had no other governing body to which they could turn.

Aref—Amos, Mary, Izaat, and Rhoui—A family of Arabs new to the story. They are fictional. Amos represents the Arab Nationalists opposed to Haj Amin. His children take different views of that same movement.

Atah Beseder—Are you alright?

Behatzlaka—Good luck.

Ben Gurion, David—One of the most influential leaders of Zionism, David Ben-Gurion declared Israel an independent state in 1948 and served as the first Prime Minister and Defense Minister. Born and raised in Poland, he emigrated to what was then part of Turkish Palestine in 1906 and became active in the Zionist movement, gaining fame for his vision, energy and sharp oratory. During World War I Ben-Gurion lived in the United States, but most of his adult life was spent in Palestine and Israel as a military and political leader. After serving as Israel's first Prime Minister he retired in 1953, but he re-entered politics and served as Prime Minister from 1955 until he voluntarily stepped down in 1963. After his last term as Prime Minister he remained active in Israeli politics until his retirement in 1970.

Bevakasha—Please.

Daniels, Hannah and Ephraim family—Our main characters from Volume One continue to play important roles in Volume Two. They now have a family of four children: Beth and David, children Hannah brought to Israel from Europe in Volume One, and the recently born twins, Joseph and Jacob.

Elohim Yakia, Today Rabah—Dear God, Thank you.

ETZEL—also known as the IRGUN, or Irgun Zvai Leumi— National Military Organization. A militant nationalist group in prestate Palestine that advocated the use of force and terrorism to achieve independence. The group split into two branches, ETZEL and the even more extremist LEHI (also known as the Stern Gang).

Eretz Israel—The Land of Israel.

Ezeh Yofi—How wonderful.

Haganah—Jewish underground defense force during the mandate—precursor to the Israel Defense Forces or IDF.

Hi Shamer—Be safe.

Husseini, Haj Amin—As a new and important character to the events of the War of Independence, Haj Amin is covered in greater detail in the chapter notes. Suffice it to say that he was the major force behind opposition to the Zionist movement in Israel and is considered a national hero in many Arab circles even today.

Husseini, Abdul Khader—In the 1930s, Khader led the Jihad al Muqaddas, a radical nationalist organization that expressed its wishes through clandestine violence. Haj Amin assumed control of the society in 1935 but Khader was its chief military leader of the Arab nationalist movement. He led Haj Amin's loyalists in the rebellion of 1936-39 and punished opposition Arab leaders nearly as much as he did the Jews. Because his actions alienated the Arab population he was betrayed and nearly killed, but escaped to Syria. From there he went to Iraq where he spent four years in prison for participating in an anti-British uprising. He spent time in Germany learning war tactics and the use of explosives and returned to lead the much-diminished Husseini loyalists in 1947. Because of his small numbers, Khader understood the importance of the roads to his success, but honored Haj Amin's wishes to attack larger settlements and cities as well. Had he not been thus distracted, and had he received the promised weapons and equipment from a bickering Arab League who feared Haj Amin's success nearly as much as they feared the Jews, the borders of present-day Palestine might be quite different. He is considered a national hero by Palestinian Arab nationalists today. He died at the Battle of Kastel in April, 1947, and is buried in the Dome of the Rock Mosque, a rare honor.

Jewish Agency—The Organization created during the Mandate period for facilitating the Jewish national home of Palestine. During the period of this novel it is the governing body of the Jewish people. Its head is David Ben Gurion. The organization of the Agency in the years prior to partition gave the Jews the advantage in having strong institutions in place when needed for war and the new state. The Arabs, on the other hand, lost their Arab Higher Committee for the critical years of development from 1938 to 1947. It was lost because Haj Amin Husseini used it as his nationalist movement against the British in the rebellion of 1936–39.

Jihad—literally "struggle," required by Muslims to improve themselves; the word is also used to describe a holy war against the enemies of Islam. It is considered by some right-wing Muslims as the sixth pillar of Islam and is probably the most abused concept in that faith.

Ken Atah Tsodeq—Yes, you are right.

Kibbutz—A settlement in Israel where all that is produced in the fields and factories is owned collectively by all members.

Lahitraot—Good-bye.

LEHI—(Lohamei Herut Yisrael)—Fighters for the Freedom of Israel, founded in 1940 by breakaway group of ETZEL (Irgun) members; also known as the Stern Gang after its founder Avraham Stern.

Mandate, British—The authority given by the League of Nations after World War I, which gave the British administrative power over Palestine to prepare it for self-government.

Moshav—Village of of immigrants combining cooperative and private farming. First established before the first world war.

Mossad—During this book it is the government organization responsible for the secret emigration of Jews from foreign countries. Its full name was Mossad le-Aliyah Bet. Later it becomes Israel's intelligence service.

Muslim Brotherhood—Islamic National movement founded in Egypt in 1928. Aimed at giving "new soul" in the heart of this nation; to give it life by means of the Koran; wanted Egypt to become an Islamic kingdom.

Naomi—Also came with Hannah out of Berlin, and like Aaron stayed in Europe to help immigration. She does not arrive in Israel until this book.

Palmach—Special elite squadron of the Haganah founded in 1941.

Pogrom—a wave of anti-Jewish violence in places like Russia, Poland and Germany.

Poh—Here.

Sabras—Palestinian-born Jewish youth; from the cactus fruit that is tough and prickly outside, sweet and succulent inside.

Salaam—Hello in Arabic.

Schwartz, Aaron—Came with Hannah our of Berlin, but stayed in Italy to help with immigration. Went to Israel in 1946 where he found a job working for one of the Jewish newspapers and continued training within the Haganah. At the time of this volume he is a young sergeant, a true Zionist, prepared to fight for his country.

Shalom—Hello in Hebrew.

Steinman, Rachel—She and Hannah become good friends in their escape in Volume One. In Volume Two she is only mentioned. She is in one of the settlements in the Negev, has found a man she loves who has two children. She comes back to the forefront in Volume Three.

World Zionist Organization—founded by Theodor Herzl in 1897; active as the Jewish Agency of Palestine until 1929.

Yigal Yadin—born in Jerusalem and joined the Haganah in 1933. He became a key figure in the Haganah leadership, was its operations officer, and helped devise and implement many of the strategies used in the War of Independence. Following the establishment of the State, he was named the second Chief of Staff of the IDF, and served in that capacity from 1949–1952. During his tenure, Yadin reorganized the standing army, the system of compulsory military service, and the reserves.

Yiddish—A Jewish language spoken by Central and Eastern European Jews and brought to Israel by them.

Yishuv—The Jewish community of Palestine before the establishment of the state of Israel.

Zohar—Also came with Hannah out of Berlin but remained in a DP camp in Italy to teach school. She decides to emigrate to Israel during the period of this book. She is aboard the Pans Cresecent when it is captured by the Brits and its passengers interred on Cyprus. She will rejoin us in Volume Three.

PROLOGUE

Jerusalem, October 1841

Elder Orson Hyde walked out of Stephen's Gate and stared up at the city wall. Though he knew these were not the same walls Jesus had looked upon anciently, he felt awed at the sight of their harsh, firm beauty bathed in the light of a nearly full moon. They had seen hundreds of years of war and turmoil, peace and promise, and much more was yet to come, for there was much prophesied about Jerusalem and its role in the world. These walls would yet see the final destruction of the wicked and the coming of the Son of Man.

He walked down the poorly maintained road into the Kidron Valley, across the stone bridge, up a winding, rock-strewn path, and through an old gate in a wall of stone. Here in the Garden of Gethsemane, he delayed briefly, his thoughts on Christ and His sacrifice. Shedding a few tears, he took a small branch from one of the trees and climbed to the crest of the Mount of Olives.

It was from here that the Lord ascended to Heaven and, according to prophets older than the walls of the city across the Kidron, the place where Jesus would come again to save His people from their enemies one last time.

And he was here. To the west he could see the distant Mediterranean Sea; to the east, the Dead Sea valley. It was not an unfamiliar sight. He had seen it all in a vision eighteen months earlier—witness that he was to come, witness to the need to begin something new for the house of Israel.

He sat down on a large rock and watched the city come to life as the sun rose behind him. Over the last few days he had mingled with Arabs in traditional bright colored garb, Turks in their conical hats and loose pantaloon trousers, and Jews in more European attire. It was a city of twenty thousand people with dingy, narrow streets, each emitting a thousand different smells. It had all been strange, but then most of his trip had been that way.

Taking out a piece of paper, he smoothed it flat and dipped his pen in an inkwell he had brought and began writing his prayer. Now he must do what he had come to do. He cleared his mind then began to write the prayer God had revealed to him.

"O Thou! Who art from everlasting to everlasting . . ."

His greeting petitioned God to listen to his words. Then he consecrated the land under and around him for the gathering together of Judah's scattered remnants, the building up of Jerusalem again—though now trodden under the feet of Gentiles—and the rearing of a temple that would honor God's name and work.

Pausing for a brief moment, he thanked God for his safety in the midst of a tumultuous land and asked for that continued kindness on his return home. He then spoke of the promises the Lord had made to Abraham, Isaac, and Jacob wherein He would remember their scattered seed who waited for the fulfillment of these promises. He asked that God grant removal of the barrenness and sterility of the land and let springs of living water break forth to water its thirsty soil that it might flow with plenty to eat when possessed by its rightful heirs, those returning prodigals who would come home.

He concluded his prayer by remembering the Saints at home, especially his family. He then prayed for the Saints and the leaders of the Church who were being persecuted. Finally he spoke words that would bless members of the Church forever. "And let this blessing rest upon every faithful officer and member in thy Church. And all the glory and honor will we ascribe unto God and the Lamb for ever and ever. AMEN."

Standing, Orson piled stones, that by ancient custom established by Jacob and Joshua would witness that he had fulfilled his mission.

As he viewed the city from his lofty position one last time, he knew Jerusalem would never be the same. Slowly but surely the hearts of the dispersed of Judah would turn to this dusty, dry, and sparsely-inhabited land, and it would become "a cup of trembling unto all the people round about, . . . a burdensome stone for all people" (Zech. 12:2–3). Though the entire world would be gathered against them, they would survive this time. They would prevail.

The words of Zechariah came to mind wherein that ancient prophet said that the governors of Judah would reestablish a nation that would become "like an hearth of fire among the wood, and like a torch of fire in a sheaf; and they shall devour all the people round about, on the right hand and on the left" (Zech. 12:6). With only seven thousand Jews in all of Palestine and its ancient beauty all but gone, Elder Hyde wondered how they could become that nation.

He took a deep breath. He did not know, but he knew it would be. Somewhere, somehow—even now—the hearts of dispersed Judah would begin to change until Judah returned like a flood to this land. It would not be pleasant; it would certainly not be without war and mayhem in the lives of both Jew and Gentile, but it would happen. The hardships she would endure to prepare this land for the return of her King would make the Jews shudder if they were able to see them. What lay ahead to bring them home would be as difficult as anything Judah had ever endured in her history. Eventually, she would become a humble nation prepared for the Gospel by the coming of the Lord to drive away both her pride and her enemies.

Elder Hyde started down the slope toward the road. Once on it, he turned south and began a final trip around the city.

SEE CHAPTER NOTES

CHAPTER 1

November 29, 1947

Silently unfolding the first slip of paper, Assembly President Oswaldo Aranha paused, the heaviness of the impending vote weighing on him. This vote—the vote for partition—would establish separate Jewish and Arab states in Palestine. It had already been delayed once, leading to a three-day break of intense lobbying and promise making. Aranha himself had lobbied hard with the Catholic countries of South America. The moment of truth was at hand.

"Guatemala."

Aranha's heavy silence now transferred to the old skating rink, the improvised assembly hall of the United Nations. For this one moment, the delegates, the spectators, even the reporters in the press gallery, were silent, almost in awe.

Quietly, Dr. Jorge Garcia Granados rose from his seat. As he rose, a piercing cry in Hebrew came from the spectators' gallery. *"Ana Ad Hoshiya!"* O Lord, save us.

"Guatemala votes for partition."

Almost 5,700 miles away, Hannah Daniels squeezed Naomi Stavsky's hand. They stood huddled around an old radio with a number of their fellow outcasts in a small garden in Tel Aviv, concentrating on the most important moment in Jewish history since Joshua crossed the Jordan River to capture the Promised Land.

The United Nations' vote to partition Palestine, if successful, would effectively give them the opportunity to create a Jewish state. It had not come easily. Over the last two years Hannah had watched as

Britain had remained intractable in its policy, Foreign Secretary Ernest Bevin insisting that British interests were more closely linked to Arab nationalists than to Jewish Zionism. Most in Israel considered the arguments he spewed forth dirty water—nothing but a cover for a deeply ingrained anti-Semitism. Regardless, much of the world had slowly turned against the British, the United States especially.

"The United States of America votes for partition." There was applause by all those who gathered to hear the news as it blared from the radio in the garden.

"That's nearly enough," Naomi said to Hannah.

Hannah could only nod. It was going well; they were close! She put her arm around her young friend and pulled her in. Naomi had only recently arrived from Europe where she had been a part of the underground for nearly two years now. She and dozens like her had led Jews out of Displaced Persons camps to the shorelines of the Mediterranean where they had put them on boats similar to—and even larger than—the one on which Hannah had escaped, sending them on their way to Palestine. Though hundreds had made it to Israel's shores, many more had been caught by the British and interred on the island of Cyprus where more than fifty thousand waited in camps similar to those they had escaped in Europe. Still more continued to wait in those DP camps hoping the doors of legal immigration would finally open and they too could escape the squalor of the camps of postwar Europe. Though all such people would not come to Palestine, many would, and their ability to do so without further British interference depended on this vote!

She glanced at her young friend. Her hair was lighter, but her eyes dark brown, set to the side of an aquiline nose. Taller than Hannah, she was thin with no sign of any fat, though she had matured in recent years. More noticeable to Hannah was the way Naomi carried the emotional and spiritual growth gained by literally walking thousands of miles over valley and mountain to lead others out of the camps. Smart, determined, and confident, Naomi was a far cry from the self-protective introvert Hannah had first led out of Berlin. She and Hannah had grown close those last few months in Italy, and even closer through their constant letters to one another. Now she was here. It was wonderful!

Hannah would not be in Tel Aviv were it not for Naomi coming in by ship that morning. Her own home was in Jerusalem where she and Ephraim had found a place in the Jewish Quarter of the Old City. It wasn't much, but it was home, and David and Elizabeth were there now, anxiously awaiting Hannah and Naomi's return.

"England abstains."

"Fancy that," said one man cynically.

"Still want to hold on do they. Well, we won't let them," cried another. With that there was applause.

Though Britain had announced two weeks prior that it would withdraw all its troops from Palestine by August 1, 1948, many Jews—especially the leaders—were doubtful they would actually go. Palestine was the most important part of the British Empire's tenuous hold on the Middle East. To walk away might cause them to lose their grip entirely, and few believed that was what they intended. If partition were successful, many Jews were afraid the disgruntled British would allow disorder, either to show their displeasure or to try and force a reconsideration. After all, if Jews and Arabs started massacring one another, someone would have to step in. With the British already here, the UN would surely give them what they wanted—a trusteeship and the freedom to clean out the rebels.

"The Brits at least stayed out of the vote," Naomi said.

"Tonight. Tomorrow they vote with their favors." By giving the Arabs the advantage in the coming fight, the Brits could still beat back any Jewish national home.

"When will Ephraim be back?" Naomi asked.

"In the next few days," Hannah grinned. Just the sound of his name gave her joy. He was the miracle in her life. She missed him terribly, but the Jewish Agency, the representative government for the Jews in Palestine under the British Mandate, had sent Ephraim to contact old friends in postwar Europe to help open the doors for arms purchases, especially planes. Without such weapons, any Jewish State promised by the UN would never become a reality, would never survive the coming war.

War. She dreaded even the thought of it. The Arabs were armed with weapons her people could only dream of. To survive the next few months would be critical. While the British prepared to leave, while the Jews still had some peace, they must buy and ship an array of weapons to Israel or lose their state to the Arab nations the moment they crossed the borders.

Another vote, another celebration. A vote for partition would only open the door for statehood, not guarantee it. The Jews would have to come to a peaceful solution with the Arabs, who would not even speak of peace, or they would have to fight. And if they could not show the world that they had the ability to hold such a state, the UN could reverse its position as easily as it had granted it.

"How much arm twisting did the Americans have to do to push this vote through?" Naomi asked.

"A great deal, and because of it those countries would be glad to have a clear chance to reverse their vote."

"I hear that the President had trouble with some in his own cabinet."

"Secretary of Defense James Forrestal is the most opposed. But there are others, and they are avid Arabists for the same reason as the Brits—influence and oil. Ephraim thinks they've already laid plans for bringing about reversal and may have even secretly promised the Arabs to try." The cry of a baby immediately turned her toward the house as another round of applause greeted words announced by the radio. Inside she found the twins still lying on the bed in her host's bedroom, Jacob wide awake. She picked him up and cradled him in her arms, her warmth giving him immediate comfort.

When planning their marriage, she and Ephraim had wondered if they would ever have children. Who really knew the effects of the Holocaust? She smiled. The twins had been a double gift from God, but a challenge to care for. She glanced at Joseph where he lay on the bed. Alike down to the shape of their nose and the length of their feet, even she had difficulty at times knowing the difference. Only the slight cowlick in Joseph's hairline gave him away.

She pulled Jacob even closer as she returned to the yard. How she loved them!

As she left the house, a clock on the cupboard revealed that it was near midnight. The crowd in the yard had doubled and was overflowing into the street. All were silent, straining to hear the radio. A barrel-chested man with a bald pate turned to her and said hello as she approached.

"Yitzhak, nice to see you." Hannah smiled.

"I see Ephraim has not returned."

She shook her head. "If we win tonight, his work may take even longer."

Yitzhak only smiled agreement. Yitzhak Perlman worked as an arms procurement agent for the underground Jewish army known as the Haganah. Because of those connections, he knew of Ephraim's mission to Europe and how such missions would make the difference between victory and defeat. It would do no good to have the UN resolution if they must fight the Arabs with little more than rocks and sticks.

"What will happen tomorrow, Yitzhak?"

"Haj Amin will start a strike, then a riot, then a war. What else?" He forced a smile.

"Yes, what else," she replied.

For months the Jews had continued to hope for a peaceful solution, but with the Arabs, especially Haj Amin el Husseini, Mufti of Jerusalem and self-proclaimed leader of the Palestinian Arabs, making rash statements about never allowing a Jewish state in their midst, it was difficult.

"He began fanning the flames of passion against Jews years ago. Now his men—his Holy Strugglers, he calls them—train and arm guerillas both here and across the border. He will set them loose on partition, and by their violence, they will make it hard for the UN to resist reversing what happens tonight," Yitzhak said.

"He is a butcher," Hannah said through a granite jaw.

"He is a nationalist, just like you and me. And he hates Jews because we threaten to take what he thinks belongs to him."

"He sided with Hitler in the war, Yitzhak. That makes him more than a nationalist patriot. Do not forget that he called for the absolute annihilation of the Jews and supported the Nazi resolution to the Jewish problem."

"No one said he was a patriot, Hannah," Yitzhak smiled. "He is Mufti, a holy man to all Islam, a defender of the faith who is justified in fighting the infidel and destroying them all. We are next on his list. He has been planning this for years, and even though the British recognize him as the butcher you know him to be and will not allow him into Palestine, he runs things here for the Arabs through the

Arab Higher Committee. It is him we have been fighting since 1920, and now he will see the chance he has always wanted. He will not miss it, and it will be him and his beliefs we will have to defeat more than all other Arab Armies. Until we do, we will not have peace in this land."

"I wish all Jews saw him as the danger. They do not see the danger. They think there may be a few events—a riot or two—but the British will stop it, and we will find a way to peace. Because of it, they will not be ready, and many will die."

"Yes, I know. They think this is a great opportunity for Palestinian Arabs as well as for us, and that the Arabs will see it that way. Most will not. They do not like our foreign ways, and they especially do not want us buying their land. Because of this, many will fight us. Others will not. They will wait to see. Many others will run at the first sign of trouble, thinking they can return later. They have done it for generations. They do not realize this time will be different."

"Some will fight Haj Amin," Hannah said.

"Some. We try to make treaties with those who hate Haj Amin or who believe their lives will be better under us, but they are few—most are Christian Arabs. Islam, at least Haj Amin's rendition of Islam, will prevent most from supporting us. Holy War in defense of one of their holiest cities is strong medicine. They will also remember what happened to those who opposed him in 1936–39. Six thousand Arabs died in those years, four thousand of them at Arab hands. Fear of him will be strong." Yitzhak smiled. "I do not wish to be depressing on such a happy night. *Behatzlaka*, Hannah. Be safe." She watched as Yitzhak left the yard and headed toward Haganah headquarters while turning her attention back to the radio.

"Here it comes!" someone said in a hushed voice.

"Where do we stand?" asked another.

"Thirteen against is all I know," answered another.

"How many does it take?" said Naomi as she slipped her arm around Hannah's waist.

"Two-thirds majority vote," Hannah whispered.

"The General Assembly of the United Nations—" the radio broadcaster began. The yard went silent and someone reached for the knob of the radio in an attempt to get more volume. "—by a vote of thirty-three in favor, thirteen against, and ten abstentions, has voted to partition Palestine."

Jewish Tel Aviv exploded in joy. Naomi hugged Hannah and the baby, and tears filled their eyes as they realized that, at last, the chance for real freedom had come! People gathered arm in arm and began a march toward the main street of Tel Aviv, a street that ran parallel to the ocean for the length of the city itself. Suddenly the air was filled with a chorus of voices singing the "Hatikvah," the Zionist anthem. In Russian, Czech, German, Hungarian, Yiddish, and Hebrew, hymns pummeled the air with their joyous sound. The yard emptied, leaving Hannah and Naomi standing alone, watching as the crowds passed by, dancing and celebrating.

Hannah could tell Naomi wished to be away, to be caught up in the joy of it all. "Go," she said softly. "I'll be fine. I have the children."

Naomi looked apologetic. "Are you sure. I—"

"Go!" She laughed. "I'll be here. But remember, we must leave for Jerusalem early. I need to get back to David and Elizabeth."

Naomi was suddenly gone, her long legs carrying her into the street where she locked arms and was swallowed by a crowd of happy faces. Hannah watched until her own body was caught up by the sounds of the "Hatikvah" and she danced about with little Jacob in her arms, his wide eyes looking up into hers. She lifted him to the sky and swung him gently around as tears rolled down her face and watered the thin grass of Eretz Israel.

Freedom! At last they had a chance for real freedom! No longer would they be forced to live in a world that did not want them and used them for a scapegoat for all its ills. No longer would they be subject to the whims of kings, czars, and dictators.

She thought of David and Elizabeth and wished now that she had brought them along. But there had been only one seat in the car of a friend, and she and the twins took it and a little more. David was eleven now, Elizabeth nine. Both had become her and Ephraim's children by legal adoption when their parents' names were finally discovered on lists of the dead compiled by the Allies cleaning up the savage slaughter of Jews in Germany, Poland, and half a dozen other countries. Now, here in Israel, they had a new life—going to school; learning history, art, culture, and even Arabic; joining a new generation of Jews in Palestine, strong, vibrant, and now, free! Free! The crowd along the street was reduced to a few hurrying individuals trying to catch up. Hannah could hear the distant sounds of celebration. Tired and sobered by her joy, she sat down on the small bench by the door and listened. As she did, the sound of distant shofar horns broke through the night air, giving her chills. The *shofar*! The horn used by Moses to signal the house of Israel's departure from Egypt! How long did it take the children of Israel to come to their promised land? How many lessons did they have to learn before they were ready to enter? And how quick did they lose sight of their God and turn to their idols?

It sent chills down her spine. If there was one thing Hannah had discovered over the last two years, it was that Judah, even after thousands of years, was still undecided about serving God. Many Palestinian Jews refused to live according to even the most basic commandments issued from Sinai. The Zionist movement was not a religious movement but a political one. Without God at its center, could they survive what lay ahead? Could they really return? It saddened her, but she had come to realize they couldn't, completely, but they could begin. God wanted them to begin and would help them begin. Her new faith—and her old—testified of it, but a physical gathering was only the first step. Next would come the more important spiritual one. It was this return for which her heart longed and which she hoped to see in her lifetime.

She had memorized the words Nephi quoted from Isaiah. Looking down at a still wide-awake Jacob, she spoke them.

> But, behold, Zion hath said: The Lord hath forsaken me, and my Lord hath forgotten me—but he will show that he hath not.
>
> For can a woman forget her sucking child, that she should not have compassion on the son of her womb? Yea, they may forget, yet will I not forget thee, O house of Israel.
>
> Behold, I have graven thee upon the palms of my hands; thy walls are continually before me.
>
> Thy children shall make haste against thy destroyers; and they that made thee waste shall go forth of thee.

Lift up thine eyes round about and behold; all these gather themselves together, and they shall come to thee. And as I live, saith the Lord, thou shalt surely clothe thee with them all, as with an ornament, and bind them on even as a bride.

This night was just a small sign that God had not forgotten them. Would she live to see it all? Or would it be Joseph and Jacob, her blood and Ephraim's blood? She wasn't sure, she just knew it had now begun, and nothing—not even the Arab world around them—could stop it.

She attuned her ears to the sound of the *shofar* again, the call for a return to Israel. It must have been a glorious day when they left the slave pits of the pharaoh to go home to their Promised Land, but it too must have been a day filled with apprehension and fear of the unknown.

SEE CHAPTER NOTES

CHAPTER 2

Ephraim sat back as the radio announcement came through in his sparsely furnished hotel room in Prague. He wondered where Hannah was, what she was doing, how the kids were. How he longed to be with her at this moment.

The chance for a Jewish state. How glad she would be!

He smiled. He could almost see her dancing in the streets, celebrating with the throngs of jubilant Jews whose dreams had finally come true. He lifted his soda and saluted the distant shores that had become home.

Turning off the radio, his heart sobered by the increased weight of this landmark decision. There would be war now, and many of those who celebrated would not live to see real freedom. Instead they would die for it. The thought made him ache.

Ephraim shuddered at the thought. Many would die in this war, Jew and Arab. There was no longer any other solution.

Over the last two years of adjusting to life in Palestine, Ephraim had found himself overrun with differences of opinion on how the split between the two peoples had begun and who was at fault. He spoke with friends. He read the histories and had the histories read to him. Sami Khalidy, president of Jerusalem's Arab college, would translate the Arabic histories; Hannah would translate the Hebrew. It was a complicated story of intrigue, broken promises, frustration, and anger. Out of it had come intransigence, greed, fanaticism, and now war. As in all wars, the many would pay for the sins of the few.

His experience in World War II had taught him to hate war. He hated what it had done to thousands of innocent people like Hannah. He hated how many good men had been forced to die to stop what one madman had started. As in the days of Captain Moroni, a greedy, power hungry man had started it all, and before his war was over, every life in the known world had been abused. Thousands were forced from their homes and the land devastated to such a degree that many had been forced to move away and start their lives over. Book of Mormon? World War II in a nutshell. Now here it was happening again.

Ephraim was haunted by thoughts about what lay ahead. With Germany it had been pretty clear-cut who was right and who was wrong. This time it wasn't that easy. This was going to be a war between two peoples who both felt they had the right to a piece of real estate small enough to fit inside Rhode Island, and at least one of the combatants wasn't willing to share. Did one side have a stronger argument than the other? He had listened to Hannah and Sami give their reasoning dozens of times, and to him it all came out the same. They should share and be happy; they were both being given a state for the first time in their rather colorful and questionable histories.

But as far as whether or not he would fight, the real clincher for Ephraim was his solid belief in the Jewish right of return. Scripture, ancient and modern, was filled with it. Even the Koran alluded to it. So much so that Arab leaders like Feisal Hussein, King of Iraq and Syria, had said at one time that he welcomed the Jewish return, and he was sure they could live together. Other Arab leaders had said the same thing—until guys like Haj Amin Husseini had started ranting about it.

Ephraim didn't want to fight. He still hoped they wouldn't have to, hoped they would make peace, even though he knew such was wishful thinking now. But the fight that was brewing did pose some interesting questions. Some Church members questioned if this was going to be Armageddon. Ephraim didn't think so. It was too soon to be Armageddon. First the Jews must return to their Promised Land, an event prophesied and prayed for on countless occasions. The Holy Land itself had been dedicated for the return of the Jews ten times since Elder Hyde's initial dedication in 1841. The most recent dedication by Elder Widtsoe in 1933 petitioned the Lord to bring the Jews home to the land He had promised them.

More importantly though, the Jews must turn to Christ and accept Him as their Redeemer. Elder Widtsoe had even promised them that if they would accept Christ, peace would come to their land and their persecutions would cease. But that had not yet happened. Following the Holocaust, too many Jews—like David's older brother, Aaron— had lost faith in their own God, let alone the God of the Christian nations that had persecuted them for so long. Jews were returning to Palestine, but it was a faithless, political return and not the humble, spiritual return required of the Lord. And this little parcel of land in the Middle East would not have peace, only war.

It would be a bloody war, and Ephraim was frightened for his family. But it wasn't *that* war. One of those "wars and rumors of wars" he supposed, but not Armageddon. That gave him both comfort and disappointment. The return of the Jews was going to be a lengthy process, and peace would be elusive. He and his family—down to his grandchildren, probably longer—would be dealing with war as long as they stayed in Palestine or Israel or whatever the Jews decided to call their new state. That would make for a hard life.

But he knew it was to be his life—and Hannah's and their children's. The return to ancient Israel was in their blood. They were Ephraim and Judah. They had not only a responsibility to work for a return, but he had learned to love Palestine. He couldn't see himself ever leaving it except for an occasional trip back to the states to see his family or go to the temple. It was where he wanted to be, even if it meant having to fight for the right to be there.

Ephraim got up and looked out the window. For him the question was no longer one of whether the Jews were to return, but whether or not they could. He knew that Ben-Gurion and the Jewish leadership hoped for a political solution while planning for a military one. He also knew they had hoped for the first so strongly that they had procrastinated the second. Of course, there were other reasons for putting off war. They were poorly equipped and even more poorly financed. Fortunately, the Arabs would not attack until after the British left the country, and that would give the Jews time to do more. But it was a daunting future fraught with *what ifs*. What if the *Yishuv*, the world Jewish community, refused to give them the money they needed? What if the world refused to sell them the arms even if they had the money? And what if the British refused to let them send the arms into Palestine until it was too late?

One thing that Ephraim understood clearly was that the United Nations did not authorize war in the Middle East by authorizing partition. They wanted Jew and Arab to work out their problems peacefully, and because this was their position, they would not readily allow the formation of an open and operational Jewish Army. They were just naive enough, because they did not live in Palestine, to believe that their wishes would be adhered to, and stubborn enough to enforce embargos that put the Jews at a large disadvantage. For that purpose, Ben-Gurion had begun making plans for secret arms purchases and deliveries. Just in case. For Ephraim, it was the only policy that made any sense. If they wanted to return, they must be prepared to make it work.

Ephraim believed they could. In the last two years he had discovered a people who had the heart, the will, the insatiable desire for return. Though all Jews did not have these, thousands—even millions—did. It was why he had given his heart and soul to aid them, but he also knew they would need weapons. Sooner or later they would have to fight for their state. Without guns and planes, cannons and tanks, a man's heart would not be enough. Haj Amin would get weapons and he would use them, and he would force the rest of the Arab world to use those they already had. He wanted to win and he would bring every weapon into play he could think of.

With a deep sigh, Ephraim glanced at his watch. A little after midnight Palestine time. Ehud Avriel was flying in to Prague tomorrow night. Ephraim had located several contacts through his old friend Joseph that would help, but once he introduced them to Ehud, he would be flying back to Palestine. He had done all he could. Now it was time to turn it over to more qualified hands.

The knock on the door had him out of his chair reaching for his handgun. He stood to the side of the door and asked, "Who is it?"

"Joseph," the quiet voice responded.

Ephraim tucked the gun in his belt and opened the door. Joseph quickly slipped inside and removed his raincoat. "Miserable weather," he said, forcing a smile.

"We could use a little of it at home," Ephraim said. It had been a dry year in Palestine. Some wondered if they would have enough to get them through the next summer.

Joseph smiled, removed a paper and handed it to Ephraim. "Here it is. They are not true *Messerschmitts*—the ones the Germans used. They are copies made by the Slavs, but they are better than Piper Cubs."

Ephraim looked at the paper and grinned at his old friend. Joseph had helped him round up Nazis in Berlin at the end of the war, and he had done such a good job that American Army intelligence had put him to work full time. Now he was one of the top leaders in the new West German intelligence organization. Not bad for a former *Wehrmacht* soldier who had no future after Hitler and the Nazis had ruined his country. He had helped Jews then; now he was in a position to help them again and was doing everything in his power to help create a new home for those his country had so badly offended. Joseph, like thousands of Germans, would do penance for their crimes, but not all would do more than ask their God for forgiveness as Joseph was.

"Excellent, Joseph." Ephraim grinned, putting the papers in his valise. "Ehud arrives tomorrow. He'll need a lot more than these to save our new country."

"If he has money, he can have whatever he wants."

"That might be a bit of problem. How long can you get your friends to hold them?" There were some funds, enough for a few initial payments, and more were promised, but it would take time, time to convince the greater *Yishuv* of the need to support their cause with gold and silver. For now they must play a delaying game in which they tied up orders of weapons while putting off payment. Such tactics couldn't last long—not in postwar Europe—but they had little choice. He could only pray that Ben-Gurion and his finance secretary would find their trip to the United States in a few weeks a profitable one.

"I will see that they hold them. Do not worry," Joseph said. "These planes are for you, no one else."

"Thank you, Joseph. You're a good friend to me and all Jews."

"Then you are going back tomorrow."

Ephraim nodded. "My children need a papa."

"And Hannah needs a husband," Joseph paused. Joseph lifted the sack he carried. "These are the items you asked to be found. For the children." He gave them to Ephraim. "That they still exist is a miracle, but many Jews are finding remnants of their past. Bits and pieces, but they help to remember."

Ephraim took the sack and looked inside. He could not believe they had been found. "This must have been a good deal of work, Joseph."

Joseph only shrugged, a sheepish look on his face. "I only wish I had found some of them alive."

"Thank you. From the bottom of my heart, I . . ."

"Do you hear of . . . of Rachel?" Rachel had been with Hannah since the hospital and release from the death camps. She and Joseph had been friends as children and, though on opposite sides of the war, had rekindled their friendship after the war. It was obvious Joseph still hoped for something more, but old wounds were still too sore for Rachel to respond to his affection.

"She lives on a *kibbutz* in the Negev. She's responsible for settling new immigrants and is happy." He could not bring himself to say more. It would only disappoint Joseph to know that Rachel had found someone.

"You must come and visit, Joseph."

"Someday. For now, my country . . . the communists need attention, Ephraim. If they get a foothold . . ."

Ephraim put a hand on his friend's shoulder. "I understand. When you can, come."

Joseph nodded, then hugged his friend. Had it not been for Ephraim Daniels, he would not have survived after the war. He was sure of it.

"You still go to Church?" Ephraim asked.

Joseph smiled. "What else would the branch president do?"

Ephraim laughed. "You're a good man, Joseph. Be safe."

Joseph nodded, turned the knob, and opened the door. "Take care, Ephraim. This war will not be as easy as the last for you. Your American industry is not building the planes you will fly, and these Messerschmitts are not of German quality. They have many problems and crash easily. You must be very careful . . ."

"I will. I'll kiss the kids for you."

Joseph nodded and was gone.

Ephraim turned to the picture on the small table next to his bed—Hannah, David, Elizabeth, and the boys. He would see them in a few days. His shoulders lifted a little. It was a silver lining in an ever-darkening cloud.

SEE CHAPTER NOTES

CHAPTER 3

The vehicle bounced over the old road and Aaron had to brake to keep it from careening into the sandy desert on each side of them.

"How much farther?" the man next to him asked.

"Not far," Aaron said, keeping his eyes on the thin line of light before him.

They had come to the Negev to bring a paper to David Ben-Gurion, leader of the Jewish Agency. The paper was a draft of the official declaration by the Agency congratulating the United Nations on their vote and welcoming their support of a new Jewish state. Produced by others, it needed final approval by Ben-Gurion himself. "I hope he is still awake," the man said. Gershon Avner was a young bureaucrat of the Jewish Agency and obviously afraid of the man who had pushed, pulled, and shoved the Jews of Palestine toward a new state.

They arrived at the Hotel Kaliya near the Dead Sea just after two in the morning and went immediately to Ben-Gurion's room.

Gershon hesitated before the door, then knocked. It was several moments before a woman opened the door and let them in.

"We have won, I . . ." Gershon began uncomfortably.

"So what if we won?" said Ben-Gurion's wife, Paula. "Let him sleep!" But she had already opened the door of the bedroom and let them enter. Again with reluctance, Gershon stretched forth a hand and shook his leader's shoulder.

Ben-Gurion turned over. He was plagued with chronic back problems and had been ill to boot. He had gone to bed early knowing that sitting by the radio would not change the outcome, which he already knew anyway.

"Mazel tov," Gershon said softly, "It is over. They have voted for partition."

"As if it means anything," Ben-Gurion snorted as he sat up and got out of bed, putting on his bathrobe before adjusting his glasses and taking the draft Gershon had in his hand, his hair in its usual chaotic disarray. He read for only a moment then spoke.

"And the Arab reaction?"

"They declared the resolution invalid and walked out of the hall."

"You cannot blame them. They do not understand why they should be made to pay for the Holocaust."

"They said that any efforts to implement the resolution will result in war," Gershon added.

"Then it is war we will have," Ben-Gurion said. He shook his head. "This will not do. I will need paper," he said, looking around the room.

Gershon grabbed what few sheets lay on the table and handed them to his leader who began writing feverishly. After he had thrown several drafts away he spoke again. "More paper. This will not do."

Aaron watched as Paula Ben-Gurion looked frantically for something on which her husband could write, Gershon helping her.

"More paper," Ben-Gurion said with great impatience.

"But there is nothing," Paula said with frustration.

Gershon grabbed a strip of brown toilet paper from the bathroom and handed it to his boss who immediately started writing his measured words again.

As he finished, the door burst open and a happy group of youth from the nearby potash works came dancing into the room. Aaron could see that Ben-Gurion was not pleased, but then everyone knew that their leader was not given much to outward celebration. Instead he thrust his fists into his pockets and dutifully let them circle him before Paula began motioning them back the way they had come. When the door was closed, Ben-Gurion sat down, a sad look to his face. He quickly waved Gershon from the room and Aaron followed.

"Awfully down in the mouth," Aaron said stiffly.

"He knows better than anyone that tomorrow or the next day or the next, those same young people, and many more, may wish this day had never come."

"You can't be serious?" Aaron said. "This is the greatest day in our history since . . . since . . ."

"Moses. I know. I hear it all the time. But you will try to remember that today is not only a night of freedom, but also the beginning of war. Some of those young people will die for the new state, and Ben-Gurion knows it."

Aaron felt the sudden rush of reality course through him. War. He shook his head. "The Arabs have big mouths, but they are not fools. Now that the world has shown their support of us, they will make peace."

"They have said too much already. And remember, the Mufti does not want peace. He will fight us. And very soon. Our only salvation is that he is less ready for war than we are."

"Better to have war than to take any further abuse at the hands of men like Hitler."

Avner did not respond at first, his mind challenged by what he knew lay ahead. Finally he took a deep breath. "Yes, you are right. But it will not be so easy to watch others die around you, will it? Your friends are in this too, Aaron. You may survive, but they may not. You must try to understand the weight he carries. He knows that this vote does not guarantee a Jewish state. That, my friend, will be built with the mortar of young blood. Your blood and the blood of family and friends."

Walking out of the hotel, they got in the jeep Aaron had commandeered earlier in the night from a British officer's apartment. A necessity sometimes when your army is still supposedly nonexistent and transportation is at a premium.

"Come, we must get back to Jerusalem," Gershon said, pulling Aaron out of his thoughts.

"Gershon, I . . . uh . . . I want to do more. I . . . I am the youngest sergeant in the Haganah. I earned it—you know I did— but ever since coming here, I . . . it is as if they do not trust me."

"They trust you, Aaron, and you will receive more responsibility, especially now. The war has no respect for age and will make old men of us all. Wait a few weeks."

Aaron nodded, forced a smile, and started the engine. "A promise then. At the first possible moment you put in a good word for me."

"Yes, yes, a promise. Heaven have mercy on the Arabs, but you will get the action you seem obsessed with."

Aaron laughed lightly and popped the clutch, throwing the jeep in reverse. It was then he saw Ben-Gurion rushing out the door in their direction. He pushed on the brake and waited.

"Need a ride," Ben-Gurion said, hopping in the back of the jeep. Aaron glanced at Gershon, then at the leader of his people. There were Arabs between the Hotel Kaliya and Jerusalem, and most of them were not happy with tonight's vote.

"Uh . . . I will defend you with my life, but even then I am afraid we are outnumbered several thousand to one between here and Jerusalem," Aaron said.

"Go," Ben-Gurion said gruffly. "They are still in too much shock to start killing us tonight."

Aaron couldn't help the smile as he rammed the gearshift into second and started for the main road. He liked David Ben-Gurion.

CHAPTER 4

Doctor Amos Aref watched the sunrise from the balcony of his small home in the Christian Quarter of the Old City of Jerusalem. Soon it would be time to go to the church for prayer, then to the office. But this morning, he could not force himself from the chair.

"Father." The voice came from behind him, but he did not move. He felt the warm touch on his shoulder and forced himself to reach up and gently rub the soft skin of his daughter's hand, the pain in his chest subsiding.

"You have not slept all night. You must try. You cannot go to the office until you do."

He patted her hand. "It is all right. I am well enough. We must go to the church and pray. It is our only hope now." Born in the late 1800s, Aref had lived through the tumult of war and rebellion for nearly 65 years. He had fought with the British to free his people from the rule of the Turks. For years he had remained firm in his belief that the British would finally give them their own government and let them be. Then came the Jews. Initially they lived together in peace—went to each other's celebrations, spent evenings together as families. But the Zionists changed everything. Greedy for land and power, they continually demanded more. The Jews had been nothing but a minority in a land owned by his people, a minority he felt should be given the same rights, freedoms, and opportunities that all minorities should receive, but he was not willing to give them the land.

Mary gave no answer. She understood her father's pain. Her entire life, he had taught her how precious the land was and how much it meant to the family. To see it given to others was frustrating for all.

"There is still time for peace, Father. Still time for negotiation." She wanted to say more, share her true feelings, but it would only make him angry. She had silently rejoiced at the announcement. At last her people would have a chance for a state of their own. But her father, like most Palestinian Arabs, saw it only as a loss, not a victory.

"Negotiation? Hah! Those of us who have tried to negotiate have lost, Daughter, lost! The war eagles have won, and they will turn this land into a battleground drenched with blood. A holy war! That is what will come."

A devout Christian, her father hated only one thing more than losing his country—war. Opposed to Haj Amin, he had been forced to leave the country in 1939. Half a dozen of her father's closest friends had not been so lucky, dying in the purges of that same year.

"I thought we were rid of him three years ago, sure they would try him at Nuremberg, but he survived. It is proof the devil takes care of his own. A butcher! Fighting for our people and us! Has God once more gone to sleep? Has he forgotten us? Every Christian in this land is at risk if the Husseinis come to power."

"And every Jew," she said softly. She understood her father's deep hatred for Haj Amin, and she knew it had only become worse since her two brothers had told them they intended to join Husseini's forces if the United Nations gave the Jews their land. "He will not come to power, Father. God has not forgotten us."

"The Jews or Haj Amin. It isn't much of a choice, is it, Daughter?" he said in soft cynicism. "Have you seen Izaat and Rhoui lately?"

"I will see them at the shop today. Did you want me to tell them you wish—"

"No, they are not to come here again until they come to their senses!" When her brothers had declared their allegiance to the Mufti, it had nearly killed her father. She remembered him saying he would rather see his two sons in the grave than fighting for the Husseinis. He had reminded them of the Arab lives Haj Amin had taken, of the way he had ruined their chances with the world community because of his support for Hitler and the Holocaust, of the fact that he continued to refuse to give Christian Arabs the same rights and privileges as Muslim Arabs. His arguments, agreeable to Mary, had landed on her brothers' deaf ears. They knew all these things, but they no longer mattered. Angered by the way events in the world were rolling over Arab rights in Palestine, they allied themselves with the man they felt had the best chance of getting those rights back. Her father had kicked them out of the house.

Mary hadn't been here then. She had gone away to London for schooling, returning only when her father had gotten quite ill and refused to let Izaat, Rhoui, and their wives care for him.

Her eighteen months at Oxford had been wonderful. She intended to return to England as soon as possible, as soon as her father was well. She missed school. She missed the open and exciting environment at Oxford. She missed the thousand new ideas she hadn't even thought existed. Politics and culture, music and dance, even philosophy and religion excited and tantalized her mind and senses.

Mary had been raised on a steady diet of her father's viewpoint and had never considered other ideas. After discussions and heated debates with Jews, Christians, Arabs, atheists, and numerous others who wanted to talk about Palestine, she had come to understand the Jewish point of view much better. Tired to the bones of having others always dictate to them, use them, and rule over them, the Jews sought their own place in the world. It was no different than what she and her father wanted as Palestinians. The trouble was they both wished for it in exactly the same place, and both were unwilling to move over and make room so that the other could live in peace. Now they were ready to go to war over it.

Worse, the real cause of unrest was the lunatic fringe. Haj Amin on one side; ETZEL and LEHI on the other. Both refusing to negotiate. Both wanting everything. Both willing to use violence to anger the people and force a war of annihilation. The majority of Palestinians, both Arab and Jew, didn't want to fight and kill each other, but the fanatics seemed to live for it, constantly making devils out of their opponents, finding fault, telling lies, stirring up dissent and unrest until the hate boiled over and the mob did their dirty work for them. It would be no different this time.

Mary felt her father's heart beating through the tips of her fingers where they touched his neck. A bit irregular, even weak, but he had just finished a bout with the flu. He was still regaining his strength. She kissed him on the top of the head.

"Will you go to the office today?" she asked.

He shook his head. Except for Sundays, he always went to the office for at least a part of the day. His flu had been cured for several days now, and the sick of Jerusalem were endless. Her father did his best for any who needed his help. Even Jews. His refusal to go was an indication of how very hard this was hitting him. She sat down on the chair opposite him. "Father, your patients need you. Please, do not let this setback—"

"Setback?" He took a deep breath as if to control his emotions. His voice was very tired. "Dear Daughter, I love you, but you understand nothing. This is not a setback. It is the end." He paused, his voice weakening. "Would you mind if we went to the church later? I think I will rest."

"Father, you have not missed prayers since I was a child."

He patted her hand. "I am all right. I just want to be alone, to think. You are right. I did not sleep much last night, and I must. Then we will go to the church. Now go to the shop. I know you have work."

"Will you be all right? You seem very tired, and—"

"I am fine. Now go."

She kissed him one more time, then stood and left the room. Lifting her shawl and purse from the stand-alone rack near the door, she left the apartment, glimpsing him still sitting in his chair on the patio as she closed it behind her. Descending the steps she walked hurriedly down the street, turning back only once to wave at him. He smiled and waved back, then she turned and picked up the pace.

A moment later she passed the street that led to the Church of the Holy Sepulcher, the church to which they usually went to pray. Crossing herself, she turned left, then right and walked through the semi-crowded street toward her brothers' shop, greeting people as they went about their business in a manner more reserved than usual.

God, Allah, Jehovah. Each of them would be receiving prayers this morning, and each would be asked for protection even as those who prayed planned the death and destruction of others. There was only one Eternal God, and though they called him by different names, it would be that single God who would hear such prayers. How could He possibly favor one child over another? How could humans believe that He would? That was what made most wars of this kind so horrible. They were started, fought, and claimed for God, as if doing so somehow made them agreeable to Him.

Stopping at the corner of the Street of the Jews, Mary stared down its narrow corridor. It was still open, but she did not see the usual black suits of the Orthodox who often came this way to do their shopping. They were not passing through the Old City to get from the small piece of the Western Wall where they prayed to their homes in *Mea Shearim* or another orthodox enclave.

As she turned into the street of their business, it seemed unusually quiet, the shopkeepers reserved, even tense. She noticed that some sat with weapons on their laps or against the wall next to them. No wonder the Jews did not come this way. Distrust where there had been friendship. Hate where there had at least been respect. She felt empty.

She stretched her legs to cover more distance. She must get to work, busy herself, and take her mind off these things. Surely not everyone would lose their heads. Some would find a way to peace.

She thought of her two brothers, Izaat and Rhoui. How would they react to this blow? They were both stubborn, proud men who spoke against the Jews much too often, especially Rhoui. They considered themselves soldiers of the Grand Mufti now. She could not understand how they could follow such a man, but they were her brothers, and she would continue to try and love them, even if she did despise the Mufti and their decision to serve him.

She arrived at the shop. There were a number of men sitting on small stools and chairs on the cobblestone street and around the entrance to the shop discussing last night's announcement and Jewish celebration. Even from fifty feet she could hear Rhoui shouting denunciations and calling for action. It made the hair on the back of her neck stand on end. She tried to slip past all of them and into the shop without being noticed, but Izaat saw her, stopped the conversation with a wave of the hand, and welcomed her.

"Hah, little Sister! You have come to make us rich men!" he said with a big smile.

Raoul Khatib said hello and added a slight honorific bow. Raoul was her brothers' choice for her. A good choice from their perspective, and from the perspective of most Arab homes, both Christian and Muslim. At twenty-five, he had his own shop, was smart, aggressive in business, and needed no accountant to keep him from ruining what he had gained. He was of average height and build with dark hair and eyes and a handsome face. But she did not love him and had little desire to be more than friends. Though her brothers had tried to get their father to influence her, he had resisted their attempts—at least for now—and she was relieved. There was something about Raoul that made her nervous. She hadn't exactly identified why, but it was as if there were an emptiness in him, a cold sort of cruelty.

"Good morning," she said in Arabic. She did not avert her eyes as a good Arab woman would. She did not hold to the old tribal traditions as she once did and felt no allegiance to them. On more occasions than her brothers liked to remember, she had let her feelings be known to others, and because of it she had been ridiculed and spit upon while being belittled, even chastened. Today she was in no mood for even the slightest harassment, but nothing was forthcoming, and she went past them and to the back of the shop where a curtain covered the door to a small storage room and an even smaller office. Removing her sweater, she glanced in the broken piece of mirror she had propped there, checking to make sure all was in order. Mary did not consider herself a good-looking woman. Her face was much too round, her legs too short, and her waist at least an inch too thick to create an image of beauty, but she had learned to make the most of what she had. Staring back at her were dark eyes and olive-colored skin. Her figure was hidden by the loose fitting Arab dress she wore. She removed the traditional headscarf she wore in public out of respect for her father. Shaking out her hair, she found herself wishing for the millionth time for the courage to stop abiding this tradition.

Sitting down at the small desk, Mary began her work while trying to ignore the voices of the men outside her brothers' shop, but it was difficult.

"It makes no difference what the United Nations say! Who are they that we should do as they tell us, Allah?" She recognized Rhoui's voice. The use of the word Allah by a Christian was not uncommon in Arab Palestine because of the mix of the two religions, but Rhoui had begun to accept more and more of Islam over the last few months because of his support for Haj Amin, and, from what Mary had heard, he had converted. That explained his absence from mass or confession for the last few weeks, but he had not openly proclaimed this change in religions. Maybe it was only rumor.

"We must fight. It is Allah's will," said another. "They will desecrate our mosques and our women. If we are men, we will never let another Jew into this city!"

"The war has already begun," said another. "The Mufti has called for *jihad*, and every one of us should be willing."

"For Paradise and 70 virgins, eh Musa," said Izaat evenly.

All laughed, but Mary's ears waited to hear the rest of her eldest brother's words.

"Buy your weapons, prepare for fighting, but remember, this circle will grow smaller. You, Raoul, you have much to live for. If we allow the Jews a homeland, if we have our own state at long last without war, you will go very far. You sell goods they like, and they will make you a rich man. Everyone will profit. Maybe then you can even marry my sister, eh?"

More laughter, then the firm voice of Raoul.

"I do not want the Jew's money if it costs us our country. I will die driving them and anyone who sides with them from this land!"

Mary frowned at the statement. Such bravado! Such a fool!

"Yes, I know, but the cost may be your life. It is one thing to give up their money, but your life? That is quite another. And you, Rhoui. You have three small children. Is this anger you feel worth leaving them fatherless?"

"You speak foolishly, Brother. The Jews will never settle for only part of Palestine. They will want it all, and with time they will get stronger, not weaker. I would rather die now giving my children a future than sit idly by and see it taken away by my enemies." It was said with great force and made Mary swallow hard. Rhoui had become a true believer. There was no other way for him now. He was convinced that war was the only way.

"Very well, and the rest of you? Talk is easy, it is dying that is hard. Are you ready to become martyrs? Do you believe as Rhoui? Will the Jews ruin us? Has not their economic drive given us all better shops and more money to buy clothing for our families and nice schools for our children?"

The answer was more subdued but unanimous that money could not repay for the loss of their pride and their land. Their fervor made her even more nervous. She had know all of these men since childhood, and they talked of war as if it were some sort of lark, a trip into the hills for target practice. Izaat was the only one who seemed to be questioning this foolishness.

"Is it true, Izaat, that you have been asked to lead a group if a strike is called?" asked Raoul.

"It does not matter who leads, but if there is a strike called, it is a call to war by the Mufti and the Arab Higher Committee, and I will go."

"And us with you," Raoul said with bravado. The others chimed in.

Mary nearly bit the end of her pencil off. Strikes? Riots? She had been only eight years old when the last strikes occurred. The city was practically shut down, many people died, and she remembered the hardship on them as a family. Her father had been so afraid during that time. Then he had left. The Mufti blamed opposition leaders like her father for the loss of his rebellion. And her father thought it would be better that he go away for a few months. It had lasted more than a year.

She could stand to listen to their talk no more. She must go someplace else. Grabbing her shawl, she went through the store to where the men stood.

"You leave already, little Sister," Izaat said with a smile.

"I have errands to run." Then she thought of her father. "Izaat, may I speak with you?"

A bit annoyed, Izaat pulled away from the group and joined her. "What is it, Mary?" he said a little coolly.

"Father is very upset this morning. Could you go by the house and . . ." She noticed that another man had joined their group, and the men were talking in more hushed tones.

Izaat's brow wrinkled, "Is he still ill? Why now?"

"He is better, and he needs someone to talk to. This might be the time to make things right."

"I haven't changed my mind. I fight for Palestine."

"Izaat, he is your father. Please go and see him."

"He would only try to stop us from fighting for Haj Amin." Izaat's eyes remained cool, determined. He was not a tall man, but he was powerfully built with a barrel chest and thick biceps. He had worked as a stevedore in Jaffa port for a year before their father encouraged him to buy the shop. Mary knew few men who could match him in strength. But his head often turned as hard as his muscles, and though not given to hyperbole and excited argument like Rhoui, he could be as pigheaded as any man she knew. Only she and their mother had learned how to break through his granite exterior.

She gave him her warmest smile and put a hand on his arm. "Father knows that the time for talk has ended. He knows you are committed. I am sure you will be able to talk of other things. Go see him, Brother. You will be glad you did, and it would make me very happy as well."

The cool exterior visibly warmed, and he nodded. "I must meet with Emile Ghoury, then I will go and see him."

Emile Ghoury, secretary of the Arab Higher Committee and a trusted Husseini lieutenant, was the man responsible for any fighting in the Old City. Mary's heart missed a beat, but she said nothing. To argue with him about it would be fruitless and only change his mind about their father. She nodded agreement and started down the street, glancing over her shoulder to see Izaat return to the group. The stranger was obviously a Muslim villager and his gesture indicated he was telling them something important. It made her bristle, and she picked up her pace.

The further she went, the more she noticed other groups of men gathering about shop fronts and tables, all talking in the same hushed tones. Their talk of war was obvious, but when? Where? She knew there had been attacks, isolated incidents by hotheads, thieves, and fanatics. Most expected these things—they were common to Palestine, much too common. Decisions or statements that displeased one side or the other always brought such reactions these days, and their response was usually violent. But this was different. This gave her a feeling of impending doom and it made her skin crawl.

All the way to Damascus Gate the feeling was the same. Even outside the walls there was a hushed tone and merchants left their wares unattended to gather in small groups. She covered her face and moved close enough to one that she could hear.

"The Mufti? But he is not in Palestine. Surely he will need to come before—"

"We are his hands!" interrupted a hard-looking man at the center of the circle. "We are Allah's warriors, and we must fight. Prepare yourselves and be ready! We answer their resolution tomorrow, and we answer it with blood! Already the Syrians attack in the north. Raids only, but soon, when the British leave, they will come into Palestine like a flood! Our Arab brothers are with us, and some cross the border even now to join us. Even Khader is returning. For now we strike like vipers, but soon it will be as many as the hoards of Genghis Kahn who drive the Jews into the sea!"

The group of men all nodded agreement. One caught sight of her and gave an evil look that said, *Move away, Woman. This is not your affair.* She turned and went up the steps to the street.

Crossing, she practically ran to the post office and mailed her letters. As she left the building, she felt dread about returning to the Old City and the shop. It was coming, and she was frightened. She needed to think, to find a place to find some peace and calm her feelings.

She thought of the tomb. Turning back, she went to Jaffa Road and then north, walked a block, and turned into a narrow street. After only a short distance, she knocked on the gate door of the Garden Tomb, then waited.

Since returning to Jerusalem from England, she had come here on several occasions to think and read about Christ. Inside the walled compound was what the Anglican Church considered the tomb of Jesus, even though most Catholics and Protestants believed that the tomb was located in the Church of the Holy Sepulcher. Her first visit here had been one of skepticism and curiosity, but she had felt such peace here that she could not resist the thought that it might be the spot where such holy things occurred. Returning when she could, she had become convinced.

The door opened, and Arthur Sommers stood before her, a smile on his face. Welcoming her, he opened the gate wide enough that she could step inside and out of the noise of the city. He then left her alone, returning to his duties.

Turning left, she walked down a bit of an incline where steps were being built as a part of the restoration. At the bottom and in front of the tomb entrance was a sitting bench carved from the rough stone surrounding it. She sat down on the rock wall and removed her headscarf. She felt her fear melt away as she settled into the quiet environment of the garden. Closing her eyes, she let it wash over her like water, cleansing her of her fears and worry.

After nearly twenty minutes she heard soft footsteps on the steps and opened her eyes to see a young man pass by her and approach the tomb, then disappear inside. She had been there and knew what he would see—a burial chamber to the right and left of a middle or wailing chamber. The one on the right still had a part of the stone on which the dead person would be lain and was thought to be the chamber to which Jesus was taken and then resurrected on the third day.

The young man came out a few minutes later, a sober look on his face. He noticed her and smiled before turning toward the steps. Dark hair, khaki pants and shirt with the long sleeves rolled up. His face was tanned, and very dark eyes sat above chiseled cheekbones. It was obvious he was a Jew, and an attractive one at that.

"Why does a Jew come to a Christian holy site?" she asked.

He turned back. "Your Savior would not approve?" he replied with a wry smile.

"If I remember my history, it was your people who first disapproved. Of Him."

"On the contrary, we believe he was a good Jew and his early following was made up of Jews. We have no quarrel with that. It was the Jewish leaders who disapproved, probably because they felt threatened. After his death, more Jews turned away because his followers tried to make more of him than just a good Jew. It is that we disapprove of, just as we disapprove of Muslims making more of Mohammed than he really was." He spoke in English with an accent she knew was European. His voice was pleasant enough to listen to, and she was impressed with his understanding of at least some of what transpired. But he was haughty—a typical Jew filled with pride because he was a Jew. Silliness.

"They are not the same. Mohammed was a man, Jesus was God come to earth."

"Hmm," he gave a tolerant smile. "From what I've been told, you will be hard pressed to prove that, even in your own scripture. As I understand it, Jesus and God are not one and the same, but two separate and distinct individuals, one called Jehovah and the other Elohim."

"You came here for a reason. Apparently it is not because you are a believer," she said coolly.

"A friend of mine—an American—told me about this place months ago. He said he thought it was the real tomb of Christ. He is also the one who taught me what I just told you. If I were a believer in your Jesus, it would be that one I would have to believe in." He shrugged. "As far as coming here, curiosity got the best of me, I guess." He looked around at what could be seen of the garden. "Except for the people who work and live here, there don't seem to be many others who believe as you and my friend do."

She looked down at the dusty stone floor between her and the tomb. "I suppose they are occupied with the announcement of your new state." She said it coldly.

"Christians? Probably in mourning," he turned. "I should be getting to my duty." He started toward the gate again.

"Will you drive us out of our homes?" she asked without thinking.

He stopped and turned back, staring into her eyes as if searching for something or trying to make up his mind what to say. Finally he took a deep breath.

"I don't know. War is not that easily manipulated is it? I don't think most Germans wanted to massacre my people when Hitler came to power, at least that is what I choose to believe. But in time, in the heat of war, many changed their minds. If war comes . . . I cannot tell you what we will do anymore than you can tell me if your holy strugglers will drive my family from their home."

"I would not take away your home," she said.

He smiled slightly, "No, I don't suppose you would, not any more than I would take yours. But I fear your leaders will not be so kind."

"And yours?"

He hesitated. "I'm not sure of them, either. As I said, war changes things, people."

"Yes, I know. I have a brother who lusts for Jewish blood as much as the Inquisitors of an earlier age did." She forced a smile. "You spoke of a family?"

"I and my brother are the only survivors from my family, but we are part of another now; a mum and dad, a sister and two new brothers. Twins."

"Are you afraid for them?"

He hesitated again, thinking. "Yes," he said softly. He started up the incline, then stopped again. "If what my mum tells me is true about what happened in this place . . . I see why she and Ephraim love to come here. It is very . . . peaceful." He disappeared from view, and she stood and went to where she could see him.

"Are they Anglican?"

He laughed lightly. "No, nor are they Catholic or Protestant."

"Then what are they?"

"Saints, both of them." He walked away and disappeared through the gate, leaving her even more curious. Quickly ascending the steps Mary ran after him. He was almost to the street when she yelled her question. "What do you mean, they are saints? All good Christians . . ."

He did not hear her and disappeared around the corner. She felt disappointed but didn't know why. What was it about him that would make her feel this way?

She took a deep breath. It did not matter. He was a Jew. He was gone. That was as it should be. But his mother was a Christian. Though strange to some, it was not so to her. Her mother had been Muslim, her father Christian. She supposed that was one reason it was so easy for Rhoui to gravitate to that religion. She just wished he hadn't gravitated to the fanatics who used it for their own purposes.

Wrapping her scarf over her head and then around the lower section of her face, she started for the street. Her father would be ready for something to eat now, and he would still want to visit the church. She felt better, stronger. She always did after her visits to the tomb.

Mary crossed Suleiman Street and entered Damascus Gate. The throngs seemed normal, the talk focused on buying and selling goods. It eased her mind further, and she let it drift back to the mysterious Jew. He had not been tall, but he was not short either. Thin, but muscled, with dark hair and eyes. He could pass for an Arab, she thought, but she had known him to be a Jew immediately. It was his clothing. Khaki shirt, long sleeves rolled up past the elbow, and khaki pants with military style boots. Yes, many wore such clothing. It was the closest thing to a military uniform they had in their *Haganah*. And yet he had not frightened her. In fact, she had felt quite safe. Curious.

As she pushed her way through the crowded, narrow streets, the thought occurred to her that she would see him again. It was a strange thought for an Arab woman, especially now, but she couldn't help it. She *wanted* to see him again. She pulled her scarf a little higher around her nose as if it would keep her thoughts from being discovered. If her father knew—and her brothers—that she entertained thoughts about a Jew, they would surely lock her in the house until she were an old woman!

The thought gave her even greater pleasure, and she found the sudden necessity of mentally kicking herself back to reality. This was no time for such daydreaming.

She went up the stairs of their apartment, pausing at the door, getting final control of her thoughts and feelings. Then, turning the knob, she entered. Her father still sat on the small patio, his head slumped forward, sleeping. She put her scarf on its hanger, straightened her hair in the mirror, and went to him. Stooping down in front of the chair, she smiled up at him and was about to ask him if Izaat had come when she saw that his eyes were open and fixed.

"Father," she said, touching his arm, sudden fear rushing to her chest.

His arm slipped out from under her hand as his head fell to the side.

"Father!" she screamed it as she tried to catch his slumping body and ease it to the floor, tears springing to her eyes with the sudden realization that he was dead.

"Father! Wake up!" she pleaded as she gathered him into her lap. "Please, you can't leave me now!" She shook him lightly, trying to wake him, but he didn't move. He couldn't be dead. She would not let him be! She shook him again. "Father, oh Father!" She turned toward the balcony and screamed for help as she held him tightly, her tears cascading down her cheeks and dropping onto his cold flesh. The door opened, and she felt the presence of others as they rushed into the room. She screamed at them to help him. Several knelt down and tried to calm her as grief thrust itself over her like a wave of the sea. She had left him! He had died alone! How could she have not felt it coming? Not known he needed her?

She felt strong arms try to pull her away, heard the voice of Izaat, but she would not listen. She held tightly to her father, refusing to let go. Izaat pulled harder, forcing her free of him and gathering her up from the floor and into his arms. Suddenly the room darkened around her, sounds blurring. She fought it, tried to stay conscious, get back to the lifeless body on the floor, but the darkness gathered strength, enveloped her, and forced itself mercilessly into her heart. Then there was nothing.

Izaat took her from the room and lay her limp body on her bed. He instructed his wife to care for her as he returned to the room and worked his way through the crowd to his father. He had come too late. He should have ignored the meeting with Emile and the others. Mary had asked him to come. She must have sensed this, and he had delayed. Now his heart ached. Picking up the lifeless body as gently as he could, he held him close and kissed his forehead, tears rolling down his granite cheeks. The wailing began, the crowd following him from the room, down the stairs, and into the street. As he worked his way toward the Church of the Holy Sepulcher, the crowd grew and the word spread.

Amos Aref had gone to Paradise.

SEE CHAPTER NOTES

CHAPTER 5

Hannah and Naomi each carried one of the twins as they walked the short distance to the bus station. Hannah purchased tickets, and they sat down to wait.

"How long?" Naomi asked, rocking Joseph gently in her arms.

"Half an hour. It's the bus from Netanya. It will make a stop here before going to Jerusalem. Once we're aboard, it's about an hour and a half to Jerusalem."

Naomi nodded. She was used to waiting. Over the last two years she had spent more time waiting than she cared to remember—for Jews to gather to their assigned meeting place; for guards to look the other way so they could cross over borders; for boats that sometimes came and sometimes didn't. Waiting was a part of life.

A woman sat down beside them, parking her luggage in a second seat. She seemed frightened.

"Atah Beseder?" Hannah asked in Hebrew.

"All right, you ask? Am I all right?" Her eyes rolled. "It is starting," she said in a harsh whisper. "They shot a young man just outside of Tel Aviv this morning. Just shot him in cold blood. Shot at others to. Like snipers they sit on their houses and try to pick us off! They are planning more. Some say they will attack Tel Aviv tomorrow or the next day. I go to Jerusalem. It is safer there."

Hannah could only smile. Safe. There was no place in Palestine that would be safe now. "Do you know who the man was?" she asked.

"Moshe Goldman, may the Eternal give him peace. He was a neighbor. Just twenty-five and a good boy. Oy, they will kill all the good boys."

Hannah reached over and touched the woman's arm. "Please, won't you hold the baby for a moment? I wish to talk to the ticket agent."

The distraught woman reached for Jacob, her face immediately softening. "Oy, such a dear boy!" Hannah went to the ticket line and waited her turn. She inquired about the coming of the bus from Netanya, then returned to her seat, noticing that the numbers were quickly growing. The place was abuzz with talk in half a dozen different languages, four of which Hannah understood. Most of these people were anxious to get back to their homes and were leaving Tel Aviv's beaches or visits to friends and family early. The anxiety of war was setting in.

Hannah gestured to take the baby, but the woman had him asleep and pulled Jacob close, unwilling to give him up. Hannah smiled and sat down across from them. A young lady sat in the chair next to her, ticket in hand, calm and poised. Her tan skin set off blue eyes and blonde hair in a thin, plain face.

"Shalom," Hannah said. "Do you live in Jerusalem?"

The girl shook her head lightly and said no, but her face flushed. "I go there for my wedding."

"*Ezeh Yofi!* Oh, how wonderful!" Hannah said. They talked for a moment and Hannah found out her name was Shoshanna Farhi; she was twenty-two, and her wedding was still several weeks away. Attempting another question, Hannah noticed the bus approaching and stood to get the baby. There were no reserved seats on buses, and if they didn't want to stand the entire trip with babes in arms, they had better get moving. Naomi had already picked up her bag and was headed for the door, Joseph under an arm. Hannah received Jacob back with less reluctance this time as the woman was quickly trying to get to the bus herself. Hannah turned to pick up her suitcase, but Shoshanna already had a hand on it and smiled.

"Let me help," she said.

They hastened to the bus and a short line while an even longer line formed behind them. Hannah handed her ticket to the driver. She was relieved to see Naomi saving her a seat near the center of the bus. Shoshanna gave Hannah her luggage, but all seats were taken except for one a few seats in front of them. She stepped toward it, but another took it first, forcing her to stand just a few feet behind the driver. A moment later the bus pulled from the station and headed for the main road to Jerusalem.

As they turned onto the highway that would lead them past Lydda Airport then into the canyons of the Jerusalem/Tel Aviv Road, Hannah felt anxious. The road to Jerusalem was narrow, winding, and set between steep hills lined with half a dozen Arab villages. Its craggy, tree-lined side hills had been used for ambush before, especially during the rebellion of 1936–39. Bullets randomly fired at the completely filled bus would surely take a life, and with the babies along, it concerned her deeply.

In the morning paper there had been a call to remain calm, a reminder that a declaration of partition did not mean war, that negotiations with the Arab states were continuing and leaders were sure a settlement could be reached. Hannah hoped so, but she also knew Haj Amin had begun stirring up his people, vowing to begin the fight and drive the Jews back to Europe. She had tuned into Cairo radio and heard the latest of his speeches to that effect. The man was not about to settle for peace.

Hannah noticed the plane coming in for a landing and stared at it carefully. A small passenger plane with Greek markings. She thought of Ephraim. Tomorrow he would come home. It brought a smile to her face, and she let her mind wander as she stared out the window.

They had been happy from the moment he had pulled her out of the sea to the safety of Eretz Israel's soil. Married at Jerusalem by British authority on January 22, they had moved into a small apartment in the Jewish Quarter of the Old City where they became an immediate oddity. First, they had not been married under Jewish law, something for which some of the rabbis had never forgiven them; and second, Ephraim had started holding Church meetings at their home, inviting all his neighbors to attend, another thing for which some of the rabbis would probably never forgive them, especially Rabbi Salomon—the most prominent Rabbi in the Old City and the most stern and unbending.

Ephraim's missionary effort bore little fruit, however. Though many were curious at first, Rabbi Salomon threatened them with excommunication from the synagogue if they continued coming to Ephraim's meetings. Consequently such get togethers amounted to

44	Robert Marcum

themselves, David and Elizabeth, and an occasional visitor from America or England who belonged to the Church. They were usually in Palestine on business, doing archaeological work, or busy with political matters, but they had seen Ephraim's posting on the bulletin boards of the British headquarters building or the King David Hotel. His success amounted to Hannah and the two children being baptized in May of 1946. Only going to the temple in Salt Lake City a little over a year later was better.

After that their lives seemed more settled, even peaceful. All of them continued to work with the underground immigration program, and Ephraim began flying mail in to some of the settlements with one of the small planes owned by a private company. Then the Haganah approached him. Still a clandestine organization within Israel, they wanted his help in organizing an air force. His nights were spent in meetings with everyone from the head of the Haganah, Yitzhak Sadeh, to the premier leader of the Zionist movement, David Ben-Gurion.

Shocked back to the present, Hannah gasped as she saw the truck swing on to the road in front of them, immediately recognizing trouble. As the two men in the back raised weapons to fire, she screamed, "Naomi, get down!" Accustomed to such commands, Naomi was on the floor as the first bullets pierced the window, hitting Shoshanna Farhi and two others. Seriously wounded, the driver lost control of the bus, and it swerved, hit the side of the road, then slid down the embankment. Hannah felt it begin to tip. She pulled Jacob close, trying to prevent him from being pummeled by the chaos of bodies and metal. When the bus finally careened to a halt, she was buried under the weight of several screaming passengers. It was a fight to keep her and Jacob from being crushed in the panic of everyone trying to get free. She heard the explosions and felt the bus shake as more bodies were thrown on top of them.

Then it was quiet. In shock everyone lost their voice, fear making their mouths dry and their lungs ache. Hannah pushed and shoved to get free, felt the warm stickiness of blood but didn't know if it were her own or another's. A strong arm reached down and pulled her free, and she found herself in the midst of horror. Smoke lay thick in the air, people moaned, others screamed, as the living realized they must get free.

"*Poh!* Here!" someone hollered from above. She looked up and saw a man against a clear blue sky reaching down. But how could this be? How could . . . ? She shook her head, trying to free it of the cobwebs.

"Give me the child, quickly!" the voice repeated in Hebrew.

Hannah glanced down at Jacob who was screaming and frightened. She came to her senses and handed the boy to the strong hands reaching down to help her. As she turned to find Naomi and Joseph, she saw others scrambling to get free through broken windows. Naomi was on her knees, shaking her head slowly left to right, while staring down at little Joseph.

"No," she said. "No! Joseph! Open your eyes! Joseph, please . . ."

Hannah thrust herself over a body and around those exiting through the side of the bus. She knelt beside Naomi. Joseph's forehead was covered with blood, and Naomi had been hurt as well. Hannah took her child, "Naomi, get up. Quickly! We have to get out of here," she said with shaky composure. Inside she was shattered. She could feel no breath from her little boy's mouth, could feel no movement in his little body. She pulled him close. "Breathe, Joseph. You must breathe."

Nothing. She pulled him up to her lips and, squeezing his little mouth between her fingers, blew air into his lungs and pulled back.

Nothing. Naomi was now outside, but Hannah ignored her pleas to follow. Again she gave her baby air, and again. Suddenly he coughed, then again, and again. Then a cry.

"*Elohim Yakia, Todah Rabah!*" she said loudly, as Joseph started to scream. Standing, she lifted him to Naomi who disappeared from the window. Strong hands reached down and grabbed her, pulling her free. Her last view was of Shoshana Farhi, lying in a pool of her own blood, her eyes staring into the distance.

A moment later she was standing on solid ground, Joseph back in her arms, a cloth pressed tightly against the cut on his head. Naomi came to her knees beside them crying, shaking a bit but her fear for Joseph relieved by his blinking eyes and loud cry. Hannah put her hand on top of Naomi's. "It's all right. Joseph is fine. Find Jacob, Naomi. Find Jacob."

Naomi's breath caught, and she nodded, then stood and went for Jacob.

Moments later a dozen cars were on the scene. People came to help, and among them was a doctor. He treated the most serious first but finally came to Hannah, Naomi, and the two children. When he was finished, he had stitched a screaming Joseph's wound with half a dozen stitches. Naomi's own took a dozen more, and Hannah had received attention for a knot on the back of her head the size of an egg. Loaded quickly into trucks, the more seriously wounded were returned to Tel Aviv for care. When asked if she wanted to go with them, she shook her head. "We go to Jerusalem," she said, looking down at her son, who was now sleeping. "We go home."

Five minutes later they were in a large army truck driven by British soldiers. She quickly learned they had been en route to the airport when they saw the scene and came to help. "Our orders don't include getting you back to the city, but they don't say we shouldn't either," one of them said.

"What happened?" Naomi asked.

"Arabs. Unhappy about things is my guess," said a second soldier. "Don't worry, ladies, they won't attack us. You'll be safe as if you was me own mum." Hannah was grateful for the arrival of these soldiers.

The truck left the scene, and Hannah watched it slowly fade behind them. It was then she remembered Shoshana Farhi.

Her marriage had been only days away.

SEE CHAPTER NOTES

CHAPTER 6

Aaron left Haganah headquarters on Montefiore Street. Still no real orders. Everything seemed a bit confusing, the excitement of the announced partition almost causing atrophy as people celebrated, seeming to think a declaration would end any dispute. It wouldn't last long. The Arabs had already attacked a bus on its way to Jerusalem from Tel Aviv, and a sniper near Jaffa had shot a man. East Jerusalem—the Arab sector—seemed quiet enough, but he was sure it was just the calm before the storm. The denunciations by world Arab leaders were heating up the airwaves, and Haj Amin had denounced the whole affair through his headquarters in Cairo, though the report said he was in Lebanon somewhere. He called for *Jihad* from all Muslims. Typical for a butcher like Haj Amin Husseini. If the British could keep him and his followers out of the country, calm things down, there might be a chance for peace. But Haganah intelligence—SHAI—was already reporting border crossings by large groups of armed Arab fighters, and the British were making no more than a show at stopping them. Apparently the Arab Higher Committee's offer to pay was working, and with partition less than a day old, it did not bode well for a peaceful solution.

He headed toward the Old City. As he reached the corner of Suleiman Street and Jaffa Road, the wailing of an Arab funeral service filled the air. He looked to his left and saw the procession coming toward him. It was impressive with hundreds of people crowded around the body, held aloft by mourners. Possibly an Arab dignitary. Whoever he was, he was popular with his people—and the British.

There were dozens of guards along the road and at least six armored cars leading or following the procession, their gunners at the ready and watching the rooftops and the crowd as if expecting trouble, as well they should. The Arabs were stirring the pot, and some among ETZEL and LEHI had issued statements that the war for Jewish Independence was only just beginning and that blood would run in the streets.

He let his own eye wander across the crowd that lined the street. The Arabs were on the far side, thick in number, but the Jewish presence on his side of the street was nearly as large. No one seemed interested in starting something. The body being passed over the heads of mourners was the center of everyone's attention. The devotion by both Jew and Arab at a time when unrest was high piqued Aaron's curiosity even more, and he stepped to a spot where he could see better.

A priest of the Roman Catholic Church led the procession, surrounded by several others carrying ornate receptacles and dressed in their priestly robes. Most of the mourners were dressed in black, the women with their faces at least partially covered by headscarves or veils after the Arab tradition. Except one.

She walked behind the bier, her black hair blowing in the cool wind of the November day, her dark eyes filled with the sadness of loss instead of the peace he had seen just last evening at the garden tomb. As before, her beauty made his heart skip a beat and his eyes take a long admiring look.

Two men walked beside her. The younger of the two was probably in his late twenties and wore an Arab *kaffiyeh* and a business suit. His face was hard with anger, and he often glared at the Jews who had come to honor the man lying still on the bier. His wife and children walked behind him, their faces filled with sadness.

The other wore a dark maroon, conical shaped *fez*, the head covering introduced under the Turks fifty years ago but still popular with some Palestinians. He too was dressed in a dark suit and tie and carried a small child in his arms. Two older children and a wife followed, and their age would put him in his mid to late thirties. Stocky and powerfully built, only his eyes were filled with shocked sadness.

The woman wore a black dress of European cut that fit her well, the calves of her legs showing. It wasn't typical attire for an Arab woman, especially under these circumstances, and from the defiant look on her face, she didn't care. This was a woman with spunk and determination. She intrigued him even more.

The crowd of mourners continued to grow, and Aaron noticed they were of all kinds—Arab Muslims, wailing and wanting to touch the bier after their tradition; Christians, much more somber and quiet; and orthodox Jews, their vocal mourning rivaled that of the Arabs, but they did not approach the bier. The law of clean and unclean, though ancient, still held sway in orthodox Jewry.

As more Arabs joined the procession, the crowd swelled and British guards closed ranks on this side of the street, trying their best to keep the two peoples separated. Even Jews wanted to join in and pushed forward, forcing their way past the guards and into the procession. The British grabbed several and thrust them back. A few altercations began until one of the commanding officers saw they were not trying to make trouble and told his men to let them go. With that came a sudden push toward the family as all joined together to pay their respects. Aaron was moved forward, caught up in the flow as it pressed into the street. He was nearly even with the bier, fighting against the wave of humanity in an attempt to reverse his direction, when he saw the girl only a few feet away. Tears streamed down her cheeks, and a firm, yet proud, set to her jaw reminded him of Hannah. Though she looked pale and tired from her loss, she held her head high, her back straight. He watched as the younger of the two brothers handed her a scarf. She shoved it away, making him angry. He pushed it toward her again, and she shoved it away a second time. It was obvious she was embarrassing him by her refusal to wear the headscarf, obvious that it angered him nearly to the point of losing control. Then the elder brother whispered to her, and she reluctantly took the scarf, wrapping it around her neck in mock refusal. He said something else but it did no good and he gave up. He was also angered by her stubbornness, but there was little either of them could do.

"Who is it?" Aaron shouted at an old gentleman next to him.

"Dr. Amos Aref. His office is in the Old City. He treated both Arabs and Jews. A good man, may the God of Moses and Abraham bless his family."

Aaron stepped closer to the old Jew talking as he kept walking, his eyes on the girl. "Is that his daughter?"

"Yes, and his two sons. The one in the *kafiyeh* is Rhoui. A nationalist and supporter of the Arab Higher Committee. They say he has converted to Islam because of its teaching on holy war, and because the Catholic Church has let it be known that they do not support a war against the Jews. The other is Izaat. Also a nationalist, but much more level headed. He is shrewd, tough, but fair-minded and will be a good leader of men in any battle. A dangerous man if he is your enemy."

"You know them well."

"I am also a doctor. Amos and I worked together. Our wives . . ." He cleared his throat. "We were very close friends for many years."

"How can a Christian support Haj Amin?" Aaron said stiffly.

"Most say they support the Arab Higher Committee, not Amin, and the Committee has promised Christians a say in the new government if they fight now."

"Are they fools? Everyone knows Haj Amin pulls the strings of the Committee."

"This may be true, but it is their way of getting around a ticklish subject. Besides, there is no other Palestinian representative other than Haj Amin. They really have no other choice."

"Only because the Mufti butchers candidates, or has them run out of the country. Have they forgotten?"

They were only a few feet from the family now, the crush of the crowd pushing them along the street toward the Mount of Olives.

"Mary is Amos's only daughter. She went to England for education. As you can see she does not hold to the Arab traditions, or the Christian ones. She has always been a headstrong girl, but until she went to London she never questioned such things." There was a worried wrinkle to his brow, a wrinkle created when one generation cannot understand why another cannot see things as they do. But Aaron understood. He had broken with the traditions of his own religion, as most Zionists had. What good were they when God seemed to value tradition more than he did human life?

"Rhoui and Izaat will be furious with her for making them look bad in public. The way she dresses and acts is a humiliation for them," the doctor said.

"What will they do?"

"If it were left to Rhoui, he would banish her to another city. But Izaat is the oldest." The man shrugged. "He will decide, but this is no regular woman. She may not abide by either decision. She loved London. She will probably return there."

Aaron watched as the crowd continued down Suleiman Street. "There are so many people. Under present circumstances I would not think they could walk side-by-side with us."

"Because of the coming war?" he frowned. "Yes, in a few days they will be shooting at each other, but those who knew Amos would never do such a thing at his funeral. He was a peace-loving man. It must have broken his heart to . . ." His voice trailed off and he cleared his throat again. "He supported the opposition to Haj Amin for years, but he was broken by the lack of progress and the insistence of the Jews to lobby the UN for partition. He has been out of the public eye for many months now. Just another sane voice shouted down by the fanatics. It is a sad day."

"Then his sons disagreed with their father. What about his daughter?"

He paused as the bier pressed ahead and they began to lose ground. "Amos has had nothing to do with his sons since they declared their support for the Committee and Haj Amin. Mary is her father's daughter."

A fight broke out behind the procession, young hotheads using the wake to start throwing fists at each other. The British moved quickly to separate the half dozen combatants before more joined in. All were pummeled into submission with batons, then dragged away and put in the back of a waiting truck. Two more tried to free their friends and others joined them. All at once the British had their hands full, and Aaron found himself on the fringe of a riot. He took the old gentleman's arm and pulled him away to safety. They gained the sidewalk at the corner of King David and Suleiman streets and quickly slipped inside the foyer of a small hotel. Looking out the window, they watched as the British circled the small group of fighters and quickly gained control, the procession moving forward without most even knowing what had happened.

The old gentleman sat down on a soft red leather chair to catch his breath. Aaron sat in a similar chair across from him.

"What you see is only a beginning. Tomorrow . . ." His voice trailed off, his face pale with sorrow.

"What of tomorrow?" Aaron asked.

"Enough of war. Your accent tells me you have not been in Palestine long. A survivor of the German war is my guess."

"Berlin. I arrived only a year ago after spending the previous year helping others leave Europe."

"I thought so. I have lived here all my life. I have seen everything change."

"And you wish for the old days," Aaron said a bit cynically.

The old man gave Aaron a tolerant smile. "Sometimes. Especially when I think of the price you and others will pay for your dream of a Jewish state."

"We are willing if it means freedom from the tyranny of others," Aaron said firmly.

"Yes, I am sure you are. Your experience in the camps has given you the strength necessary to fight, but it also clouds your vision."

"It seems to me our vision is perfectly clear. We are a persecuted people and always will be until we have a place of our own with laws that can protect us from massacre by those who blame us for everything from the collapse of their economy to the death of their savior."

"But what is your insatiable need to drive away the people who have lived on this land for generations? Can you not see what you ask them to give up?"

"It is not their land and never has been," Aaron said adamantly. "Though they have lived on it, they have never been its owners. Other governments—the Romans, the Turks—"

The old gentleman raised a hand. "Please, I know the history. But it is this very attitude I speak of. You use this argument to defend your position, and in doing so, you refuse to see what you are doing to men like Amos and his family." He sat back in his chair. "Argue as you will, you will never convince the Palestinian people you have a greater right to this land than they do. If the world wants to be so generous with Palestine, why not give it to the people who have lived on it for the past thousand years? What gives them the right to give it to you? That is how they think, and nothing you say will convince them otherwise." He leaned forward again. "You must learn to see it from their perspective, young survivor, or you will never have peace in this land. Never."

Aaron felt both anger and confusion. He stood to leave. "They can have their own state, a first for a people most Arabs consider to be Syrian or Lebanese or Jordanian, or they can go and live with those who claim them as brothers. It is their choice, but we have no place else to go, and we will fight them if they try to shove us out. It is a very simple proposition."

"Is it so simple?" The old man got to his feet slowly then looked directly into Aaron's eyes with sadness. "When you take away a man's home, he will hate you for it and then he will fight you to his last breath to get it back. It is not the Arabs of other nations you need to fear, nor is it Haj Amin and his mercenaries. They will lose heart for the battle eventually, because it is not their land and their home. It is the people of the land who will fight you. They will never go away, and their hatred will only grow as you push them into a small corner of the country they think is theirs." He took a deep breath. "It is prophesied that we will return, and thus it must be, but it is also prophesied that it will be a day of sorrows. I wish only that you understand why this will be so."

"I do not even know your name," Aaron said.

"Yehuda Messerman. I am a doctor, but I do not do much anymore. My hands . . ." He looked at them, shaking his head. "Old age has made them less steady than they used to be." He forced a smile, then left and the door closed behind him.

Aaron followed, watching Dr. Messerman disappear into the crowd. He started back, a bit unsettled by the old man's words. The battle for the land he was fighting and would fight had always been an end point for him—the culmination of events that would give them peace and freedom. It was obvious Dr. Messerman didn't agree. Surely he was wrong.

Unlike Haj Amin, Aaron's people didn't want to butcher Arabs in the streets or make them subservient or second-class citizens. Everyone would benefit from a Jewish state, if they were willing. Surely, eventually, they would see this.

The procession was out of sight, the street normal except for police vans a hundred yards east of where he stood. The hotheads would be taken to jail and probably released before the sun set. The British were keeping the peace as they had done for more than thirty years. He wondered how much longer that would be possible, how much longer they would try. He crossed the street and walked south toward Jaffa Gate and along the Old City wall. At the gate, he turned left and entered the Old City. Immediately sensing hostility as Arab merchants and bystanders glared at him, uttering venomous words, Aaron kept to the right and walked down Patriarchate Street instead of going through the souks to the Jewish Quarter. He saw an Orthodox Jewish family fifty steps ahead of him with half a dozen Arab youths taunting them. One threw a stone at the man, then ran away in fear of a reaction. There was none, and another boy was emboldened to throw a stone of his own. This one struck a young Jewish boy of the family in the head and caused an immediate outcry of pain. The father and mother quickly pulled him along, attempting to get away, but the Arabs were merciless. Seeing their success, others joined in as a mob mentality quickly took over. Aaron looked about for British help, saw no one, and knew he would have to do something.

"Hey!" he yelled as the boys moved closer, preparing to attack the family with more stones. "Hey!" he yelled again. He ran after them and grabbed an Arab boy by his shirt collar before he could get away. The others scattered, fear in their eyes as they realized they were no longer preying on a Jew unwilling to fight. He shoved the boy away, and he stumbled after his friends while yelling Arabic curses over his shoulder. Once out of Aaron's reach, he threw his stone. It hit the ground five feet in front of Aaron and then careened to the left, hitting the wall. Aaron feigned as if to chase the boy, and he took off like his pants were afire.

Aaron turned to find the Jewish family already far ahead, scurrying like frightened rabbits for the safety of the Quarter. Continuing his walk, he picked up the pace. He could chase away children, but if their older brothers or fathers decided to take up the argument, he would be at a distinct disadvantage.

He warned several passing Jews of the hooligans without much effect, then turned into the Jewish Quarter and headed down the street toward Hannah and Ephraim's apartment. Entering the Street of the Jews his eyes caught sight of a woman hanging children's clothes on a line that stretched across the street one story up. She was humming a song he didn't recognize, but it gave him comfort, and he was grateful for the normality. With Messerman's words and the rock-throwing children still fresh in his mind, he couldn't help but wonder how long such would be the case. The Arabs had a propensity toward a very quick graduation from stones to bullets as seen in the riots of 1936–39.

At the corner he nearly bumped into the man he had just helped in the street. He hadn't noticed before, but he wore the garb of the Neturei Karta, a fanatic party within orthodox Jewry that believed only God himself could give Israel to the Jews, not the Zionists. They had lived in the Jewish Quarter of the Old City and in other places around the city for several generations under Arab, Turkish, and British rule and saw no reason for things to change. Though in the past there had been some deaths due to Arab riots, the Nuturei Karta saw them only as a punishment for their lack of humility before God, not because of any Arab hate for them as Jews. Aaron, like most Zionists who had opted to leave God in heaven and out of their lives, saw their argument as the same apathetic and naïve attitude that had led so many of his people to the gas chambers of Germany. He excused himself and kept going.

"We don't want you here," the man hissed in Hebrew. "The God of Moses will protect us, and we have pacts with the Mufti."

Aaron couldn't help himself and turned back. "Where was the Mufti, or your God for that matter, when those boys attacked your family?" he said, then he walked away.

"All you do is make trouble! Next time I go that way they will watch, and they will throw more rocks. It is better to leave it alone. We have an agreement. They will not kill us."

Aaron stopped in his tracks, the anger rising into his stomach. "No, just humiliate you. And this time they declare they will drive you from Jerusalem. What then?"

"They say this only because of you Zionists. Go away and things will be like they were. You force them to break their pact with us. It will be your fault they come to kill us—your fault they break the agreement."

It was all Aaron could do to start walking and keep quiet. He had argued with such men before. It did absolutely no good. If it wasn't God, it was the British, or the pact, but they always had an excuse for not joining the Haganah or even giving it much needed support. Because of it, Jerusalem was ill prepared for what lay ahead and would be the most at risk, especially the Jewish Quarter of the Old City where the Old Stones—the old orthodox community—were strongest. What would it take to get them to open their eyes? Would it take the death of this man's children to get him to see that this time the Arabs meant to annihilate the Jewish community? How could they make a pact with or believe in one made by the Mufti?

He turned the corner and nearly knocked someone to the ground, excused himself, turned around and nearly bumped into another.

"You are deep in thought."

Aaron looked up to see a friend standing a few feet ahead of him.

"What? Oh, *Shalom*, Abby. How are you?"

"Less occupied than you, thank goodness. You nearly knocked that poor man to the ground because of your stupor," he frowned.

Abraham Marshak was the son of one of the Old City's rabbis and just the opposite of the man who had just denounced Aaron. Lubovitcher Orthodox, Abby had joined the Haganah with his father's permission. The Lubovitcher were not like the Nuturei Karta. They believed God expected Israel to fight for their land as well as pray for it. Though shunned by Rabbi Salomon for their views, Abraham's people had remained steadfast and even made some headway with others.

"I am fine. I saw the argument with Saul. Do not mind him, he is Rabbi Salomon's disciple."

"How is the Rabbi?" Aaron asked out of a sort of cynical curiosity.

"Still trying to control the Quarter. You forget, little changes here. Rabbi Salomon sees to that."

"Still controls the charitable funds, does he?" Aaron said.

"Still. The other rabbis are tired of it. They look for ways to show their displeasure. That helps Haganah efforts, if nothing else."

"Is he still currying British favor?"

Abraham nodded. "He does not believe they will ever leave. Therefore, we must not do anything to injure their feelings and chase them away. He does not see that he is nothing more than their toady."

Abby also studied archaeology under Professor Sukenik, one of the most noted Bible archaeologists in the world and the father of Yigal Yadin, one of the youngest and, according to rumor, one of the brightest leaders in the Haganah. As usual, Abby had something under his arm wrapped in sheepskin.

"Still digging I see," Aaron said with a smile.

Abby returned the smile, clutching his find a little tighter. "And you? Are you still working at the newspaper?"

Aaron smiled, lifting his hands for Abby to see. There were dark spots on them, especially under the fingernails. Ink from the printing press. After his return from the Negev with Ben-Gurion, he had spent the rest of the night circulating a special edition of the paper hailing the partition vote and what it meant for all Palestine. It was in such demand, even members of the staff had not received a copy. He hoped that Hannah had been able to get one.

"I see. He still hasn't made you a reporter then."

The smile dissolved. "He wants me to take some classes, learn to write Hebrew first."

"Then you better do it. You don't want to wash ink off your hands the rest of your life," he said in his typically direct manner. In fact Aaron didn't know many Orthodox Jews who were not direct, even rude. He supposed it was their nature. Say what you had to say and say it in the fewest possible words.

"Why not? You seem to want to wash dirt off yours until the day you die."

Abby didn't smile. "There is a difference, I—"

"I was joking with you, Abby."

"I haven't seen you for awhile. Since you found a place of your own, you don't come to the Old City that often."

"Mum needed the space for the babies, and I like my privacy." He paused, thinking of Messerman's words. "What is being done to defend the Quarter? You know the Arabs will come."

"Starting last night, we are putting guards on the roofs and in the streets that lead directly into the Arab sections of the Old City. Tomorrow we meet with Haganah commanders over Jerusalem to decide on other measures."

"Are they convinced more needs to be done?" Aaron asked. Because of the intransigent attitude of the Old Stones, those who had lived and studied Torah in their Yeshivas for generations, and its crowded narrow streets, Aaron knew that Haganah leadership did not think the Old City defensible. They could not afford to pull limited resources from other places to defend people who refused to defend themselves.

"Not yet, and when statements like those Rabbi Salomon made today reach Haganah ears, they will not be any more willing to defend this place than they have been."

"What did the good Rabbi have to say?"

"That partition is not the wish of the Almighty, and any sane Jew should fight it. Once again, my father was the only dissenting voice, though others privately support him."

Aaron shook his head lightly in disbelief. "The Rabbi will get them all butchered if he doesn't change."

"More begin to realize this. Several of my friends have asked to join the fight. I am arranging weapons and some training."

"We will need more than a few," Aaron said.

Abraham only nodded. "I must hurry. This . . ." Abby lifted the package, "It is important. Eleazar waits for it."

"Title to all Israel, I hope."

"Were the Eternal One so willing. *Behatzlaka*, Aaron. Good luck," Abraham said.

"*Hi Shomer*, my friend. Be safe," Aaron responded then headed in the direction of Hannah and Ephraim's apartment. It was getting late, and he had to hurry if he wanted something to eat. The sun was low enough in the sky now that it did not shine in the street, and he felt the chill of the winter air. He should have remembered his coat, but he had left a jacket at the apartment on his last trip. He would use it to return to his apartment in the New City.

Reaching the stairs, he took them two at a time and knocked. He heard stirring inside, then the door opened. When he saw the bruised and scraped face of his mum, his mouth dropped open.

Hannah smiled and motioned him in. Naomi sat on the couch, her forehead covered in a bandage but a glad smile on her face. He could see she was happy to see him and smiled back. Then he saw Joseph and felt sick all over again. "*Zeh Lo Tov*. This is not good, Hannah."

Hannah calmed him with the touch of a hand. "He is alright. We all are."

Naomi stood, a bit nervous. It had been a long time. Aaron smiled at her. "More beautiful than I remember."

"You have always been blind, Aaron, but I am glad of it." They embraced and kissed each other on the cheek. Then he stepped back.

"Now, tell me what happened."

Naomi glanced at Hannah who gave her a nod. When they finished he was sobered. His thoughts of the war had always been sterile. Reality was a different thing, and the words of Gershon Avner resounded in his ears. *It will not be so easy when those you love are among the dead.* It had nearly happened.

"You must leave this place. It is not safe here. There is no one to stop even the smallest Arab attack, and already they are preparing for just that. You must come with me tomorrow to West Jerusalem, and from there to Tel Aviv."

Hannah gave him a tolerant smile, her eyebrow raising slightly as if to say he was surely kidding. Tel Aviv would be no safer than any other Jewish city in Israel. "You must be hungry," she said, handing Joseph to Naomi.

"Mum, you aren't listening," Aaron said with firm irritation.

"Later. For now, visit with Naomi. She has come so far. You *are* hungry, aren't you?" she asked, moving into the kitchen.

"I was, but I seem to have lost my appetite."

"Knowing you as I do, it will come back. David should be here soon, and Elizabeth."

"Are they at school then?"

Hannah nodded as she began pulling food from cupboards and the small icebox.

"What are you hearing, Aaron? How bad . . . in other places in the country . . ." Naomi asked.

He had been there when the report about the bus had come through, but he had not thought . . . He breathed deeply. "Another was attacked after your bus. A woman was killed. Another person was shot between Jaffa and Tel Aviv. A total of seven casualties today that we know of."

"Then it has begun," Naomi said.

"That is why we must move Hannah and the children out of here. Jerusalem will be their main target, and the Old City will get the worst of it."

"Then we must defend Jerusalem, not flee it," Hannah said from the kitchen.

"What will the British do?" Naomi asked.

"They will stay neutral unless a massacre is about to take place."

"They have never been neutral," Hannah said. "They do what they consider best for them at the moment. For that reason they stop massacres. It would be bad press to do otherwise. Mark my words, Aaron. They will be pro-Arab unless their actions, or lack of action, will humiliate them in world opinion. They love Arab oil more than they love Jews."

"Mum, you know that all the British are not pro-Arab. You—"

Hannah came to the door. "It is true. We do have some friends among them, and between them and the ones we can buy, we just might get enough help to save a few hundred of our people." Her face showed her distaste. It was one of the few subjects that brought such anger out in her. "You know as well as I do that most will obey orders, and orders from England will be pro-Arab. Others, some in very important positions in this country, are as anti-Jewish as the Nazis and will look for every opportunity to make our lives miserable." She forced a smile. "Come and eat."

They sat down to the table and Hannah bowed her head. Aaron and Naomi followed suit. Though they were not believers in her new faith, they showed her this respect.

She gave thanks for their safety, especially in Joseph's case, and acknowledged the need for divine help in what lay ahead. Then she asked for protection for those of their family and friends who were not with them, especially Ephraim, before she blessed the food and closed.

She gave them a warm smile. "I am so grateful you are both here. What a wonderful day it makes!" She handed Aaron a plate of cheese and breads and Naomi helped herself to some olives floating in brine.

As they ate they talked. "I met a man today at a funeral. He is a doctor by the name of Yehuda Messerman. Do you know him?" Aaron asked Hannah.

"Two months ago the babies were sick and he was recommended. His office is here, in the Quarter, though he lives in Katamon."

"Katamon is mostly Arab," Aaron said.

"And close to the Quarter. Katamon is one of the few places that both Jew and Arab have lived together for five hundred years, though I admit there are fewer Jews there now than there used to be. Since the riots of '39, many moved into the New City."

"And a strategic location overlooking West Jerusalem. There is already talk of—" He bit his tongue as he realized he was discussing military matters he shouldn't be.

"Talk of making it Jewish?" Hannah asked. "Do not worry, Aaron. You are not revealing secrets most people have not already thought of, both Jew and Palestinian."

"Dr. Messerman believes the Arabs will never stop fighting."

"And you do?" Hannah asked.

Aaron looked down at his plate with a shrug. "I suppose I never really thought about it much. War has winners and losers. The losers adapt or they leave."

"As we did when we left Europe." Hannah sighed. "Yes, many will leave, and many will adapt."

"And what will happen to them?" Naomi asked. It was apparent she had not really thought of this either. She, more than most, had dealt with the displaced persons of war, and the displacement of anyone concerned her.

"I don't know," Hannah said, her brow deeply wrinkled with hard thought.

"This is not Europe, Hannah, and we are not Nazis. If they want peace, they can have it, and no one will have to leave."

"You try to salve your own conscience, Aaron. You know Haj Amin wants war and will have it. Do you think that the attack on our bus was only anger at the United Nations' decision? Already it begins." She shoved her plate aside, her appetite gone. "Do you remember the bombing of Berlin?"

Aaron fiddled with his fork while nodding. "It still haunts my dreams."

"And the result?"

"Thousands, millions, left the city."

"And do you think the Allies bombed Berlin only because of its factories?" She sat back in her chair. "The Nazis lost heart for the fight as the Allies dropped more and more bombs on them. They ran. The only difference is they had somewhere to go when it was over. We and the Arabs of Palestine do not."

"You are wrong," Aaron said. "The Arab countries will take them, assimilate them."

"Are you sure?"

Aaron didn't answer.

"The United States is a benevolent country, and yet how many of our people did they take when Hitler's regime was defeated?" Hannah pressed.

"A few thousand," Naomi responded. "But they are taking more now."

"And Great Britain?"

No response, the two of them just giving the other a side glance.

"And you think the Arab countries around us will do this better? You deceive yourselves." She leaned forward. "War is a horrible thing. Never, in any instance, has a war been fought when the innocents are not severely harmed. This will be no different. Many people will lose their homes. Their lives will change as dramatically as ours did in Poland and Germany. The rich will use their money to escape, and the poor will die because no one cares about them. There will be camps, and sorrow, and governments will debate what to do while more die, just as they did with our people. I wish it would not be so! I wish the Arabs would make peace, but they will not, and this will end badly for us or for our Arab neighbors. It is always the same."

There was silence for a long moment.

"Many of our people gave up," Hannah continued. "They died. Survivors refuse to give up. We did not give up and will never give up. There will be survivors among the Arabs and they will fight for what they think is theirs until they can't fight anymore. If this is what Dr. Messerman told you, he is right."

Aaron sat back, a wry smile on his face. "You can't be serious, Hannah. If we defeat the Arabs, if we build a strong army, no one will question our right to be here, and no one will dare go to war with us."

"How many Jews do you think will ever live in this land?" Hannah asked.

"Millions. Ten or twenty at least."

"If every Jew in the world comes here, maybe, but most won't. Cut it in half and you might be close. How many Arabs are there in the countries around us?"

"Hundreds of millions," Naomi responded with a subdued voice.

"They can fight us every year for a millennium and still never use up their numbers."

"Then we conquer them," Aaron said weakly.

"They will be conquered, Aaron, but not by weapons of war. Do you know who they expect to usher in the thousand years of peace?"

They looked at one another. Neither knew.

"Yeshua, a prophet in Islam and the one they think will destroy the anti-Christ in the Day of Judgment and inaugurate the Second Coming. Our people know him as Jesus, the son of Joseph the carpenter. If he were to come and show his power among them, do you think they would stop fighting?"

"The Jews do not accept him, Hannah," Naomi said.

"And if he saves them from utter destruction, do you think they will accept him then?"

Both looked at their hands but did not answer and each fidgeted, a bit nervous at the turn of the discussion.

"The wicked will never accept him," Hannah went on. "They will die for their pride. But the righteous, on both sides, will accept him, and when they do, He will usher in a period of peace like the world has never seen," she said softly. "Then Judah will finally return. Not before."

There was another long moment of uncomfortable silence. Naomi leaned forward, looking deeply into Hannah's eyes while wrapping her hands around those of her friend. "We have waited for thousands of years for this Messiah, Hannah. He never comes. Always we wait. Always he delays. I want to believe your words, but experience and history tell me your God, if He exists at all, does not care about the Jews."

"Yes, I know," she smiled. "But there were other things also prophesied to take place first. Isaiah—"

Aaron pushed his chair back forcefully and went to the window. "Isaiah! Isaiah was nothing more than a wild man driven crazy by the desert sun and his hate for our people. An ascetic at best, a lunatic at worst!"

"His words have not failed, Aaron," she said as calmly as she could. "In time, all of them will be fulfilled."

"Time?" Aaron said even more frustrated. "When are you going to stop giving your God more time?" He turned back. "We have no more time! If He is the Savior for Judah as well as Mormons, He should have come ten years ago, when He was needed most by our people! We are tired of waiting and empty promises!"

The air was tense as Hannah thought of what she could say. Naomi was looking at her hands, staying out of the way, hoping Aaron would calm himself. She had seen these discussions before, and always they ended badly. Hannah was such a believer and Aaron so much her opposite that it never seemed to end well when they discussed God and religion.

Hannah took a deep breath. There wasn't much she could say, and she almost regretted bringing it up again. Aaron would need a sign before he believed in God again. It would take a miracle to touch his heart. What could she say that would make a difference to him? Nothing.

"I know it sounds crazy, but I believe it, and I've told you how you can believe it too. There is a price to be paid for this knowledge, and until you pay it you will never understand what I am trying to tell you. Never." Hannah stood and took her dishes to the sink.

There was another long silence, but the tension seemed to melt away in the warmth of Hannah's words. Naomi looked at her friend and felt that strength and wished for it. Secretly she had tried to pray, but she never seemed able to get past the first few words without anger and bitterness. In the Nazis' camps she had prayed day after miserable day, but nothing had happened, even to those she knew to be good people. God seemed to have deserted them, even though Hannah's new religion seemed to teach it a different way. How could you forgive God such callous desertion? Hannah had, and Naomi's amazement at that was the only thing that kept her from completely turning her back on God.

The door opened and David and Elizabeth appeared, chattering at one another in Hebrew. Naomi was even happier to see them than she would have been had things been less tense.

David looked at Hannah and stopped midsentence. Elizabeth turned to see what had caused him to shut up so abruptly and saw the bandages.

"Mother! What happened?" Elizabeth cried.

"*Atah B-beseder*?" David stammered. His speech was still imperfect, the stutter a constant he had to deal with every day, but Hannah was grateful he was speaking at all. When they had first met, she didn't know if he ever would again.

"Fine! We had a bit of an accident on one of the buses," Hannah said, "but we're fine." She glanced at Naomi and Aaron for support.

"*Shalom*, David," Aaron said.

"*Shalom*, Ari," David replied without taking his eyes off Hannah. "You w-were on the b-bus they attacked."

Hannah forced a smile while taking David's hands in hers. "It is all right, David. We are safe."

Then Elizabeth saw the bandages on the baby's head. "Joseph!" she exclaimed in a mournful tone as she quickly picked him up, holding him close.

"A bump on the head, that's all." Hannah said evenly. "Now, you have guests. Where are your manners?"

David's face was firm as granite, his anger evident in the set of his jaw. In his eyes she could see the hatred for those who had tried to harm her and the boys, and she stroked his arm. When he was like this—sullen, hateful, but holding it all inside—it was hard to get through to him. "David," she spoke softly. "Everything is fine."

There was no answer. He was dealing with his anger in his own way. She pulled him close and kissed him on the forehead. The war had hurt him the most deeply, and she wondered if he would ever really get over it, especially now that it was starting all over again.

Finally he relaxed a little and then laid his head on her shoulder. "I should have g-gone w-with you," he said firmly.

"Next time. I won't leave you behind again. I promise."

"I should have b-been there to p-protect you and the t-twins. I should—"

"It's alright, David. It wasn't your fault. We only have a few bumps and bruises. I needed you here to watch after Beth, remember? Now, Aaron has come to see you, and we have another guest. Say hello."

David turned and faced his brother, forcing a smile "How are you, Ari?"

"Good," Aaron smiled. "Are you keeping up in school, shrimp?"

"St-straight A's," David said, forcing another smile.

"Oh, right," Beth chided while still checking Joseph's wound tenderly. Beth had grown accustomed to David's mood changes and knew that treating him normally was the best thing to get him past them.

"She's just jealous," he said. He turned to Naomi. "Hi," he said, a bit sheepishly.

"Hi."

"You've ch-changed. You're much more b-beautiful than I remember."

Naomi smiled at his directness. "And you talk more than I remember. The last time I saw you, speaking was not a favorite pastime."

"I know, b-but, I have a lot more t-to say now." He kissed her on the cheeks in a gentlemanly way. Hannah breathed more easily. He would be all right now.

"Bebe said you would b-be more b-beautiful," he said.

"Bebe?"

"He means me," Beth said, sticking her tongue out at David. "He gives everyone nicknames. You heard him call Aaron, Ari, and he calls Rachel, Rach, and Hannah; well he does well by her. He calls her mum, just like Aaron."

"And Ephraim?"

"Eph," David grinned. "Or P-pops—d-depends on if I w-want to make him mad."

"I see, and I suppose you will be giving me one as well," Naomi said. "What will it be?"

David gave her a devious smile. "It will d-depend on how you answer one question."

"Which is?" Naomi asked.

"W-will you marry me? Then I can c-call you dear, or hon, or love, or something like Eph calls Mum."

Naomi and Aaron laughed.

"You are going to get my hand laid against your backside if you're not careful," Hannah said playfully.

David turned to his brother. "I asked her first, remember that," he said.

Aaron put his hands in the air, "Far be it from me to interfere with true love."

Hannah noted that Naomi lost the smile, but then forced it back. So old feelings still existed, at least for Naomi?

She looked at David, relieved. He was back to his normal self, the anger once again tucked away in a semisafe place. "Wash up you two. Time for something to eat."

They went to the sink and began to wash with a damp rag. Water was precious and would become more so. They had been instructed by Haganah leaders in charge of all Jerusalem to save water for weeks now. The pipeline into the city ran through the Arab section of East and North Jerusalem, and if war broke out, they would surely cut it off, but once more some could not bring themselves to face the reality of it. To prepare for war was to give up on peace, to admit that everything was about to change. Therefore, some saved water and some didn't—an attempt to keep things normal.

"They are both a good deal taller," Naomi said, looking at David and Beth. "Especially Elizabeth. She is almost as tall as David."

"B-but not as g-good looking," David said with a teasing grin.

Elizabeth stuck her tongue out at him as she dried her hands.

When Hannah had first met Beth she had been told that she was short for her age, probably due to malnutrition. Since coming to Israel, she had stopped having nightmares and her appetite had doubled. It was obvious David's trauma would take a good deal more time to heal, but for the most part they were both happy, well-adjusted children. They had a mother and father again who were doing their best to help the two children put the past behind them. Now a new war could ruin it all. Somehow she must see that it didn't. Somehow, she must protect them, especially David. The thought nearly overwhelmed her. How did you protect a child from war? There was really only one way. You took them away, but she could not bear the thought of leaving her home, her country. She had worked so hard to get here, to build a new life. To think of leaving it was nearly unbearable!

But she would if it meant saving Beth and David. She would.

They sat down around the small table and the two children began eating the remaining food. Naomi filled them in on what she had been doing in smuggling Jews out of DP camps and aboard ships headed for Palestine. She figured she had sent more than ten thousand people here over the years, though she did not know what had happened to most.

"Some are interred on Cyprus, caught by the British. Others must be on kibbutzim across the country. Possibly we will meet again. Who knows?"

"I met one of them," David said. "She t-taught in our school when our regular t-teacher w-was sick. She knew Zohar and you. She said that you w-were a very t-tough lady, very smart, that w-without your help they w-would never have gotten out of the camps. Her name was Natanson, I think."

"Mismia Natanson. She was a wonderful help." They could see the memory was a fond one.

"Tell me about the Holy City and Palestine," Naomi said. They did for about twenty minutes.

"There are so many things to see, but one of the most beautiful is the Sea of Galilee. You must go there," Beth said. "And Jerusalem, well it is Jerusalem, and there is such an excitement here all the time. We love it."

"Except now w-we have t-to fight for it," David said sadly.

"Do you want to fight for it?" Naomi asked. "Ephraim could take you somewhere else," she glanced over at Hannah.

"No, we-we'll fight. This is our home now, and w-we won't let them t-take this one, w-will we, Mum?"

"No, David, we won't," Hannah forced a smile, her previous thoughts hurting her conscience a little. She hadn't thought of asking them if they would ever leave, only of saving them. How would they feel if she told them they must go to America? What would they say if she and Ephraim thought it best to run from the battle?

She didn't want to think about it.

They had been speaking for nearly two hours when the babies started crying, time for their feeding. She stood and took them to her room while Elizabeth and Naomi cleaned up the kitchen. Aaron and David went out on the steps and sat down. Aaron took out a cigarette and lit it.

"You know Mum and D-dad d-don't like that," David said. Aaron looked at his little brother, then tucked the cigarette into his shirt pocket. "Thanks," David smiled.

"You're welcome. Mum is right, you know? They are bad for you."

"I know. I t-tried one."

"You what?"

"T-tried one. You know—lit it, p-puffed on it like you d-do. How c-can you stand those things? It made me g-gag."

Aaron laughed. "Yes, well serves you right. They're only for grownups."

"Not very g-grown up, if you ask me. Sucking on a w-weed like that. You c-could get b-better stuff from your thumb."

"What's happening around the neighborhood?" Aaron asked, changing the subject.

David saw the question for what it was, but he didn't mind. "W-war, that's what. Everyone's g-getting ready. All my friends' p-parents are planning to g-get out at first sign of b-blood. No stomach for fighting."

"Don't they know that once they start running, it will be just like Germany?"

"I t-told them, Ari, b-but most of them never w-went through what we did. They d-don't understand and they're scared, j-just like we w-were at first. I remember how scared I w-was, and I know why they want to run."

Aaron put his arm around his little brother. He remembered too. As much as he wanted to forget, he still remembered.

"It isn't the same, David. We can fight this time, both of us, and we have lots of help." He pulled David even closer. "If they come here, I'll come back. I promise."

David only nodded, biting his lip. "My friend says the Haganah w-will send some p-people in here t-tomorrow. Is that t-true?" He tried to stop the stuttering, but it was hard! And the more he tried, the worse it seemed to get, at least sometimes.

"I don't know, but I would guess they are right. You help them, and they'll keep everybody alive."

"And where w-will you be g-going?"

"I have an assignment tonight. I suppose they will tell me then. Hopefully I'll be here, in the Old City."

There was a long silence. "Y-you need to get b-baptized, Aaron."

It was out of the blue, and it surprised him. "I just had a bath the other day," he said with a wry smile. David didn't return it, and Aaron could see this was serious for his brother. "Baptism is a Christian rite, David. I'm not Christian."

"B-besides b-being the Son of G-god, Christ w-was the g-greatest Jew who ever lived. You want to b-be a g-good Jew, you need t-to follow Christ."

"Mum's words?"

"No, mine. Mum doesn't t-tell me everything to say. I got baptized b-because I know it's right." He took a deep breath, concentrating. "Not j-just for sin, but b-because it shows Jesus you mean b-business when it comes to following Him. I mean b-business because I know he's w-waiting on the other side and has things for me to d-do there as much as here. If you d-don't get baptized, you have t-to wait around over there until somebody d-does it for you. I w-would do it, but I can't until we g-go back to the states and see Eph's folks again and g-go to the temple. So g-get it done yourself, or k-keep out of range of Arab guns. You hear me?" He stood and ran inside.

Aaron sat there stunned. After a moment of trying to piece together David's words he looked up to see Naomi.

"He's just scared for you, that's all," she said.

"You heard."

"The window was open a little. Hannah's changing a diaper. Do you mind if I sit down?"

"I'd be disappointed if you didn't." As she sat down beside him, half a dozen people scurried by without noticing them.

"What did he mean, he could be baptized for me?" Aaron asked.

"I don't know. You'll have to ask Hannah."

"It's okay for David to do that stuff. I mean, Hannah's his mom for real now and she has the right to teach him what she thinks, but—"

"But it's not for you?"

"Yeah, not for me." He removed the cigarette and was about to light it, but then shoved it back in his pocket.

"What Hannah says makes sense sometimes."

"Only because she is Hannah and we love her."

Naomi had no response. Maybe he was right.

"I have to run," Aaron said without moving.

"Is this a personal trek or do you want company?" she said enticingly.

"Business. Haganah business. Maybe another time," he said sincerely. He got to his feet. "Tell Hannah I'll see her in the next few days." He started down the steps, then turned back. "It's good to see you again, Naomi. Real good."

She watched him walk down the narrow street. At one time, Aaron had fallen in love with her. While they were working in the underground in Europe, he had tried to advance their relationship. But she had been too busy, too afraid, too unwilling to commit. Slowly she had forced herself to face her fears, but by the time she had, Aaron had given up. They remained friends, though she had hoped that somehow time and being away from one another might rekindle a dying flame, it had not. She had pushed him away, and now it was too late.

The cries of the two babies brought her to her feet to see if she could give Hannah a hand. As she did, she took a breath of air and let the scent of the Old City settle in her chest. It was a wonderful mixture of a dozen different foods mingled with the cool mountain air of one of the world's most ancient and sacred spots. And it was a city preparing for war, a war that would once again divide Jerusalem, neighbor fighting neighbor, friends turning to enemies.

The cries subsided, and Naomi leaned against the wall and watched as the last of the sun's rays disappeared over the city. She found herself hoping this night would never end, that this same peaceful quiet and wonderful evening would extend into eternity. Oh, how she wished for it!

"*Shalom.*"

She looked to the bottom of the stairs to see a young man about Aaron's age looking up at her. His face was in shadow, but the voice sounded gentle, and she found it interesting that it gave her comfort instead of alarm.

"*Shalom,*" she responded.

"You are a friend of the Daniels?"

"Yes, and you?"

He stepped into the light of a window where she could see that he was dressed in a black suit and wore a fedora, the typical attire of an orthodox Jew from Hungary or Poland, and had the usual heavy beard and uncut locks at the sides of his face.

"I am Abraham Marshak. We live only a few doors down. Yes, our families are friends."

"Nice to meet you Abraham. My name is Naomi. Naomi Stavsky."

"Ah, Aaron has spoken of you. You work with Palmach, in Europe."

"I did until a few weeks ago. I thought I might be more useful here."

"Yes, that may be," he said sadly.

Naomi thought she detected some reluctance but said nothing. The very orthodox of Poland were the ones she had the most difficult time dealing with in the DP camps. They believed that all things were God's will; they accepted their lot too easily and would not fight for their freedom. It had been such men before the war who had accepted ghettos and camps much too easily.

"Well, good night, Naomi Stavsky, and welcome to Palestine, such as it is. God go with you."

"Tell me, Abraham, do you have a weapon?"

Abraham turned back, a curious look on his face. "And if I do not?"

"Then others will have to fight and die for you. Do you consider such a position a righteous one?" She couldn't help needling him. Somehow the Orthodox had to get the idea that they must fight for their rights if they wanted them.

"You do not wish to take this role?" he asked evenly. "I thought Zionists could save all Jews."

She flushed, unable to respond.

"I am sure that if I but trust in you, everything will be alright." He smiled slightly, then turned and walked away.

She felt her face burning. Such men ought to be horse whipped! She watched him enter one of the apartments a few doors away as Hannah came onto the small porch.

"Who were you talking to?" Hannah asked.

"Someone named Marshak?"

"Abraham or Eliahu?"

"Abraham," she said.

"And he has upset you. That is not like Abraham."

"It wasn't him. It's his . . . his refusal to fight."

Hannah laughed. "Abraham? Well if he refuses, he has a strange way of showing it. Abraham is a member of Haganah and will probably be very important in the defense of this place. Though a rabbi's son, he is Lubovitcher and has no aversion to defending the Old City."

Naomi felt hot all over again. She had been a fool! How could she face him now? Well, she wouldn't. She would be assigned somewhere else and that would be that.

Hannah laughed again then said she was going to bed, that there were blankets on the couch when Naomi was ready. Naomi gave her a hug and thanked her before Hannah disappeared inside, leaving Naomi still embarrassed.

After a few minutes of further useless rationalization she gave up. When she turned to go back inside she caught a glimpse of light where a door was opened and saw that it was that of the Marshaks' apartment. She squinted into the darkness and could make out Abraham as he left the doorway and disappeared down the narrow street, dressed in plain clothes and no fedora.

He also carried a weapon.

Her curiosity getting the better of her, she quickly descended the steps and followed. Her training in the hills and towns of Europe had taught her that moving about quietly gave one a great advantage, so she removed her leather shoes and went barefoot. She got close enough to him that she could follow but not close enough to be detected. They worked their way through maze-like streets, and she began losing track of where she was in relation to Hannah's apartment. At the moment she decided this was foolish and she'd better try finding her way back, Abraham was joined by half a dozen others, all dressed the same, all carrying weapons. Abraham gave orders and they split by twos and went in different directions. Abraham and another climbed a set of stairs to their left, went to a balcony railing, climbed up, grabbed hold of the roof and easily swung themselves up. She could hear the slight clatter of their feet as they worked their way along the roofs of the buildings. She kept up with the sound for a hundred feet then lost it. Had they come to a stop? She looked down the street in the direction she thought must be north. In the rays of a partial moon, she thought she could make out a sign written in Arabic that separated the two Quarters. She remembered seeing it earlier in the day when she and Hannah had walked from the bus station. At least she knew approximately where she was.

"You should not be out so late." Startled, she reactively turned and slammed both her palms against the body, driving backward until he was against the wall, then she grabbed him by the throat. She found herself staring at Abraham Marshak up close, then noticed the touch of cold steel in her stomach.

She let go and backed away. "You shouldn't sneak up on someone like that."

"You should mind your own business," he replied. "Now, go home."

She turned and started away, then turned back. "I was wrong about you. You are a fighter." She started walking again.

"Where did you learn to attack that way?" he asked.

"From Palmach training in Europe," she said, continuing to walk away. "I'll be seeing you, Abraham Marshak."

And she left him behind.

SEE CHAPTER NOTES

CHAPTER 7

December 2, 1947

Aaron refolded the paper as he stood on the street next to the newspaper vendor. The hot invective and rhetoric had reached new heights, and that was not easy. In Cairo, ulamas—learned and respected holy men—drafted decrees calling for jihad, justifying the absolute annihilation of the Jews with the authority of the Koran. Haj Amin was promising immediate action, and the Arab states were backing him with their own threats of "annihilation" and "a war to end all wars." They complained of being thrust into a position of continuing Hitler's dirty work by the community of nations, and declared that if the partition resolution were not reversed, they would have no choice but to rain down further fire on the heads of the Jews.

But Aaron and every other Jew knew that the Arabs would go to war only as a last resort. For now they would satisfy their people with their vitriolic statements and by supporting, at least in their daily news releases, the Arab Higher Committee and the Palestinian people, whom they called on to rise up and defend their own land.

Of course the Arab Higher Committee was nothing more than Haj Amin's puppet, and Aaron knew that any rising up would be done by his men and under his commanders. He just wasn't sure where it would begin. But if the Mufti stayed true to form, the strike initiated the previous morning would lead to a riot.

Aaron walked to a nearby café for breakfast and a cup of coffee. As he was about to finish, a man entered the place with the news that Arab merchants in East Jerusalem were covering their shops with iron shutters with crosses and crescents painted on them so as to distinguish them from Jewish businesses.

"Are you sure?" someone asked.

"Positive. I just drove my cab through there and saw it with my own eyes. They intend to take action today, I swear it. This strike is about to become a riot."

"I came past Damascus Gate as well," said another. "They are giving speeches. Very caustic. They are igniting the fire."

"Did they have weapons?" asked a third.

"I could not see, but I am sure—"

"They can do nothing," said the café owner. "The British will stop them."

"The British?" the first guffawed. "They will aid them. I tell you they will riot today, and I pity anyone who is in their way."

Aaron looked around him in disgust as he paid for his food and coffee. They talked, they saw the signs, but none were willing to act. They simply did not want to believe.

"You are Haganah," the café owner said to Aaron as he took his money. "You should go and do something. Your people promised to protect us if they rioted. Now you should go and do it."

"Yes," said another, "you promised. A friend of mine was threatened with a gun by one of your men when he tried to remove his goods from his shop. They made him put them all back. Now you should make sure he does not lose everything."

Aaron felt anger stir in his chest. "And I suppose you will come as well?" "Me?" The owner laughed lightly. "I am not a soldier." He said it in a cynical tone that only made Aaron angrier.

Aaron leaned forward, his face only inches from that of the owner who backed away slightly. "You are a fool. You will be a soldier before this is over." He turned to the others. "All of you will be, and you will die if you do not fight. Do you think the Arabs are playing games this time? You have heard the broadcasts, read the newspapers. You know it is different this time, much different. Haj Amin and the Arabs mean to destroy us, and the British are mad enough to let them. And because you do not volunteer for the Haganah here in Jerusalem, because you use a hundred excuses and refuse to fight, there will not be enough of us to keep you safe this time. Not near enough!"

He stalked from the store, leaving them speechless. As he reached the corner someone grabbed his arm, and he turned around to find himself facing both the café owner and the cab driver. Both had apologetic looks on their faces. The owner spoke first.

"You are right. It is different. We hoped . . . We thought . . . Anyway, what can we do?" he asked.

Aaron still wasn't sure they were serious, but as several others joined them, he became convinced. "The rioters will go to the Commercial Center. I know the Haganah will be spread too thin and will need help. We can go there and give them a hand. Do you have weapons?"

Two nodded, and Aaron told them to go and get them. "But be careful of the British. They will confiscate them if they catch you. The rest of you find something—a heavy stick, a knife, anything to defend yourselves and others. Meet me at the hat shop on Princess Mary Street in ten minutes."

They dispersed quickly—nodding, determined. Aaron felt a surge of excitement as he turned and ran down the street toward his apartment. He would also need a weapon.

* * *

The Haganah in Jerusalem was poorly trained, poorly led for the most part, and poorly equipped. After all, they were still an underground army of volunteers who trained when they could. To make matters worse, they were few in numbers.

SHAI's intelligence reports did little to help. They indicated that the strike would lead to demonstrations only on the third day and Haganah leaders took them at their word. Believing they still had another day to bring in reinforcements or to give warning, they did little more than soothe the fears of panicked shopkeepers.

It was ten, just twenty minutes after Aaron had left the café with his bagel, when the first attack took place. Asher Lazar and Moshe Shamir worked for *Ha'aretz*, a competitor of the *Jerusalem Post* where Aaron worked. They were traveling down Mamilla Road when a band of shrieking Arabs with knives and clubs rounded the corner.

"What the devil?" Moshe exclaimed in Hebrew. He watched as fellow Jews started running for their lives, entering buildings, slamming doors, and locking them. In seconds, the street was deserted of Jews, and they were left facing the angry mob.

"Get out of here, Moshe! Now!" Asher said.

Moshe tried to start the car, but it stalled. In seconds they were surrounded.

"Asher, run for it!" cried Moshe as he jumped from the car. He ran up the street to safety, thinking Asher was behind him. When he was fifty strides away he looked behind him and saw that the mob had gotten Asher and his friend had disappeared into a labyrinth of clubs and fists. Moshe ran toward the Commercial Center screaming for help.

Aaron and his newly acquired platoon of civilians saw him. Aaron, recognizing the reporter, grabbed his arm. "What is wrong?" he asked.

"Asher . . ." Moshe said, pointed desperately back the way he had come. "The mob . . . they are in . . . back there! Back there! They killed him!"

Aaron ran down the street. Those that followed hesitated, the sudden fear wrenching at their stomachs. When Aaron looked back he saw only the taxi cab driver and the café owner were still with him. The rest had stayed behind, one helping the distraught Moshe while others ran in the opposite direction.

They turned to face the mob coming their way. There were hundreds. Aaron's heart seemed to stop as he realized his old German luger would do little good if they kept coming. Then out of nowhere half a dozen British policemen entered the street and spread out as if to disperse the mob, but as the mob advanced the Brits quickly moved aside without so much as pulling a weapon. So much for help from the British.

"Well, Haganah boy, we're in it now," said the cab driver as the mob picked up speed.

Arabic screams of revenge filled the air and chants of "Death to the Jews" and "The Nazis were right" filled the air. It was then Aaron saw him.

He walked at the front of the group, knife in hand, the conical fez still on his head. The man from the funeral, the one Messerman said was Mary's older brother. What was his name? He could not remember. It did not matter. He was here. He was killing Jews. He was the enemy.

The mob ran toward them from a hundred yards, Mary's brother leading them in their yell of death to the Jews.

Aaron raised his weapon again. This time he aimed high and pulled the trigger. The sound of the shots echoed in the valley formed by buildings, and the mob came to a silent, confused stop.

He was about to fire again when shots were fired from behind them. Aaron turned to see a dozen Haganah men rushing down the street toward them. The mob lost their courage and began running the opposite direction, past the British police and toward the Commercial Center.

All but one. Mary's brother stood there, alone in the street. Was it defiance or frustration? Aaron could not tell, but he aimed his luger at his barrel chest just the same.

After another moment's hesitation, he sneered and ran to catch up to his comrades. Then they were gone. Aaron let his weapon fall to his side, quietly relieved. He had never killed a man before and was glad he hadn't been forced to, especially not that man.

"*Atah Beseder?*"

Aaron forced a smile for his Haganah commander, Tsvi Sinai. "*Beseder.*" He noticed only Tsvi carried a weapon. "They beat up Asher Lazar and may have killed him. Back there, by that car," Aaron said. He noticed people coming back onto the street—cautious, but their curiosity getting the best of them. Those that were with Tsvi quickly ran toward the motionless man.

"They don't have the guts for a real fight," said one.

"Looting and murder, that's all they want. Fight back and they run like chickens being chased by a fox," the taxi cab driver added.

"Not all of them," Aaron said soberly. Mary's brother would fight, and had he not been leading a mob of college students—had it been armed men, trained in fighting—things might have been different. He shuddered at the thought.

Aaron saw two British policemen coming their way, their own weapons drawn.

"They will arrest us for carrying weapons."

"They should have arrested everybody in that mob," Aaron said.

"Come on, let's get lost." They turned and started back.

"Shoot them in the legs," yelled one of the British police. "We'll take them alive."

Tsvi grabbed Aaron by the collar and pulled him into a store, the café owner and cab driver right behind them. They quickly went through it, exited into the next street and mingled with the crowd until they were sure they weren't being followed.

"I need to report to Amir. We need many more men. Consider yourself under orders, Sergeant Schwartz. Go to the Commercial Center. Do what you can." He left them through a cross street, disappearing in its shadows.

"Thanks for sticking with me," Aaron said to the others as they set a quick pace for the Center.

"*Atah Tsodeq*. You were right—without each other, we lose everything."

"What are your names?" Aaron asked.

"Ze'ev," replied the cab driver.

"I am Bartok. Nahum Bartok. You are welcome to free coffee in my café anytime you want it."

A British armored car came into the far end of the street and quickly approached, the crowd of people opening to it like the Red Sea before the command of Moses.

"Come on. We don't want to get caught. We need to get to the Center."

Suddenly heavy gunfire broke out from the north, near the post office as far as Aaron could tell. It was getting worse. This was no strike, and it was quickly moving beyond a riot. It was Haj Amin's attempt at starting a war.

"Hey!" yelled the café owner. Aaron turned to see him in the clutches of two British policemen with two more quickly rushing him. He had to duck to the left to avoid them.

"Run!" said the café owner as he grappled with his captors. Aaron glanced over his shoulder to see the cab driver slug one of the policemen, knocking him to the ground. Then there were four others all over him and the two men did their best to fight free. Aaron hesitated. He should help.

"Run, you fool! You have the gun!"

Aaron ran. The cab driver was right. It was the weapon that would get them all a prison sentence. He scampered through the crowd of shoppers and thought how odd that so many were going on with their lives as if everything were normal. Didn't they know what was happening? How could they just ignore it? But, then, it had been this way for years. Fighting, small uprisings, the British moving in to quell it. This *was* normal.

He ducked inside a Jewish dry goods shop, feigning an interest in items on the shelf while watching out the window. Two men rushed by; he sighed relief. He slipped to the back of the store and found the door, grabbed the knob and turned it. Locked. He started back to the front. The two soldiers just entering fixed their eyes on his. He turned back. The locked door was his only way out.

* * *

Ten minutes before the Arabs had launched their riot, Mary walked out of the Christian Quarter and into the street that fronted Jaffa Gate, receiving several derogatory remarks for her dress. She didn't care. She was tired of caring for old traditions that didn't matter and old religions that didn't work. She needed to find food and intended to do it where the sneers about her appearance were less obvious. She pulled her wool coat around her neck against the chill as she crossed the street and entered the Commercial Center.

Izaat and Rhoui had been furious. She didn't care about that either. They had told her to stay in the house until she could comply with what she was told and until they decided her punishment for her behavior at the funeral. She hadn't said anything in return simply because it would have done no good. They could throw their lives away in defense of an Arab world that was archaic and ridiculous, but she wasn't about to go with them.

Shop owners were sweeping, laying out goods, preparing for the day. She loved coming here. Owned by the Palestine Land Development Company which had bought it from the Orthodox Church in 1922, it contained large Jewish wholesale stores, dozens of small shops owned by both Jews and Arabs, Arab auto garages, and a delightful open market.

She was not surprised that many of the shops, especially the Arab ones, were not open—this was the second day of the strike, and only the very strong or very foolish Arabs would turn a deaf ear to it. The

Jews, on the other hand, were still trying to go on with their lives, knowing that the worst might happen but hoping their Haganah and the British would protect them. She had come to support them and to tell her brothers and the whole of Arab Jerusalem she did not care for their strikes or their hatred of everything Jewish.

She passed the first of the shops and took notice of the mixture of concern and nervousness on the faces of the Jewish owners. They were watchful, fidgeting. She tried to give them a comforting smile, but it did no good. It made her heart ache to see them so afraid and wished it could be just another normal day, the streets filled with Jew and Arab looking for food and a good bargain. She wondered if it would ever be that way again.

She came to the open market, relieved to find it at least partially stocked by farmers ready to sell their goods. Most of them were Jews, but she did see a few nervous Arabs as well. If they didn't sell their goods, they didn't eat. It was a risk they had to take.

She began picking over their goods, and though there were no tomatoes or corn, she found good quality cucumbers and carrots, along with cabbage and a few oranges. She was paying for them when someone tapped her on the shoulder. She turned to find Dr. Messerman facing her.

"Hello, Mary. How are you?" he asked, a slight smile on his lips.

"Well enough," she said with a smile. "And you?" she counted out the coins requested and dropped them into the hands of the eager seller. She received her items in a paper bag and a verbal blessing to be safe.

"I didn't get to speak to you the other day, at the funeral. I am sorry about your father. He was a good friend for all Palestinians, Jew or Arab."

"Thank you," she said turning away. She didn't wish to be rude, but sudden tears overwhelmed her; she had to move away to keep them from erupting onto the street. As she pulled a hanky from her coat pocket and dabbed at her eyes, Dr. Messerman stepped to her side.

"Crying is a good thing for pain."

"Yes, it makes it worse." She forced a smile. She heard the distant sound of gunfire and felt the hair on the back of her neck bristle. Shouting came from Jaffa Road. It was getting closer. She glanced that direction and saw the British police hurriedly evacuate the street as the mob suddenly appeared. The British made no effort to stop them, and Mary turned to go the other way, grabbing Messerman's arm as she did. "Come quickly! We have to get out of here!" she said sharply, looking over her shoulder at the same time. In confusion, the doctor glanced back and saw the mob erupt in screams as they ran into the Center. The two of them started to run through the narrow corridor, jostling with other shoppers scrambling to get away, the place erupting in chaos. Mary pulled Dr. Messerman into a side corridor, then into a small shop where she sometimes purchased underclothing. The Jewish owner was ashen faced as he tried to get the door closed behind them and lock it. An Arab man, his face hidden in his kafiyeh, lunged at the door and knocked it open with a crash, the glass flying in every direction, the owner slammed to the floor. He lay there dazed as Mary pulled Dr. Messerman into the back room as two more rioters came through the shattered door and began breaking the glass windows and throwing everything off the shelves. Suddenly the place was filled with young people grabbing for the goods, pillaging, stealing, battering the owner. She closed the door to the backroom and locked it as several ran toward her. They pounded on the door, then used their weapons to try and break through. Sweat poured down her face as she and Dr. Messerman backed into a corner opposite it, praying it would hold. The slamming against the door shook her to her toes, but the door held. She clutched her package of cucumbers and gritted her teeth as she crossed herself in prayer.

Then she heard the shot.

Everything came to a sudden halt—the noise, the movement, even her own breathing. She watched as the doctor looked with shocked and pain-filled eyes down at his side. Red flowed through his shirt where his coat was open. He cautiously felt it with his hand. Then he fell to his knees and toppled to the floor, shock and pain taking all his strength.

She blinked several times, hoping she would wake up, that somehow the nightmare would end. She shook her head in denial, the words "No, No," erupting from her throat like a burst in a water pipe. She went to her knees beside him, oblivious to the sudden return of the noise and banging on the door. She rolled him over and quickly pulled his coat away. Blood covered his shirt but his eyes opened to thin slits and a smile formed on his lips.

"I . . . I . . ." pain etched his face, and his body stiffened against it.

"Bevakahsa!" she pleaded. "Please. Don't talk!" she said. "I . . . I will get you help." She started to get up, but he caught her arm and held it in a death grip.

"No," he said gently. "I . . ." He forced a smile. Then his eyes closed and his head fell to one side. Desperately she searched for a pulse as the banging on the door began to disintegrate into shards of wood all around her.

* * *

Aaron was in a full run when he lowered his shoulder and slammed into the door of the shop in which he was trapped. It gave way and blew into the alley outside the building, giving him freedom. He looked both directions and then went right. He reached the street to find himself in the middle of the Commercial Center, the mob all around him. He ran into a man wearing a kafiyeh and quickly threw him back into the alley, slugged him in the jaw, and knocked him unconscious. Grabbing the kafiyeh, he wrapped the long end around his face, then removed the man's long coat, slung it over his khaki shirt and at least part of his pants. Running into the narrow street of shops, he lost himself in the crowd while glancing over his shoulder to see if the police had followed. He saw them come to the head of the street, then turn back. They had no stomach for the mob, and the Haganah was conspicuously missing as well. Outnumbered several hundred to one, there was little he could do, and he turned to the business of trying to stay alive. It was clear that his disguise worked when another Arab threw him a small radio freshly looted from a Jewish shop. Aaron saw the owner recoiling behind his counter, saw the looter wield a knife from under his jacket and stab the Jew. He took four steps inside the shop, slamming the door behind him. The looter, about to render another deadly blow, turned in surprise.

"What?" he questioned in Arabic.

Aaron grabbed his hand, wrenched the knife free and threw it to one side, then used his fist to knock the man senseless. He quickly stooped down and checked the shopkeeper's wound. Deep, but not deadly.

"Can you walk?" Aaron said in Hebrew.

The Jew, his eyes wide and filled with confusion and fear that bound his tongue, didn't respond. Aaron removed the covering from his face.

"I am a Jew. Can you walk?" he said again.

The man nodded, his body shaking, nearly out of control. Aaron helped him to his feet and to the room in the back of the store. "Lock yourself in here," he said, grabbing a piece of cloth from one of the shelves and pressing it against the wound. "I'll go for help and get you out as soon as I can."

The man nodded, taking control of the cloth and grimacing in pain. Aaron retraced his steps and was quickly in the street. Looking for help, he saw a group of British policemen near a shop to his left. Opening his mouth to yell for aid, he heard an order shouted for the armored cars to break down a shop door. The front of the store disintegrated as the vehicle slammed into it and the Arab rioters were quickly inside looting coats, shirts, blankets, everything in sight. Aaron found himself livid with anger. These Brits were showing their true colors. As the policeman gave the order to burn the shop, Aaron crossed the street and slammed his body into the soldier's back, nearly snapping him in two. The man went down with a scream, Aaron quickly on top of him. He knocked him unconscious with a nearby stone left by the looters, then stood up, defying everyone around him. They seemed to back away, blinking with confusion. Then it dawned on him that his disguise had them baffled. He quickly turned and made a dash for open ground. By the time the others realized what was happening, he already had a fifty-yard lead. He could only wonder if it would be enough.

* * *

Tears were dripping off Mary's cheeks when the first mobster broke through and stood over her. Two others quickly joined him and began pulling her from the room, screaming Arab obscenities as they did. She found herself being pummeled by fists until she screamed at them in Arabic and began fighting back, the anger exploding in her chest. They pulled back and she scrambled to her feet, shoving one of them back against the counter. His kafiyeh fell to one side and she recognized Raoul. She attacked with renewed fervor, using her fists to pound his chest and face, yelling her own curses at him and what he had done. Only the quick reaction of his fellow murderers kept her from scratching his eyes out. When they had a firm grip on her, he slapped her fiercely across the face. She swaggered as she fought the darkness while mustering the energy to spit in his face. He hit her again, harder. This time the darkness exploded into her brain and she felt her body give way. She went limp, and they let her drop to the floor, unconscious.

Raoul stood there for only a moment, his fingers wiping saliva from his eye. He raised his leg to kick her in the ribs, but the voice from the doorway stopped him. He looked up to see Izaat and stopped breathing.

"She was helping a Jew. Our orders are to kill anyone who—"

Izaat took two steps and hit him full in the face with his rifle. Raoul was knocked against the counter and melted to the floor, blood gushing from a long open cut that went from his nose to his ear lobe. He shook his head to keep conscious but did not look up, afraid another blow would follow. Instead Izaat knelt by his sister and turned her over. She was alive. He ordered everyone out of the store and it quickly emptied, the group rushing to join the rest of the mob as they burned, pillaged, and brutally beat anyone Jewish who had not been able to escape or hide. *Mobs,* Izaat thought. Once they started, it was like spreading wildfire, burning everyone it touched with its insanity.

But it was war.

Izaat looked over at Raoul with hate-filled eyes. "Leave the Old City. If I see you again, I will kill you!"

Raoul struggled to his feet and stumbled out of the store, his eyes fierce with rage as he tried to stanch the bleeding of his nose and face caused by the gun butt. Then he was gone, the crowd of looters sucking him in like quicksand.

Izaat knelt down, picked up Mary, then started from the store and toward Jaffa Gate. The place was ablaze around him, people running, screaming, looting. A Jew struggled to get free; five men jumped him, beating him mercilessly. It was horrific.

But it was war.

She should not have come here, he told himself. She should have heeded his warning to stay away. But she had not. He didn't think . . .

He should have thought. He should have locked her in the house. How could she have been so foolish?

The blow came from behind and knocked Izaat to his knees. It was all he could do to keep from dropping Mary and stay conscious. Another blow knocked him over, and he couldn't help it as Mary fell free of his grasp and hit the stones of the street. He rolled over to look up into the face of Raoul. Though his vision was hazy, he could see that he had a club. It had blood on it. He was about to use it again. And Izaat couldn't stop it.

* * *

Aaron leaned against the warehouse to catch his breath, his eyes searching the street behind him. Nothing. They had given up. The place was ablaze now, the people running through the streets like waifs from a nightmare, their bodies trailing smoke caused by the fire and their shrieks like those of demons. He had to get back to the shopkeeper. He pushed himself from the wall and stumbled up the street toward Jaffa Gate, bumping into victims trying to get themselves and others out of the Center and struggling against the seeming endless numbers of looters. Three times he used his disguise to help Jews break away from elements of the mob, their heads broken or faces bloody with the beatings they were given. Twice the mobbers had nearly turned on him until he brandished his luger and they turned and ran away to find an easier target.

He saw Mary's brother near the exit on Jaffa Road. He was carrying an unconscious woman. So it wasn't only Jews who had been victims. Aaron did not feel sorry for him.

He saw the man lurking in the shadows behind Aref and knew immediately he was stalking the Arab. Mystified, and curious, he kept silent. Then the man attacked, pummeled Aref with a stick the size of a man's arm and knocked him to his knees. Aref tried to keep from dropping the woman he carried, but the second blow knocked him senseless and both toppled onto the cobblestone street. Aaron reacted, hitting the assailant from behind as he was about to deal a fatal blow. He threw him to the ground, knocking the club free, and immediately grabbed for his luger. As the man scrambled to get his bludgeon,

Aaron hit him on the back of the neck. The Arab slammed into the cobblestones and didn't move. Aaron, grabbed the club and threw it as far away as he could while looking around to see if the attacker had friends or if others were concerned. Looting had everyone's attention.

He went to the unconscious Aref and checked for a pulse. He would survive. Then he went to the woman and turned her over to find himself looking into the face of Mary, her eyes blinking as if coming out of a bad dream. Then they closed again and her head fell gently to one side. He checked her pulse, relieved to feel a steady beat in the wrist of her arm.

"Hey, Arab!"

Aaron looked up to see a British policeman coming his way, totally ignoring the pandemonium around him. He was looking at a diamond necklace and shoved it into his pocket with a smile. Aaron saw that it was the same soldier he had nearly broken in half a little earlier and made sure his kafiyeh was in place before looking up and answering in Arabic.

"Yes, your honor?"

"Jews fought back, eh?" He gave a mocking smile. "Must 'ave been a hundred of them, from the look of your friends. Get them out of here, do you 'ear? Soldiers will be comin', and we don't want you gettin' arrested now, do we?" He grinned.

"No, your honor." He said, relieved the man hadn't recognized him. As he picked Mary up and stood he noticed the insignia on the policeman's arm and the name on his badge. Foley! The man who commanded the police force responsible for the Commercial Center. He would make sure someone heard about Foley.

Aaron carried her to the top of Jaffa street then to a small strip of grass next to the Old City wall near Jaffa Gate before returning for her brother. There was a pool of blood around his head and he was still unconscious. The smoke was thick now, and people were running out of the Center to escape. He picked up the heavy body and fell in with the mass of looters now loaded with everything they could carry. It was then he noticed the assailant was lying unconscious on the street and in danger of being trampled. He could not work up any sympathy.

When he reached the grass, he saw that Mary was sitting up, her head in her hands. When he lay her brother down she looked up, then forced herself to her knees and grasped her brother's hand, checking for a pulse.

"Why did you do this?" she said coldly.

Aaron hadn't expected the question and it made him angry. "If I had, I would not bother to carry the two of you to safety." He started to walk away.

"I'm sorry," she said. "You are right. You could not have done it." She was relieved to find a strong pulse in Izaat's wrist but was worried about the wound to his head. She had helped her father enough to know that his condition needed more attention than she could give him. "He needs a hospital."

Aaron turned back. "So do a lot of others. Your brother went in there to kill Jews. In the process one of his own kind decided to break his skull. He can wait his turn." He walked away.

"There is another man, a Jew. He was shot in one of the shops," Mary said. "You should go after him. He is a friend of my father. A doctor."

Aaron immediately remembered Dr. Messerman. "Where?" he questioned, turning back.

"The lingerie shop near the open market. I was with him. My brother must have found me there. Another man . . ." She tried to remember what happened. She remembered Raoul, remembered him hitting her. But that was all. She shook her head. "It is not important. Go."

Aaron wanted to ask more but quickly ran back into the Center. The fire was worst near the market.

* * *

Ephraim descended the steps of the Greek airliner and took a deep breath of air. He had come to love the smell, the feel, of this place. He was glad to be home. He presented his American passport to the British officer at the customs desk.

"You 'ave been travelin' a lot lately, Mr. Daniels," the man said.

"Went to see the Pope in Italy," he said with a smile.

The soldier hung onto his passive face. "'Ave a good day, then," he said, turning to his next customer. As Ephraim walked across the room to the front door, he felt someone touch his arm and turned to see another British soldier grinning at him.

"Awrite, laddie," he said.

"Jack," Ephraim said, shaking the extended hand. "How are things?"

Colonel Jack Willis, second in command of the Highland Light Infantry, was one of the few fair-minded British officers Ephraim knew. They had first met just after Ephraim arrived in Israel. He had been helping rescue some refugees from a boat when they got separated from the main body of rescuers and had to hide without making connections. He tried to lead them to the road, but one exhausted woman was so weak she had to be carried, and the other man and woman could go no more than a hundred yards without a rest. Jack had shown up in a troop transport truck when it was dark and there were few cars. Instead of arresting them, he took them to Tel Aviv and saw that they were fed before pulling Ephraim aside and giving a hundred pounds of his own money for further needs.

Jack and Ephraim had become good friends since then. Though their personal lives were far different, they met often on Sundays for lunch and conversation. Ephraim was pleased to be greeted by a friendly face upon his return to Palestine.

"Can I give ye a ride tae Jerusalem?" Jack asked.

It was more a statement than a question, and Ephraim wondered why the pressure. He didn't have to wait long to find out.

"The Arabs killed seven of yer folk yesterday an' they're hintin' at more today. A ride wi' me an' my men will be safer than wi' a bus."

Ephraim nodded as they walked to Jack's jeep. He noticed that there were two trucks filled with troops parked behind them. He and Jack got in the back of the jeep while another soldier got in the passenger seat next to the driver. Everyone was armed, and Ephraim could feel the intensity of their mood in the tips of his fingers.

A few minutes later they were headed for the main road leading to Jerusalem. Ephraim's eyes caught sight of the burned-out bus as they turned on the highway.

"Happened yesterday. Three butchers attacked wi' machine guns and grenades. Three civilians killed," Jack said soberly. "Ye're in fer a bugger of a war, laddie. These Arabs think anyone is fair game, whether they be carryin' a weapon or nae."

As they started up the steeper portion of the canyon, Ephraim knew they were being carefully watched.

"Intelligence reports tell us the Arabs are massin' fer some attacks in the suburbs of Jerusalem and Tel Aviv, but a few have been ordered tae begin harassin' traffic along the roads. Even now it isnae safe. Snipers sit up there an' take pot shots at anyone who isnae British or Arab," Jack said. "They'll close it if they can. MacMillan says we keep it open unless it means losin' men."

As commander of troops in Palestine, Sir Gordon MacMillan was a no-nonsense military man who followed London policy makers as if they were gods. He irritated Ephraim to no end. "Your government has to keep that road open, Jack. If it doesn't, they'll starve us out." He took a deep breath, knowing he was talking to the wrong man. "Sorry, I know your hands are tied."

"The wee jimmies in London dinnae give ye much hope of winnin' this little fray, an' they arenae in the way tae back a loser." After taking a deep breath to get control of his anger, Jack leaned closer, speaking in a low tone. "If ye an' Hannah need anythin', ken me that. I'll do what I can."

Ephraim nodded, his eyes on the hillside of the deepest part of the canyon. He saw movement and the occasional glint of sun on metal. As the sound of a rifle shot echoed through the canyon, Jack swore as he turned around to see if anyone was hit.

"Tryin' tae irritate us, are they?" he said.

Unable to see all the vehicles, he told his driver to pull over and get a position where he could. Ping! A second shot bounced off the metal of the front of his jeep, making him swear again. He yelled an order for one of his machine gunners to fire at the ridge of the hill. Ephraim watched as a dozen Arabs suddenly found legs and fled. Jack ordered a cease-fire and the canyon echoed, then went silent. The Arabs had decided to lie low.

Jack ordered an advance and the vehicles picked up but little speed as they arduously worked their way to the top of the canyon. Passing the Arab village of Kastel, Ephraim could see that the number of men in the village had grown a good deal. Haj Amin was moving in forces.

"If ye want an experienced opinion, Husseini will go for the big kill. When he does nae get it, he'll go back tae what he knows best. Ambush. That's what he an' his folk do best. It is their bread an' butter, an' eventually he'll come here in force and try tae close Jerusalem. I've seen it in a dozen backwater countries just like this one, an' it's always the same. Ambush is the only real war they can fight, but they can do it well." He ordered his driver to pull over and his men to spread out and confiscate any weapons they could find. It was a cursory search, and they came up with nothing and were back in the trucks five minutes later.

"They're here. Hidden, but they have them," Jack said as he motioned for the convoy to get moving again.

"We all have them," Ephraim replied. "You'll have your work cut out for you if you try to get them all."

"Then civil war it will be. The orders I received this mornin' leaves this sort of thing up to my discretion. A lot of my countrymen dinnae like what yer ETZEL an' LEHI did to their friends over the last few years, an' they plan tae make it tough fer ye an' easy fer the Arabs. Some of us will try tae be evenhanded. Some will hit the Arabs hard an' take it easy on ye. But the outcome will be the same—war. Guerilla war, but folk will die just the same."

They drove into Jerusalem as Ephraim thought about what he had just felt in the canyon—the anxiety, the desperation, the fierce desire to survive.

The vehicles behind the troop transports began peeling off along other streets as they approached Bevingrad by way of Jaffa Road. As they arrived at the main gate of the British compound, Jack could see transports racing out and heading for the Old City. He pulled over to question one of the guards.

"The Arabs continued their strike this mornin'. Now they're riotin'. 'Ead for the Commercial Center. Our lads don't seem to be able to stop them."

Jack told his driver to move ahead and signaled the soldier-laden trucks to follow. They saw the smoke coming from the Center first, then the rioters carrying away all the loot they could as British troops kept Jewish men away, beating and arresting them. Jack leaped out of his jeep and ordered some of his men to hold back anyone who tried to get through along Jaffa Road from the Arab Quarter, then told the others to follow him. With Ephraim at his side, Jack found the commander of the troops and asked him what was going on. Ephraim noticed that the man outranked Jack by one level, and from the snide look on his face, he wasn't about to let Jack forget it.

"Are you lost?" the British officer asked.

"Maybe. I thought there was a British Army around here. Ye know the type—peacekeepers, dedicated men of honor. Have ye seen any?"

The jaw hardened. "I suggest you go back to Bevingrad, Willis. My orders are clear. We are not to put our men at risk needlessly while keeping the peace." Jack stepped toe-to-toe. The other officer flinched but then hardened further. "Back off, Colonel, or I'll 'ave my men arrest you on the spot."

Ephraim noticed Abraham Marshak standing under guard near the wall of the Old City with about fifty others. His nose was bloodied and the hatred in his eyes was palpable. The others had the same look, all of them obviously frustrated and outraged by what was happening. It was all Ephraim could do to keep his own anger under control; Jack's statement about some of his fellow British soldiers being collaborators was very real. This Brit's interpretation of neutrality was doing a lot of damage and had to be stopped now. Ephraim started for the entrance to the Commercial Center. The officer shouted a command and one of his soldiers stepped in Ephraim's way; two others pointed weapons at his stomach.

"Arrest—"

Jack silenced the officer with a right hook to the jaw. The man was lifted off his feet six inches, then landed with a thud on his back. He didn't move. Jack then turned to the men holding Ephraim. They and the rest of the Brits under the unconscious man's command had shock written across their mugs, though some seemed satisfied at the turn of events. He picked three of these and told them to take charge of the Colonel and see that he got back to Bevingrad and put in a cell until this could be sorted out. "Anyone who cares tae challenge that order can step forward now." He was looking directly at the men holding Ephraim back. One glanced at another and the three of them lowered their weapons and stepped back.

Jack turned to the Jews being kept out of the center. "Ye have the apologies of the British government. Go help yer people. If a British soldier tries tae stop ye, I'll shoot him." He looked at the soldiers to be sure they heard what he said.

Initially, stunned by the sudden turn of events, Abraham and the other Jews hesitated only a moment, then started into the Center.

Ephraim and Jack watched them go and were ready to follow when a woman's voice stopped them.

"Your police will stop them."

They turned to see a woman near the wall, a wounded man next to her. They were Arabs.

"I saw many of them helping the mob. A policeman in charge asked the man you hit to keep everyone out. He said the Jews needed to learn a lesson."

Jack hesitated when another voice chimed in. He turned to see Aaron carrying a wounded man out of the Center. "She's right. I witnessed it myself. The policeman's man is Foley, and he is helping the mob break into a warehouse just down the street."

While Ephraim helped Aaron with the man he carried, Jack ordered one of his sergeants to take his men and arrest any British involved in the looting. They rushed into the Center as Aaron spoke again. "These two men need a hospital."

Mary gave Aaron a relieved smile that gave rise to a layer of goose bumps on Aaron's arms.

"He's right," Ephraim said. "This one's been shot, and even from here the Arab looks like he could use a few stitches in his skull." He looked at Aaron, "It looks like you've had a busy afternoon."

Jack peered down the street. There were ambulances standing idle, waiting orders that hadn't come. He gave them, then went into the Center to make sure his orders were obeyed.

Aaron pulled a blood-saturated rag from Dr. Messerman's side and checked the wound while Ephraim helped a moaning Izaat sit up.

"Bad bump on the head," Ephraim said matter-of-factly. "Probably a concussion." Izaat tried to brush his hand aside, an angry disoriented look on his face. "Relax," Ephraim said, pulling his hand away. "You need medical attention."

"Not from Jews," Izaat hissed.

"Hush, Izaat," Mary said angrily. "These Jews have saved your life."

Ephraim and Aaron glanced at each other, then stepped back and out of the way as two medics joined them and each took charge of one of the wounded.

"What happened?" Ephraim asked.

Aaron started his story as the medic called for a stretcher bearer for Dr. Messerman who was finally conscious but convincing no one that he was fine. They were hauling him off to an ambulance and Izaat was getting his head stitched up when Aaron finished. Ephraim saw more wounded being carried from the Center and said he was going to help as he started toward the entrance. Aaron nodded but stayed.

Izaat angrily tried to get up before the bandage was in place and Mary told him to sit still or she would club him again. Aaron couldn't help the smile. His estimation of Mary seemed to have been correct. She was fearless.

"You want me to stay among these Jews who tried to kill me?" Izaat said angrily.

"You were attacked by an Arab, not by us," Aaron said. "And if I hadn't stopped him, he would have clubbed you to death."

"That is a lie," Izaat shoved the medic to one side and used the wall to get to his feet. He was unsteady, his head spinning, but he forced himself to stay on his feet.

"You have a concussion," the medic said. "You should be in a hospital."

"I do not need a hospital," he said angrily. He tried to walk but teetered and fell, holding his head. The medic called for stretcher bearers as Mary scolded Izaat and told him to be still before he made things worse. Izaat, dizzy and sick to his stomach, didn't argue this time, and the stretcher bearers were soon loading him as well.

Mary turned to Aaron. "I am sorry. His anger makes him a fool. What . . . what did the Arab look like who attacked my brother?"

Aaron described him.

"Raoul," she said with some bitterness, then shoved it aside and smiled at them. "Thank you for your help. I should go with him."

"Look in on Dr. Messerman for me, will you?" Aaron smiled.

"You know him?"

"We met at a funeral."

Her face showed curious confusion.

"I'll explain sometime, Mary Aref."

Mary nodded slightly, then went after her brother.

He didn't want her to go and blurted out the only thing he could think of. "Where do you live?"

She turned back, a half-smile creasing her lips, her eyes glinting in the setting sun. "In the Old City. The Arab Quarter on el Saraya Street above the old bookstore of Musa Hadad."

He knew the store and nodded as she turned and walked away. He watched her until she was in the ambulance, gave him a slight wave, and the doors closed. El Saraya Street was filled with shops he had visited a hundred times. He wondered why he had never seen her before and if it would be a difficult street for a Jew to visit after today.

Jack came to his side, breaking up his thoughts. "I'm sorry about this, laddie. Real sorry."

Aaron nodded. He knew Jack, and he knew the apology was genuine. "Give me a hand?"

Aaron looked up to see Ephraim a few feet away, his clothing already stained with blood and ash. Aaron and Jack joined him and they trudged back in the Center, spending the next three hours helping the injured and wounded, putting out fires, and giving comfort where they could. It was late in the day when the three of them finally set their own weary bodies on some ancient stones jutting from the ground near the Old City wall.

"Thanks, Jack," Ephraim said, "but you'll probably get court-martialed for hitting that officer."

"I'll nae be charged. That officer knows I'll have his head if he presses it." Jack pulled a blade of grass and stuck it in his mouth. "The Mufti is behind this, an' it's only the beginnin', ye know that."

"Yeah, we know."

"Bad showing by yer Haganah. One concerted counterattack an' the Arabs would have run fer the hills."

"We're still learning," Aaron said.

"Ye'd better pick up the pace, laddie, or there won't be enough Jews left tae form a minyan fer prayer." He stood. "Time tae go." He paused. "One thin'. Console yerselves wi' the thought that the Arabs will lose if this is the best they can do. Looters cannae fight a war. They're cowards." He smiled down at them. "I'm at yer service. Anythin' ye need . . ." He looked over at the Commercial Center. "Anythin'." He turned and started for his jeep, barking orders for his men to follow. Tired and nearly as dirty as Jack, his men dragged themselves into the back of their trucks and followed Jack's jeep out.

Ephraim pushed himself to his feet and picked up his discarded duffel bag as Aaron joined him. They started along the road toward home, Ephraim mentally filing away Jack's offer. It was obvious they were going to need all the help they could get.

"*Shalom.*"

He looked up to see Hannah standing in front of them. "Hi to you too," he dropped the bag and took her in his arms. As he kissed her he noticed the bruised face.

"What happened?"

"I walked into an open door."

"Don't lie in front of the children," he said.

"She was on the bus that was hit on the road to Jerusalem," Aaron answered for her.

"I saw it," he said, worried. "How are the twins?"

"Fine."

Ephraim put an arm around her, picked up the bag and they started moving again. "How did you know I was here."

"Abby told me." She glanced over her shoulder at the Commercial Center. In a single day the Arabs had dealt them a stiff blow. How could they survive if they couldn't even defend a few shops? She let it go. They would survive. Somehow.

"Abby says the ETZEL retaliated. They tried to burn down the Rex Cinema."

Ephraim laughed lightly. "Good choice. After all, who needs a movie? This is as Hollywood as it gets." He took a deep breath. "They ravished women, beat up old men, and deprived every Jewish store in there of their livelihood. Burning the Rex hardly seems like an appropriate response."

"It doesn't sound like they even did that very well. A few rolls of film and the walls of the projector room were all that was damaged," Hannah said. "How did the two of you get involved in this?"

Ephraim went first, then Aaron. He didn't tell her everything, but she sensed he had come close to getting himself killed.

"The Mufti means business," Ephraim smiled. "I suppose we should start taking him seriously." They came to Jaffa Gate. It was blocked by British policemen working more at keeping Jews out than in quelling the demonstration beyond the gate. The chants from the mob made Hannah's hair curl.

"I used Zion Gate to come out," she said.

"A good choice. These people want blood."

"They'll close the gate down before long. Cut off our Quarter from the outside city," Aaron said.

"If the British will let them," Hannah said.

"If you saw what we saw today, you'd bite your tongue," Ephraim said. He took Hannah's arm and they crossed the street, staying behind a row of police vehicles and trucks. The street became relatively calm, but remembering what he had seen in the canyon, Ephraim kept his eye peeled for snipers along the walls and rooftops.

He relaxed a little as they turned the last corner and entered the Gate. Though it faced an Arab section of the New City, it was peaceful. He wondered how long it could last.

They entered their street and Ephraim spied Elizabeth standing on the second-floor porch of their apartment, watching them.

"*Shalom*," he said with a broad smile. He loved Beth and David like they were his own now, and it did his heart a world of good to see her.

"You both need a bath," Elizabeth said in Hebrew.

"Thanks for noticing," Ephraim grinned. "I suppose you've made arrangements."

He spoke it in good Hebrew. He had learned the language quickly, having been attuned to it from the start.

"There is a water shortage, remember. You will have to use the wash cloth, like the rest of us." She gave a false frown. As he stepped closer to make a response, she pulled a bucket out from behind her back, and before he could say a single word, he was drenched in water. He sputtered as the black ash washed into his mouth, down his torso and legs, and onto the street. It felt wonderful, even though the evening was turning quite cool.

"I don't suppose you have any more . . ." Aaron started to say.

David suddenly appeared and poured another bucket. It cascaded off Aaron's shoulders and down his back. In the cool of evening, it chilled him to the bone while waking up his tired muscles. When he could open his eyes, both children were grinning. David tossed something else and Ephraim reached out and grabbed it. A bar of soap. "Wh-when you are finished, you c-can give it to Ari and c-come in the house. Not b-before. Mum's rules," David said.

Ephraim starting rubbing the soap against his skin, making vocal sounds that were remarkably off-key. Sour faces popped out of windows and doors as neighbors slammed their shutters closed.

"That's enough. People will think we've lost our minds," Hannah said with a grin.

Ephraim chuckled, looking up at his two children. "That felt wonderful, even if it did turn me to an ice cube. Thank you."

Aaron caught the soap Ephraim tossed him and grinned. It was wonderful to be alive, to be cared about.

"You're still not clean," Elizabeth said, eyeing the two of them critically.

They each looked at their skin.

"She's right," Ephraim said to Aaron, who only shrugged, muddy, black ash clinging to him.

"Nah. I've been in the sun too long. That's all."

"Come on. Let's go inside and get you a shower," Hannah said to Ephraim. He started around and up the steps after her. David and Elizabeth disappeared inside while Aaron sat down to take off his wet shoes.

Ephraim stood still, water dripping down his legs and onto the steps. "It's nice to be home."

She turned into him and he pulled her close. "Can you stay this time?"

"Avriel is handling things in Europe, Schwimmer in the States. Yes, I'll be home for a while. At least until they need pilots to fly everything in here. Till then just the regular mail route and supply drops."

"But that could prove dangerous. The Arabs—"

He put a finger to her mouth. "Shhh. Let's keep the Arabs out of the house tonight, okay?"

She nodded, her eyes filling with love. How could she be so lucky?

"Excuse me," Aaron said, slipping by. "It's getting cold out here, and I don't have the hot flames of love to keep my feet from freezing to the stones." He quickly disappeared inside.

They started up the stairs again. It was wonderful to be home.

CHAPTER 8

Mary sat at the table but couldn't eat, her mouth too tender to move her jaw and her stomach too full with the bile of anger.

She had returned from the hospital with Izaat clutching her arm for support. He refused to stay in a Jewish hospital for one minute longer than it took to bandage his skull and give him an aspirin for his throbbing head. The British soldiers only shrugged their shoulders and let him go.

Dr. Messerman was still there. His wounds weren't life threatening, though it might be several days before he left the hospital.

When they had arrived home, Izaat's anger had burst out of him like water under heavy pressure. Nearly out of control, he had cursed her for what she had done, for even being in the Quarter. She listened, tightly clamping her mouth lest her anger make things worse. But then he had told her that she had tarnished their father's name by her actions, and she could hold it back no longer. She got to her feet and confronted him, her face stretching up toward his in defiance. "And yours have tarnished the name of God and His Holy Son, not to mention our father's! You and the Mufti's henchmen have killed innocent blood, Izaat! Do you think this pleases Father? No, he is turning over in his grave at your words." She crossed herself. "May he rest in peace," she said it reactively, taking a deep breath and forging ahead.

"Half the families who owned those shops were our friends yesterday. Today you beat them, burned their stores, robbed them, and some of your new friends even raped their women! Then they tried to murder Dr. Messerman, a friend of father's and of all Arabs.

This is what killed our father, Izaat! This hate and support for Haj Amin and his butchers!"

He had come at her as if to hit her but got control as he raised his hand. Instead he slammed it on the table top. "Enough! We asked them not to seek partition! They rejected our pleas! We ask them to quit bringing more of their people here and stealing our land and our country. They refuse! Enough is enough! We will take it no longer! We will fight them! All of them! Whether they be a doctor or a store-keeper or any other Jew." He stood and went to the window, calming himself, his wife pale, but submissive as always, quickly gathering some dishes and taking them to the sink, where she busied herself.

"*Our* country? When has it ever been our country, Izaat?" She asked it as calmly as she could. "When has there been a time when we have not been ruled by someone else? First the Romans, and last the British. Was there something I missed? A time when Palestine *belonged* to our people? Even in 1920 we claimed allegiance to Syria. Only when they were defeated did we start calling ourselves a separate people. Only then did it become *our* land. And who are we? What gives us the right to claim this land any more than the Jews?" She paused, leaning forward across the table. "Even now the world does not recognize us as a separate people, and for them to give us a separate state is a blessing, not a curse. It is the first real step in becoming what you want for us. Why do you and others insist on giving it up by this . . . this fighting? Can you not see that to do this plays right into the hands of the Arab countries around us who want to split us up like a cooked chicken, each devouring a part? By your actions you will bring about an end to the very dream you seek."

She stood and went to the patio door, staring into the dark street below, trying to get control. "The United Nations has given us a chance, and what do we do?" she asked in a calmer voice. "We listen to Haj Amin, a man who wants to be king of all Arabs, who wants to extend Islamic rule to every nation. Another ruler! Do you think he will give us the land once we win it for him. He is Herod the Great all over again. We are fools!"

Izaat cursed in Arabic. "You understand nothing! If we let them in, they will drive us out. Even now they prepare for it."

"Did they attack us anywhere in Palestine since the vote? Did they shoot at our buses and burn our shops? They would live in peace if you would let them. But you want war. You want it because Haj Amin tells you to want it, and when it is finished you will have nothing because you are all greedy fools who cannot see when you are well off. And if they prepare their Haganah, it is because of what we do, what we say, not because they want to drive us from the land."

"The land is everything, Mary. Everything. It has fed our people for two thousand years. If the Jews get their state, how do we feed ourselves? Where do our people go?" His voice was tired, confused. He ran his hand through his hair, his head shaking as if to throw aside at least one of the opponents battling for his allegiance. "The Jews must be driven from this country before they have it all. If we do not do it now, if they defeat us somehow . . ." He seemed to shudder. "They will take it all, Mary, and they will burn *our* shops. It is them or us, and I will not let it be us!"

"Then our rulers will be the Arabs or Haj Amin. What a horrible choice." Mary took a deep breath then knelt before her brother and took his hand in hers. "Dear Izaat, your love for our people makes me blush with pride, but have you forgotten who it was that killed our own people in the 1930s when they refused to support his revolt? Even our own uncle was butchered. Surely it would be better to deal with the Jews. They want peace. They are willing to work with us. Please, can you not see that war with them will bring catastrophe to this land—either from the Mufti or from the Arabs. And if we lose this chance for peace . . . if they believe us an eternal enemy . . . even the Jews will lose patience, and you are right—the warriors among them will use it to drive us out completely. The Jews, Izaat, are our only salvation, but we must deal with them now."

He seemed beaten, confused, so tired he might sink to the floor, but then he stiffened. "No, you are wrong." He pulled his hand away. "You will never speak such words again in father's house. Do you hear me? Never!"

She could not believe her ears. She stood and turned from Izaat. "If our father is displeased with what is being said here, it is your words that would cause him grief, not mine. Have you forgotten his words to you about your support of Haj Amin and violence?"

Izaat stood, his face livid with anger. Turning Mary to face him, he slapped her across the face.

Mary touched her face, tears racing to her eyes at the sting of what he had done. He held her tight against him as he apologized and begged her forgiveness. She broke away and ran for her room, slamming and locking the door behind her. Throwing herself on the bed she let the tears flow.

"Mary, please, I . . . I am sorry," Izaat begged at the door. Mary did not answer. At that moment she did not want to even hear his voice and covered her head with a pillow to shut him out.

It was nearly ten minutes before she lifted the pillow and sat up, drying her eyes. She could hear Izaat talking to his wife in the other room. From the tone of the conversation, he was getting another tongue lashing. It surprised Mary. Her sister-in-law Hanan, the traditional, obedient Arab wife, was not one to talk back. A moment later a door slammed and the outer room grew quiet, though Mary knew Izaat was still there. A moment later there was a light knock on her door.

"Mary, I ask your forgiveness." There was a long pause. "Please, open the door. I wish only to talk." Another pause. "You may be right about some of this, but can you not see that we have no choice? Yes, the Arabs will come, and they will try to take the land, but that is why I must fight now. We must show the world that we are a people, that we have rights, and that they cannot take them away as easily as they might take a toy away from a child. If we do not fight now, we are nothing, and they will see us as nothing. We will be just more Arabs to be pushed and shoved about. I do not love Haj Amin, and he will never be our king, but he is the only one we can turn to now. There is no other voice for the Palestinian people."

She knew he was sincere, but she was still too hurt to open the door. "Go away, Izaat," she said evenly. "Just go away and may the saints help you understand the evil that you do." A moment later she heard the door to the apartment open and close. He was gone.

Mary hurried to the window and watched him walk down the narrow, dark street. She still loved him and was more afraid for him than she had ever been. He had never hit her before, never even raised his voice at her. The hate, the anger she saw tonight frightened her. Was this the man he was becoming? No, he had apologized. He was genuinely sorry. Possibly hitting her had awakened him to what he was becoming as much as it had her. If so, the sting was worth it. He could change. He would change. She could not bear the thought of him hating her this way.

And Rhoui was even worse. He had come to the house earlier livid with anger. He had wanted to horsewhip her on the spot then banish her to Beirut or Damascus, but Izaat hadn't even let him in the house. Izaat was good. She had to trust that his hitting her was an anomaly, a freakish turn of nature caused by pressure and frustration, because he was all she had to hang on to. Rhoui she could not trust. His hate was so deeply rooted that his very presence frightened her.

Then there was Raoul. To think that any notion had been given to a union between them gave her chills. Thank the heavens that she had discovered his true character. How she prayed she would never see him again.

Her stomach churned. Her father's death and now this. She felt frightened, alone, and vulnerable. Rhoui or Raoul would find a way to torment her. She must get free of this place for a little while at least, but where could she go?

She thought of several places—even London—but there were still things she must do here. A visa, her passport needed renewing, and her father's inheritance to her and her brothers was still in need of attention. She decided on her aunt in Katamon. Yes, it would be a good place. It was a heavily-populated Arab area outside the city walls. She would be safe there and could plan while still being close enough to her home she could return when she wanted. She would send a message to her aunt tomorrow to see if she had room. In a few days she would go there, away from at least some of this madness.

She closed the windows and shutters against the cold night, locked the door and bolted it, and went to the bathroom. She ran the tub full of water, the steam rolling off its surface like a pleasant fog.

In desperate need of more pleasant thoughts, her mind settled on the Jew who had saved them. He had been the same one she met at the tomb. He knew her name and was apparently at her father's funeral, a friend of Dr. Messerman. The thought of him caring enough to be there made her heart quicken.

She stood, trying to shove it aside as she undressed and slipped into the hot water, the warmth rushing up her legs and spine as she immersed herself. Oh, how good it felt!

She closed her eyes and let the warm fluid clear away the ache in her bones and comfort her soul. She could still picture the young Jew standing there as she had waved from the ambulance. He was very handsome and she wondered if she would ever see him again.

A sudden wind rattling the windows startled her. The water was quickly cooling, so she finished washing herself and pulled the plug from the drain, then stood and reached for a towel. The rain began striking the window as she finished drying and quickly slipped her shivering body into underclothes, nightgown, and a heavy cloth robe. She hastened through the house a second time, making sure all windows were closed tight, then checked the small kerosene furnace. Huddling near it, she reached for her father's papers she had been sorting. All his financial papers were in Izaat's possession, and he was working to get it organized and divided according to their father's will. Before her lay his writings, letters, and other personal papers accumulated over the years; she was trying to make sense out of them. In the process she had found they gave her great comfort, drawing him close through this look at the past.

She saw the picture of her parents and pulled it from the papers. It was of their wedding at the Church of the Holy Sepulcher. They looked so young. She touched their faces with her fingertips. Oh how she missed them! Though her mother had been gone for ten years, a day never went by that Mary didn't feel her presence. If she could but feel those arms around her now. If she could just have her father hold her close and chase away the fear and anger in her heart.

But it could not be. It would never be again.

She pulled a hanky from her purse and tried to stop the flow caused by her reverie. It had been a tear-filled day. When she cleared her eyes, she tried to concentrate once more on the papers before her.

It was then she heard the soft tapping noise on the glass doors from the balcony. She listened more intently. Just the wind, or the rain, she thought. She picked up the small book of her father's notes on meetings with Jewish leaders and began pulling the ribbon from around its folded pages.

There it was again. Fear wrenched at her stomach. How could this be? There were no steps to the balcony, no ladder, no way of getting there. She scrambled to her feet and quickly went into her father's room. Opening his top drawer, she removed the old pistol and a small box of bullets. Fumbling, then dropping two of them, she was slow to put one in the chamber. She clicked it shut and tried to cock it. Old, rusty, and heavy, it wasn't easy, but once she had the hammer back, she took a deep breath and went back to the sitting room. The tap was louder. Yes, there was someone there.

"Who is it?" she rasped. She pointed the antique weapon at the doors. "Whoever you are, I have a gun, and I know how to use it!" She tried to control the shaking in her hands and the beat of her heart. She felt hot, flustered, frightened. Was this Raoul coming to finish what he had started at the lingerie store? The door rattled and a small voiced seemed to hiss from the other side.

"Open up, please. I . . ."

"If that is you Raoul, go away or I'll shoot! I swear I will!"

"Mary Aref," the voice said with more volume. "It's Aaron—the Jew who pulled you and your brother out of the Commercial Center."

"You! What are you—"

"It is very wet out here, and I will catch my death of cold if you don't open this door soon. And what will the neighbors think if they see me standing here."

She dropped the gun to her side and quickly unlocked the door. He stepped inside, his body dripping wet and shaking against the cold slush that hung on him like a coating of wet sugar. Mary was too astounded to speak or move as he closed the door behind him, then went to the furnace and warmed his shivering hands.

"I apologize about the entrance, but if you are like everyone else in this city, you have nosy neighbors, and I thought you might like my visit to go unannounced." He smiled.

"What . . . what on earth . . . what are you doing here? Have you lost your mind? If you are discovered, they will beat you to death and cut you to pieces." She was pale with fear. "You cannot stay! You must, go. Now!" She reached for the knob.

"The sleet has stopped. I might be seen if I leave now." He turned, facing her, warming the back of his legs and creating a puddle of water near the base of the furnace. His hair was matted to his scalp and even curlier than she remembered it, but his dark eyes danced as he watched for her answer.

She lifted her hand from the knob. "This is madness! You are a Jew, I an Arab! Our people are trying to kill one another, and you come here like a thief in the night." She shook her head disbelievingly. "Your mother has surely raised a fool."

Aaron smiled sheepishly. He hadn't taken the time to think about it. He had just decided. The rooftops were close enough together that he had been able to come without hindrance from the Jewish Quarter. Though he had seen several gunmen—from both sides—he had been able to avoid them, find her street and the shop, then the balcony. Though he had been forced to go back to the roofs and lower himself to it from there, it had been easy enough, and he hadn't once stopped to think how impulsive and dangerous it had been. He had wanted to see her again, that was all. And when he had finished with his meeting with the Haganah he had come. It had been simple enough then. Now that she mentioned it, he discovered she was right. It was really quite foolish.

"I assume we are alone? That your brother will not come from one of these rooms and shoot me where I stand," he smiled.

She couldn't help herself and smiled back, then changed it to a frown. She knew little of this man.

"They are in there, asleep," she said pointing to her own bedroom door.

"They?" he said with a concerned raise of an eyebrow.

"My brother and his wife."

"Then he is out of the hospital?"

"Yes, of course. A slight concussion and twelve stitches. But he's alright, and if he hears you in here . . ." she waggled the heavy gun at him.

Both brows went up as Aaron looked at the ancient weapon. "Careful! That gun could fire just from looking at it." He took three steps and put his hand around the gun before she could react. Gently he removed it from her grip, their hands touching as he did. He lay it aside, his eyes searching hers. "You're lying," he said returning to the stove. "I couldn't get to the balcony at first, so I tried the window on that side. There is no one there."

She felt somewhat foolish. Folding her arms adamantly across her midsection she gave him a forced scowl. "Do all Jews break into the homes of defenseless women, or are you the exception?"

"The exception, I would imagine," he said with a wry smile. "Especially defenseless Arab women."

The blood went to her face as she flushed with frustration. "Get out!" she said firmly. "Leave now before I scream and they rip you to pieces." Her arm extended a pointed finger that punched at the door. He looked at it, then at her, then shrugged as he moved to the door. "Mary Aref. I wish to see you again. I will be visiting Dr. Messerman at the hospital tomorrow. Possibly I will see you there." He turned and smiled at her while reaching for the door handle.

"Wait!" she said, having second thoughts about him leaving that way. "You must leave the way you came. The man who lives in the back apartment watches everything since my father's death. The self-appointed protector of my virtue."

"He has no concern on that account," Aaron said. "I am—"

She was flustered again. "You don't find me appealing?"

"Oh, no. That isn't what I meant . . . I . . . ." It was his turn to feel foolish and it brought a smile to her face.

"Ah," he said, relieved. "She can smile! My efforts have been wonderfully rewarded. Now I can leave, a happy and contented man." He started across the room and reached for the balcony door. As she turned to face him, he took one quick step, wrapped an arm around her and kissed her gently on the lips, then opened the door and left.

It happened so fast that Mary stood speechless. She was at once exasperated, flustered, and pleasantly surprised. Her hand went to her lips as if to check them for traces of his, while her mind leaped to anger at his taking such privileges without permission or even the slightest indication that she was agreeable to such a thing. Which she surely was not! She grabbed the doorknob and flung open the door. Stepping onto the dark balcony, she looked right and left, then over the edge, but found no sign of him.

"Tomorrow," he said.

She glanced up to see him looking at her from the edge of the roof, a playful grin on his face. Then he was gone.

"Never!" she yelled, then instantly slapped her hand over her mouth. Surely the whole neighborhood had heard her. She glanced left and right, across the street at the apartments there, but saw no one. "Never!" she said in a loud defiant whisper. But there was no answer. She waited. Nothing.

She growled, tramping inside and slamming the door behind her. There was simply nothing else to do.

CHAPTER 9

Living in a city spiraling toward war is a strange thing. One day you bargain with the Arab or Jewish shopkeeper, laugh and talk of families and work, while the next you are locked out. As Hannah went out for bread and vegetables each day after the looting of the Commercial Center, she saw more and more shops in the Jewish Quarter locked up, their owners gone. They had left the Old City during the night. Then had come the barricading of the streets that led into the Arab sections of the Old City, the beginning of shooting, and the usual friendly bustle replaced with fear, mistrust, and empty streets.

Hannah and her family, and anyone who had been a Jew in Europe during Hitler's reign, had felt the anguish of a city afraid before. They had lived in Berlin and Krakow where Germans and Poles had turned on them like wild dogs, even neighbors betraying them into the hands of the Gestapo. Survivors of the Holocaust understood hate and how it forced friends apart, made neighbors turn on neighbors or move out altogether. For survivors, it was sad to see so many decide they would leave Jerusalem so quickly, but they understood. Had the Jews fled quicker from the Germans and the Poles, more of their families might still be alive.

Hannah discussed daily events and their ramifications with several neighbors at the outdoor market in the Street of the Jews each day. It wasn't safe to walk out of the Quarter as gangs of Arab youth hung around the street to beat up any Jews who dared to try.

"The bus," one Jewish woman said. "You take the bus. Rocks can only break windows, not your head if you take the bus."

They had laughed nervously at the remark. They all knew it would only get worse, that even the bus wouldn't be safe before long. Some talked of leaving themselves—of taking vacation now instead of in the summer, of visiting relatives in far away places until things got better. That's when Hannah drifted away to do other things. She could not bear the thought of leaving. It was her home now, and she was not about to give it up without a fight. She and all the Jews of Krakow had done that, and they had lost everything—their homes, their dignity, and most had even lost their lives. The Arabs who listened to Haj Amin believed they could do it again, but she and thousands of others who had come out of the camps would not allow it. Never again.

To those remaining, Rabbi Salomon had finally quelled the thoughts of leaving with his Shabbat sermon. He explained that the Hasids had lived in the Old City for generations. They had friends among the Arabs and the British. They had no need to be afraid. It was only the Zionists the Arabs disdained, and if they kept the Zionists out, the Arabs would not shoot at them or take away their homes. Those with thoughts of leaving felt so guilty after his sermon that most stayed, though some feared horribly for their lives. It divided the Jews of the Quarter about the role of the Haganah. Some said they should go, some that they should stay. It was a daily argument, and Hannah made sure they understood her position: to run was no solution, but neither was staying unless they intended to fight. The Arabs would come, just as the Nazis had, and they had better be ready. The end result was that Rabbi Salomon was not happy with her position and had stopped talking to her, again.

Hannah spied Binyamin Holtzberg, the Haganah commander for the Quarter, buying some apples from a vendor and took the time to greet him, then ask questions. His answers were not comforting. Gun emplacements were cropping up on the roofs of the Arab Quarter and they were preparing for battle. Only last night there had been several attacks and attempts to advance.

"There is a Palmach Unit here now. They are lodged at the Misgav Ladah Hospital," Binyamin said. "They heard banging at the gate separating us from the Arab Quarter. It sounded as if someone were breaking in. They found some Arabs in the street but chased them away. We are trying to coordinate our efforts with them, but we need many more or the roofs will soon be crawling with Arabs. I have asked Aaron to stay and help us. He has agreed."

Hannah nodded. Aaron had asked his commanding officer for an assignment here before Binyamin's request. It was home.

Everything was so uncoordinated now, especially here. The Haganah had so few recruits from the Quarter that you could count them on one hand. Nonreligious fighters were brought in from outside the Quarter. They came not knowing the people, not understanding them. They were not like the rest of Palestine. Few of the Old Stones of the Quarter believed as the Zionists. Most were very religious and did not want outsiders coming in with their bad habits and lack of morals. They only wanted to be left alone and relied on the British— and unwavering faith that their Arab neighbors would not turn on them—as they had done for years. She could understand that desire to believe in others. She had been that way, but she had learned.

"Avraham Halperin developed a plan for the defense of the Quarter. Are you familiar with it?" Hannah asked. From the look on Binyamin's face it was obvious he was not. "Aaron knows of it. You should talk." She paused. The second bus from the New City arrived. It had several broken windows and they could see immediately that there had been a serious attack. So much for safety on the buses.

The wounded and frightened people stepped quickly out of the bus and into the arms of waiting friends and family. Hannah could see many would need immediate medical attention. She and Binyamin joined with others to try and help, but they had little in the way of first-aid equipment. Binyamin sent a young boy to Misgav Ladah Hospital to fetch more, along with medical personnel who could treat some of the more serious wounds. Ladah Hospital was more of a clinic than a hospital, but there were supplies there and several trained nurses. The doctors usually came every other day from the New City. This was not one of those days. Dr. Messerman was still in the hospital because his wound had infected, and no one else practiced in the Quarter.

"What happened?" Binyamin asked the bus driver as he tried to patch up the deep cut in his forehead.

"A mob at Jaffa Gate. Rock throwers. The British drove them away by firing their weapons over their heads." He shook his own. "If they had not, we would have been butchered." Two nurses and several aids came running, carrying boxes of supplies and wielding stretchers. The male aids, assisted by others, began hauling the worst cases back to the hospital. Hannah was about to bandage a young girl's arm as one of the nurses knelt down beside them and examined the wound.

"A busy morning," Hannah commented.

"Very. Patients have been coming all morning. Two were severely beaten by Arabs who broke into the Quarter during the night. Four others had bullet wounds. We lost one of them." She showed Hannah how to bandage the wound, then went to the next victim. They both knew it was just the beginning.

The girl's mother rushed up as Hannah finished the bandage. Hugging her daughter in near panic and thanking God profusely for his kindness, she then inspected her for any other wounds while apologizing for sending her to the New City. Her husband, an ultraorthodox Jew, joined them and cradled her in his arms. As they began a quick departure, the mother scolded him for taking so long, then for keeping them in the Quarter. They were leaving right away she said loudly. As the family disappeared in a curve of the street, Hannah noticed several men walking toward the bus. One of them was Aaron. He had a half a dozen others with him, their faces tired and pale. She noticed blood stains on their clothing, and three had bandaged arms and cut faces.

She walked around several groups of people to where Aaron had stopped to talk to Binyamin, her eyes worriedly checking Aaron's body for wounds. The worry in her stomach settled a little when she found none.

"We were shot at from the village of Silwan. We returned fire and Moshe was hit," Aaron said. Hannah stayed back, knowing Aaron would not want her fawning over him right now.

"Where is Moshe now," Binyamin asked, obviously controlling a desire to panic. Things were quickly spiraling out of control. The Haganah had given him only twenty-five men, and already they were fighting battles that had seriously wounded one of his men and taken the life of another.

"They could not treat his wound at Misgav Ladah, so their ambulance took him to Hadassah. We rode with them just in case, but as you can see, we didn't have our weapons." He looked at the injured men. "We were attacked at Sheik Jarrah. This time they threw rocks. Next time it will be bullets."

Hadassah Hospital was the largest Jewish hospital in Palestine and had good surgeons and the latest in medical supplies and equipment. Any critical injuries would be taken there, but it sat on Mt. Scopus with Arab East Jerusalem at its foot. Sheik Jarrah, the most populated section, sat astride the road to Hadassah and had many loyalists to Haj Amin Husseini among its residents. It was a hotbed of Arab discontent, and to go there now was very dangerous, especially without weapons. Hannah knew they hadn't had a choice. The British had set up numerous checkpoints and were confiscating weapons and arresting their owners, their usual response to riots. But it would not be enough this time. Haj Amin wanted civil war; chaos and weak attempts at confiscating weapons would not be enough.

"You had better get a hold of Amir, Binyamin, get more help in here. They are testing us. If they find us weak enough, they will try to take the Quarter."

Rabbi Salomon had walked up to the small circle of men and shook his head adamantly. "No, this is not the solution. The British will protect us. We do not need any more of your Haganah here."

Rabbi Mordechai Salomon, the "father" of the Old City Jews, was chairman of the Quarter's Jewish Council and mandated by the British as its only representative. "The British have informed me that the army will arrive tomorrow to protect the Quarter and our families. They are better prepared to keep the Arabs in line. They have been doing it for years."

Hannah admired the way Aaron and Binyamin held their tongue, but they had orders to work with the Rabbi; she didn't.

"The British are leaving. What then, Rabbi?"

"You are wrong. They will never leave. Once it is shown that you Zionists cannot protect the Holy City, the United Nations will demand that they stay." He said it as if to sweep her aside like some insignificant mosquito. He had always treated her this way, but then she did not feel singled out so very much. It was the way he treated anyone who challenged him.

"And this?" She waved at the injured people and the badly damaged bus. "Is this my imagination?"

"There are a few fanatics, angry at you Zionists, not at us. It will not take long, and they will settle down again. I have seen it many times. It will pass."

"I saw it, too. In Krakow. They turned our Quarter into a ghetto, then hauled us away to camps and butchered us."

His face hardened at her example. "The Arabs are not Nazis. They are our neighbors. We have lived with them for generations."

She felt the anger boil in her stomach. "Yes, as the Poles were ours. And have you forgotten Haj Amin? Have you forgotten his effort in Germany? Do you refuse to hear the radio broadcasts, the words he uses against us? They are no different than Hitler's. No different! And the men who stir this up, who fire into the Quarter from Arab rooftops—apparently they do not wish to be your neighbors anymore. They will not think twice about shooting you or anyone else when they overrun this Quarter."

"Haj Amin does not lead the Arabs here. The Arab Higher Committee—"

"Are his stooges and everyone but you seems to know it," Hannah reacted.

Flummoxed, he turned his back on her, speaking directly to Holtzberg. "The British lieutenant named McCloud is responsible for the Quarter. He will send in a sufficient force to protect us and see that those who want to leave for a time do so safely. He asked that I speak to you so that no unfortunate shooting takes place when they come."

"If they leave us alone, we have no quarrel with them. But if they try to take our weapons, we'll fight them."

Rabbi Salomon stepped close to Holtzberg. "Do not turn the Quarter into a battleground, young fool. There is no need to fight the British—or the Arabs for that matter. Not here."

"Trust them if you like, Rabbi, but we will not. Not after what happened in the Commercial Center and a dozen other places in the last few days. Or have you forgotten that British soldiers stood by and watched the Arabs slaughter our people, some of them from this Quarter. Now they confiscate our weapons while leaving the Arabs alone, even aiding them. I do not relish their protection, and the sooner they leave the better."

The Rabbi was flustered again. Used to getting his way, being obeyed, he grew angrier. "My people do not need you. We have never needed you. If you cause trouble, I will have—" He bit his tongue.

"Have us thrown out?" Holtzberg gave a wry smile. "You might bully these people into submission, buy their allegiance with the funds you control, but that will not work with us. Beware, Rabbi, of biting any hand trying to help you. It may not be able to pick you up when you trip over your own mistakes."

The words seemed to shake the Rabbi, but he quickly recovered his pride, said something in a language unfamiliar to most before turning on his heel and walking away.

"Never heard that language before," one of the men said.

"Armenian, one of the six he knows," Hannah said. She had heard it enough in the camps to understand the Rabbi wasn't giving them a blessing.

"What did he say?" the man asked.

"You don't want to know." She turned to Holtzberg. "Beware of him, Binyamin. He will do whatever is necessary to protect what he believes God has given him. His pride won't let him do otherwise, and that is what makes him dangerous."

Holtzberg nodded. His interview with the Rabbi when first assigned had been positive, but since then things had begun to change. The Rabbi's world was disintegrating like a sandcastle in a storm, and he was hoping someone would throw up a dike and stop the waves. Who could blame him for thinking the British provided the safest of stone walls between him and the floods of war? But what wall they represented would soon be gone, and the Rabbi's world would still be in danger. Hannah was right, what then? Only the Haganah, and it frightened Binyamin that he and his men were all that would be left. There simply were not enough of them.

He turned to Aaron. "Who replaced you when you took Moshe to Hadassah?"

"Abraham Marshak, Naomi, and three others."

"Good," Binyamin started away, then glanced over his shoulder. "Get some sleep, then meet me at Misgav Ladah at three. I may have new orders for you." He hastened away and disappeared down a side street that led to Ladah Hospital.

Aaron dismissed the others, then put an arm around Hannah's shoulder as they started for the apartment. "Have you heard from Ephraim?"

"He will be back this afternoon." Ephraim was flying supplies into some of the settlements. The Old City was not the only place that was under attack. Ambushes had taken place in at least ten places during the night. Some needed more ammunition; others just needed their mail. "You said Naomi was with Abraham?" She tried to hide the apprehension in her voice. He tightened a comforting grip around her shoulder, and she knew she had failed, at least partly.

"She's Palmach, Hannah. Of all the units of Haganah, that is the one that emphasizes duty. Besides, you would have to tie and gag her to keep her away. We both know that."

They reached the street of the apartment where Beth sat on the steps entertaining one of the twins. Even from a hundred feet away she could hear his giggles. Everything here seemed so normal.

"Can we save it, Aaron? Can We?" she asked with frustration.

"I don't know. All we can do is try."

They both understood what a blow it would be to the morale of the entire Yishuv if they lost the Quarter. Jews had inhabited it continuously for centuries, and it held some of the most ancient and important synagogues in the entire world. To lose it would be a right hook from which it would be difficult to bounce back.

"They were putting out feelers last night to see how far the British will let them go," Aaron said. "We must do the same."

Beth saw them and started in their direction, holding the baby up and pointing while whispering something in his ear. He looked toward Hannah as if understanding Beth's words.

"Do you remember the tunnels Avraham Halperin told us about when he was Haganah commander over the Quarter?" Aaron asked.

"Yes, I remember. The ancient tunnels built centuries ago. He told us there are caves as well, and possibly an old Roman street buried under the rubble of centuries of ruins."

"The Arab emplacements can look into the main streets of the Quarter. They will be able to control those streets unless we find a way to thwart them."

Beth was nearly to them, and Hannah could see it was Jacob she carried. Seeing Hannah, he kicked his arms and legs excitedly. "By traveling underground," she responded while smiling at her son.

He nodded. "If the ancient road runs as Avraham Halperin says it does, we can build other tunnels and access most parts of the Quarter and some parts outside it. It may be a way for us to get supplies in if the Arabs cut off the Quarter when the British leave."

She took Jacob from Beth. "Have you been a good boy?" she kissed his cheek.

Aaron suddenly reacted to movement on the distant rooftop, pushing Hannah and Beth toward the wall. Hannah nearly fell and he steadied her as the crack of a rifle was heard, a bullet ricocheting just behind them. Aaron opened the door to an apartment and shoved them both inside, following and slamming the door behind them. Beth was near tears, her face pale with fear. Hannah, her breath coming in quick rushes, had to sit down on the old couch, her legs too weak to hold her. She saw the old woman staring at them in shock from the small kitchen.

"A sniper," Hannah said in a whispered tone, explaining to her friend Mithra why they had suddenly become her guests.

"Hannah?"

"Yes, yes, Mithra. It is me."

Beth went to Aaron, who held her close, trying to dispel the fear they both felt.

"And how do we find this ancient road?" Hannah said, after catching her breath.

"Maps, Mum, maps. Ancient maps held by Abraham Marshak's boss. You and Ephraim are his friends. Could you . . ."

"Today. I will go today," Hannah responded.

Aaron nodded. If he hadn't seen the movement . . . If Beth and Jacob had been alone . . . The thought made his stomach cramp.

Tonight he must get rid of that sniper.

* * *

Naomi kept her head down as she and Abraham worked their way across the roofs then down the ladder to a street where Arabs couldn't see them. It had been a long day and they were exhausted.

They started walking back toward their street, Abraham carrying a rifle. She had left hers with her replacement. So far neither had been forced to use their guns, but they knew it was only a matter of time. The Arabs were increasing their positions daily and working them forward. Only the Jews' own hastily installed emplacements prevented any further encroachments, and their proximity now meant fighting.

"The synagogues should be used, Abraham. They would give us an advantage against the Arabs."

"Rabbi Salomon will not give permission. My father will talk to him again today. Maybe the wounding of Moshe and the shooting into the streets will convince him."

"Will you take your father's place someday?"

"It is intended that I do so. I am ready to accept the responsibility, but it is a bit frightening to think of it."

"Why?"

"There are many people in my father's synagogue and many problems. To counsel them, have them depend on you for help in more ways than most imagine, is a great weight. I would rather be an archaeologist."

"You would be good at that as well. Would your father be disappointed if you chose that over being Rabbi?"

"Yes, very. There are no other sons in our family. It would force the people to find a new rabbi. That would be very hard for everyone."

"But possible."

"Yes, possible."

Naomi liked Abraham. They had spent many hours together over the last week, preparing emplacements, doing guard duty, making bullets and homemade hand grenades. He was the most direct man she knew, but he was kind and good-hearted as well. He would make a good Rabbi.

"Maybe you could do both," she said.

"Maybe," he paused. "A Rabbi needs a wife. It is another hurdle for me. I know only one woman I think I could love."

Naomi's breath caught in her chest reactively. She did not know he had someone he cared for, but it also surprised her that she cared he had those feelings for someone.

"I am sure she would be agreeable. Have you talked to her?"

"It is not done that way here, Naomi. When I give the word, my father will approach her father and they will make a marriage contract. Of course, it used to be that the woman had little choice, but now that is not so. She could say no, especially this woman. That is why I have done nothing." He hesitated at a street corner. "I must go this way, report to Binyamin that we are off duty but will return tonight. Is that agreeable to you?"

She nodded. "I'll meet you outside Hannah's apartment."

He nodded and started away. He was a handsome man in a plain sort of way, but he would make a good husband to a Hasidic woman. She could not see Abraham being overly demanding or forcing a woman to bend her will to his. It would be a partnership, but there would still be restrictions because of the place he held in the community and because he was orthodox. It was not a lifestyle meant for anyone who was not Hasidic.

She continued walking toward Hannah's. She found it interesting that she was a bit jealous of Abraham's love for another woman. They were friends, nothing more, and yet in a way she had hoped it might be more. Was it because of her disappointment with Aaron? Was she looking for some sort of acceptance because she had discovered he was no longer interested?

That was silly, she thought. She did not know it was over with Aaron. They had spent so little time together, she could not be sure those feelings didn't still have a chance of igniting again. She felt passion toward Aaron, and that was not what she felt with Abraham. And passion for the one you married had to be there, didn't it?

She shook it off. She could never be the wife of a Rabbi. She was not a believer, and a Rabbi's wife surely must be a believer. Why was she even thinking of such a thing?

She walked faster, changing her thoughts to the letter she had sent to Haganah command. She had asked for an assignment to SHAI but had heard nothing. She would be good at intelligence work. She hoped she would hear soon. Though she wanted to help defend the Quarter, SHAI was her dream.

And it didn't include any rabbis.

CHAPTER 10

It was nearly four when Aaron awoke. He quickly dressed and went into the kitchen for some bread and cheese. Beth and David were studying their scriptures at the table, the twins were asleep, and Hannah had gone to the New City to see about the tunnels. He sliced off a chunk of bread, then a piece of cheese and leaned against the small counter as he ate.

"It does not mean that," Beth said a bit irritated.

"It d-does. Look. Read it for yourself, then look in Isaiah. You w-will see. This is not the g-gathering of the Jews talked about by the p-prophet, in either b-book. That c-comes later."

"Then what are we doing here?" Beth said in frustration.

"Pr-preparing a p-place so that it c-can happen. Like Mum said, Isaiah is t-talking about a spiritual g-gathering. This isn't it. Zionists aren't even religious." He looked up at Aaron. "Look at my brother. He never p-prays, thinks synagogues are w-works of art, and hasn't read T-torah even once. All Zionists are like that."

Aaron almost choked on his bread, clearing his throat with a quick sip of water. "All Zionists are *not* like that. You, Beth, Hannah, and Ephraim are all Zionists, and there are others who are believers as well." He shook his head. "And you are wrong anyway. I have read Torah, at least some of it, and some of your Book of Mormon, too, so watch your tongue." He smiled.

"You?" Beth said incredulous, "read Torah and this?" She raised her copy of the Book of Mormon. "You're lying."

"Am I? Lehi takes his family and flees Jerusalem in a time not so different from this. The city is under siege, the populace wicked, and God needs someone to survive and take his record—called the brass plates, as I recall—and find a different place to live. He goes south, into the desert, then builds a boat and sails into the sea. They find a promised land and, well, need I say more?"

Beth's mouth dropped open slightly. "He has read it."

"Have you g-gotten to the Isaiah ch-chapters yet?" David challenged.

Aaron had read about the brass plates and the prophets who wrote in them and assumed something from Isaiah would come later, but he just hadn't gotten there yet. "No. It took me nearly a year to get through the first fifteen chapters of the book."

"You really read slow," Beth said genuinely.

Aaron chuckled. "I haven't had much time for reading."

"You really should make more, especially for the Isaiah chapters. They talk about what is going on in Palestine now. It's important," Beth said, then turned to David. "Then you can straighten out your little brother!"

David made a face at her and she stuck her tongue out at him.

"I hate to shatter your dream, Beth, but from what Ephraim told you the other night, I think David is right."

"Y-you heard that?"

"I'm not deaf, David. The door was open between the bedroom and this room. Of course I heard it."

"Do you believe it?" Beth asked, looking a bit shattered.

"I don't know that it matters, does it? Either way we're here to stay, but I don't think there will be much of a religious revival in Judaism until we feel safe. Even then, can you see Rabbi Salomon and the rest of the orthodox changing?"

"But it will take too long that way," Beth said, frustrated. "Jesus needs to come soon, and . . . and . . ." She was near tears, as she had been since they had been shot at earlier in the day. Shaken, afraid, this was her way of trying to get comfort again. "We . . . we'll never feel safe until *He* comes!" She lay her head down on the table in tears.

Aaron sat down in the chair next to her and rubbed her hair, unsure of what to say. This was work for Mum and Ephraim, not him. Beth was right, he was not religious, not like them, and he was afraid he'd screw up Beth's faith if he said the wrong thing now.

"If Jesus is Messiah," Aaron hesitated, choosing his words carefully. "If He is, you have to trust that He will come at the right time, whether now or later. In the meantime, we must do what we can to prepare for Him, correct?"

Beth lifted her head and rested her chin on the table, wiping away the tears with the palm of her hands. "Yes, I suppose. But what can we do? Everybody seems to hate us so much. Just because we're Jews and because we *want* to prepare a place for Him, they shoot at us. If He came now, if He showed them we are His people, they would stop, wouldn't they?"

Aaron sat back looking into her dark, questioning eyes. "Yes, I suppose they would." He suddenly realized how afraid she was. She, like the rest of them, had been through the misery of Hitler's war and here was the same thing staring her in the face again, threatening for a second time everything she had learned to love and live for. How could he help her when he lacked faith himself?

He thought desperately for words then remembered something Hannah had told him and Naomi only a few days ago. "Hannah says that the coming of your Messiah is not a single event, Beth. It is many events that culminate in His final coming. There will be war and hate and a struggle between good and evil. You are a part of that struggle, and you have to be strong if you want to see Him again, either when He comes or by going where He is. Hannah says it will be alright for you if you just keep believing and working to that end. Do you remember?"

Beth raised her head off the table and snuffed her nose, her eyes searching his. "Do you believe it, Aaron? Do you think Hannah is right?"

His mouth felt dry. There it was, the question he had always avoided—wanted even now to avoid—but if he did, how would she react?

"The war in Germany taught me hard lessons, Beth. I'm still not sure what I believe. I just know I am in the middle of a fight that is important to our people, and if God does exist, it must be important to Him too. For now, can that be enough?"

She nodded slightly, then seemed to think of something. "Wait." She slid off the chair and ran into the small bedroom she and Naomi shared. As they waited, David spoke.

"You d-did good." David smiled.

"Thanks."

"Some of the b-boys I know say you might need runners, messenger b-boys, to b-bring you ammunition and orders and stuff because you don't have field radios. I w-want to help."

Aaron nodded. He knew Holtzberg had put out the word, but he had hoped David wouldn't hear. "It is meant for older boys, but I'll let you know."

"I'm the f-fastest boy in the Quarter and I know every street, every b-building. I have b-been exploring it since we moved in. I c-can do it."

"I know, but Mum has to give her permission. You know that."

Beth came back in the room. She had a small book in her hand and laid it on the table in front of him. It was a breast-pocket sized copy of the Book of Mormon. He had seen Ephraim's and knew they were a special edition made for those in the military, but it was Hannah's larger copy Aaron had always used when no one was around the house.

"I bought it in America, in Salt Lake City. It fits better in my purse, but I want you to have it."

He picked up the book, thumbed the pages and noted that many verses had been marked in red pencil. He shook his head. "I can't. You have already marked things important to you. I don't want—"

"I have them marked in this one," she said pointing to the larger copy on the table. "When you finish reading it, you can give it back if you like, but I want you to take it. It will give you more time to read if you have it with you all the time."

He smiled. "All right." He dropped it into the pocket of his khaki shirt and patted it. "Thank you. It is a wonderful gift." He stood as the door opened and Naomi came in. She looked exhausted.

"*Shalom*," he said.

"*Shalom*." She smiled back.

"Just on my way to see Binyamin. The bed I used is probably still warm, and it looks like you could use it."

She nodded thanks, smiled at Beth and David, then started for the bathroom. "I'll wash first and grab a bite to eat."

"I can fix you something," Beth said.

"I would like that," Naomi responded as she closed the bathroom door.

"Will you two be alright until Mum comes home?" Aaron asked.

They looked at him with humor in their eyes. "We babysit all the time, Aaron" Beth said. "Of course, we'll be all right."

She was a changed little girl, the tears of only a moment ago a fading memory. He felt relieved. At least he hadn't made things worse. Grabbing his jacket he gave them one last look before leaving the house. David was reading and Beth pulling some food from the icebox. Neither saw the slight smile he gave both of them. He loved them.

Slipping out, he was careful to keep to the wall as he descended the stairs to the deserted street. The windows on the far side were shuttered now. The sniper had fired a dozen shots at different targets since the initial shot fired at them. He wondered how many other streets were under this kind of siege already and if anything had been done to remove it. He kept an eye on the far rooftops, looking for a sign of the enemy. Nothing. There was only one way to get them to reveal themselves, and he wasn't willing to take that chance. He kept close to the wall and ran for the corner, ducked around it and immediately noted the change.

People were out here, unafraid. Streets running east and west were not in danger, at least not yet. He walked to the middle of the street and looked in both directions. If the Arabs took the southern end of the Armenian Quarter they would be able to fire into east-west streets as well, and it wouldn't take long to get snipers on the roofs to the east either. Surrounded. They must get men on the roofs quickly. He walked to the end of the block, looked around the corner, and found the street deserted. As he looked north, he could see sandbagged emplacements on the rooftops in the distance. He darted across the intersection and walked into the Misgav Ladah Hospital, finding Binyamin and a dozen others talking seriously in the waiting area.

Binyamin looked up and smiled at him. "Good. You're here. These men will go with you into the Arab Quarter tonight." Aaron noticed that all of them were strangers. He nodded to them his pleasure at their arrival.

"How did you get in?" he asked the closest.

"Taxis." They smiled.

"They weren't agreeable at first, but when they saw our guns, it was a quick trip," said another. "The Arabs scattered at Jaffa Gate when they saw we were armed, but a few took potshots at us too. It will only get worse."

He was even more pleased to hear they had weapons. He looked at Binyamin. "What do you want us to do?"

Binyamin pulled out a map and began his instruction. As Aaron listened, it was obvious that the Arabs had a dozen emplacements on the rooftops, that Binyamin had placed several of his own to counter them, and that his next step was to send a message.

After the shot at Beth and Jacob today, it was a message Aaron was happy to deliver.

CHAPTER 11

Hannah knocked on the door of the small apartment on Hamigdal Street. She and Ephraim had been here several times, but their contact with Eleazar Sukenik took place mostly on archaeological digs. The main one they had helped Eleazar with was the uncovering of some ruins in Jericho Valley thought to be the remains of the winter palace of Herod the Great.

She heard stirring inside, then the key in the lock turned and the door opened. Eleazar stood in the doorway, an annoyed look on his face until he saw who it was.

"Hannah! Come in, come in!" He opened the door wider and she walked past him to the living room. Closing the door, he ushered her into his den at the back of the house. "I am glad you have come," he said. "I have something you will like to see."

His excitement was always contagious, and he knew that Hannah had developed the same insatiable desire for the ancient world as he had. Before the birth of the twins, it was often she, Ephraim, and Eleazar who were the first at work and the last to leave his digs, and they had many long talks about his discoveries.

As they entered the room twice the size of the living area, she was once again amazed at how he knew where anything was. The walls were lined with shelves filled with books in half a dozen different languages and boxes filled with notes on 4 x 6 cards, endless scraps of paper, and even on cardboard—whatever had been handy at the time.

Hannah immediately noticed that the long table that extended the length of one side of the room was devoid of its usual pieces of pottery shards and other finds from the Jericho dig. They were replaced by an ancient parchment scroll—a very old and very fragile piece of parchment scroll. Her breath caught in her throat as she saw it. "What on earth? Where . . . what . . . is all this?"

"One of the great finds of this century," he said with reverent excitement. "I purchased these yesterday from an antiquities dealer named Kando. You know him. The one from whom Ephraim purchased the coins of Jesus' day." He looked at the scrolls fondly. "This is a copy of the Book of Isaiah written completely in Hebrew. We have nothing like it."

Hannah felt her heart race as she stared at the ancient document. She knew not to touch it, so she bent closer, staring at the words on the page. It was ancient Hebrew and beyond her ability to read, but from the look of the parchment and ink, they were extremely old.

After a moment she looked at her old friend. "Are there more? Where were they found?"

"More? Yes, some were purchased before I was called in to look them over. When I saw them, I bought them immediately, but I could not get Kando to tell me who has the others."

"How many?"

"Four more at least, and there may be more where these were found, but we will not know for some time. Jericho is dangerous now, the hills filled with Haj Amin's butchers," he said in frustration.

"They were found in the hills outside Jericho," she mused.

He nodded. They had discussed the area before, had even considered looking in the caves of the area themselves, but had neglected doing so. Now she ached for having put it off. Eleazar had told her and Ephraim about documents written by the church historian Eusebius around A.D. 300 stating that a Greek version of the Psalms had been discovered in the Jericho caves during the reign of Antonius, son of Severus who ruled from A.D. 198 to 217. That had led him to read further, and he'd discovered that a Nestorian Patriarch had described the discovery of a large cache of Hebrew manuscripts in a cave near the same ancient city. It seemed the caves of the dry desert surrounding Jericho were a chosen receptacle of such things.

"You are a blessed man, Eleazar." She smiled. "I wish I had time to look more, but I have come for something else, something very important."

His eyes showed a bit of disappointment, but he nodded lightly. "Anything I can do, you know I will."

"Do you have any maps of the Old City showing the ancient Roman road and other tunnels?"

"Ah, the tunnels. There are many." He thought a moment, then went to a box and pulled out several rolled up maps. He placed them on his desk and unrolled and rerolled them until he found the one he was looking for. He spread it out and put books on its edges to keep it from rolling shut.

"Hezekiah's tunnel is the first of note, but it is outside the Old City, so I will assume you are not interested in it. During the time of the great rebellion in A.D. 66, a number of tunnels were built to hide from the Romans and to prevent their siege engines from getting next to the walls. Rather ingenious really. They would dig the tunnel using wood to support the roof. Then when the Romans rolled the siege engine used to breach the walls into place, the Jews would start the beams on fire and leave the tunnel. When the beam burned, the weight of the machine would cause the tunnel to cave in and the machine would tumble to its destruction, taking hundreds of soldiers with it. Some of those tunnels may still exist, though we do not know their exact locations. It only delayed the inevitable, but at least it left some a place to flee when the Romans finally breached the walls, seized the temple and destroyed it, and massacred thousands. History tells us that two of the rebel leaders were caught in the tunnels. One hiding, the other chipping away at another tunnel under the wall by which he and a few remaining supporters could flee from the city. They were both imprisoned in Rome after being displayed in the parade honoring Titus and his final victory of this land."

He pointed at the map. "The main tunnel that still exists would be the old Roman Cardo or road that you mentioned. It was built when the Romans rebuilt Jerusalem and called it Aelia Capitolina. It began here, near Damascus Gate and ended in the Jewish Quarter. Five hundred years later the Byzantines added to it, extending it further into the Quarter. In subsequent destructions of Jerusalem, the Cardo was covered with debris, or buildings were built on its columns, and the beams provided a ceiling for at least portions of the street. Some of them were found a few years ago, but the openings were sealed by the British and would be most difficult to find without their knowing. If you can gain entrance to them another way, they could be used and others cleared, but it will be a good deal of work."

"We need protection from snipers, a way to move about without getting killed."

"It is a good idea." He paused a moment. "Some of them may attach to Zedekiah's Cave, located under the Muslim Quarter. If they know of such entrances, they could use them to get past your sentries just as you could use them. That would mean a good deal of trouble for you."

"You have been in the cave. Do you think the tunnels connect?"

"I never saw anything, but there are so many holes and passages," he shook his head. "It is not impossible."

"Any suggestions on where to dig to find a new way in?"

"Start here," he pointed at a spot on the west side of Hurva Square. "You should find the Byzantine portion of the Cardo. From there," he shrugged, "who knows?"

She gave him a hug and then took one last look at the ancient scrolls on the table. "You should get them to a safer place, Eleazar. This war . . ."

"I have already made arrangements. The God of Moses bless you, Hannah. Say hello to Ephraim and the family for me. Especially David. He has a talent for this sort of thing. He will make a great archeologist someday."

Hannah nodded as they said goodbye at the door, then rushed back toward the bus stop. She had said nothing to Eleazar, but she had been in the basement of the Hurva Synagogue at one time looking for Abraham Marshak. Workmen had been repairing one of the walls. She had noticed then that there seemed to be an opening behind that ancient stone work. Possibly finding the tunnels of the Old City would be easier than Eleazar thought.

The number 2 bus was nearly empty, its broken windows an apparent warning sign to those who might ride. She and half a dozen others hunkered down in their seats as the bus started toward Jaffa Gate. As they turned to enter, she saw a British armored car and several jeeps full of soldiers sitting along the street. Fifty or more were in position to keep an eye on the milling crowd as a deterrent to stone throwers. She recognized Jack Willis among them, giving orders with a stern look of determination. Thank goodness there were still a few British willing to keep the peace! As they passed by, she waved and yelled his name out the broken window next to her, but he didn't hear, the angry crowd drawing his attention as they pushed toward the street.

As the bus came to nearly a standstill, she saw several groups of Jews with pushcarts, hurrying between the British guards and toward the gate and the New City beyond, their faces full of fear as taunts from the pressing crowd were hurled their way. She saw one Jewish boy of about twelve stick his tongue out at the mob, then stiffen his neck and defiantly march closer to the soldiers. Several arms tried to grab at him as they cursed his parentage, but the soldiers pushed him back into the center of the street where his frightened mother grabbed hold of him and gave him a well-deserved tongue lashing. The first stone came from the back of the crowd and others quickly followed. Hannah arose in her seat to see several Jews hit, then bolt for the gate. Jack shouted an order and the troops turned on the crowd and fired their weapons into the air. Most of the Arabs ran for the side streets, but a few remained to fling a last stone at the soldiers or the escaping Jews.

She sat down and put her head on her arm. The chaos was getting worse by the day.

When they arrived at the bus stop inside the Old City, British soldiers immediately boarded the bus and began a search.

"What is this?" Raffi, the bus driver, complained.

"We have orders. If we are going to keep you Jews and Arabs from killing each other, we have to keep guns out of your hands."

"Then search the Arabs too," Raffi complained. He was still complaining when Hannah got off the bus and headed toward Hurva Synagogue. As she approached the entrance, she pulled the scarf from her shoulders over her head, then entered the building. Several men were praying in the main hall while half a dozen others stared at the dome above them in hot discussion. One of them was Binyamin, another Abraham Marshak. The others were rabbis. She avoided the men's section but remained close enough to hear their conversation. They were discussing fortifying the synagogue, using it as a place of defense. The rabbis weren't happy with the prospect and argued against it. She couldn't blame them. The Hurva was one of the oldest synagogues in the city, built upon the ruins of one established in the 1200s by Nachmanides. After his death, it went into disrepair, then started crumbling and was not used until a Russian rabbi brought a sect here and bought the land on which the Synagogue of Nachmanides had stood. They were poor and could not afford to restore it, and as it fell further and further into dilapidation it became known as "the Ruin" or Hurva. Blood, sweat, tradition, and history filled the air, stones, and very foundations of this building. She could understand the reluctance of the rabbis to give it over to the Haganah, especially since they had so little faith in the Zionist army.

The discussion finally broke up and Abraham, his face red with frustration, joined her.

"The dome of this place is higher than any other. Snipers who try to take the rooftops close to this section would be easy targets from up there." He looked toward the dome.

"They will relent, Abraham, in time. When they see that there are no other choices," Hannah said.

"It does not matter if they relent. We will use it, with or without their permission." He said heatedly. He then took a deep breath. "What can I do for you, Hannah?"

"I need to get into the basement," she said.

"The basement? But what for?"

"Get the key from the Rabbi, and I'll show you."

He walked back to the group of rabbis and talked with them. One reached in his pocket and gave Abraham a large key while glancing over his shoulder at Hannah with concerned curiosity. Abraham returned and walked through the outer hall to the basement. He opened the door, found two candles, and lit them with a book of matches from his pocket before they descended the steps to the basement. Hannah held her candle up and tried to get her bearings.

"Where was it they did the repair work about six months ago?"

"Around this way." He led her to the left, then through a low door into a second room where he approached fresh brickwork that had not been plastered yet.

"Unless I have lost all sense of direction, we are facing west. Is that right?"

"Yes, that is right. Why do you ask?" he said a bit impatiently.

"Because on the other side of this wall there is a tunnel, probably a part of the Cardo that the Romans built. If we can get to it, clear it, we might be able to connect important parts of the Quarter to one another and get around without exposing ourselves to snipers. It could also be used to move men and weapons about, even create a way to resupply the city. Can you get permission to take a portion of these bricks down?"

He didn't know what to say and only nodded.

"Good. When you have it, we'll start looking."

"I . . . I had forgotten about them," Abraham said, exasperated with his own lack of vision. "Avraham Halperin told me about them when he was here last, but I had forgotten. The Cardo runs under the Arab portion of the Old City. We could surprise them," Abraham said.

"Or they could surprise us," Hannah answered. "Get permission to break through that wall, Abraham. Let's see what we can find."

As Hannah disappeared up the steps, Abraham pushed his candle closer to the wall as if it might suddenly reveal what lay just beyond its thickness. Then he turned and quickly followed her. After setting a time to meet that night, she left the building, and he turned back to find the rabbis. There was a lot to do.

SEE CHAPTER NOTES

CHAPTER 12

Aaron's squad of outsiders had taken commando courses at Gush Etzion and were well versed in night fighting, but they did not understand the Old City's layout, and he worried that they might get lost if he split them up. Instead they went to the Street of the Jews, climbed to the rooftops, and quickly made their way across them until they sneaked between two new Arab emplacements. Once in the Arab Quarter, they lowered themselves back into the city streets and went about putting fliers on the walls of the buildings in several of the main shopping areas. The fliers warned the Arabs that if they continued to shoot into the Quarter, they would be forced from their homes by an all out Jewish attack. If their Arab men could not protect them from a single squad who came in the night, how could they protect them from an entire battalion? All of them knew the scare tactics wouldn't stop the sniping, and they would have to come back, but all agreed that warnings were a needed first step.

When the fliers were posted, they broke into several shops without homes over them and quietly made a mess of things while stealing what food they could carry back with them, another sign that they could come and go as they pleased. While his men did the damage, Aaron went down a street, turned right, and found Mary's house. It was dark. She was either in bed or gone, but it did not matter. He had no intention of repeating his visit of a few nights ago. He only wished to leave her a message. He had been unable to go to the hospital to see Dr. Messerman and wanted to apologize in case she had. He hoped to set up another meeting.

Quietly climbing the stairs, he slid the note under her door, then went back and joined his men who were just finishing posting fliers and raising a little havoc. Suddenly they heard men approaching and quickly went inside one of the shops to let them pass.

"We should cut their throats," one of his men said.

"We are not to kill them, just send a message," Aaron said firmly.

The voices passed, and he and his men set about to leave when someone spoke. "Hey, there is a trap door here, behind the counter."

Aaron removed his flashlight, placed it under his shirt to filter and dim the light, and then inspected the door. Lifting it, he peered into a dark hole that had a familiar smell to it. "Gun grease!" he said.

"What? Are you sure?"

"He's right. I've smelled it a hundred times. They cover the weapons in it when they ship them."

Aaron removed his pistol and started down the steep ladder. When he was below floor level he uncovered the flashlight and scanned the room. It was filled with odds and ends stacked around the walls in cardboard boxes, but the crates in the middle of the floor caught his attention. There was a rifle sitting atop the closest, and it was still covered with gun grease. He examined it as one of the men came down the ladder.

"British," the man said. "Some soldier wanting to make a few pounds probably sold them to the Arabs." He saw some smaller containers near the table and hoisted one to its top. "Ammunition!" he said as he pried the lid off.

Aaron was still examining the rifle, then stood and took a handful of bullets.

"These we have to take back," the man said. "We can't just leave them here." He picked up the second box and opened it. "Grenades!" Two others had joined them and one quickly removed the lid of the gun crate.

"A dozen rifles, six in each box."

"And enough bullets to kill a thousand of us," said the first stiffly.

"Get everyone else down here," Aaron said. He grabbed some boxes off the shelf and emptied their contents on the floor. This was a shoe and clothing store. They could use the cloth to wrap the guns. As the others came down the steps, he told the last to close the door, then threw them each a cloth, ordering them to grab a rifle and start wrapping it.

"Now, fill your pockets with bullets. Then we must go."

"What about the grenades?"

"Each take a couple. Leave the rest. We need to destroy this little armory just in case we missed something. And they need to know we can do this anytime."

Two minutes later, they were climbing the ladder back to the main floor of the shop. "I'll give you five minutes to get back to the Quarter, then I blow this place and follow? Got it?" They nodded and he assigned Alex to lead. An instant later they were gone.

He sat back against the wall, the grenade in his hand. He had two more grenades in his pockets and a rifle. He used the four remaining minutes wiping it down enough that he could use it if needed. He was catching his breath as the second hand on his watch ticked off the last few seconds. He stood, pulled the pin, took a deep breath and wiped the sweat from his eyes.

"Now or never," he said. He threw the grenade into the cellar and ran for the door. He nearly stopped breathing when the knob slipped through his greasy fingers, but he didn't hesitate. Slamming his body against the door, it broke into pieces and he was stumbling into the street. He had taken half a dozen steps when the explosion ripped upward and blew out the windows of the store. The rest of the grenades blew up a second later and the front of the building disintegrated behind him, lighting up the street and making him a target. He dove for another doorway, waited, then ran again when no bullets ricocheted around him. He was up the steps and swung over the edge of the building to the roof when the street below filled with men yelling at one another in confusion. As he dragged his feet over the edge of the roof a bullet struck the heel of his shoe and blew it off. The pain in his foot from the concussion left him wincing, but he got to his feet and ran for the Quarter, trying to keep low and not make an obvious target.

Angry voices yelled in Arabic from a dozen different directions and bullets careened off everything around him as he zigzagged across the roof and leaped for the next building. He hit hard, rolled, and slithered behind a water tank as they honed in on him. Catching his breath, he waited until there was a lull, got up, and started running again. He remembered that the second street he had to fling himself across was wider but still doable—unless they shot his legs from under him. On the other side he would be in the Quarter. The bullet struck the rifle butt just as he was about to jump and tossed him off course. He knew when he jumped that he would never make it. He threw the rifle ahead of him and grabbed the edge of the roof as he plummeted toward the ground. He tried to pull himself up but didn't have enough leverage. Swinging his body left, he tried to grab the corner with his foot but missed. Arabic shouting was getting closer. He reached down, pulled a grenade from his pocket, pulled the pin and tossed it back the way he had come. The explosion lit up the night sky as strong arms grabbed him and pulled him up. Several of his own were positioned along the roof, returning fire as he and his comrades darted for cover.

Once behind a solid wall that stuck up beyond a flat roof, he caught his breath while bullets struck around them. "Thanks," he gasped.

"You're welcome," said one of his men. "Let us go, shall we?"

"Good idea." He gave the word to retreat in Hebrew, and they began working their way in the darkness to the far side of the roof and down a ladder. At the bottom they collapsed on the pavement to catch their breath.

"I don't think that is a message they can misread," one of the men said.

"Especially the owner of the shop," said another. "Aref, that was the name on the door. The Aref Brothers Shoes and Clothing."

Aaron felt sick inside. Mary's brothers? Probably. What a way to treat the future in-laws. No matter. The Aref brothers were the enemy, and the weapons belonged to them. They above all men needed to be sent this message. Besides, Mary probably wasn't going to give him the time of day anyway.

"They had it coming. We're supposed to hit them back hard when they attack us, and they have been. It was a good operation," Alex said.

"They might counterattack. Let's get back up there," Aaron said. The others looked at one another, then nodded or shrugged agreement. Though tired and ready to tell their heroic story to others, they would do what he said. Sergeant Schwartz had proven his worth.

* * *

Izaat stared at the blackened corpse of the shop. They had been lucky. The fire hadn't spread to other buildings, hadn't turned into the disaster it might have been.

He was angry. Angry with the Jews for selecting his shop as a target. Angry with Rhoui for disobeying him about hiding weapons in the basement; angry at God for bringing them to this. But the Jews had escaped, and God was unreachable, so he had taken out his anger on his brother. It had only worsened their strained relationship.

He looked down the street to where Rhoui, Mary, and others warmed themselves over a contained barrel fire. Their faces were blackened with soot from their efforts to save the shop, and their shoulders slumped with the reality that they had failed. He took a deep breath and joined them.

"We should counterattack," said Rhoui through a clenched jaw. He did not look at Izaat, their shouting match still too fresh.

"It will be foolish. They will be waiting for us," Izaat responded, knowing it would not be enough for Rhoui. He was right. His brother bit his tongue, gave both Izaat and Mary a stifling glare, turned on his heel, and walked away.

"Rhoui, wait . . ." Mary said.

"It is better that he go. Neither of us is in the mood to talk tonight."

Mary turned back to the fire. Rhoui had ignored her the entire time, refusing even to acknowledge her existence when they were standing right next to one another while putting out the fire. His hatred was so strong, it had made her bristle with its electricity.

Their latest encounter hadn't helped. She had been at the shop when Rhoui brought the weapons into the cellar. She had tried to prevent him, tried to talk sense into him, but he hadn't listened, and had pointed his weapon at her to shut her up. The look in his eyes had sent her running for the door, and she hadn't been back since. Now everything was gone. Nothing remained but ashes and soot.

"They nearly caught the one who did this. If they come again, we will be ready and they will pay for their effort." The one who spoke was new to the city, sent by Abdul Khader along with nearly fifty others, ostensibly to mount an attack on the Jews and to protect the

Quarter. All Mary had seen over the last two days was men stealing from Arab shopkeepers as if they were owed a living. Fruit, vegetables, clothing, even furniture had been taken, and yet all they did was sit about and incite hate with their lies. None were on the roofs, and none were working. They told others to do those things while they sat about. That's what Mary saw.

"And you will be there to make them pay?" Mary asked with disdain. "You and your friends will finally quit lying about why you are here, quit stealing from us and go to the roofs to defend our honor and our virtue? Well, at least one good thing has come of this disaster."

The mercenary's face flushed with anger and he sputtered, then glanced at Izaat and quickly smiled. "You are but a woman and do not understand war. We are not sent to do your fighting for you, only to advise you."

"Ah, to advise us. Then you should receive an advisor's wage. That should cut your stealing by half at least."

The man's hand went to his pistol handle. "Tell your sister to keep her place or I will—"

"You will do nothing," Izaat said. His gun was already in his hand, the barrel pointed toward the ground. "She is right. If you and your friends wish to stay, you will go to the roofs like the rest of us and you will take orders from us. When you do these things, you will get food—not before—and the next time we see you stealing from one of our people we will shoot you."

The mercenary's eyes hardened. "We are under the orders of Haj Amin Husseini. If you refuse us what we need—"

"We refuse until you earn your keep. If that is not acceptable to him, he must be the tyrant the Jews claim him to be. If you wish to stay in *this* part of the Old City, you will do as I say. If our terms are not acceptable, you can go into the Muslim Quarter, and I will not see your face again."

There was really no dividing line between the Christian and Muslim quarters, but Izaat was beginning to think now was a good time to create one. With the influx of Haj Amin's mercenaries, things had quickly turned sour, their desire to take over obvious and blatant. It was worse in the Christian Quarter, and many of his people had complained to him about it.

The man backed away from the fire, hesitated as if to challenge Izaat, then turned and strutted down the street in a huff.

"Do you know who that was?" asked one of his friends.

"I am too tired to care. Tell the men still willing to fight with us that we meet in the central chapel of the Church of the Holy Sepulcher tomorrow."

"But—"

"No buts, Sami. You and the rest of the men in this section of the city asked that I lead. If that is still your wish, you will do as I say."

Sami nodded as he swallowed hard. "That was Tal Abu Falal. He served under Abdul Khader Husseini in the events of 1936–39. If he tells Khader of this—"

"Then Khader will know we mean business here and will not be bullied by his men." He turned to another man. "Theodosius, you are a builder. For a fair price you can rebuild this shop. It shouldn't cost more than 2000 British pounds. Agreed?"

"Agreed, but this is foolish. The Jews will come again. Possibly we should wait until the end of the war. Possibly you should spend your money on weapons, or on sending your wife and children away until this is finished. That is what I intend to do, and very soon."

"And if I leave and you leave, and we take our families, how many more will follow?" He shook his head. "No, we must stay. Our people look to us. We must not act as if the loss of a single shop can chase us away." He paused. He was tired, frustrated, angry. But Mary's words from a few nights before were finally making sense. "My friends," he said softly. "We are fighting for our homes, and if we leave them, we will lose them either to the Jews or to men like Falal—Arabs who have only one thing in mind, taking Jerusalem for themselves."

"But I thought . . . they . . . we need them, Izaat."

"Do we? Mary is right. They do not fight. They steal from us and lay about, eating our food as if it is owed to them. Three houses have been deserted by our people today because of the shooting last night. Who inhabits those houses today? Falal—a member of the Husseini clan—and his friends. Do you think they will give them back when they already talk as if they now own them? They are here for advantage, nothing more."

"But how . . . how do we keep them out?" Sami asked. "They come and we cannot prevent them. They could just as easily turn on us as—"

"The Jews? You are finally seeing what I am trying to explain, Sami. We must protect ourselves from them as much as from the Jews. That is why I must rebuild this shop and why we must keep our people here. We will show our neighbors that we can protect them from all their enemies, whether Jew or not. As to how we keep them out it is simple. We barricade the entrances to our streets and allow no one through unless they are willing to fight with us and take food only when it is given."

"But will they not fight us?"

"Do you think Haj Amin wants the world to know he leads a divided camp? He will leave us be or he will negotiate. Then we will tell him what his men do. If he is honorable, he will stop it. If not, we should fight him anyway." He put a hand on the shoulder of Theodosius. "Two thousand British pounds. Will you begin tomorrow?"

Theodosius nodded. "I will. We will spread the word about the meeting in the morning, but everyone will not agree . . . and . . ."

"Let me worry about that."

"The Jews attacked us, Izaat. We should respond," Sami said.

Izaat handed him one of the fliers posted by Aaron's men. "They attacked us because we shoot at their people and make it obvious we intend to take their homes. If we retaliate, they will come again. We must decide if that is what we want. If it is, I will lead you against them, but we had better think about it carefully. I'll see you tomorrow." He put an arm around Mary and started down the street. The others stayed behind, discussing what he had said. They were worried. He was not.

"You surprise me, Izaat. I thought you supported Khader's men coming here."

"I did until I saw what they were like. I have been looking for a way to get our men to stop them before it spirals out of our control. This provided that opportunity."

"But Sami is right. It might be dangerous for you. Falal impresses me as a man who will look for a way to strike back at you."

"We will see."

Mary knew that was the end of it, but in the pit of her stomach she was not so sure. There were other, more dangerous ways for a man like Falal to get his revenge. "Be careful, Izaat. This is a man who would shoot you in the back if he had a chance."

Izaat nodded. "I wish only to know if my sister has forgiven me. What I did was a horrible thing, and since it happened I have been forced to look at myself and what I was becoming. Can you forgive me?"

She had also done a lot of thinking. Though her fear of Rhoui and Raoul remained, it had quickly dissipated for Izaat. She had already forgiven him and had even gone to his house to tell him so, but he had not been there. Off to Ramallah to try and get weapons, Hanan had told her. After that she had decided to leave it be and let it work itself out. She was glad that time had finally come. "It is forgotten, Izaat. That was not you, and I know it."

"Thank you," his shoulders seemed to come out of a slump.

"I may go to Katamon for a few days and stay with our aunt. She needs help with the hotel," Mary said.

"You need not do this. I was wrong and too easily offended. Your words hurt because they were true, at least some of them. We were wrong to attack innocent people as we did. I see that now, and we are at least partially wrong for trusting ourselves to Haj Amin's men, but you are wrong about the Jews. They will take everything if they can. What they did tonight makes that obvious to me, and it should to you."

"But you said it yourself, they are only attacking because of what our men do," she said as calmly as she could. She did not want to fight with him again.

"We are at war now, Mary. There is nothing to do but protect ourselves and try to stay alive. If the Jews come, I will fight them. I must."

Mary could see that Izaat had changed. His initial anger at partition had been cooled by what he had seen at the Commercial Center, but now he was trapped, and both of them knew it. All of them were. Things had already escalated beyond their control, and men like Falal and even Rhoui would not allow peace. "Our streets are the farthest away from the Jews. Can you not stay away from the rooftops—the sniping—and just defend our homes if the Jews come?"

He put an arm around her. "We will see. I will do my best not to attack or shoot at innocent people, but beyond that I can make no promises. War, fighting, may not give me that freedom. There is only so much a man can do."

She put her arm around his waist. "I am proud of you for trying, Izaat. Thank you." They were at the stairs that led to her home when she turned and spoke a hope she had in her heart. "Possibly the British will intervene and peace will come before . . . before things get out of control."

He forced a smile. "It is something to pray for." Izaat knew it would never happen. Neither side wanted the British to stay, and if they did, it would be a war much worse than what lay ahead of them. He kissed her on the forehead and started to walk away

"I love you, Izaat. Be careful," she pleaded.

"And I love you."

She watched him disappear in the night before turning up the stairs to find her bed, exhaustion settling in on her like a heavy, wet blanket.

She found the note when she opened the door and turned on the light. She must have missed it in her hurry to get to the shop. Closing the door, she broke the wax seal and opened the letter. It was carefully printed in English.

Dear Mary,

I apologize for dropping in on you the way I did the other night. I know it was bad timing and bad form. Forgive me.

I do not know if you went to the hospital to see Dr. Messerman. I could not because of duty here in the Quarter, but I wish to see you again. The Church of the Apostle of Christ in the Armenian Quarter is on neutral ground. Sunday? After morning mass. I hope you will come.

Aaron

She had been to see Dr. Messerman who was healing quickly and would leave the hospital by the end of next week, and she had been disappointed that Aaron had not come, but also relieved. He was Jewish, she Arab. It would not work.

She felt flattered that he was still trying, that he cared that much. But only for a moment. She realized he must have been with those who had blown up their shop.

She carefully tore the letter into small pieces and threw it in the garbage.

Izaat was right. They were at war and he was a Jew who must fight them. She would never see him again. Never.

* * *

Abraham used the sledgehammer one more time and broke the last of the brick into a dozen pieces. The rabbis leaned forward to stare into the hole as the dust cleared. They had kept this little venture to themselves at Abraham's request. There was no sense letting the whole world know what they were doing unless it proved worthwhile. This was especially true of Rabbi Salomon, who surely would have thrown rocks at the idea from the outset.

Hannah stepped forward with her lantern and held it near the hole as she and Naomi peered in. They could see nothing but a black void beyond the wall. Hannah excitedly told Abraham to widen it. With renewed energy he broke away another section of the wall.

Hannah handed him the lantern. "Please," she said.

His eyes showed their gratitude, and he quickly stuck the lantern through the hole, then peered in.

The space was filled with debris, but there was enough space between it and what appeared to be the ceiling that he could make out what looked like a perfectly carved column bracing a stone crossbeam. He wriggled into the space and pushed himself through the debris until he reached its crest and peered into a wider hole.

"*Oy vay!*" he cried. "You are right! It is the Cardo!"

Hannah and Naomi were on his heels and quickly lying on the rubble pile to each side of him, staring into the debris-filled hall that lay before them. Their eyes scanned the room, picking out half a dozen columns that lined what must have been the Roman street. They were in extremely good condition and bearing a good deal of weight from above.

"This must be the part the Crusaders roofed," Abraham said.

"Abraham, what is it? What have you found?"

Abraham turned back to see one of the rabbis looking at them from the hole. He told him and the rabbi scurried in to join them. A moment later, all three of the rabbis lay on their stomachs, their dark suits brown with dust, staring at the discovery.

"How far does it go?" one asked.

"It used to run all the way to Damascus Gate, but some of it has probably been replaced by buildings. It is hard to say until we explore it."

"I'm ready," Naomi said. She pushed herself over the crest of the debris and went carefully down the far side, Hannah and Abraham right behind her. Hannah immediately saw pottery shards that she was sure dated a thousand years or more and picked one up. "Crusader period, I am sure of it," she estimated. Abraham took it from her while helping the rabbis come down to where they were.

"Early Crusade," Abraham said. He picked up another. "This one is Byzantine, A.D. 500 to 600. Look at it! The paint is still intact."

Naomi was already walking north where the space widened, leaving the archeologists to their finds. She went a hundred feet over rocks and other debris until she came to the end of the room. Climbing to the top, she used her flashlight to see if she could find any space; nothing but solid rock, at least this high. They would have to clean out the debris to know for sure.

"Look!" Abraham shouted.

The others quickly joined him to find a room with steps leading down below the debris.

"A shop," Abraham said. "In Roman times the Cardo would have been lined with them. My guess is that on the other side of that wall back there we will find the basement to someone's home." He shined the light on a wall at the back of the room he had found.

They searched the main Cardo for another twenty minutes before Naomi and Hannah felt cool air blowing from the debris beneath them near the northwest corner of the wall. They started moving rocks and were soon looking into another empty space. Abraham joined them as Naomi wriggled through the hole and into a long narrow room. After Abraham followed, they walked to the end, only to discover that it turned left. They were in a tunnel.

Naomi yelled for Hannah and she quickly squirmed through the narrow space and joined them, and the three walked a hundred feet before coming to an end, then searched the walls as they came back.

"Look," Hannah said. "This is a seam. Two walls join here."

"Two different buildings, more recent stone. Basements of the Quarter." He went to the other side of the tunnel and scraped away dust, looking carefully at the chisel marks he found. "This side is older." He flashed his light around the room. "See that dark substance? Soot—from a fire. That part of this room probably dates back to the second rebellion when the Romans destroyed the place and burned everything."

The flashlight dimmed. "Come. Time to go." They went to the entrance to find only two of the rabbis still with them. The third had gone back, the dust and close air getting to him. They hurried back and scrambled up the debris, then slipped out through the hole in the wall of the synagogue. The rabbis helped them throw the remnants of brick into the hole, sweep the floor, and move a cabinet in front of their creation all while listening intently to Abraham's excited discussion of what they had found. Finally they brushed themselves off as best they could before climbing the steps to the main floor. Abraham swore the three to absolute secrecy for now, telling them that they needed time to decide what to do and to explore more of the ruins. They agreed, then disappeared into the night, excitedly chattering in Yiddish.

"Will they keep it a secret?" Naomi asked.

"For twenty-four hours. That should be enough. We'll need tools and a work schedule. The trouble will be clearing the debris without ruining the artifacts. I will have to supervise everything. Everything! And I must let Eleazar know. He will want to come—to see it—and to help."

He chattered so fast and was so excited he reminded Naomi of a little child about to play his favorite game. This was the work that really made him happy, gave him vigor. It was wonderful to see.

"It is a great thing," he finally said, taking a deep breath. "And yet it has taken war for us to look under our feet for an important piece of the past. Our forefathers fought for this city just as we do now. They barricaded themselves in against the Romans and fought to the death. The burnt house we saw down there belonged to real people, people who died for Jerusalem. Now we're defending it—at least part of it—again."

The night was black, clouds covering the stars. It felt safe. As they neared their street, more people were standing about discussing an explosion that had occurred in the Arab section of the city. Hannah got a lump in her throat and her mouth went dry as she remembered Aaron was part of a group sent into that section. She said a quick goodbye to Abraham and Naomi and hurried up the street to her apartment ahead of them. Possibly he was at home.

Naomi listened patiently as Abraham outlined everything he must do to make the tunnels safe without destroying the artifacts. When he finally hesitated long enough to catch his breath, she touched his arm gently.

"You would make a good rabbi, Abraham, but you have a passion for discovery that is wonderfully refreshing."

Abraham reactively pulled his arm away, feeling at once shocked at her closeness and gratified by her remark. He was orthodox and women did not touch men who were not their husbands. As she turned away a bit embarrassed, he wished he had not offended her.

"I . . . I am sorry. You surprised me, and—"

"Don't apologize, Abraham," she said recovering from the feeling of rejection she knew was not intended. "I forgot your beliefs for a moment, that is all. I am the one who should apologize."

He felt hot all over, unsure what to say. They had discussed many things over the last week as they worked through assignments by the Haganah, but they had never been quite so close—though he found himself wishing to be most of the time. He had never dealt with women one-on-one before, except his sister. Being around Naomi flustered him. He had to get his composure, say something.

"Will you . . . ah . . . assist me . . . in the tunnels, I mean?" he blurted out.

She smiled. "I would be honored, at least until I get another assignment." She paused. "I sent a letter requesting a position with SHAI."

His shoulders slumped a little as he unsuccessfully tried to hide his disappointment. "You would be very good with SHAI. You are a very perceptive woman." He hesitated. "Naomi, was your family . . . before Germany . . . were they good Jews?"

"They were not like you or most others in the Quarter. You are very strict, my father was not. We went to synagogue, and we celebrated Shabbat, and the holy days were important, but my father would never have kept me from dating young men—Jew or not—and he would not have made a marriage for me." She stopped a moment. It had been a long time since she had thought of those days, refusing to go back as if doing so would only bring more pain. Now it was a pleasant memory.

"We had a mezuzah on the door frame of every room and kosher food was eaten most of the time, but if we were at a friend's house who was not a Jew, my father said it was more in keeping with God's law not to offend them than to worry about a plateful of pork. Does that make me less in your sight?"

"My father has often accused me of being too liberal to be a good rabbi. He may be right."

"Yes, I have noticed you are not so concerned about some things as others are in the Quarter, and I am glad. I don't think I could be around you if you were always correcting my eating habits, or how I dress." She smiled at him.

"I think I am pleased at this, but I am not sure. For an orthodox Jew to be complimented for being unorthodox is a little confusing."

"I don't know how you do it, Abraham. Can God really be pleased with such strictness and concern for so many laws?"

"Halakah—the law of the rabbis—keeps us focused on God, Naomi. By doing what God asks in the small things, I honor him. Each action of prayer, each bite of kosher food reminds me of him, of his greatness. Can this be bad?"

"Bad? Probably not, I just couldn't live that way, that's all. And if there is a God, I have a hard time seeing him expecting me to. I would be so busy trying to remember what I should and shouldn't do that I would be miserable all of the time."

He laughed lightly. "Yes, it probably does seem like a burden to others, but for us who have learned to worship God through the detail of our lives it is not that way. We find joy in piety." He paused. "Your statement gives the impression you are not sure if there is a God."

She didn't answer immediately. When she left Germany with Hannah, she had not believed, could not believe. She hated God then. "The camps drove me away from our God, Abraham, not closer to Him, but Hannah—well, she makes me doubt my doubt."

"Yes, Hannah can have that effect. At times she reminds me of a protestant evangelist with her passion and forcefulness. At others I swear I can feel God in the room when she speaks of what she knows." He paused. "When she first moved here, she was not well received. She was married to a gentile, had left Judaism for Christianity, and refused to sit quietly, like most women who live here, when affairs of importance are being discussed. Rabbi Salomon was furious with her when she and Ephraim started holding meetings in their home. He still is, although there is little he can do other than shun them."

"I've seen his haughty treatment of her and the kids. From what I hear, he would run Ephraim out of here if the law would let him."

"She is a blood Jew. He is married to her. His citizenship is guaranteed and so is that of the children born to her. Their faith might be different, and he might prevent them from attending synagogue but there is little else he can do." He sighed. "Someday Rabbi Salomon will see in Hannah Daniels what many of us see. She is good, and you can't help but love her for it."

Naomi was surprised at his frank and tender words. It must have shown because he laughed lightly. "I don't know anyone who helps more people in this Quarter than Hannah—sometimes whether they like it or not. And I don't know anyone who makes you feel as good about yourself as she does, even when she is chastising you."

Naomi laughed. "Yes, I know." Naomi found herself drawn to Abraham. He wasn't at all like the Orthodox Jews she had known in Hungary who had seemed so cold toward everyone and so contrary in their strict interpretation of Torah law and adherence to Rabbinical regulations.

"You are Lubovitcher Hasidim, are you not?" she asked.

"Yes, why do you ask?"

"You and your father are quite different from Rabbi Salomon and the Satmar Hasidim."

He smiled. "Yes, quite different. We are the two political extremes in Hasidic Judaism. Of course, between us are a couple of hundred other groups as well. It makes for interesting debates in a community like this where you have all kinds."

"The three men who went with us tonight, they are Lubovitcher Hasids as well?"

"Two of them. The other, Isaac Shlomo, is a follower of Rabbi Nachman of Breslov, Ukraine. His group is small, but he has a say in the Hurva synagogue. Breslov Hasids don't have an official rabbi, so they are free to go to any Jewish guide or teacher they choose. Reb Isaac and those who came with him from Ukraine follow my father."

"Rabbi Salomon would have little patience for our being together like this, talking, would he not?"

"Yes, and for me it is joyful—a good thing—and it makes me happy. This can only bring me closer to God, so it must be good."

She laughed. "I am guessing that is a compliment."

"Yes, of course." He paused, getting his composure again. "You understand that my nervousness at your touch was not because I find you repugnant. It is quite the opposite, but Hasidic Jews consider a touch between a man and woman so sacred that it should never take place except in private, between the two of them, after marriage. It is a principle of great importance to us."

"Please don't be offended, Abraham. I understand your belief, and yet your Hasidic teachings also place greater value on men than on women. You do not regard the intellect of girls to be equal with boys so you do not give them the chance for education. You consider it sufficient if a girl learns about the Torah, the religious holidays, and the dietary laws. You want them to have babies and take care of them until they leave home. You don't even give them an equal place in the synagogue. Your protection of them morally is to be commended, but your determination of their worth leaves me cold. I could not live in a home where I was not treated as an equal, where my husband felt I was not worthy of learning just as much as he is, or where my role is to serve him and keep a clean house and hardly anything more."

There was a brief silence. "I suppose this is the reason a Hasidic man should marry a Hasidic woman. If you are raised with these beliefs, it is not so difficult," Abraham said softly. With Naomi so close, he felt pained at that truth, but there it was. He could not ignore it as much as he had tried the last few days.

"A well-matched couple can make an enduring marriage, is that it?" she said evenly.

"Yes, I suppose it is."

She stopped. "Then a Jew could never be happy with a gentile."

He turned and faced her. "You mean Ephraim and Hannah."

"Yes. I have never seen two people so happy together. They adjust to each other's needs, they talk things through, they work together, and though they each brought many differences to their marriage, it works."

"But are they so different than we Hasids? The core beliefs they cling to are the same. If my father told me I was to marry a Satmar Hasid we could make it work, even though she may be from Hungary and I from Eretz Israel and her feelings about many things may be quite different from my own. We also would have to make adjustments, just as Ephraim and Hannah have, but because our core beliefs are the same we would do it. Do you think it would be so easy for them if she had remained a Jew and he a Mormon?"

She hesitated but then firmly stated, "Yes, I think they could. They love one another. That would be enough."

"We're here."

She looked around and saw that he was right. They were standing outside his door.

"Good night," he said as she started away, her stomach churning. "Naomi." She turned back. "I wish love were enough, but it isn't." He disappeared behind the closed door.

Naomi didn't know what to think or feel, but she knew he was probably right. To make a marriage really work, both partners would need the same root beliefs, whether they were atheist or God-fearing Mormons. Why at this moment did that disappoint her so much?

She climbed the stairs to Hannah's place, but before entering, she breathed deeply of the night air and remembered something that had happened several years earlier when they were trying to leave Europe. They were at the house in the Austrian Alps and Emil Silberman, the father of the twins who had come from Berlin with them, had upset Naomi by talking of the camps as being God's will. He was a good man and meant no harm, but she had become so angry with God for his apparent disregard for her people that it had sounded worse than it really was. Hannah had followed her to the porch and then tried to explain what she had come to understand about God. Naomi had listened but hadn't really heard, her anger creating too much of a barrier to accept Hannah's words. Except for a few. "God will give every single person every opportunity to become as He is. Sometimes it isn't what we want, and sometimes it hurts more than we think we can bear, but hard things prepare us to be like Him in a life still ahead of us. Give Him a chance, Naomi. Give Him a chance to make gold out of sand."

She had never thought of life in that way, nor of the possibility there might be a reason for suffering and death, not until then. It had been a seed she wanted to nurture but couldn't at the time, and she had tried to cast it off as just another excuse for a God who didn't exist or didn't care, but it had stayed with her, making her doubt her doubt. Though it hadn't turned her back to Judaism, it had softened her heart and given her some degree of peace. At least she didn't hate God anymore; she just wasn't sure she could ever really, fully believe in or trust Him again—not yet at least. That left her in a sort of limbo that was at once frustrating and annoying. It seemed like she was a tree with no roots, or better, a world with no sun. Her life was acceptable, but she wished for more light to warm her all the time.

Strange that she think of this now, but there it was. She put her hand over her mouth to cover the yawn. When she and Abraham had gone to investigate the tunnels, they had told Binyamin they could not go to the roofs. He had let them off only when Abraham told him what they were up to. She was grateful now that she would get more rest. She had been in Eretz Israel for a little more than a week but probably hadn't slept more than a dozen hours.

"*Shalom,*" came a voice from the dark at the bottom of the steps. "You're up late." It was Ephraim.

"You too. How was your day?"

"Long, and yours?" Ephraim said.

"The same." She told him about the tunnels, the morning attacks, Binyamin's assignment for Aaron. "He still isn't back."

"Is that why you're waiting up?"

It wasn't, at least not consciously, but she was a bit worried.

"He's fine," Ephraim said. "Come on. You better hit the sack."

"Is that another one of your American euphemisms," she gave a wry smile.

"Yeah, but you get the picture."

"Yes, and it is a pleasant one. But I want to ask you a question first."

He sat down on the steps. "Shoot. Oops, I mean, fire away." He grinned wide enough she could see his teeth in the dark.

"Is love enough for a good marriage?"

The question caught Ephraim off guard. "Well, it certainly helps," he said lamely.

She laughed. "It was a dumb question."

"A dumber answer. Let me try again." He took a deep breath. "When I first met Hannah, all I wanted to do was help her because she was hurting, inside and out. I fell in love with her later, when I saw how strong, how determined she was to make something out of a nothing life handed to her by the Germans. I was in awe of her. That's not to say I wasn't physically attracted—I was—but not in a purely physical way. She had just come out of the camps, skinny as a rail with sallow skin and hair that needed work." He chuckled. "She thought she was borderline ugly, but she wasn't, not to me. There was something about her eyes, her smile, her touch that gave me goose bumps, and when you throw that into the mix along with awe, you come up with a pretty big bang."

"She said you almost didn't ask her to marry you."

"She's right, because love wasn't enough." He hesitated, trying to get the words right. "We came from two different worlds. Worse, I was a Mormon, she wasn't. Marrying in the faith is just as important to my religion as it is to orthodox Jews."

"So I have heard, but you went ahead."

"Yeah, I did, but not just because I loved her. If that had been it, I would have gone home to the States, hard as it might have been." Another pause. "Hannah had already committed to baptism, but the paperwork was slow in coming. I wanted her in the water before we marched to the altar, but it just wasn't working out that way. Finally I wired Church authorities in Salt Lake and told them my dilemma. They said to go ahead with the wedding—the papers were on the way. Five months and two lost letters after we were married, the papers granting permission for the baptism finally got there and she and David and Beth were baptized. Actually it worked out pretty well. Beth and David weren't ready for baptism earlier. They just didn't know enough to make a decision. They were ready in May and all of 'em went into the water at the same time. It was one of the greatest days of my life."

"Why is marrying in the faith so important?" she asked, the edge of frustration in her voice.

"You've seen what I'm like, Noami. I want the kids to study the scriptures, come to Christ, and eventually participate in what we call the saving ordinances of the Church. Can you see me holding sacrament meeting here in our home while Hannah is off shopping somewhere? Or conversely, if she had remained Jewish, can you see me standing idle while she and the kids run off to synagogue, or looking on while David went through a Bar mitzvah? We have a nice mix of Judaic and LDS traditions in our home, but we agree on them. We have them because we both want them, because they fit what we want to teach. We celebrate Hanukkah and Christmas, but the real tricky stuff, the stuff that makes a difference is the doctrine and belief in Christ. It would be impossible to mix modern Judaic belief about Jesus with my belief. For the most part they're incompatible, and our kids would grow up doubting both. It's the teachings, the doctrines that make the difference on family unity and success in the home." He smiled. "Whew. That's what we call dumping your bucket. Just another American euphemism. Did any of it help?"

"Yes, thank you," she said softly.

"Naomi, may I make an observation? Love is a powerful force and just as necessary to a long and successful marriage as having the same religion. I see some in Abraham's faith marry without even knowing each other, and I get nervous about it because I know that if something other than the same religion doesn't develop, they might live in the same house all their lives but it will never be successful. You have to have both, and it takes effort to have real love in a relationship. If Hannah and I didn't love each other as deeply as we do, our religion might force us to stay together, but we would both be miserable. That's no way to live."

She nodded. "Thanks, Pops," she said.

"Watch your tongue, young lady, or I'll wash it with soap." He smiled. "Come on, let's get some sleep." He stepped up and opened the door, then let her go inside the darkened apartment. As they tiptoed to their separate rooms, she found herself understanding why Hannah loved him so much. Ephraim Daniels was a rare find.

Undressing, she pulled on the nightgown Hannah had made and sent to her last Christmas, then climbed into bed next to Beth, trying hard not to wake her.

She and Abraham might learn to love one another, but she could never be Hasidic. At least she didn't think she could. No, she couldn't. It was time to stop the fantasies and get on with her life. She should hear on her request to be assigned to SHAI soon, and she would go to Tel Aviv. Besides, though she would never admit it to others, she still had feelings for Aaron, feelings too strong to ignore. Maybe in time . . .

Her eyes felt heavy. She was tired. She needed sleep. Thankfully it came quickly.

CHAPTER 13

Shalom Dror, newly appointed leader of the Michmash battalion was given responsibility for the entire city of Jerusalem as Yisrael Amir tried to shore up his command and prepare Jerusalem for guerilla warfare. It was Dror who responded to Holtzberg's request for more men by sending those who went with Aaron into the Christian Arab Quarter.

Disguised as a doctor, Dror entered the Old City the day after Aaron's excursion to assess what had happened and why, then what else might be needed. It made Aaron a bit nervous. The Haganah had been clear—defensive operations only. He was a bit concerned about how Dror would interpret what he had done in blowing up the Aref brothers' shop.

Dror was meeting with Aaron and his men when Rabbi Salomon came into the waiting area of Misgav Ladah Hospital unannounced.

"These irresponsible acts of yours are provoking the Arabs into action. We are on good terms with our Arab neighbors and have lived amicably with them for generations. If your Haganah does not bother them, they will not bother us. I demand that you remove your men."

With that Rabbi Salomon turned on his heel and left Dror with a smile on his face.

"Sergeant Schwartz, I think the Rabbi would define your action as provocative and very offensive. What do you think?"

The others tried to hold back the chuckles but some weren't very successful. Aaron didn't know how to respond, so he lowered his head and pushed dust around with a toe.

Dror removed the smile from his face and the others cleared their throats and did the same. "Your action was impulsive but correct. The sniping and attempts by the Arabs to push into the Quarter, their raids and thievery, will be answered decisively. Past experience has proven that Haj Amin's men must be given wounds to lick before they learn their lesson. Further, we noted this morning that several hundred more Arabs left that section of the Old City. They don't seem to have confidence in the ability of Khader's men to protect them. That affects morale among the Arabs while giving our own people confidence in us—something the poor showing at the Commercial Center dealt a blow to."

Aaron breathed a little easier and looked up from the floor.

"However," Dror went on, "the Arabs will retaliate and escalate the fighting. I will send you a few more men and what weapons I can, but you boys had better prepare for the trouble your attack has caused or it won't be Arabs fleeing the Old City but Jews. Understood?"

"Yes, sir," Aaron said. The others echoed his response.

Dror left the city after another few hours of meetings and planning. The men he promised came the next day in two buses to Zion Gate where a British officer was bribed to let them pass. The next day Yis'rael Funt, who was replacing Holtzberg as commander of the Quarter because Holtzberg was needed elsewhere, set up his headquarters in Misgav Ladah Hospital as Holtzberg had done. He immediately sent his men to reinforce the eleven positions set up during the last few days along the roofs that bordered Arab sections of the old and new cities. That evening, as Hannah lit the third Hanukkah candle and prayed for the safety of her family, Funt's men celebrated with parties at their posts. When Aaron, who was on the front lines with his new platoon, saw that young women were joining Funt's men, he registered a complaint with the new commander that got nowhere. Moments later, as he was about to remove his men to a different post before they mutinied, shots were fired from the Arab Quarter with cries of "The Jews are burning Al Aksa!" The candles lit by Funt's men and the dancing and celebration had been misinterpreted.

Aaron's men dove for cover, but Yitzhak Solomon, the young soldier who had discovered the trap door two nights before, was killed.

The shooting died down long enough that Aaron could remove the body and send it back to Ladah Hospital, but at sunrise the firing began in earnest and they hunkered down. Funt's lack of discipline was going to make it a long day, and Aaron found himself regretting Holtzberg's reassignment.

* * *

Tal Abu Falal had found Rhoui at home just hours before the battle had begun. "It is time that you took your brother's place," Falal told him. "He is weak! If he is allowed to mislead your fighters, you will lose the Christian Arab Quarter of the city for good. At first light I will attack the Jewish Old City with my men. Bring those who are willing and fight with us. With our victory, your strength will be greater than your brother's and the men of the Christian Quarter will follow you."

Rhoui, still angry at his brother, let Falal's appeal to his ego work its way under his skin and into his soul. He agreed—Izaat was out of control and must be stopped.

Now they were near the gate that separated the Jewish Quarter from the Arab section of the Old City. They had been fighting for nearly seven hours but unable to break into the Quarter. Morale was running low. Already the Brits were moving into the Old City on both sides of the gate to force a truce, and Falal knew they must break through now or pull back. The thought of failure was more than he could stand, and he was frustrated and angry.

"Your men are weak cowards," he yelled at Rhoui.

Rhoui bit his lip. He was disillusioned with Falal's ability as a soldier, but he knew of his ability with the pistol he carried in his hand. To say the wrong thing now would be to invite sure death.

"I will give you one more chance. Then I will report to General Khader of your cowardice and have you shot. Is that understood?"

Rhoui glanced at the others who would go home if they thought they could reach the door without Falal or one of his men shooting them. They knew what he knew. This man was a fool, an idiot. He had given them orders that had no chance of overrunning the Jews, his own cowardice obvious as he took the easy tasks for himself.

"Yes. What do you want us to do?" Rhoui asked, hiding his disgust.

"I will take my men to the roof. We will cover for you. You and your men will use these explosives," he pointed to a box on the floor, "to blow the lock on the gate then attack the shops just the other side of it where the Jews are weakening. Then we will join you and push on into the Quarter. Once we have established our authority over some buildings, we will barricade the street further. The British will not dare remove us after that."

Rhoui only nodded. It was a good plan, and he knew it. He had suggested it first thing this morning. Instead, Falal had tried half a dozen other maneuvers on the rooftops where the Jews were concentrated and waiting. If he had listened, they would already have half of the Jewish Quarter in their possession.

Falal and his men left the building and went to find a way to the roof.

"We should never have listened to you, Rhoui," Sami said. "I was wrong to think Falal was a soldier. He is a fool."

"Be quiet, Sami, or I will shoot you myself. The Jews are our enemies. We must fight them. Falal finally sees that my plan is best, and now we will make it work. This is our chance to defeat the Jews, and we will not run. To do so will only verify Falal's feelings about us."

"He is right, Sami," Raoul said. "This is what we must do, and if Izaat were not such a coward he would be here to help us. Now we will show the Jews what we can do to them, and it will be Rhoui who leads us. After that we should get rid of Izaat!"

"You can show them without me," Sami said, starting for the door. Raoul started to raise his rifle, but Sami expected it and had his own raised and ready. "You might shoot me, Raoul, but you will die as well. Lower your gun."

Raoul lowered his weapon and Sami backed out of the room and was quickly gone.

"He is a coward!" Raoul spit on the floor.

"Never mind. Get ready," Rhoui said harshly. "I will deal with Sami later." He checked the chamber of his weapon and made sure the clip was completely filled with bullets. He told the others to do the same. It was the one rifle left from those that the Jews had stolen from his shop. Luckily he had taken it home.

It had been a day of near misses. Twice, a bullet had passed through his loose shirt and once he had stumbled in the street to have bullets strike on all sides without hitting him. How long could his luck hold?

The firing on the rooftops started. Rhoui pointed at Raoul and told him to take the small package of explosives. They went into the street and worked their way toward the gate. No bullets struck near them, an indication that either Falal had the Jews pinned down with his fire, or the Jews were waiting for a clear shot when they got to the gate. When they were near enough, he told Raoul to take the explosives to the gate. Raoul hesitated.

"Do not call Sami a coward and then refuse an order," Rhoui said coldly.

Raoul gave him a cold stare, then shoved the explosives at Rhoui. "If you wish to lead us, Rhoui, if you want to replace Izaat, you will go."

Rhoui felt sweat drop from his brow, but he grabbed the package angrily. "I will not forget this failure to obey an order, Raoul." He did not hesitate, but ran toward the gate, zigzagging as he went. Bullets struck the pavement, forcing him to take cover against a wall, catch his breath, then force himself to go again. He reached the gate and quickly placed the explosives on the lock, tying them there with a piece of wire as bullets hit the gate above and to his side. Shaking, he pulled a match and tried to light the fuse but the match broke. He felt a bullet zip past his ear and went to the ground, covering his head. The fear of imminent death gripped him and he could not move.

"Light it!" Raoul yelled. "Do it, Rhoui, before they kill you!"

He had a sudden hate for his friend. It was *because* they might kill him that he could not move.

A bullet hit his leg and he cried out as Raoul and the others returned fire. With all his effort, Rhoui reached for another match, struck it, and lifted his hand toward the fuse. He was shaking so badly that the fuse would not catch, and he pulled himself up, trying to calm himself as the match went out. He pulled another from his pocket, took a deep breath, and lit the fuse, then got to his feet and hobbled toward his friends as they covered for him. He reached the shops and was helped inside the first one where they hunkered down for the explosion.

Nothing.

Carefully he peeked out the window at the gate. The dynamite was gone! How could this be? A second later he saw someone moving on the other side of the gate, saw the explosives flying through the air toward them and screamed a warning just as he saw Falal on the edge of the roof firing his rifle. The explosion blew the window in just as Rhoui ducked down, the glass flying over his head and against the far wall, where several shards lodged themselves in the plaster.

As the dust cleared, he touched something running down his lip and found that the concussion of the explosion had made his nose bleed. Others in the room moaned back to consciousness as Rhoui slid up the wall into a fully sitting position, shaking his head against the ringing in his ears.

Raoul got to his feet and checked himself for damage before he looked into the street to find Falal lying face down on the cobblestone pavement. His men were in disarray, some wounded by the explosives, others disoriented by them. He heard the sirens of jeeps and looked down the street to see the British emptying several vehicles and rushing toward them. The men who could struggled to their feet and disappeared. The ones who were too hurt to get away would be searched, their guns confiscated, then given aid and sent home. Raoul turned and headed for the back of the store, found a door and was gone, leaving Rhoui bleeding on the floor. He struggled to get up and follow and was nearly there when a British soldier burst through the door, his weapon in hand.

"Get your filthy 'ands in the air, mate," he yelled. Rhoui raised his hands and rested them on his head, balancing on one leg as the pain in the other was too much. The first battle for the Jewish Quarter was over. They let Rhoui go the next morning.

CHAPTER 14

Rabbi Salomon was furious. Feeling the Haganah was responsible for the violence in the Old City, he asked for more British policemen to patrol the Quarter and wrote a letter to Dror once again asking that they be removed completely before they got everyone killed. When Abraham told him it had been the Arabs who had attacked, and had the Haganah not been there they would have pushed into the Quarter and butchered half its number, he only scoffed. Young Marshak was a fool and knew nothing about Arabs, especially these Arabs.

It was even with some reluctance that Rabbi Salomon allowed them to continue clearing the tunnels and making new ones, but he was forced to accept the reality of the danger, regardless of fault, when snipers shot and killed or wounded several civilians.

The British found themselves in the middle of a war and sent a new commander along with additional troops and orders to bring an end to the fighting. Lieutenant Colonel McCloud laid plans to control the Haganah by removing its most influential members and confiscating their weapons. Three days after the battle at Jaffe Gate, the new commander moved a platoon of the Highland Light Infantry into positions between Arab and Jewish front lines. He then raided each Jewish post, confiscated their weapons, and detained nine fighters, six of whom were released within a day. The other three were questioned at CID headquarters and let go later. Aaron was not on duty at the time, nor was Funt, and when Funt learned what the British were doing, he ordered Aaron and other leaders to take a low profile until things cooled down. No Arabs were arrested and none of them lost their weapons. It was obvious that McCloud was either very stupid or very pro-Arab, but the outcome was the same. It put the Haganah at a distinct disadvantage.

Each time the Arabs attacked, the Jews would retrieve their weapons from hiding and fight back. In the very process of defending themselves, the British would move in, confiscate their weapons, and throw a few fighters out of the Old City. Slowly the Haganah was being disarmed and disabled.

But they found a lieutenant under McCloud's command who, for a few gifts he could give to his Jewish girlfriend, was willing to try and make things bearable for both himself and the Jews. Responsible for disbursement of troops to hot spots, he made a pact with the Haganah. When the Arabs attacked, the Jews would shoot back to keep them at bay while someone sent a predetermined coded message to the lieutenant who would immediately bring troops to their aid, driving back the Arabs. Of course, he did not take Arab weapons or arrest Arab fighters, but at least things were even now. Unbeknownst to McCloud, who stayed outside the Old City at night, his troops became a much needed addition to the Haganah.

This wasn't the only help the Old City's Haganah received from the British. Mid-December, a British major, captain, and lieutenant suddenly appeared at Misgav Ladah and asked for Aaron, then requested a tour of the Jewish positions. A bit apprehensive at this sudden development, but knowing that their guns were well hidden, Aaron took them to the roofs where his men were positioned to keep an eye on the Arabs several rooftops away.

"You have good positions there and there," one of them pointed, "but you are weak here. A platoon could come between those boys there, and the ones you have over there." He then proceeded to advise Aaron on how he could solve the problem before they moved on. By the time the "tour" was over, Aaron had been grateful for the scraps of paper he had in his pocket. The British filled them with expert suggestions that would help them hold their positions and thwart any attacks.

"Do you attend that synagogue over there?" the major asked, pointing to the southern dome of Nisan Bek Synagogue.

"No, most of us don't see much of the inside of a synagogue."

"You should," said the officer with a smile. "It would make a very good fortification." He then proceeded to tell Aaron that he and his companions had visited Nisan Bek that morning. They gave Aaron a list of suggestions for its fortification. As they started to leave and Aaron was trying to put his chin back in its proper location, the major turned to him and said, "Regards from Jack Willis. He sent us along to see how you chaps were doing and asked that we advise. Follow those suggestions, and you'll get along fine. Oh, and tell that lad over there that the hiding place for his gun is not a very good one. From the backside of the sandbags, the barrel can be seen. He'll lose it to McCloud if he isn't careful. Good luck to you." Then they were gone.

As time passed, the Brits seemed divided pretty much down the middle to Aaron. Like Jack and his friends and the lieutenant, some were quite helpful while others did their best to impede them and favor the Arabs. The trick was to use the former and avoid the latter. For that purpose, the discovery of the Cardo by Abraham and Hannah had become invaluable.

Abraham had quickly organized the digging schedule, and the volunteers methodically cleared a part of the Cardo. From there they broke through walls and used the basements of homes to honeycomb the Quarter while continuing to search for other tunnels and clear out more and more of the Cardo. These were used to avoid the British and the growing number of Arab snipers and gave the people hope and safety. Even Rabbi Salomon had grunted approval, though he continued to refuse to give full cooperation. Over the next two weeks, the numbers leaving the Jewish Quarter of the Old City went from a flood to a trickle. The Cardo enabled the Haganah to move from place to place without the British, who intended to arrest them and confiscate their weapons, having the slightest idea where they were. It gave them the ability to fortify different locations under attack without being seen as well, and with as few men as they had, such ability was critical to survival. The Quarter was quickly becoming a passable fortified city.

* * *

Though the Arabs were not having their weapons confiscated, they were having problems, and Izaat was caught in the middle of them. Izaat held his meeting with the people in his part of the Arab sections of the Old City and immediately discovered that most were planning on moving out. After nearly an hour, he convinced most to hang on and then organized the men for the defense of their homes from both Arabs and Jews. He assigned some to go to the roofs of the part of the Christian Quarter he controlled but ordered them to fire only if they were fired on, to attack only if they were attacked.

"We have too few men to risk losing anyone in a foolish attack that will get us nothing in the end," he told them.

"And if Khader's men order us to join them?"

"Send them to me. If I deem it necessary to the defense of our part of the Old City, we will organize and I will lead you myself." They nodded agreement.

Izaat then assigned others to arm themselves and prepare to guard the shops against theft by Khader's mercenaries. "If they do not pay, arrest them at gunpoint and bring them to me. My father's office will be our new headquarters."

"And if they resist?" said another.

"Shoot them." He could see some apprehension at the answer. "We all believe Abdul Khader to be an honorable man. If this is true, he would want us to take action against thieves."

"And if they complain to Abou Dayieh, Khader's commander over the Old City?"

"I will go to Abou Dayieh and explain our rules. If he does not like it, he will arrest only me and you can then comply or leave the city as you wish." With that promise, they seemed once more agreeable—all except his wife Hanan, who cringed with each of his promises.

That night they threw up partial barricades and built sandbagged emplacements that would help them defend their homes while giving their people greater peace that incursions by the Jews into the Arab sections would not reach them. They went to bed that night and all slept better except Izaat. He had put his people and himself at risk and even now harbored doubts about his right to do so. He decided that Hanan and the children should be prepared to leave the Old City immediately if he were ever arrested. Awakening her, they spent the next hour going over plans for her departure, where the money and papers were, and how to get to the bus station or the Lord Governor's office if she felt in danger. She had cried herself to sleep in his arms.

Abu Falal had moved several of his men into houses in his area, and though Falal was dead from his foolish attack on the Jews, most of his men remained. When they came out the next morning and started helping themselves to food, Izaat's men worked up the courage to surround and disarm them before marching them off to the office of Izaat's father where Izaat paced to calm his anxiety. He heard them arguing, then saw them through the window. Placing himself behind his father's desk, he tried to look busy, looking up only when they entered.

"What is this?" one of Falal's men hissed at him. "You dare to arrest us?"

He ignored the man's statement and asked his own men what the problem was. His carpenter, Theodosius answered.

"We caught them stealing again. They refuse to pay."

"Is this true?" he asked the man who had hissed at him.

"We defend you. We deserve to be fed."

"And what of the money Abou Dayieh gives you for such things?"

The man looked annoyed. "It is not enough."

"And he told you to steal from our people to make up the difference, is that it?"

"It . . . it is understood. We must eat, and when the money runs out we take what is needed. Consider it our pay."

"We are to pay you and starve our own children? And if we stop paying you with our food?"

"We will leave you to the dog Jews," he hissed.

"Then leave us. We have decided we do not need your protection. You are no longer welcome in this part of the Old City." He turned to Theodosius. "Take these men to our barricades and see that they are sent away." He stood and leaned across the desk, looking directly into the mercenary's eyes. "Do not come back to this part of the Old City unless you plan to pay for your food. If you are caught stealing from us again, we will exact the penalty under your Muslim law. Do you understand?"

The man rubbed his wrist. He knew the penalty.

Izaat sat down and looked at the other man. "Are you here for the same reason?"

His neck stiffened haughtily. "Abou Dayieh will not be pleased."

"If Abou Dayieh wishes to discuss this with me, he is welcome to come here and do so. I would like the opportunity to give him the bill for the food you and others have stolen from us. If he is an honorable man, he will pay. Of course, he may wish to ask you for the money it cost him. I hope you are prepared to pay it." He leaned forward, "And if you cannot pay, I think he will exact payment by seeing you in prison or worse."

"When the Jews come, we will not come to help you. Be certain of it." the man said.

"If we let you stay and eat us out of house and home, we will starve to death long before the Jews come. Further, if Falal's ability to protect us is any indication of your own, we will be better off to take our own lives." He leaned back. "Theodosius, take these two and see them to the barricade."

Theodosius stuck his rifle in the ribs of the mercenary closest to him and prodded him toward the door. It closed behind them and Izaat got up and went to the window, his heart pounding. He watched them disappear, then crossed himself, thankful it was over.

But his relief wouldn't last long. With their first success, his men were emboldened to arrest others, and he spent his day making judgments and sending mercenaries over the barricades. It was nearly four o'clock in the afternoon when Theodosius returned to his office alone, a frown on his face.

"We have made many enemies this day, my friend," he said, sitting down.

"And our people, how do they feel?" Izaat asked.

Theodosius couldn't help the smile. "They are happier, that is true, and less afraid. They believe in us now. Before, my wife accused me of doing too little. Now she smiles at me and is happy to see me."

"Then our enemies are our friends," Izaat said.

"You know that Abou Dayieh will discover what we have done. He is not an honorable man as you suggest. He has taken food himself."

"If he comes, he will come to talk, nothing more."

"But how can this be? We reject his authority and throw his men out of part of the Old City. Surely this does not set well with him."

"That is unimportant." He paused, forming his words carefully. "Haj Amin wishes to be accepted as our leader by the world community. He is seen there as a Nazi, a butcher who wishes to take out his blood lust on the Jews. If word reached them of a war on his own people, here in the Old City, what would that do to his plans?"

Theodosius had very heavy brows and a bushy moustache that made him look a little like a walrus. As he thought the brows arched up toward his hairline. "It would only make his chances worse. But you assume that Abou Dayieh and Abdul Khader will talk to Haj Amin without striking us. You may be wrong."

"Not on this. It is too important."

There was a pause. "You know he butchered my uncle in 1939," Theodosius said.

"And mine," Izaat said. "And he will butcher us if he comes to power, you know that."

"Then we had best not help him do it," Theodosius replied. "Will Christians ever be equal in this country?"

"Muslim rule has not been kind to us, but the Jews have been known to kill a few Christians as well." He shrugged. "We shall see how it works out. But we will protect our homes or die trying. Agreed?"

"Agreed," Theodosius stood.

"Theo."

"Yes."

"I have thought through this decision carefully and tried to position us where we will earn the most gratitude when the real war begins. That will be with Abdallah who hates Haj Amin. He will reward our efforts when the Old City comes under his power, as it surely will."

"Then you no longer support Haj Amin."

"Let us just say that I am changing horses in the middle of the race. It is risky, but it can be done."

"And you are at greatest risk, my friend. If they kill you, the rest of our people will flee like dust before a wind."

Izaat leaned forward. "I ask only one thing of you, Theodosius. I have made arrangements for my wife and children to leave if it gets too dangerous. But if I am caught without warning, I ask only that you get my family to Father Fernaldo at the Church of the Holy Sepulcher."

"Consider it done. And Mary?"

"She will leave the Old City in the morning."

"You heard of Rhoui's injury?"

"Yes. He was a fool to join with Falal. They attack the strongest part of the Jewish fortifications and expect to break through with only a dozen men. Rhoui is lucky he did not join Falal. Where is he now?"

"At his home. He mends well, the bullet passing through his leg without hitting anything vital. He walks with a limp, but he walks. His wife is very nervous and wishes to leave but he will not let her. She blames you for all their troubles."

"With his agreement, I am sure. And Raoul, is he still in our part of the Old City?"

"I saw him around noon. When he saw what we were doing, he called us fools and said we would reap the wrath of Abdul Khader. He ridicules and will be nothing but trouble."

"Watch him closely. If he keeps opposing us, I will throw him out myself."

"You will be available tonight," Theodosius said.

"Here or at my house."

Theodosius got out of his chair and went to the door. "Your enemies multiply. Be careful as a mouse in a yard full of cats." He closed the door behind him.

Izaat needed no warning. For now, he felt good about what he was doing and wondered why he had ever supported the Husseinis. He supposed it was because, as he told Mary, there didn't seem to be any other choices, but this was the lie Haj Amin wished all of them to believe.

He looked at the picture of his mother and father on the corner of the desk. It had been taken long ago and showed his father at his prime. How he missed him! Would he be pleased with this action? It seemed like the thing his father would have done. He had deeply regretted not talking to him before his death and felt deep down that his support of Haj Amin had given his father a broken heart. No matter what happened, he knew that now his father would be pleased.

Izaat got out of his chair and went to the window. The street was busy, people talked and laughed, a very big difference from yesterday. How he wished their barricades could keep out the world and its war permanently.

But they could not. It would come to their streets, just as it would come to all Palestine, but for now he was pleased they could enjoy a good day.

He saw Rhoui hobbling toward the office and took a few steps to the desk, sitting down on the edge facing the door. As Rhoui entered, he stopped, then slowly closed the door behind him. His face was strained as if he were trying to control his anger.

"You are a traitor," he said stiffly.

"You look pretty healthy for taking a bullet."

"A flesh wound. The Jews are bad shots. When Haj Amin takes Jerusalem, he will drive everyone who opposes him out of the city, and you will be shot."

"Haj Amin will never get near Jerusalem."

"Not with men opposing him as you do. I have been to see Abou Dayieh. He is willing to forget this if you come now and apologize and then remove your barricades."

"If he wishes to talk to me, he is welcome to come here, just as you have."

"And our fight with the Jews?"

"Nothing has changed. Our men go to the roofs and on patrol as they always have. In fact they are more willing. They understand the need to protect their homes against all our enemies."

"And when the Jews come and Abou Dayieh refuses to protect you, what then? Will these people celebrate freedom when the Jews take everything? You are a fool, Izaat, blinded by your own ego. Without Haj Amin's mercenaries, we will lose everything. This I will not allow." He turned and left, slamming the door behind him. Izaat knew he had just made another enemy.

CHAPTER 15

In the week before Christmas, the Old City began to settle into the routine of a semisiege condition. Many of those who were afraid had left, though others still considered doing so, and would if things worsened. The British, thrust into the middle by their mandate responsibilities, kept the peace while some harassed the Haganah and others aided them. Food supplies continued to enter the Old City under British protection, though amounts began to dwindle as fewer and fewer convoys made it through from Tel Aviv with all their goods. Hannah and her family settled into life with some restrictions. Because all school teachers came into the Quarter from the New City each day and could no longer do so without extreme risk, David and Beth studied at home, watching the babies while Hannah worked in the growing tunnel system or waited to buy food from the limited supplies brought in by the British.

With the danger created by increasingly vicious attacks on anyone driving into the Jewish Quarter except British-protected convoys, Hannah and the family were cut off from regular contact with the outside, including Ephraim who stayed in Tel Aviv many nights and made his deliveries to the outlying settlements in his Piper Cub. Only when Jack Willis could get him aboard a protected convoy from Tel Aviv to Jerusalem, then into the Old City, did Ephraim make the trip.

On one of those visits he brought Naomi a letter from Haganah headquarters reassigning her to SHAI. She left with him the next morning and made the trip to Tel Aviv without more than a minor pummeling by Arabs along the highway in which half a dozen vehicles were lost and five wounded. She and all others in the Old City had heard of the increased attacks along the highway, but it was something one had to see to understand how serious the Arabs were about their attack on Jerusalem. On her arrival in Tel Aviv, she was briefed about other "hot spots" in Palestine and found that the news about attacks on the large settlements and even suburbs in Tel Aviv and Haifa were not exaggerated. In fact, they were understated. Things were heating up, and the Arab nations were planning on making it worse with the organization and training of the Arab Liberation Army. One of Naomi's assignments was to keep track of it through informants already in place and by reports from the military in the north. She immersed herself in her new work. Abraham came to mind from time to time, but so did Aaron. She worked harder to escape them both.

Secretly, and without permission, David began delivering messages for Funt's command. He avoided any that would take him in contact with Aaron, but his little deception didn't last long. Aaron saw him scooting over the roofs in midday, avoiding sniper fire, and immediately went after him. Grabbing him by the back of his shirt he pulled him to cover.

"Mum will be furious with you," Aaron said.

"Mum d-doesn't need to know," David responded.

"You can't keep something like this a secret. It is better that she hear it from you than from someone else."

David thought a moment then nodded. "I w-want you there. I w-want you to t-tell her I'm the fastest and b-best messenger you have."

"I don't know that you are," Aaron said.

"T-take my w-word for it," David replied. "Or ask Funt. He'll t-tell you." With that he was gone.

The two of them cornered Hannah that night in the kitchen and David, his palms sweating, revealed his secret. She kept her hands in the sink water and bit her lip against the words that jumped straight from her heart. It was a full minute before she could speak and the silence seemed forever.

"He's the best," Aaron said in an effort to dispel the fear he knew she was having.

"Is that good enough to keep him from getting killed?" she said.

Another silence.

"They need messengers, Mum. They d-don't have radios, or p-pigeons—the Arabs shoot them. That leaves g-guys like me and Isaac and B-benny."

"When school starts again, you're finished with this," was all she could muster. Stupid. As if school somehow made a difference! She turned from the sink and faced them. "That was a stupid thing to say." She took a deep breath while wondering how many mothers in the world had to deal with a decision like this. "You can do this if you promise me two things. You use the tunnels as often as you can, and you take no unnecessary chances, no matter the message or how important. Second, you will never, ever deliver a message during a battle of any kind." She put her hands on his arms and squeezed tight. "Do you understand? No unnecessary chances!"

He grimaced at her grip while nodding. "I'll b-be c-careful, Mum. I p-promise."

She turned back to the sink, and David left the room while Aaron found a more comfortable seat at the table. The tears ran down her cheeks and splashed in the dishwater. Had she just sent her son to sure death?

"He is only a child," she said softly as she wiped the tears away with a dry wrist.

"He's nearly twelve. In Judaism that makes him a man," Aaron replied. "When we were running from the Nazis, he was the one who always knew where to hide, and he was quick, even cunning. I saw him steal food off the tables of soldiers and escape when half a dozen men tried to get hold of him." He paused. "He'll be all right, Hannah."

She turned back to her dishes with a nod. "And you! You are even worse. The chances you take!"

"Me?" Aaron said a bit shocked.

"You and your little escapade into the Arab Quarter. You did not need to take the chance, Aaron. Was sending a message so important?"

"Yes, it was. This is a war, and soldiers fight, make decisions, and take chances. That's the way it is," he replied.

"But not you. Not David," she said. The tears were too much and her shoulders jumped with the sobs in her chest. Aaron quickly went to her and took her in his arms.

"It's okay, Hannah. I'll be careful and make sure he is careful. Funt doesn't send the young ones close to the front lines. It will be a long shot that the Arabs will ever see him." It was mostly the truth.

The babies' cries forced her to gulp back the tears, then she smiled up at him. "Promise me."

He nodded and she broke away to see to the now screaming twins.

With that the conversation had ended.

Aaron picked up a paper the next morning and read it carefully to his platoon. From what they could gather, the Arabs had cut off some of the settlements, though none had been taken. The Arab effort didn't seem to be a concentrated one, but made up of the attacks of different tribal groups with Haj Amin's mercenaries at their core. Abdul Khader and Hassan Salameh were in charge overall, while Abou Dayieh, Kemal Irekat, and several others commanded assigned areas. They did seem to be coordinating, and that was not a small thing. The tribes were as different as apples and oranges—they had minds of their own, things they would not do, even other tribes or villages with whom they would not fight. Those differences kept them at odds, uncoordinated, and less effective.

"Thank goodness for Arab tribalism," one of his men said. "It is our greatest weapon."

They laughed, but they knew it was true. If the Arabs ever started fighting as one unit they could be in trouble.

"It doesn't say how many casualties, but from what I read, it must be in the hundreds," another of his men said. "And they are picking up some pretty good loot, too. That makes more of them come, and that makes it more difficult for our men."

They were sobered by what was happening outside Jerusalem. They had been feeling sorry for themselves, feeling like they were taking the brunt of Arab wrath and nobody cared, but over the last few days they had discovered they were wrong. Others were getting hit just as hard or worse.

"If they hit other places that hard, they'll come back to us and it will be worse," one of them said to Aaron. "The Old City is about as vulnerable as anything they could take, and with five hundred fighters, we wouldn't have a chance."

"The British won't let them," said another. "A massacre wouldn't look good in the world press." He said it cynically. Nobody in this room had much love for the British.

Though the majority of British soldiers seemed to be pro-Arab, as of late they had made it clear to both sides in the Old City that any wholesale warfare would be quickly put down with a show of British force. McCloud's patrols in the streets between the Jewish and Arab sections of the Old City were mostly for show—"no more bloody battles or we'll wipe you both out." When they left, it would be a different story. Khader would change his tactics and Aaron and everyone in this room knew the Old City would get his full attention.

Could their small force in the Old City hold their own against a large-scale effort by Khader to overrun them? Aaron might be over-confident, but he thought they could. But if the armies of the Arab states showed up on the hills of Jerusalem, they'd sink like a ship with a thousand holes. They couldn't withstand an artillery attack, nor could they hold back tanks and proper military armored cars, all of which the Arabs had.

"We should do more of what the sergeant did. Blow up a few more shops and go after their leaders, and they'll have second thoughts. If we defeat these guerillas, the Arab Armies will think twice about coming in here."

There were nods by the others in the room.

"They'll just come quicker," Aaron said. Everyone looked up at him, giving him full attention. "They have said too much, made too many promises. If Haj Amin's guerillas and their Arab Liberation Army can't stop partition, they'll have to send their tanks. Are we ready for that kind of war?"

Everyone in the room knew they weren't. No tanks, no artillery, no airplanes. There was a sudden soberness in the group and no one responded. No one needed to.

Aaron found himself wishing more and more lately that a peaceful solution could be found. He didn't want to bury any more men like these. The gung-ho, brash attitude that had been a part of him only a month ago had started to unravel with the reality of war and the fear of losing everything again. But if he were honest, the biggest reason was probably Mary. For the first time he had begun to realize that real people with real feelings existed on both sides of the argument, and he worried about her—and others like her—more all the time. Yes, he dreamed of peace, but it was just that, a dream. The reality was the constant pinging of snipers, driving back incursions, and preparing fortifications. The reality was to pull your dead out of a battle while bullets struck around you and feeling you were next. You didn't handle such realities with dreams. You handled them by fighting back. And so far he felt justified. The Arabs started this war, and they were picking on the wrong guy this time. No more "turn the other cheek." That always ended up getting Jews killed. This was about survival now, and he intended to survive and so did his people. The greatest mistake the Arabs were making right now was believing the Jews would run. This wasn't Europe before Germany. This was Palestine after Germany. They were dealing with the survivors, not the ones who went off to the slaughter like sheep.

They went over their deployment for the day and then he and his men went to relieve troops along the roofs facing the Arab Quarter and Silwan to the east.

Aaron thought a good deal about Mary. He had gone to the Church of St. James in the British uniform he had been given in Italy. It still served well as a disguise, and his control of the English language made it even more convincing, but she had not come.

He had wondered if she would. It wouldn't take a genius to know that he had been involved in the destruction of the shop belonging to her brothers. He had entertained the hope that she might understand, but obviously she hadn't, and he had tried to put her out of his mind ever since. It was most difficult when he was on duty like this and, except for the occasional potshot from one side or the other, nothing was happening. To get her out of his mind, he had even tried reading from the Book of Mormon Beth had given him. Sometimes it worked, sometimes it didn't. It depended on what he read.

He got it out and turned to Second Nephi. Beth had been right. The chapters from Isaiah had intrigued him, but Nephi's explanations were what he most enjoyed. Isaiah was not easy. Nephi at least helped make sense of Israel's ancient "crazy man." He couldn't believe he had said that to Hannah. He regretted it the minute it rolled off his tongue, his frustration getting the best of him. Was he a prophet? Things he said came true.

Isaiah aside, the book was hard for him. God still didn't make sense, and if God didn't make sense, how could Christ, especially the Christ of the Book of Mormon? It claimed he was the literal son of the Father, the Redeemer, the One who would bring everyone back to God. If God didn't exist, no redeemer was needed and no sacrifice required.

But he kept reading. No other book would fit into his shirt pocket.

He reread chapter twenty-five, put the book away, and stood. He must go check on things at Nisan Bek Synagogue before going to the New City for an appointment with Haganah leaders. He left Uri in charge and knew they'd be fine without him. Going down by ladder, Aaron entered a shop that gave him access to a tunnel. Winding his way through the underground streets he came out in the square where the bus from the New City was just unloading. He was a bit surprised to see Moshe Ginzberg getting off.

Moshe had been one of two starving men he, Naomi, and Hannah had nearly been killed with in Italy. Moshe had survived and become a trainee along with Aaron and Naomi in the Palmach, but helping immigrants was not enough for Moshe, and his constant conflict with the British finally got him thrown into one of their jails. He escaped and was put on a boat to Palestine by Palmach leaders. On arrival, his hatred for the British led him to join ETZEL.

Aaron watched Moshe clear his papers through a British soldier. Odd. From what Aaron heard, Moshe was wanted by the Brits. He had led a group that bombed a trainload of British soldiers coming out of Cairo and was with another that attacked a British convoy carrying weapons and ammunition to Jerusalem. That one had failed, a number of ETZEL's men killed. Moshe had been wounded, but obviously he had recovered. And obviously he had forged papers.

Moshe noticed him and quickly came over to shake hands. The smile was just as wide as ever and the handshake just as firm. He had put on weight since Aaron last saw him, but the receding hairline and rather wide nose in a round face were still the same. Moshe asked about Hannah and the others before Aaron asked his own questions.

"What is ETZEL doing in the Quarter, and why aren't the British shoving a rifle down your throat instead of letting you in?"

Moshe smiled. "Had enough chit chat, eh, Aaron?" He put a hand around Aaron's shoulder and moved away from the bus where British soldiers were still searching for weapons. "We've been here for weeks, though in small numbers. Six men. I've come to see about establishing a complete cell."

"We know about your boys here. They stole some guns from us right after the war broke out."

"I heard. Sorry about that and about the kidnapping it led to. Just a big misunderstanding. We want things to be better this time. Maybe you can help me with that."

"There can only be one army, Moshe. We both know it. ETZEL leadership doesn't want it that way, and until they do, it will be hard to deal with anyone they send in here, including you."

Moshe's smile turned to a frown. "Sorry to hear that. We were hoping for cooperation—a two-unit system with mutual respect for one another."

"Talk to Funt. He's in command. But your people are not popular around here, and you had just as well know it. You spend too much time hitting the British, and they blame us."

"The British will stay if we don't keep the pressure on them."

"Your intelligence work is bad, Moshe. The Brits are leaving, and we don't need them making our lives miserable before they do because you boys hit them and civilians."

Moshe nodded. "Thanks for the honesty."

"Why do you stay with them, Moshe? The Haganah could use a leader like you and—"

Moshe put up a hand. "Look, I expect that someday we will all be part of the same unified force, but I don't believe Ben-Gurion is the right man to lead this country. He kowtows to the British too much and everyone knows it. If he starts treating them like the devils they are, we might talk. Until then, we know what must be done." He pulled a paper from his pocket. "By the way, my name is Clyde Stockings," he said with a smile and perfect British accent. "'Ere to see my brother, a soldier assigned to this section of the old town. 'Ave a nice day, old boy." With that he walked away. Aaron watched him go. Forgeries and sloppy British police work. He wondered if he should turn him in, then decided against it. The ETZEL would find out and come hunting him. They always hunted down those they considered traitors. In that they were like the Arab tribes, butchers of their own kind. Right now he didn't need that kind of grief.

He turned and went on his way. Things were coming to a head with ETZEL and LEHI, and it would be before this war was over. You couldn't have three armies and survive, especially if some of them were more terrorists than army.

He checked his watch. It was nearly noon. He had an appointment at Haganah headquarters in the New City at three. That left him enough time to check on the fortification of Nisan Bek Synagogue before he caught the bus at two. He started in the direction of the synagogue as he thought about why he had been summoned to HQ when he was needed so badly here. New orders? Probably, and that made him nervous. He didn't like the idea of leaving the Quarter. He had a good command—they were productive, doing their part. The Old City was stable; they were holding their own against Old City Arabs and the few mercenaries who assisted them. It was no time for a change.

He entered the synagogue and looked up at the scaffold that hung from the dome of the synagogue. The man who looked down at him was on guard duty, and from his position, he could look through the windows of the dome and see across the roofs of the Old City. He could also pick off Arabs getting too close to this section of the Quarter. The rabbis had refused them the use of Nisan Bek as a fortification at first, but when the chief Rabbi of all of Jerusalem had encouraged them to prepare and aid the war, they had been forced to reconsider. Overruled by the chief rabbi, even Rabbi Salomon had reluctantly fallen in line and given permission, making it unanimous. It had proven a good location.

Aaron saw Abraham across the room. He turned to another soldier and gave him a command. The soldier disappeared down the stairs, returning a moment later with a still sleepy Martin Gunther by his side. Martin stretched, picked up a rifle and slung it over his shoulder, and then started up the rope ladder to spell the guard in the dome, the side locks of his hair dangling in thin air.

Martin was Lubovitcher Hasid like Abraham but had volunteered contrary to the wishes of his father. As an only son, the family would have no posterity to continue their line should they lose him. Aaron understood their concern, and even he had tried to convince Martin that he should pray for victory and let others do the fighting, but he had refused.

Martin had proven to be a good shot with his rifle and took orders well unless they interfered with his prayers, Shabbat, or the reading of Torah, all of which seemed to go on constantly. He had been given to Abraham because they both lived in the Quarter, were Lubovitcher Hasids, and none of Funt's other commanders had the patience for him. Even Abraham ran a little low on it himself sometimes, but so far he had endured.

Aaron slipped over next to Abraham and both watched Martin climb the rope to the platform. "How are things?" Aaron asked.

"Busy," Abraham responded. "Arab snipers infiltrated the Armenian Quarter last night and have taken a position in the tower of the Church of St. James this morning. They've been picking away at our people in this end of the Quarter all morning. We've registered a complaint with the Brits, but they haven't cleaned them out so far, and I don't suspect they will. Not soon anyway. Lassiter is running the patrols this morning."

He paused as the two men on the narrow scaffold exchanged positions. It seemed to bounce around much too freely. As the other man descended the rope, Abraham cupped his hands and hollered. "Martin, watch yourself. They've been shooting at us all morning from St. James."

As usual, Martin waved understanding. Martin didn't speak much, preferring a wave or a nod instead, one of the outcomes of living in a Hasid home where silence was routine.

"If you're not careful, Lassiter will march in here and disarm you instead of the Arabs in St. James," Aaron said. Lassiter had been assigned to the Quarter by McCloud only two days ago and was trying to make a name for himself by harassing as many Haganah men as he could find, arresting them for interrogation, then letting them go free outside the city walls. Itching for an arrest that would stick, he was making a nuisance of himself, and Aaron and Funt both registered complaints. But McCloud, who disliked them both, did nothing but urge Lassiter to greater works.

"I'd like you to take a look at something," Abraham said, starting toward the basement. Aaron took one last worried look at Martin then followed. They went downstairs and entered one of the tunnels, connected to another, then entered the Cardo. Walking north, they came to the spot where Naomi had determined there was nothing further, and Abraham got on his hands and knees and slithered through a narrow passageway they had cleared. There was more Cardo, and they were soon dusting themselves off as they stood up in the middle of the second section.

"We found a passageway that leads in the direction of the Church of the Holy Sepulcher. Ancient documents indicate that the Cardo probably went in front of it, then on to Damascus Gate."

"That would put us under the Arab sections of the Old City."

"There is little chance of digging it out in time, and I think Arab houses will stand in our way, but this . . ." They were at a wall with a crack near the floor. Abraham stooped down and put his hand over it. "Feel that?" he asked.

Aaron put his hand over the crack and felt the rush of air. "What do you think it is?"

"Possibly a fissure that could lead us into Zedekiah's cave, but we would have to dig through solid rock to get there. What do I do? Keep digging the Cardo, or dig here?"

"You ask me? You're the expert, Abby. You decide."

"Both will get us access to the Arab sectors, but this may give us a way out of the city in case we must evacuate. The Cardo will not."

"Then it's settled. Dig here."

"Thank you. I just needed reassurance." They started back the way they had come.

"The British know we have tunnels, or at least they suspect it," Abraham said.

"They won't do anything. They know they would have a war if they invade our homes, our basements."

"I hope you are right. If they close these, we will lose many more people, and our men will be in constant sniper view."

They walked a moment before Abraham spoke again. "Have you heard from Naomi?"

"No, but I'm sure she is busy."

Abraham stopped. "I am thinking of having my father approach Ephraim Daniels about her."

Aaron was confused.

"Ephraim is the closest person to a father Naomi has. Our tradition requires . . ."

"Whoa. You're thinking of asking Naomi to marry you?" he smiled more than he should have and Abraham's face clouded. Aaron cleared his throat. "Sorry."

"You do not think she will say yes?"

Aaron measured his words carefully this time. "Not now. She doesn't know you well."

"But this is not necessary. We will get to know one another after our marriage. It is our way."

"It isn't hers, and if you don't know that by now, you don't understand Naomi. If you want even half a chance of getting a yes, you had better take your time and do a few things a Hasid would never think of."

"I cannot do this," he said adamantly, starting to walk again.

"Then forget it. She will tell you no without blinking an eyelid."

Abraham stopped then walked back to Aaron. "What are these things?"

"You have to court her, Abby. Send flowers, notes, go for walks when you can. You might even hold hands."

Abraham turned and walked away again. "This I cannot do."

"Okay, okay, forget the hand holding, but she has to love you before you ask about marriage or you better forget the whole thing." He caught up with his friend and they crawled through the small tunnel and brushed themselves off on the other side before Aaron spoke again.

"What does your father think of this? Naomi isn't Hasidic."

"I haven't told him." He took a deep breath. "This is contrary to even my better judgment, but I have feelings I cannot seem to fight and . . ."

"You're in love with her."

"Yes, yes, and I know this is not enough." He started pacing back and forth in front of Aaron. "You will find this hard to believe, but we discussed some of this once, she and I. Somehow we talked of Ephraim and Hannah and I told her the reason their marriage worked so well was . . . was because they have the same religious beliefs. Now here I am thinking of marrying a woman who is not Hasidic. Oy, I have gone crazy!"

Aaron controlled the smile. He had never seen Abraham so out of character. He put an arm around his friend and they started walking. "Relax, Abby. Take a few deep breaths will you? If she falls in love with you, I mean really falls, she might become Hasidic. Who knows? But if you don't make that happen, you haven't got a prayer."

"Do you think so? She would become Hasidic?"

He didn't, but he couldn't say it. Naomi? Hasidic? Never in a million years. But at least it would give Abraham a chance to get his life under control again. They stepped back into the basement of the synagogue. "When you can, court her, but right now let us concentrate on digging that new tunnel, shall we?"

Abby, the light of hope in his eyes, only nodded as they reached the top of the stairs. Aaron was already regretting giving him any hope at all.

The crack of a rifle echoed in the dome as they came into the central part of the synagogue. Aaron looked up to see Martin reload and fire again, then a third time before standing to one side of the window and fooling with his rifle. Probably jammed again. It was old and outdated and jammed often enough that Aaron had tried to find Martin a new one. So far he hadn't had any luck.

"What is happening, Martin? I told you we don't want trouble with Brits unless you are sure we are under attack," Abraham yelled.

Martin didn't answer but lifted his rifle, stepped to the broken-out window, took careful aim, and fired again. Then he lowered his rifle and seemed satisfied. He looked down at Abraham and Aaron with a grin on his face, but as he was about to speak, he was jerked to the left and thrown from the hanging door. He landed between the reader's platform and the first of two benches that faced it, just a few feet from Aaron who stood there in shock. He rushed to Martin's aid. He turned him over and saw the blood on the front of his shirt. Stripping it aside, he found a wide hole in Martin's midsection.

"Dead, aren't I," Martin said, his skin pale and waxen.

Aaron was stunned, his stomach clenching tightly. He stared at the gaping hole as if doing so would change reality.

"I . . . I shot . . . one of . . . in the tower . . . St. . . . ." Martin grabbed Aaron's coat and hung on as the pain of dying made him shudder.

"Don't die on us, Martin. We'll get you to hospital."

Abraham knelt beside them with a first-aid kit, desperately using a dry cloth to stanch the bleeding, his eyes filled with the anguish of knowing there was little hope.

"Tell Father, I . . . I am sorry, but I would not have made a good rabbi anyway." His smile waned and he seemed to look at something beyond them, then his eyes glazed over. The air released from his lungs with a gurgling sound Aaron would never forget.

"Martin!" Abraham said shaking him lightly.

"He is gone, Abby. Let it be," Aaron said, sitting back, shocked by his own words. The others had gathered round and Aaron looked into their faces. There was shock there, and fear on the faces of the new men. It was obvious they hadn't seen one of their number die. Aaron looked down at the lifeless body. He had seen death so many times in Germany, it had become second nature to him, and he had learned to shrug it off as easily as rain. Why was losing Yitzhak and Martin different? Why did these hurt when he had seen so much death and was past feeling such things?

"O God Who art full of compassion," Abraham started the Jewish prayer for the dead. ". . . Who dwellest on high, grant perfect rest beneath the shelter of Thy divine presence, in the exalted places among the holy and pure, who shine as the brightness of the firmament, to Martin Gunther who has gone to his eternal home . . ."

Aaron had heard it more than once in Germany. At least this time the dead man had taken an enemy with him. He listened while others knelt and prayed for Martin or stood by in stunned disbelief. When Abraham had finished his prayer, they both stood.

"Abraham, British troops are coming. We have to get him out of here." Abraham looked at Aaron with a blank stare, then realized what he was saying.

The British had probably heard the shooting and would investigate. Lassiter had snooped around the synagogue looking for weapons a dozen times but had been thwarted, only angering him more. He had threatened to close down the synagogue if he ever caught them using it for military purposes, and they had used extreme caution and a vigilant warning system to prevent it. If Lassiter found Martin, he would have his pound of flesh and more.

"Is it Lassiter?" Abraham asked regaining his senses.

"We can't wait to find out, sir," one of his men said.

Aaron outranked Abraham and issued commands. "Get Martin down to the tunnels. The rest of you," he said loudly. "Hide your weapons as you usually do and get that platform down and put away."

They scrambled, putting their guns behind false panels and sealing them shut while two men took Martin's lifeless body down the stairs.

"You have blood on you, Abraham. Go!" Aaron said.

Abraham hesitated, searching Aaron's face.

"I'll take care of it. You go with Martin. His father will need you there, not me," he said to the unasked question. Abraham went for the stairs as Aaron took a seat on a bench and pulled Beth's book from his pocket. Then he saw the pool of blood on the floor near the front of the reading platform. Grabbing the lectern next to the niche where the ark of the covenant was kept, he placed it over the blood, then stood in front. He faced the benches as if to lecture. The lectern was solid on all four sides clear to the floor and would hide the blood unless moved. Hopefully Lassiter wasn't a student of Judaism and wouldn't know the lectern was out of place.

"You will need this." He turned around to see Rabbi Marshak, Abraham's father standing in front of him with a prayer shawl in hand. He had forgotten that the rabbi was in the building, and his face was red from having disturbed the lectern in his synagogue. He took the shawl and put it over his head.

"You should also have tefillin, but under the circumstances it probably isn't that important," the rabbi smiled. "The British know even less than you what is needed."

"Sorry, Rabbi, I—"

"No need to apologize. I gave my permission already." He touched Aaron's arm. "And so did Rabbi Gunther. He will understand. After all, it's for the good of Eretz Israel, is it not?" He turned and went to a seat in front of Aaron and along with everyone else put his scarf over his head and pulled his Torah out for reading. Aaron adjusted his own shawl and opened his book as the room filled with the sound of prayer. A moment later Lassiter and a dozen men walked in with the clatter of leather soles on the wood floors.

The prayer stopped and everyone looked at the Brits as if they were intruding.

Lassiter looked about the room, up at the dome, then at Aaron whom he disliked with an obvious passion. "Someone fired from one of them windows. Killed an Arab in the tower of St. James."

Aaron smiled. "And what was he doing in the tower of St. James?"

Lassiter went red in the face. "No matter what 'e was doin'. 'E was shot from this place, and we've come to take the guilty in for the killin'."

"Nothing here but worshipers, as you can see," Aaron said. "Your sources, are they Arab, Jewish, or just guesswork?"

His face went redder. "Don't you get smart with me," he hissed.

"My apology. I thought the question was a good one. I was about to read a verse if you would like to join us."

Lassiter's face turned the color of a ripe strawberry, and Aaron thought his eyes would explode.

"Search them! Search the whole place!"

His men spread out and began searching.

"This platform will come down and stay down." He said looking up at the hanging door.

"Sorry, the workmen need it. If you will note, we are replastering the dome with your government's permission. We have the paperwork if you would like to see it."

"Never mind. You," he said to one of his men. "Climb that rope and see what you can see from that scaffold." The soldier grabbed the rope that hung a few feet from Aaron and started shimmying up it.

"It works better if someone holds the bottom. Steadies it for the climber," Aaron said.

Lassiter grumbled at one of his men to grab the rope. It did help. When he was at the top, he stood on the shaky platform and started to look out through one of the windows. A bullet struck the frame and threw splinters into his cheek. He yelped and stumbled back, nearly falling off the platform. He cursed in pain as he came down the rope at record pace.

"Probably some Jew in the Hurva," Aaron said to Lassiter. "Best run and check it out, don't you think?" His voice hardened.

Lassiter's eyes grew dark with anger. He stepped to where Aaron was and quickly whipped his pistol across Aaron's face, cutting his forehead and knocking him to one side. "Use a civil tongue when you speak to me," he said coldly.

Rabbi Marshak was on his feet and had Lassiter by the arm before he could swing the gun again. "Use that weapon again, and I will report you to your commander." He held Lassiter's arm in a firm grip.

Aaron felt the wound and shook off the nausea it caused while watching Lassiter take on the look of the devil himself as he faced the rabbi. "Let go of my arm, old man, or it will be you next!" He pulled his arm free and brought it back for a swing at the rabbi. Aaron, still weak and partially stunned by the blow, was about to take action when the rabbi gave him a hard look to keep out of it. As the hand came down he grabbed the arm and stopped it cold. "You don't want to do that, lad. I am a rabbi, and they'll take away your stripes and put you in jail for pistol whipping a rabbi."

Lassiter's face didn't change for another ten seconds as he thought it through, then he ripped his arm free from the rabbi's grip for a second time. Except for the man who was pulling splinters from his face and the one helping him, Lassiter's men watched their leader. Some looks were passive; others showed disdain. It was these that Aaron knew Lassiter would have to satisfy, and he knew how he would do it.

"Take this one into custody," he said to one of his men while pointing at Aaron.

Abraham's men stood as if to defend Aaron, and Lassiter's men responded by raising their weapons. Aaron quickly lifted a hand to calm them all. "Let it be. I was going into the city anyway."

"If you take him, and if any harm comes to him, I will see you locked up for it," Rabbi Marshak said.

Aaron smiled. "The sergeant won't touch me, Rabbi." He turned to Lassiter. "Will you, sergeant?" He stepped closer so that only Lassiter could hear the rest. "Jack Willis is coming to dinner at my father's house this Sabbath. If I am not there, in the same condition you see before you now, he will come looking for you, Sergeant, and when he's done with you, you won't want to be in the army anymore. You will be demoted so low, latrine duty will seem like holidays."

Lassiter swallowed hard but kept his face granite hard while holstering his pistol. "Take 'im," he told his men. His tone was much more civil this time.

The room emptied and everyone followed them down the street to the British vehicles. Aaron turned to Rabbi Marshak and thanked him, then told him to let Abraham and Funt know.

"I'll see you in a few days, and tell Hannah not to worry."

Rabbi Marshak could only nod as two of the Brits took Aaron by the arms and pointed him to the back of the truck. They let go long enough that he could get himself in, then two soldiers followed and the tarp was pulled down. Rabbi Marshak was relieved to see that Sergeant Lassiter got into a separate vehicle.

SEE CHAPTER NOTES

CHAPTER 16

Hannah was tired of the British army, regardless of the fact that Jack Willis and others were friends and were helping them as much as they could. To have their men constantly searched and hassled while little was done to the Arabs was horrible enough, but to have Aaron hauled off the way Rabbi Marshak described made her blood boil. It was times like these she clung to Ephraim's most recent words: "The British government has only one thing on its agenda—leaving Palestine." As far as she was concerned, the sooner the better. Then they would have only one enemy to fight.

She was trying to remain calm, but there were too many instances of British collusion and deceit to make it easy. In a war where any complicity with the Arabs took place, then went unpunished, it was difficult to believe it wasn't policy.

She took a deep breath while pulling her wool coat tighter against the biting chill of a December morning. She had not heard from Aaron since his capture twenty-four hours earlier. Ephraim had sent word with the bus driver that Jack Willis was looking into his whereabouts and would contact them as quick as he could find out something, but there had been nothing so far. As a result, she hadn't slept much last night, and she wouldn't until she saw Aaron's face again, though Jack's involvement did bring some comfort.

Climbing the stairs from the tunnels to the small shop, she greeted the owner and slipped into the street, proceeding toward the Arab bakery a block away. She always went shopping early. The tunnels were less dusty and the few streets she had to walk less dangerous, snipers picking later hours when targets were plentiful along the few streets where tunnels weren't available yet.

The bakery she was going to was owned by one of the last Arabs living in the Jewish Quarter. Most others had already left, their lives becoming more uncomfortable each day because of the growing unrest and mistrust engendered by fear. At first the pressure had come from their families living outside the Quarter who feared for their safety. Then it had come from radicals who either wanted to use them to get inside the Quarter to attack Jews, or threatened them with death if they stayed. Most began leaving, and after the Arabs started shooting and attempts were made by them to take the Quarter, all but a few simply locked their stores and slipped away in the night. As Jewish support began to wane, then turn against the few, they began joining the exodus. Now only Ahmad the baker and his wife Lilya remained. Stubborn and unwilling to give up the shop they had worked for all their lives, they continued to resist the growing pressure, but Hannah knew it was only a matter of time. After all, even Jews were leaving—more than five hundred in three weeks. If they didn't feel safe, how could an Arab?

Seeing the bakery was still open, Hannah breathed relief and entered. There was no bread on the shelves, and the sweet smell of Ahmad's wonderful breads was missing. Lilya looked up from the box she was packing and gave Hannah a somewhat defeated smile. "We have no flour. Without flour we have no living. It is time we left."

"No flour, but why? The British brought sacks in yesterday."

"All was given to the Jewish bakers and to individuals by Rabbi Salomon. We were told that until more came in the trucks, we would not get any. That will not be soon." She bit her lip against the tears. "We go to my sister's in East Jerusalem. Maybe . . . maybe when the fighting is over . . ." She couldn't hold them back any longer and burst into sobs. Hannah took her in her arms to give her comfort. "It is better. My husband received another threat from our people. They want our cooperation. If we are outside the Quarter, they cannot make us do such horrible things as they ask."

Hannah knew she was right. As things got worse, Lilya and Ahmad would be most at risk—from both sides. It was better.

Lilya sniffed her nose then looked with a serious countenance upon her Jewish friend. "You also should leave this place. Both of us attended the funeral for Mr. Goldman and the boy from the Arab butcher shop just outside the Quarter. You heard the Rabbi and the Mulla. It will only get worse. Go to Ephraim in Tel Aviv," Lilya pleaded. "They cannot destroy that city, but here . . . They will come, soon, Hannah. Do not be here when they do." She turned away and busied herself once more. Hannah could only say goodbye and leave the shop. Lilya was right. Jerusalem was vital to Haj Amin's plans. It was one of the most holy cities in Islam. To control it would give him inestimable power in the Arab and Islamic world. To get that control he must drive out the Jewish population and break their resistance here more than anywhere else in Palestine. And because the Jewish Quarter sat near the mount, it must be taken above all.

Abraham Marshak came across the street, a rifle cradled in his arm.

"Ahmad is leaving?" he asked.

She only nodded.

"Then that is all of them. It is too bad."

"It is worse than that. More and more we live in a divided city. Jewish taxis refuse to go into Arab streets, and Arab taxis take no one into Jewish neighborhoods, especially here. The blue buses of the Israeli line have changed their routes, as have the silver buses of the Arab line. Roadblocks and barricades cut off Arab centers from Jewish ones. Once again, it is worse here, and it is just like Krakow in the beginning of Hitler's war. I learned to hate Poles, and they learned to hate me. I had wanted it to be different here, but it is the same. It will be horrible."

"I must go. As you know, they bury Martin Gunther today," Abraham said.

"What time will they go? Where will they bury him?"

"At two o'clock in the cemetery across the Kidron Valley."

"That is Arab territory. It will be very dangerous," Hannah said.

"The British have promised Rabbi Salomon that they will protect us."

"And you believe them?"

"We don't have much choice. Martin deserves a righteous burial and the promise was made to Rabbi Salomon." He shrugged. "They curry his favor. They will probably keep their promise." He walked back across the street as Hannah thought of Martin, a rabbi's son willing to talk religion with her even though his father did not approve. Kind, quiet, even spiritual, but still full of curiosity and love for his people.

She said a silent prayer for him and his family as she turned to go home. She would pay her condolences to Martin's mother on the way.

She wiped the tears from her eyes as she entered a small grocery store. The grocer nodded and she slipped into the back where a guard was posted at the door leading to the basement.

"Guards now," she said.

"The British have asked about noises. Our leaders think they may suspect we are digging and will try to find out more. A precaution against them shutting us down."

She nodded while stepping aside so a family of four could pass. It would be just like the British to shut them down, regardless of the lives it might cost. It was a good precaution.

She descended, turning right and peering into the dimly lit tunnel. Once she had her bearings and her eyes adjusted, she began walking.

Hannah passed through the basement of the house belonging to Martin's parents. Rabbi Gunther and his wife were already receiving guests, half a dozen people ascending the steps to their living area. She could hear the cries of the mourners as she quickly stepped through the small area and back into another tunnel. This was not the time to pay her respects. She bumped into Rabbi Salomon.

"Rabbi," she said.

"Hannah," he responded coldly. "You see what your war is doing? A fine young man, dead, and for what? For your Zionist beliefs. Fools, all of you." He tried to go around her, and she took a step to one side, then reconsidered and held her ground. She could not let the Rabbi think that Martin Gunther had died for nothing, that his sacrifice was a mistake. It was not.

"Rabbi, do you know why Martin wanted to fight? Your Arab friends at the Commercial Center attacked his mother and they shot at his sisters from the rooftops. He felt the need to protect you and the others who study Torah in your Yeshivas, and he wanted to protect the Hurva and Nisan Bek and the other synagogues. He was willing to fight so that you could continue to pray and worship as you like and . . ." The Rabbi tried to step around her, his face flushed with anger. She moved so that he couldn't without touching her, knowing that was something he wouldn't do. ". . . *And*, Rabbi, he died because he loved Israel. It is sad that you regret his death, because in doing so, you belittle it. You couldn't do worse if you spit on his grave." With that she stepped aside to let him pass, but he didn't move. Though his face was still red, his eyes showed confusion, recognition that her words had hit a rather large nerve.

Others approached. There was suddenly a crowd, everyone wondering what was happening. Finally, he regained his composure and walked past her without a word, clearing the way for others to pass.

"By the way, Rabbi, if the Arabs are such good friends of yours, why don't you walk in the streets? *Hi Shomer,* Rabbi. Thanks to men like Martin, you still are." He hesitated at the bottom of the steps then climbed them and disappeared through the door to Martin's house. Hannah went on through the tunnels.

When she arrived in the basement of the apartment beneath hers, she quickly ascended the stairs and knocked.

"Come," a gentle voice said.

Hannah entered Mithra Birkelau's small kitchen and found her playing with the twins. Only a few days earlier she, Beth, Jacob, and Aaron had run into this same apartment escaping a sniper.

Mithra was nearly seventy years old, a survivor of the camps at Dachau. Her wrinkled skin reminded Hannah of dried earth in a sun-baked riverbed, but she had a youthful vitality that was remarkable. Her blindness was another witness of German atrocities, her eyes burned from their sockets by a vindictive guard the day the Nazis deserted Dachau. But she had never let it ruin her spirit. She was a truly amazing woman.

Beth and David sat at the kitchen table taking turns reading aloud from Torah. She wanted them to be as well versed in Jewish scriptures as they would be in the Book of Mormon. Without such knowledge, rabbis and Yeshiva students wouldn't give them the time of day. How could you convert a rabbi if you didn't know a rabbi's scriptures?

"*Shalom,* Mum," David said as he turned the book over to Beth.

"*Shalom,*" she answered, her eyes taking in the scene. Mithra was down on her hands and knees tickling Jacob's stomach and making him giggle. She then switched to Joseph's tummy, getting an outright laugh from him.

"You spoil them, Mithra. They want to be played with all the time," Hannah smiled.

"Their laughter is music to these old ears," Mithra said. She sniffed lightly. "I do not smell any of the Arab baker's sweet breads. He is gone, isn't he," she said matter-of-factly before giving Jacob another blow on the tummy.

"Yes, Lilya was packing when I got there. They received no flour."

"The British cut back the supplies again. They will continue this, you know. It is their way of applying pressure to force all of us out eventually," Mithra said. "But, I will miss his breads." She pushed herself to her feet, reached out to find the edge of her rocking chair, and sat in it. "It is probably a sin to admit it, but the Jewish baker isn't nearly as good at baking. Not nearly."

David got up from his chair and headed for the basement door as Beth marked their spot and closed the book, about to follow.

"Where are you going?" Hannah asked.

"To help in the Cardo. A new tunnel," David said. "There is still much t-to do, and w-we are late already." He disappeared down the steps.

Beth gave Hannah a quick kiss on the cheek and followed. The door closed behind them. He ran messages for the Haganah at night and carved out tunnels during the day. The boy had endless energy. She just prayed it didn't get him killed.

Hannah turned to the twins, the first sign of a dirty diaper reaching her nostrils. She picked up Jacob and checked him first.

"Moddel came by. She needed flour as well. Apparently she was not there when the truck came yesterday," Mithra said.

"You don't have much more to give, Mithra. Please send her to us next time," Hannah begged. Jacob was soaked, and she decided to change him before moving on to Joseph, the probable source of the growing smell in the room.

"You have many more mouths to feed than I."

"And a lot more flour. Promise you will send her upstairs."

"She will not come to you, Hannah. She thinks . . ." Her voice trailed off.

Hannah bit her lip against an old hurt. She knew what Mithra meant. Moddel had made it clear that Hannah's religion was of the devil and to stay clear of her. From that time to the present, Moddel—and thus her husband and children—had shunned them. Using gossip, innuendo, and terrible stories, Moddel had tried to turn every woman in the Old City against them. For nearly a month, Hannah hadn't been able to walk down the street without having everyone turn away from her. Then Mithra had intervened.

Wonderful Mithra. She had invited them for dinner, visited with them, asked questions, been a wonderful neighbor and friend. Slowly her acceptance had led to less antagonism and more friendship. Gradually, Hannah found herself being greeted in passing and even having an occasional conversation. After a year, only Moddel and a few others, including Rabbi Salomon's daughters, refused to talk to her. Hannah knew it would probably never change and had just learned to live with it. She found it ironic that she had been persecuted by Christians when a Jew, and now that she served Christ, Jews took it on themselves to make her life just as miserable.

She finished putting on Jacob's clean diaper and tickled his tummy to get a few giggles of her own. In many ways Hannah felt sorry for Moddel. She seemed very unhappy, even bitter. Hannah couldn't remember the woman ever having a good thing to say about others, and since her husband's run in with a sniper, she had only worsened.

"How is Saul doing?" she asked.

"He still cannot move from the bed, but she says his left arm does have some movement now. I suppose that is a good sign." There was a pause. "Moddel's fear is getting worse. She has to cross the street to get to the tunnels, and she won't do it until they are nearly starving. I think she wishes to leave the Quarter soon. Only Rabbi Salomon's plea to stay and Saul's inability to walk prevent her from going now." Mithra paused. "She thinks too much of Rabbi Salomon, and so does Saul. It would be better for them in the newer part of the city where the Arabs cannot frighten them so much." Hannah didn't say anything. They had talked about this before, and Mithra knew Hannah agreed. Moddel should go before her fear prompted foolish actions or a breakdown that might endanger her children.

She sat Jacob on the couch next to her and picked up Joseph. Her nostrils immediately told her she had found the offending child.

"I have to go. Joseph needs more than a fresh diaper. He needs a bath."

Mithra smiled and wrinkled her nose. "Such a pungent odor from such a sweet child," she chuckled. "Will you go to the Jewish baker's later in the day?"

"I will try. Do you have enough for today?"

"Yes, plenty."

Hannah took a boy in each arm and started for the door. She did a balancing act as she tried to hold them while gripping the knob in an awkward attempt to turn it.

"*Lahitraot.* Good-bye. If you need anything, let me know."

"*Todah Rabah. Shalom.*"

Closing the door behind her, Hannah held to the shadows for a moment before taking the steps to their apartment and quickly going inside, her heart pounding, the memory of the snipers' near miss a few days ago still haunting her. Though Aaron's platoon had driven the Arabs back the night after that shooting, they had not been able to keep them from taking another, stronger position that gave them the same view. Though it was farther away, and a more difficult shot, the effect was the same. The street was a shooting gallery, and it would take a full-scale attack into the Arab Quarter to get rid of them this time. It wasn't something the British would allow, so caution and fear were the rule of the day.

She caught her breath and slowed her heartbeat before taking the boys into the bathroom. Wiping the tense sweat from the palms of her hands she calmed herself before removing Joseph's diaper and cleaning him off, then washing out the soiled cloth in the toilet. Then she gave him a quick bath in the sink before putting on a fresh diaper and shirt. When finished, she dropped the rinsed out diaper in a lidded bucket and shut it tight. There were a dozen used diapers in it now. She would need to do the washing this afternoon.

Gathering up both wriggling boys, she took them to her bedroom where she placed Jacob in his crib with a favorite toy, then sat down in the rocker Ephraim had made for her. She started feeding Joseph and grimaced at his first suckle. Another month and she would stop nursing unless she had no other milk to give them.

Ephraim now spent most of his time at the airport outside Tel Aviv where his Piper Cub was housed. Aviron, the fledgling Jewish Airline, owned it. Outwardly, they were under contract with the British to deliver mail to the outlying settlements. He was actually flying reconnaissance over Arabs attacking Jewish settlements and dropping homemade bombs in the process.

It made for sleepless, prayerful nights when she didn't hear from him, and that was most of the time. There were no available phones in the Quarter, the lines cut as quickly as they were repaired, and the mail was sparse if it came at all. She knew Ephraim. He would help where he could, no matter the risk, and she had been in his Piper Cub before. There was little to nothing to prevent a bullet from going through his backbone when Arabs got annoyed with him.

She drew a deep breath. She had learned to deal with this most of the time through prayer and faith and just keeping herself occupied. Occasionally she would find herself beginning to doubt like she did in the camps, and only concerted prayer would bring her peace and strength.

She looked at the picture on the dresser—Ephraim next to the plane he flew in Germany. He loved to fly, and because he loved to fly there was no sense arguing to keep him out of the air and on solid ground. Besides, more people had died down here than up there. That might change in the future. The *Sherut Avir* had been organized a week ago within the Haganah, and it was under this new department's direction that plans were being readied for an air war once the right kind of planes arrived in Palestine. Whether she liked it or not, Ephraim would fly some of those planes. He was too good to do anything else.

His safety was what she prayed about the most.

She closed her eyes and said another quiet prayer for him. She had hoped they would be together during all this, but so far they had seen little of each other, even since his return from Europe. She never knew when he would come. Maybe it would be today, maybe tomorrow, but without him, the days were long. With him, they flew by. If she lost him . . . She wouldn't think about that. She wasn't going to lose him.

She finished feeding Joseph and switched him for Jacob. The boys were strong, healthy, and beautiful. This alone was a great blessing, and she must remember there were many of those. They had been protected more than once during the last month, and she must not lose sight of that.

Hannah heard someone knocking on the apartment door and quickly buttoned her blouse. While Jacob fussed for more food, she went to the door, opened it, and found Jack Willis standing on the landing, two of his men at the foot of the stairs.

"Jack! What is it? What's wrong?" she asked, her heart racing.

He stepped past her and turned back as she shut the door. "Aaron has been given a jail sentence. He's bein' taken tae Acco prison in the mornin'."

Hannah reached for a chair. She had to sit down.

CHAPTER 17

The lockup at Bevingrad was impenetrable. Aaron's trial had been short, almost non-existent. He had underestimated Lassiter. The man had friends as anti-Semitic as he who had lied about Aaron's involvement in the killing of the Arab sniper. When it was over, he had been seen doing the shooting, caught with the weapon, and had tried to escape. That explained the bruises on his face and the ache in his abdomen.

British military justice—fair, unbiased, and quick. Well, at least it was quick!

Jack had been at the trial, even registered a protest. That had gotten Aaron a one-day reprieve. Instead of going to Acco prison today, he would go tomorrow. Unless Jack or Ephraim pulled a rabbit out of a hat.

Aaron looked around him. A dozen others. Similar trials, similar verdicts. All of them guilty—guilty of defending themselves when shot at by Arab snipers, guilty of smuggling weapons aboard buses and trucks to keep themselves from getting killed, guilty of resisting British arrest, and guilty of defending their families and others against unlawful searches and seizures in their own homes. It was a side of the British military the world ought to see but probably never would.

"They're acting like they plan to stay," the man next to him said. Aaron turned to see Moshe smiling at him.

"At least through Christmas," Aaron replied touching his lips gingerly. One thing Lassiter did have was a mean left hook. The Brit hadn't touched him until they were well out of the Old City, then he had detoured, taken him to a side road and let out his frustrations for ten minutes on Aaron's body. Of course, the fact that Aaron wouldn't admit to anything probably added to those frustrations, and the spittle that ended up on the

British sergeant's cheekbone probably didn't help either, but it was obvious by the time they were moving again that Sergeant Lassiter had little fear of Jack Willis.

"The word is they set you up," Moshe said.

Aaron noticed another man standing beside Moshe and immediately didn't like him. He didn't know whether it was the sadistic grin on his face or the empty, murderous look in his eyes, but something inside Aaron said to beware.

"Yeah, they did."

"Do you mind telling me who it was," Moshe said.

"A sergeant named Lassiter."

"Yes, a bad one. Lassiter has sent more than one good man to Acco. We tried on two occasions to see that he was stopped, but he seems to have the luck of the Irish," Moshe wasn't smiling. He nodded toward his companion. "This is Avriel. Avriel, Aaron Schwartz. He and a couple other Jews saved my skin in Italy."

Avriel nodded but didn't say anything. It was then Aaron noticed both men wore leg irons.

"From the look of you, the Brits think they have quite a catch."

"They're sending us to Acco to be hanged. Caught us blowing up an armory outside Jericho." He shrugged. "Maybe they will, maybe they won't. It's a long trip to Acco," he smiled. "Now you see why my people continue to fight the British."

"Has it occurred to you that ETZEL might be part of the reason they do this to us?"

"They did it before we started fighting them, Aaron, not after."

There was the rattle of keys in a lock outside their cell, then the sound of leather shoes on stone floor. They stopped in front of their door and prepared to open it.

"Watch yourself, Aaron. If Lassiter framed you, he won't want you to live long enough for an inquiry." Then Moshe leaned in to him. "Stay close, and keep your eyes open. Like I said, Acco is a long drive." With that the two men shuffled away.

Aaron got the message. They would try and escape. He appreciated the warning. Though he trusted Jack to do his best to turn this around, if he couldn't, Aaron might need another way out. He had no plans to spend this war in a British prison.

* * *

Ephraim was steaming. Jack had sent a message about Aaron's so-called trial, and he'd taken the next convoy to Jerusalem. Riding in a truck filled with canned goods while Arabs took potshots at him and British soldiers did nothing to stop it hadn't helped his mood, but at least they had gotten through. The trucks near the end of the convoy hadn't, and only a last-minute change of heart by one of the British armored cars kept several men from being butchered by Arabs who clamored down the hillside to finish them off. Even then the trucks and goods had been left to the Arabs. By the time he arrived in the city, the taste of British justice had already soured.

Jack and Hannah were waiting when the convoy reached Bevingrad. Ephraim hopped in the back of the jeep with Hannah, gave her a much-needed hug and kiss and kept his arm around her while Jack's driver started for the office of the military governor. On the way, Jack explained in detail what had happened, emphasizing Aaron's precarious position. The sour taste in Ephraim's mouth turned downright bitter.

"So far the Governor's aide has nae indicated he can get us an audience," Jack said over the sound of the motor.

"He'll see us," Ephraim said. "I saw Naomi in Tel Aviv. Her connections to the underground in Italy are coming in handy. It seems there is a crisis brewing. About 15,000 immigrants shipped out of Romania and Ben-Gurion needed advice from someone who knew the leaders of the underground and could act as a go between. That was Naomi." He took a deep breath. "The point is, she's working directly with Ben-Gurion, and she told him about Aaron. He'll call the Lord Governor at ten this morning." He looked at his watch. "Fifteen minutes from now. The Governor will listen to Ben-Gurion."

The jeep pulled up to the building housing the Lord Governor's offices. Ephraim got out and helped Hannah as Jack joined them. They took the steps quickly, and Jack got them past the first two guards and inside the building. They hastened to the Lord Governor's suites where more guards stood at attention and the Governor's personal secretary sat behind a large mahogany desk. He stood and put up an arm as if to ward them off. Ephraim ignored him and stepped past the desk toward the Lord Governor's door, Hannah holding tightly to his hand. The guards stopped him before he completed his next step. "You received a call from David Ben-Gurion about us," Ephraim said. "We're expected."

The secretary stopped his protest, waved off the guards and Ephraim, grateful Naomi had gotten Ben-Gurion to make the call, turned the knob and the three of them entered the room. The Lord Governor was sitting behind another very large desk reading some papers. He looked up as the door opened, then stood, pointing at some chairs.

"Mr. and Mrs. Daniels, Colonel Willis. Please, be seated."

They stood in front of him. "No time for that, Governor. You have our son locked up on trumped up charges. We want his release, and you can secure it," Ephraim said.

The Lord Governor's jaw hardened. "Sit," he said. "It isn't that easy."

Ephraim and Hannah remained standing, not ready to be put off so easy. "Jack, tell the Lord Governor what you saw in that court yesterday," Ephraim said.

"One of our sergeants an' a few of his friends lied through their teeth an' got a conviction. That is what I saw, Lord Governor." He removed a letter from his pocket, unfolded it, and pushed it across the desk. "A signed affidavit by a dozen Jews present when the laddie was arrested. One of them is a rabbi an' willin' tae testify at Sergeant Lassiter's court martial." He pointed to some names at the bottom. "Those men are British soldiers who were present an' willin' tae do the same. This isnae the first time Lassiter has used his authority tae get rid of men he considers troublesome, an' I intend tae see him booted out of the army fer it. Fer now, we need tae stop this particular injustice."

With a glare, the Lord Governor took the letter and read it briefly, then sat down. "Please, will you have a seat? I will make a call and see what I can do." He lifted the phone but did not dial, his eyes going from the seat to them and back again. When they sat down, he dialed, told his secretary to call Bevingrad lockup, and hung up.

"I do not wish to give the impression that I agree with your position. It will take more than a signed affidavit to bring about your son's release," he glared at Jack again, "but I will get his transfer postponed until we can get to the bottom of this."

Jack leaned forward in his chair. "Beggin' yer pardon, Lord Governor, but as I just told ye, Sergeant Lassiter is a liar and has, on numerous occasions, made life hard fer Jews. He should be detained an' charges brought against him. Unless that happens, our position looks a bit off balance, if ye know what I say, Sir."

"I know what you mean," said the Lord Governor with some irritation, "but I can't go about having British soldiers arrested, now can I? After all, I am not responsible for these soldiers, at least not directly. Their officers are." He turned to Ephraim and Hannah. "But, I promise to see that the matter is looked into. For now let's take care of this problem, shall we?" He seemed to be looking at them for the first time. "You are a bit young to have a son thrown into Acco Prison. How old is the boy?"

"He isn't a son by blood. He's been part of our family ever since the end of the war in Germany."

"Ah, his real parents were killed by the Nazis. I see. So many of those, so many." He shook his head sadly. "But, now he is here. I assume he has papers. Legal documents, showing he came legally to this country."

The questions irritated Hannah but she bit her tongue as Ephraim answered. "He has them." He didn't tell the Lord Governor that they were forgeries, like Hannah's, Beth's, and David's.

The phone rang and the Lord Governor picked it up. The conversation was typically British. A brief discussion of trivia took place before getting to the point.

"You have a prisoner by the name of . . ."

He looked up at Ephraim for help. He had forgotten to even ask.

"Aaron Schwartz," Ephraim offered.

"Schwartz, Aaron Schwartz. He is being sent to Acco prison, but there may have been some irregularities in his trial. I want you to keep him here until we can clear up the mess. Can you do it?"

There was a pause as he listened. Then he turned away in his swivel chair. Half a dozen "uh huhs" later he turned back. "Oh, I see," he said, resigned. "And when did it leave?" Another pause. "Then they are well on their way. No, no, I'll make the call. Thank you. When he is sent back, notify me directly, would you?" They said goodbye and he hung up the phone, a sad look in his eye. He picked it up again and told his secretary to find the number for Acco prison and call the commander in charge, then he put it down and leaned forward, giving them the bad news.

"He's already on his way. An hour ago," he smiled. "But, we'll have him sent back immediately." He stood, "Where can you be reached?"

"Call Colonel Willis," Ephraim said. "He knows how to get in touch with us." Ephraim stood, Hannah hanging on tightly.

"I should mention that I am an American citizen as is my wife. Our embassy will be notified about this as soon as we leave here. I hope you understand the necessity of our doing so."

The Lord Governor did not appreciate the veiled threat, but he nodded, stood, and wished them well in a cold tone.

As they left, Ephraim patted Hannah's hand gently, sensing her tension and concern. Once in the hall he turned to Jack.

"I don't like this. I thought he wasn't supposed to leave until this afternoon." He could see that Jack was confused as well.

"They dinnae keep an exact schedule fer fear of it getting' out an' havin' the convoy hit by friends of the prisoners. It's happened a few times."

Ephraim took a deep breath, frustrated at being so helpless.

"I'll make sure they send him right back, Eph. I willnae leave here until I know it has happened. I'll let yer embassy know as well. That was a good move. It will make him think twice before dumpin' this on some clerk." He put an arm around his friend's shoulders. "Go home. See the kids. I'll be there as soon as I know he is on the road back. My driver will see that ye get there safe and sound."

Ephraim and Hannah looked at one another. There was nothing else to do. They thanked Jack and walked toward the front door. It was going to be a long day.

* * *

Aaron knew he was in trouble when he saw Lassiter watching them load while discussing something with the commander responsible for their transfer. His fears were confirmed when he was put in the truck with those convicted of the worst crimes and his shackles were locked to steel benches for sitting. As the soldier finished, he spit at Aaron's feet, a sign that whatever lies Lassiter had told him were believed.

The truck was armored with steel sides, the door locked tight from the outside. The only light came through a small, barred window in the door. He had seen a second truck for prisoners and four armored cars that could carry at least half a dozen men each. He also knew that any attempt to escape without outside help was destined to fail. Moshe was sitting on the opposite side and end from him, and Aaron watched him out of the corner of his eye for the first hour of the trip. There was no sign he was going to try something alone.

Aaron thought about Hannah, Ephraim, and the others. He felt certain they knew of his capture—Jack had been in the court, heard the lies and the verdict. He also figured that by now the three of them had tried to help but had been unsuccessful, at least so far. They would keep trying. The question was if they would succeed.

After another hour, the convoy stopped, and Aaron heard the sound of metal gates being opened before they proceeded again. After a few more seconds, the vehicles came to a halt and the motors were shut off. A voice commanded the prisoners to get out, and the doors were opened, the brightness of the sun making Aaron squint. Two guards kept weapons trained on them as their shackles were unlocked from the benches one at time and each man led out. When Aaron got his feet on solid ground again, he saw men with bowls in their hands eating some kind of soup and gnawing on stale bread. He was led away from the group and got none. Another sign Lassiter's lies were working. He was told to sit down on the ground with his back against the wall, and a soldier was given the order to shoot him if he moved. Aaron laid his head against the wall and watched the others eat. Even that poor meal made him salivate, and he gazed around him for a distraction.

They were inside a small compound with barracks along one side and a motor pool, kitchen, dining hall, and armory on the other. At the far end were the offices where several men sat on the front steps eating food of their own from a different table. The vehicles in which they traveled were parked near a gate of solid steel panels, massive bars attached from side to side against any attack from outside. He had seen this place before. They were at the old British fort in Haifa.

He closed his eyes and tried to get some rest but was immediately interrupted by a person falling over his legs. He looked up to see that a fight of some kind had broken out and prisoners were pushing and shoving one another about, even laying on a few punches. Whistles blew and soldiers came running from the four corners of the compound to attempt to reinstate order again. Aaron looked for and found Moshe being jostled about by a guard on the far side of the yard, and then shoved up against a wall. He wasn't resisting. Someone was shoved in front of Aaron, and he had to sway to his left to see Moshe. As he did he saw the guard removing his hand from Moshe's pocket. He had given him something.

The brawling prisoners, Avriel most prominent among them, were unceremoniously shoved back into their prison vehicles, and Aaron was prodded with two rifle barrels to join them. Keeping his eyes on Moshe as they were shackled, their eyes met just as the door was slammed shut and locked. Moshe gave him a slight smile, and Aaron wondered how the man was going to get his hand to his pocket. The shackles bound everyone's wrists in such a way that they had less than an inch in movement.

It didn't take him long to find out. The key, previously removed from his pocket, appeared in Moshe's hand and he quickly maneuvered it into the lock of the wrist irons, snapping them open. He reached down and unlocked his leg irons, then did the same for Avriel and worked his way up the row until he reached Aaron.

"These men have all agreed to fight, so I have freed them. You have not agreed."

Aaron's mind raced. His friends would surely get him freed, but what if they could not? Would he survive Acco, or would Lassiter's lies spread to the guards there and bring about a premature end to his life? He couldn't take that chance. He lifted his hands the inch he could. "I'll fight."

The shackles were quickly unlocked, and Moshe gave the prisoners instructions. "In less than five minutes, friends of ours will hit this convoy. If they are successful, the doors will be blown and we'll join them against any British still fighting. Get on the floor and cover your ears or the concussion from the explosives will break your eardrums."

Aaron slid to the floor and under the edge of the bench as the vehicle veered to one side, then came to a sudden stop. He heard gunfire, then explosions. Moshe was positioned at the window and saw one of his rescuers running toward the back of the truck.

"Here it comes," he said, hitting the deck and covering his ears. The explosion hit with such force that it hurt Aaron's ears anyway, along with his eyes and even his stomach. While shaking his head to rid it of the cobwebs, he saw everyone getting to their feet. He scrambled to his own before he was left behind. The doors leaned at odd angles and dust and smoke filtered light into the opening. Moshe shoved the first men out then followed. Avriel came next, and Aaron stumbled forward to go after him. He looked out the opening to see the first prisoner lying face down on the ground, but Avriel and Moshe were under a nearby truck and scurrying for the far side. He jumped and went after them as bullets struck around his feet and zipped by his face. He dove under the truck and crawled out the other side, then ran for a small ravine to the side of the road. When he hit the bottom, he was handed a gun by someone in civilian clothes and told to follow. They ran down the ravine for fifty yards, passing fighters along its length, then darted out the far side where another truck waited. Clamoring in the back as the truck pulled away, Aaron found he was lying on the floor looking up into the faces of half a dozen sweating, tired combatants. He turned over to look out the back of the truck and saw others getting into vehicles of their own and following. Two of the British armored vehicles were turned on their sides and incapacitated while two others were giving chase. A dozen soldiers were firing from behind vehicles and hillocks at the rescuers who were firing back. Then they turned a corner and the scene disappeared.

He slid over, leaned against the side near the rear, and caught his breath.

"Welcome to ETZEL," Moshe said. "You are one of us now, whether you like it or not."

Aaron kept his face emotionless, his eyes looking out the back of the truck. They were in the mountains of the Carmel Range above Haifa. It wasn't that far to Jerusalem. He looked over at Moshe and smiled as they came to a steep grade in the road and the truck began to slow.

"I think not. Thanks for the help, Moshe, but I have business in Jerusalem." With that he slipped over the back of the truck and jumped, rolling into the dried grass and shrubs at the side, then scrambling for cover. He heard Moshe's laugh and looked up to see him standing in the back of the truck.

"You're a fool, Aaron Schwartz, but say hello to Hannah. Tell her we are even now—a life for a life."

Aaron heard advancing vehicles and scurried deeper into the brush and let them pass, then waited until he was sure there were no others before clamoring up the side of the hill into the thick trees. It was a long walk to Jerusalem.

* * *

Jack came to the Old City and told Ephraim and Hannah about the escape not more than an hour after it happened. They all felt sick inside. Aaron was a fugitive now, on the run from the British as well as the Arabs, and he was with ETZEL. None of it was encouraging.

Jack sat back on the couch. "There is something else ye should know. The truck was only leavin' the prison when the Lord Governor was on the phone. He could have stopped the convoy, taken Aaron off."

"What?" Hannah said.

"It seems my government has decided the fewer men on the street, the fewer the fights, an' the less chance of the referee walkin' intae an errant punch."

"So innocent or not, Aaron was going to jail."

"Makes ye sick," Jack said in disgust. He pulled a sheet of paper from his pocket and handed it to Ephraim. "Just tae know ye that we dinnae all agree."

"What's this?" Ephraim asked.

"There isnae much I can do fer Aaron, at least right now. But I an' others are getting' a little sick of ye Jews havin' yer hands tied behind yer back an' then watchin' the referees stand by an' let the other guy beat ye tae a bloody pulp.

"The first name on the list works in our motor pool—armored cars are his specialty. He has two older models they've decided tae ship off tae Haifa early. He'll see that they disappear if ye want them."

"And the cost?"

"That they are nae used against any British soldiers. Other than that there is nae cost. This laddie's father was killed by Arabs in Arabia twenty years ago." He pulled an envelope from his pocket. "The second man on the list sends this note that ye ought tae get tae SHAI afore this evenin'. It gives the time an' strength of a platoon of the Highland Light Infantry that intends tae raid one of yer weapons slicks tomorrow. From what he says, the slick is a rather large one in the New City and will hurt yer cause a good deal if it is nae moved afore the army gets there."

"I know him. A major in the OSS during the war with the Nazis," Ephraim said taking the note. "I'll see that our intelligence people get it."

"He'll have other messages. Ye should have one of yer best contact him—quietly of course—an' set up a method of contact."

Jack leaned forward and pointed to another name on the list. "This laddie fought wi' us in World War II and has become the assistant for the Chaplain General of the British armed forces in Palestine. The chaplain receives daily reports that show what is intended in the way of British military movement on any given day, just in case his services are needed. A message from this fellow could keep ye one step ahead of our boys every day of the week."

"And he is willing?" Hannah asked.

"Willin', an' if ye talk hard enough, he might stick around after the last boat carryin' our troops sails for England. He'll retire about then an' has nae family waitin' at home."

He sat back in his chair again. "I dinnae know what the rest of the blokes on the list will do. I just know they'll do somethin' if asked." He leaned forward. "Me, included. An' tae make up fer the Lord Governor's mistake, I an' a couple of friends from the signal corps tapped his lines this afternoon. It should make for interestin' listenin'." He took the list and wrote an address on the back. "Ye will find listenin' equipment in Apartment 2 of this address. Further, these boys say they'll tap the lines of the central switchboard of the Jerusalem Post Office if ye like. That will allow SHAI tae listen in tae key Arab and British phones in the city an' on the lines that feed Europe. It should give ye some nice detail on conversations between Haj Amin and the members of the Arab Higher Committee still in town." He sat back in the chair, a self-congratulating grin on his mug. "That's fer starters. The important stuff will come later."

Ephraim and Hannah looked at one another, disbelief on their faces.

"I . . . I don't know what to say, Jack. I mean, this could get you busted right into the brig, and getting out before the turn of the century would be unlikely."

"That's what ye said about that punch I threw on the commanding officer at the Commercial Center." He grinned. "They'll have tae catch me first," he said as he stood. "I must be goin'." He had his hand on the door. "By the way, I've turned in my resignation, effective the end of March. Tell yer Haganah I'll be lookin' for work." With that, he closed the door and was gone.

Hannah smiled at the look on Ephraim's face. "You look like you just opened your great uncle's will to find you inherited all of Salt Lake City."

"This is better," Ephraim said. He stood and grabbed a jacket. "I'm going to catch Jack and deliver these to headquarters in Tel Aviv personally." He took her in his arms as she stood. "Will you be okay?"

"Fine," she lied with a smile. "If you hear anything about Aaron, you will let me know right away, won't you?"

"Right away." He kissed her. "I love you. I'll be back for Christmas Eve, I promise."

He kissed her again on the nose, then pulled himself away and opened the door. She grabbed his coat lapels and gave him one last kiss, then shoved him out the door before it was too late. As she turned around, she saw David and Beth standing in the doorway that led to the bedrooms, broad grins on both faces.

CHAPTER 18

Aaron felt the chill of the wind as the snow fell around him then began to pile up against his wet pants. He had walked through the trees for more than an hour, finally reaching the top of the mountain as darkness fell and the rain turned to snow. He was tired, cold, and hungry, and the village not more than a hundred yards away could remedy all three. The trouble was the village of Daliyat al Carmel was Druze, and not all Druze had committed to Israel.

Too cold and hungry to care if the village were aligned with Arabs or Jews, Aaron got to his feet and stumbled down the hillside to the edge of the town. There were a few souls about, but in the darkness he avoided them as he looked for an empty building and food. He found a small animal shelter filled with hay, goats, and chickens and went inside, closing the door behind him. He felt about in the darkness as the goats bleated and the chickens ran about helter-skelter, clucking noisily in their attempt to avoid him. He could only hope the wind carried the sounds away from the nearby house.

He found a stack of hay behind a solid board fence, climbed over, and fell on the soft mound. Covering himself for warmth, he immediately closed his eyes and fell asleep.

He awoke to the sound of a creaking door and voices. Moving the hay aside slightly he saw the light of a lantern and watched through the crack of the fence as a woman and young girl began milking their goats. Sun cascaded through a crack in the door, and he realized he had slept through the night and into early dawn. He kept quiet watching them, waiting for them to finish their task. They talked in Arabic but said little, concentrating on getting their chores done.

Finally the woman stood, placed the milk pail on a shelf where it could not be disturbed, and reached for a pitchfork. In one motion, she swung its wooden tines over the fence and stabbed at Aaron's midsection.

Instinctively he reached up and grabbed the weapon, even as he burst from the hay revealing himself. The woman's eyes went wide with fear, but she could not speak, nor would she let go of the pitchfork. Instead she backed away, jerking the tines from Aaron's grasp.

"Please," he said in Arabic, "I will not hurt you. I only needed a place to sleep."

At the sound of his voice, the girl turned around with a start, spilling her milk and frightening the goat. The animal bolted, running into the woman who fell with a thud. As he jumped over the fence to help her up she turned onto her hands and knees and, finding her voice, scrambled toward the door, yelling for help. The girl backed up against the wall in complete shock as Aaron jumped on the woman and slapped a palm over her lips, then pinned her down. Her eyes widened until he was sure they would pop out of their sockets, and he let go of her mouth only to have her scream again. He clamped her mouth shut a second time as something whacked his head, fluid drenching his shoulders and back.

"Leave her be!" yelled the girl as she swung the milk pail again. Spluttering, he grabbed the bucket with his second hand, then stood and backed away.

"Alright, alright!" he said, putting his hands in the air. "I mean no harm. But please, be quiet before the whole village comes down on us."

The girl helped her mother as she scurried backward to the wall. Just then a man appeared at the door with a rifle in his hand.

"No, no, wait! I don't mean any harm. This is all a mistake. I . . ."

Two more men appeared at the door and pushed in, one of them placing himself between Aaron and the screaming woman while the man with the rifle yelled at him in Arabic, "Back away or I will shoot you dead!"

He put his hands higher and did as he was told until he was against the fence of the hay bin. The woman cried, teeth chattering, her eyes rolling in her head as she was taken outside. The girl, her round, dark eyes fixed on Aaron, stayed put.

"Shoot him, Father," she said.

Aaron's eyes went to the gun. "Go, Daughter. Help your mother."

The girl hesitated, then left the barn.

"Who are you? What do you want here?"

"Aaron Schwartz. I am from Jerusalem. I got caught in the storm and took refuge here. I was under the hay when your wife used the pitchfork, forcing me to grab it. I am sorry I frightened her, but when she started to scream—"

"You put your palm over her mouth." There was a slight smile on his lips. "I saw it from outside the door." He reached over and closed the door, then lowered the rifle. The other men put theirs down as well. "You must promise a gift for her to make things right. We will accept a donkey or a camel."

Aaron bowed, "Upon my word you will have it, but I must go to Jerusalem to purchase such a gift. I have no money."

The man raised his gun but another stopped him.

"Possibly there is another solution. We heard that Jews escaped from the British yesterday. Several of the English soldiers were wounded, one killed. You are one of these escapees?" This one spoke in Hebrew, and the others deferred to him.

"Yes."

"And the others?" the man on the left said.

"They had other plans."

"The radio says they are ETZEL. Are you also ETZEL?"

"No, I am Haganah."

It was hard to tell if the man was really smiling, if any of them were, behind the heavy moustache of the Druze, their eyes in shadow.

"Not everyone in this village likes your Haganah. But those who don't are few. We will be back soon with food."

The door opened and they left before Aaron could think or react. Finally he pulled up a small stool the woman had used to milk the goats, lifted the milk pail from the ground, and began milking the nearest goat. When he had some in the bottom of the bucket, he raised it to his lips and took a drink. As the minutes passed his anxiety increased. Looking between the cracks of the barn he could see someone standing near the house across the barnyard. He opened the door a crack and took a better look. His host was standing near the corner talking to several other men. After a moment of argument, they all came toward the barn, rifles cradled in their arms. He slipped atop the gate to the hay bin just as the door opened. The room filled with men of similar height and appearance as his host. In the dim light, he found it difficult to pick the man out of the crowd.

"Instead of a donkey or a camel, we ask that you take us to one of your leaders. We wish to join forces with them against the Arabs." The man who spoke was the one who had proposed a different bargaining in the beginning.

Aaron slipped off the rail. "Wait a minute." He paused, thinking. "You want to fight with us? And if I take you to someone who can make such a deal, you will forget my intrusion?"

"Yes."

"Why are you so anxious to fight? You're in no danger now."

"Come," Hassan said. "We will show you." The group turned and marched out, Aaron following. They went down a side street until they were on the edge of the town, turning heads the whole way. He was an outsider—a tall, obviously Jewish outsider with no moustache and no white turban—and most took note. He wondered if any Arab supporters were among those who did.

They continued through the trees until they reached an outcrop that overlooked Haifa and its port. There was smoke rising from the oil refinery.

"Two nights ago, Jews of ETZEL attacked Tira south of us. They killed ten villagers. Last night the same men set off bombs at the oil refinery killing six more. That set off immediate riots in the refinery itself and 39 Jews were murdered. The Haganah retaliated, firing on buses that carried workers to their homes. I do not know how many more died, but of this I am sure—both sides will escalate, and we will have war in this region."

Another man spoke. "We do not like the Husseinis. They have tried to take away our most holy site, Jethro's tomb, and force us to worship as they worship. We would prefer an alliance with the new Jewish government, but they must guarantee that they will protect our villages and give us rights equal to any Jew in your new state."

His host spoke again. "We know the Arab states plan to send a volunteer army from Damascus. We have sent men to spy on them.

We will know when they come into Palestine, and we will fight them if they come here, but only if we have these guarantees."

Aaron couldn't believe his ears, his good fortune overwhelming. But he continued to keep his face passive. "Has any of the volunteer army crossed the border?"

The two men looked at one another, then nodded. "As a sign of good faith we will tell you where they are, but only when we speak with your leaders and have their word."

Aaron smiled. "How long will it take to get us to Jerusalem?"

"We can be there tonight."

Aaron stretched forth his hand to shake. "You have a deal."

* * *

Aaron was dressed like his four companions, his moustache made from goat's hair and glued to his skin, making him itch horribly. His lips and nose were constantly doing a little dance in an effort to scratch the itch away. His host sat next to him in a beat up German car that had more rust than metal, four bald tires, and a motor that spewed a dark gray cloud behind them thick enough to hide their vehicle from anything that followed.

They neared the village of Tira and the two men in the front seat readied the two sten guns they carried—weapons purchased only yesterday from Arabs deserting the same village for fear the Jews might return. The place was nearly empty, the houses mostly destroyed by explosive charges and fire. ETZEL had left their mark, and nearly 60 people had died from it. He thought about Martin and Yitzhak Solomon, the two he had seen die in Jerusalem. Maybe things weren't worse in the Old City after all.

They passed along the highway without trouble, reaching Khirbat Shalun by midafternoon. The car radiator was beginning to steam, and they pulled over to a spring to fill it and have something to eat.

Hassan brought out cheese and bread, and they sat on rocks near the spring to eat. Aaron looked at the ruins on the hill. Ancient Shiloh, the place where the Ark of the Covenant was kept until captured by the Philistines who returned it when plagues helped change their mind. It was from Shiloh that the Ark went before the children of Israel into battle and gave them victories, at least according to the Torah record.

"You wish for another Ark," Hassan said, cutting off a piece of cheese with a knife.

"I have a friend who tells me it wasn't the Ark but Jehovah who won those battles."

"Allah, Jehovah, it is the same. The One God went before Israel and delivered her from her enemies when she was worthy." He chewed the cheese. "That is the problem with your new Israel. They are not worthy."

"That seems to have been the story for more than 2000 years. We're never quite good enough to win Jehovah's approval."

"God's will is a mysterious thing, but just because it does not match my own does not mean it ceases to be His."

"And His reasoning for six million butchered Jews?" questioned Aaron.

"That is another thing about God's will—men seldom understand it. They do not see things as He does, therefore they cannot understand."

"You're beginning to sound like a friend of mine."

"And this friend, is he a wise man?"

"In everything but religion, I suppose he is."

"He is either wise or unwise. Wisdom does not play games with a man's character. Do not let your own doubts get in the way of his wisdom, my young friend. When you do, your own ignorance stifles real understanding." He slid off the rock and started for the car. Aaron followed.

They drove into Ramallah a little after dark. The place was a beehive of Arab activity, and Aaron dutifully noted the roadblocks, uniforms, and numbers of armed men he saw in the town. As they reached the central square, a large bonfire burned in the middle of a rally. The driver pulled the car over and shut it off, the steam indicating a need for more water. While the driver went for some, Hassan and his son Ragheb neared the chanting men in the street, curious as to what was happening. Aaron stayed put, "Death to the Jews!" repeated over and over again giving him the chills.

He saw the small convoy of cars and jeeps enter the square from the street to his left, saw the crowd turn and stare at the man in the blue and white checkered kaffiyeh sitting in the passenger seat, and heard the shrill undulating battle cries of the Arabs pierce the night air. As the car came to a stop, the man stood and waved as the crowd took a new chant—"*Abou Moussa! Abou Moussa!*" Aaron was fascinated by the adoration of these men for the stocky, round-faced man in a brown business suit—Abdul Khader Husseini.

Khader got out of the car into a sea of outstretched hands. The atmosphere was electric, an almost ecstatic euphoria that Khader could bend to his will. Mesmerized by it, Aaron got out of the car and stood on the trunk so as to see better. Khader moved to a makeshift stand on the far side of the street, climbed up, and held his hands above his head, increasing the volume of the chant and shrill battle cries to fevered pitch. After a moment, he motioned for them to quiet down so that he could speak. It went dead silent.

"Arabs of Palestine," he said, "I have come to fight with you."

The crowd erupted. He quieted them.

"To conquer with you."

Another eruption. Then quiet again.

"And to die with you!"

The place was pandemonium, the men jumping up and down, the shrill sounds emanating from them in an endless cacophony of noise. It was then that Aaron realized what he must do. Khader was only fifty yards away. Khader! The one man whose death would hurt the guerillas the most. He must find a way to stop him. Now! Here! Tonight!

He looked about. There were weapons everywhere, slung over shoulders, held in one and two hands, tucked in belts, hung from a string around men's necks—rifles and pistols, large and small, old and new. He only needed one.

Jumping down from the car, he walked resolutely toward the crowd with his heart pounding, the blood coursing through his veins hot and violent. Pushing into the crowd, he found a man with his weapon in his belt, pulled it free, and faded away in the crowd without the victim even noticing. He pushed and shoved his way toward the stand, his eyes set on Khader who continued his speech, each sentence now punctuated by the sound of weapons exploding into the air. Thirty feet, twenty-five, twenty. He was close. The crowd was tighter here, bodies packed together like dates in a tin can. He pushed and shoved, was pushed, was shoved, jostled, gained ground, lost ground, gained it again. Fifteen feet. He pulled the gun up with the next punctuation of Khader's sentence, fired it in the air, felt the recoil, and knew the weapon was ready. He aimed but couldn't keep the barrel steady. He tried to get his balance, tried to aim again. The sights were knocked left, then right. Sweat poured down his face as Khader made his last grand statement and the crowd erupted. Guns fired, nearly deafening him. He took a last aim as Khader turned his back.

The bullet launched from the barrel, but Aaron knew immediately the trajectory was wrong. It hit another man in the shoulder, and he went down next to Khader. Pandemonium struck the crowd as everyone realized he was struck by a bullet. Two men grabbed Khader and took him to the ground, covering him with their bodies as the crowd fled for cover and cries of "The Jews! The Jews!" sliced through the night air. Aaron kept his head, dropped the gun to the ground, and flowed with the crowd that was breaking back the way he had come. He was at the car in only seconds, his companions waiting. There were men running everywhere, looking, searching for anyone who looked out of the ordinary, who looked Jewish. The driver knew that to drive away now would show the obvious, and Hassan told them all to get out of the car and walk north. Each obeyed, and shortly they were a full block away from their vehicle. They turned right, went to a small inn, entered, and found seats at a table. Hassan was calm; the rest, including Aaron, tried to control their shaking limbs. Hassan ordered dinner. When the waitress was gone, he turned to Aaron.

"That was a brave thing you did, but foolish, very foolish. They will tear this town apart looking for you, and they will search everyone for Arab papers. You have none."

Aaron nodded, attempting to rise from his chair. "You're right. We should separate before I get you killed."

Hassan grabbed his arm and gently pulled him down. "Sit, fool. We know this town. Without us you will be discovered immediately, and your torture will make you wish you were back in the hands of the Nazis."

The others wiped their brows, scowling at him but saying nothing. When the food came, Hassan told them to eat whether they had the stomach or not, and as they finished, he ordered the driver to go and get the car. "If they question you, show them your papers. They will not detain you because you are my son."

"You are the sheik, the Mukhtar of Daliyat," Aaron said in sudden realization.

"This is so, but if I am found with the attempted assassin of Abdul Khader, it will mean more pain than even his assassin will receive."

The enormity of his attempt began to sink in. Time passed slowly while they waited for the car to pull up in front of the inn and the driver to come to the door. Hassan paid for the meal and they exited the building. Moments later they were limping for the edge of Ramallah on four of eight cylinders. As they turned onto the main road, they saw a roadblock of a dozen vehicles and at least a hundred men wielding weapons. As they watched, a man was pulled from his vehicle, thrown to the ground, punched and kicked, then dragged toward a small building on their left. Realizing they would never make it through, Aaron opened the car door and got out, slamming it shut, even as Hassan protested.

"Meet me on the outskirts of the town. If I am not there in an hour, I am a dead man. Contact Jack Willis and let him know. He's an officer at Bevingrad." Before Hassan could protest further, Aaron headed to the town, hoping he would see them again.

* * *

Aaron's moustache slipped off as he turned into a narrow street lined with small Arab homes of mud brick covered with stucco. He caught it and attempted to get it to stick again. But the sweat flowing down the side of his face in small rivulets would not allow it, and he stuck it in his pocket.

The street was quiet except for the barking of dogs and the sound of crying babies. A door slammed and someone cursed in Arabic, then two men came running toward him talking in excited tones. Aaron stepped into the narrow space between two buildings as they neared and watched them dash by. He stayed put, trying to catch his breath, the sounds of chaos in the distant center of town. He had run, walked, and trotted through narrow streets for the past thirty minutes, avoiding most people and hiding from others. So far, no one had stopped him or questioned his right to be there, even though he was dressed as a Druze and there were few of them in Ramallah. This alone was a miracle.

He peered from his hiding place, listened, and wondered how long before they would start a house-to-house search. He had made so many twists and turns he wasn't sure where he was in relation to where he needed to be. One thing he did know was he did not have long before Hassan would give up on him and head for Jerusalem. But without his moustache and a desire to press his luck in Druze clothing, he needed a new disguise.

He slipped from the crack and walked cautiously down the narrow street. Ancient cobblestone snaked between rows of houses two stories high with small courtyards. The windows had no glass, only shutters, most of which were closed against the cold winter air. He could hear activity—voices, the clatter of dishes, children playing, goats or sheep bleating, and chickens clucking. Most prominent were the cries of several babies and the voices of mothers giving instructions. There were few voices of men—they were off to the rally and were now helping hunt for him. He was nearly to the end of the street when he heard vehicles behind him. He turned and saw them coming to a halt at the other end. The headlights revealed men scrambling from vehicles and flowing into the street. A search party.

Darting into the courtyard of the first house on his right where he was out of sight, he peeked around the corner. They were going house-to-house. He had maybe ten minutes before they would reach him, but going back into the street meant definite capture. He looked at the house, its shuttered windows dark. He listened. No sound. Trying the door latch, it gave and he lifted it, then stepped inside, his heart racing. Glowing embers in the fireplace revealed the objects in the room—a table, chairs, cupboard for sleeping mats, and a stairway that led to the second floor. Two small children were curled up under blankets near the fire, fast asleep.

He tiptoed to the stairs cautiously and went up. The upper room was open to the lower floor so that it could be heated and light from the fire below flickered off the ceiling. No one was sleeping on the floor as he had expected, the room empty except for a bed and a clothing cabinet. He went to the cabinet, opened one of the doors, and shuffled through the clothes. A red-and-white checked kaffiyeh lay folded on the shelf. He quickly unfolded it. Removing the white turban of the Druze, he donned the freshly laundered kaffiyeh, wrapping it as best as he remembered around his head, hanging a corner over his left shoulder, the other over the right but high enough to cover his lower face. He then searched for other clothing, found some that were a little big but would do, and quickly changed. Sensing someone at the front of the house, he quickly closed the door to the cabinet and frantically searched for someplace to hide. His eyes fell on the narrow ladder attached to the wall in one corner and then found the trap door in the ceiling. He scurried up as someone entered the house and closed the door. He pushed it up and to one side as a child spoke and a woman's voice responded. He quickly climbed the last few rungs of the ladder, slipped onto the roof and closed the door behind him, staying on his knees to listen through the leather covered door. Nothing.

Getting to his feet but keeping low by hunching his back, Aaron went to the edge of the roof. Looking over he could see the search party below. Would they come to the roof? The question was answered almost immediately as a man appeared on the roof two houses away. Shocked, Aaron hesitated then went to his belly against the short wall that jutted above the roof.

"Hey! Hey!" the man yelled. "Saad, there is someone on the roof! Two houses away! Hey!" he yelled again. "You! Get up, get up!"

Aaron got to his knees and scrambled toward the back of the house as he heard running in the street. A gun fired, the bullet piercing the short wall just above him. He got to his feet, ran the last few yards, put one foot on the short wall and launched himself across the narrow space between houses and onto the roof of the next. Another bullet struck to his left as he zigged right and jumped for a house farther away. He leapt roof to roof, house to house, ducking and turning, fleeing to a house that had a lower section attached. He hit the ground at a dead run and ran through a maze of streets until he finally turned into the main road and was confronted by the roadblock for a second time. He saw a truck just pulling away from the curb and ran for all he was worth until he could grab the side and lift himself into its back.

Rolling forward, he bumped into someone, looked up and saw a man standing above him. They looked at one another for a moment, then the man went to the back of the truck and pulled down the tarp covering before turning around and facing Aaron.

"You are the one everyone looks for," he said in Arabic.

Aaron didn't answer as the man took two steps and pulled back the kaffiyeh. "You look Arabic, but you are a Jew. I can see it in your eyes."

Perhaps the man was in his middle forties, and he was large enough that Aaron knew it would be futile to run.

"I could become a wealthy man by turning you in," he said.

"You will have to kill me to get me there."

White teeth showed as the Arab smiled. "Yes, I believe you. And Khader would never pay me anyway." He paused long enough to pull back the tarp at the corner of the truck and look out. "We will be outside the city in five minutes, but there is a checkpoint between us and your freedom." He picked up a hammer and gently began knocking off the lid to a fifty-gallon barrel. "I work in Jerusalem. The pay is not great, but the man I work for is a big man—a member of the Arab Higher Committee—and no one dares to search his goods. It allows me to smuggle some things from Jordan that I sell and that provide me a good living." When it was off he pointed. "It is your turn to be smuggled. Get in."

Aaron looked at him in disbelief. "I am over six feet tall. I cannot—"

"It is either there or torture and death. Get in," he said firmly. "Now, before we get close enough to the roadblock that the guards search for you and shoot us both."

"How do I know you won't turn me over to this boss of yours?"

"You don't, but I will tell you something even my boss does not suspect. In 1936–39 I fought with those who opposed the Husseinis. Khader's men killed my father and brother. I have no love for him and was happy to hear someone tried to throttle him."

Aaron searched his eyes for a lie but found none. He stepped over the edge of the barrel and lowered himself inside, taking a deep breath as he did, the overpowering smell of fish all around him. He stood up. "That's awful! What—"

The man put a hand on Aaron's head and pushed down. "Sardines. Now get in! We are nearly there."

Aaron wriggled down as a sudden panic filled his gut. He hated tight spaces, was claustrophobic. He fought upward against the strong hand, trying to get out. The fist came out of nowhere, and he felt the crack of it against his jaw. His knees went weak, the air emptied from his lungs, and blackness filled his brain as he sunk unconscious into the barrel.

* * *

Aaron awoke looking up at the green tarp of the truck, the strong smell of fish in his nostrils. He blinked several times, wincing at the ache in his jaw. That was twice in the last two days he had been knocked about in the back of a truck. It was getting old.

He sat up, cognizant of the Arab sitting with his back against the side of the truck, a smile on his face.

"How do you feel?"

"How do I look?"

"Like death visited you but threw you back," he said.

"That's how I feel." He pushed himself across the floor until his own back rested against the side of the truck opposite the Arab. "Where are we?"

"Nearly to Jerusalem. I have wanted to do that for some time."

"Do what?"

"Hit a Jew. It felt very good."

"I'm glad I could oblige."

"You steal our country."

Aaron nodded. "What is your name?"

"It is better that you do not know. I have told my brother to drive along St. George Street. You can get out there and cross into your Jewish New City without trouble."

Aaron nodded again. "Thank you. And you?"

He did not answer but got to his feet and pulled the tarp aside. "We are nearly there. He tied back the tarp with a piece of rope. "We will not fully stop. As your people say, *Lahitraot.* Goodbye, Jew. I am only sorry you were not a better shot."

"Yeah, me too." Aaron got to his feet and stood at the back, recognizing St. George Street as they turned onto it. He stretched out a hand to shake. The Arab took it. "I hope we never see one another again until this war is over, then maybe . . . maybe we can be friends."

"Yes, maybe. *Adnan Marzouk*. If you need something smuggled after the war," he shrugged, "find me."

Aaron sat down, then jumped to the road, watching as the truck moved farther away. The Arab disappeared as he let down the tarp. Stepping onto the sidewalk, Aaron realized the street had little traffic. St. George Street was quickly turning into a no-man's-land between Jewish West Jerusalem and Arab East Jerusalem. He saw the Bevingrad compound and the central prison he had left just yesterday and turned west toward Jaffa Road, slipped into a shop he knew, and greeted the owner.

"*Shalom*," he said removing the kaffiyeh. The surprised shop-keeper smiled when he saw who it was. Five minutes later Aaron left the shop without his Arab garb, wearing the black suit of an orthodox Jew. It was better attire for the Jewish part of town. The only thing he hadn't been able to change was the strong smell of fish.

He strode to Jaffa Road and turned south. As he neared the Bevingrad compound, he switched to the opposite side of the street, while wondering what had happened to Hassan and his companions. If they went to Jack as he'd instructed, told him their story, he would have taken them to Haganah headquarters. He turned west on Mahmillah Street until he reached King George the Fifth Avenue and walked to the Jewish Agency building. He saw Hassan's old car parked in the compound as he entered the gate, immediately relieved that they had made it. At the front door, the guard asked him for ID. He removed his hat.

"Hello, Shmuel," he said with a smile.

"Aaron! What the devil? Rumor has it you're dead. How . . . Oy, you stink of fish!"

"Sardines. The latest rage in men's cologne. Jack Willis and my Druze friends, where are they?"

"In Amir's office."

"Thanks," he said putting his hat back on. He walked down the hall, relieved, tired, and eager for at least two days of sleep. He wondered what day it was and tried to count them back. December 23. It was a nice time to be home.

SEE CHAPTER NOTES

CHAPTER 19

Ephraim and Hannah each carried one of the twins as Beth and David followed them across the Courtyard of the Church of the Nativity in Bethlehem. Last year the place had been packed with people, mostly pilgrims who had come for mass and the celebration of the birth of Christ. This year there were few people and even fewer foreign pilgrims who dared venture into this troubled land.

Jack had tried to dissuade them from coming as well.

"Bethlehem is Arab Christian, the roads arenae safe, an' the mercenaries of Haj Amin have made it clear by continued attacks that they arenae honorin' the Jewish and Christian holidays of Hanukkah and Christmas," he had argued. "Surely the Son of God wouldnae want ye tae endanger yerselves an' the children when ye can celebrate His birth 'round a tree at home just as easy."

"We have no tree," she had said with a wry smile.

"Ye know what I mean, Hannah Daniels. 'Tis too dangerous."

"Haj Amin must maintain good relations with the Arab Christians if he wants their support for his war. He won't desecrate Christmas with a foolish attack on their holy sites. Nor does he wish to engender the wrath of the world community by killing pilgrims who have come here to worship. And don't forget, the Lord Governor has announced your army will be out in force as well, protecting worshipers and keeping us blimey Jews from killing Arabs, so it seems to me that the safest places in Palestine right now are places like the Church of the Nativity."

"We both know ye cannae trust the Lord Governor," he said in frustration, "But e'en if he keeps his word this time, why take the chance?"

"Because if I let fear dictate to me what I do today, it will dictate what I do tomorrow and the next day and the next, until it rules my life and I cannot function. That was Hitler's greatest weapon against my people, and now it is Haj Amin's. I refuse to let it be used on me again," Hannah responded.

He then turned to Ephraim for some kind of support, found none, and threw his arms in the air, finally agreeing to come along on one condition—he could bring other soldiers with him. Hannah had been more than happy to agree. Having one or two others accompany them on such a special occasion would be even better.

One or two? The "other" soldiers included a convoy of armored vehicles that acted as protection while they drove from Jerusalem to Bethlehem and would escort them on their return along with six well-armed bodyguards to see them across the courtyard to their destination. It was a bit much, but if it was their ticket to Bethlehem, it was worth it.

As they crossed the courtyard and Jack and his men surrounded them, Hannah noted that other British soldiers were scattered about watching for trouble. Four searched worshipers for weapons before they entered the low door to the Church of the Nativity.

"Are they your doing as well?" she said with a wry smile.

"They had already been assigned when I made my arrangements, but it is comfortin' is it nae?"

Walking across the courtyard, Hannah wished that Naomi and Aaron could have come, but Naomi was busy in Tel Aviv on assignment, and Aaron was supposed to be lying low until things could be worked out with the British or they left the country, whichever came first.

She had been in the middle of a good cry when Jack knocked on the door, engaged them in Aaron's saga and reassured them their erstwhile son was in good hands. Then the tears had really flowed.

Jack explained that Hassan had just been telling him and Agency members that Aaron had probably been captured when the boy had walked into the room, turning their wake into a celebration. After that, there had been a clamor to get Hassan to Tel Aviv to meet with Ben-Gurion and get Aaron under cover until he could get an unlikely pardon from the British or they left the country. With Lassiter still unpunished and leading a command in the Old City, Aaron wouldn't be visiting the family anytime soon—no sense giving the British a second chance to send him to Acco.

Hannah looked up at the three crosses crowning the church and belonging to the three denominations that shared it. Above the central gable was the Greek Orthodox cross, to the left, the square Jerusalem cross of the Franciscans, and to the right, the cross belonging to the Armenians. In a grotto underneath this church was the purported birthplace of Jesus, the Messiah.

They had come here for the first time more than a year ago, and though the church was a bit gloomy, they had a good experience talking about the birth of the Messiah and the events surrounding it. She wished to make it a tradition, even though Beth and David were a bit reluctant, unimpressed by the religious paraphernalia in the grotto. All of this clutter distracted them from any spiritual feelings, but Hannah wanted to make it a tradition and had insisted they return. She glanced at Beth and David. It was obvious they were not pleased.

"This way," Ephraim said, smiling and turning left.

Hannah hesitated. "Where are you going? The church . . ."

"Humor me," he said continuing to move across the flagstones. She shrugged and started after him, David and Beth suddenly hurrying to catch up. They crossed the courtyard of a second church, St. Catherine's, then went inside.

"Wait here," Ephraim said. He started for a door to their left as the rest of them watched the mass already in progress.

St. Catherine's stood on the foundations of a twelfth-century Crusader church, but it really didn't offer anything other than great acoustics. Hannah wondered why Ephraim had brought them here.

He returned with a priest who carried a large key in his hand. As they reached Hannah, Ephraim introduced him as Father Michael. He shook each hand and then prompted them to please be quiet before telling them to follow him. He went to a set of stairs and started down as Hannah pulled on Ephraim's coat sleeve, questioning the detour. He only put a finger to his grinning lips and let her go first down the narrow steps. When she reached the bottom, Father Michael opened a heavy door, reached inside, and pulled a large candle from a hidden ledge. He lit the candle and handed it to Hannah, then motioned her to enter.

She found herself in a grotto and held the candle high as the others joined her. Father Michael gave Ephraim the key and Ephraim locked the door.

"What is this place?" Jack asked.

"This is a grotto dedicated to Joseph, the earthly father of Jesus. That one is dedicated to innocents killed by Herod, and one further back is supposed to be the place where St. Jerome, bishop of Bethlehem in the fourth century, wrote the Latin Vulgate. Down that way is a door that leads into the grotto of the nativity, but Brother Michael says it could actually have been any of these three," Ephraim said.

"And without all that junk," Beth whispered.

"Amazing," said one of the soldiers.

Ephraim handed them each a candle and motioned for them to follow him. They went through a smaller grotto and into a room with a very high ceiling.

"St. Jerome's office," he said.

Hannah liked the place immediately because it was devoid of the endless paraphernalia of the traditional grotto. It was quiet, and she felt comfortable there.

"I like this place best. The stone walls remind me of Jerome's dedication to Christ. Though the Church was in full apostasy by that time, Jerome and many others did their best to hold on to what remained. Such tenacity must have been inspired, because without it we wouldn't have a Bible or any other scripture today."

Rough-hewn benches smoothed with wear stood along the walls with a rock altar at one end. Ephraim placed his candle on the altar and the others found several niches and rock abutments for theirs. Each sat down to take it in.

"Where do those steps go?" Beth asked, referring to a set of steps leading directly from the grotto to the courtyard above. Bars covered them at both ends.

"To the courtyard outside St. Catherine's," Ephraim answered. "The church had them barred to maintain some sanctity here. The priest says it also allows for air movement, keeping the grottos ventilated."

"Quite a place," Jack said.

Hannah was amazed. It was so peaceful here, and the spirit so strong. "A much better place than the Grotto of the Nativity," she said softly. "Thank you, Ephraim. This is a very nice surprise."

Ephraim smiled back as Beth removed several candles from her pocket and placed them on the bench beside her. There were nine, the same ones used for Hanukkah, which had ended only a few days earlier.

Hannah tried to meld the two holidays together somewhat by teaching the children the important parts of each. The word Hanukkah means *dedication,* and to celebrate the holiday was to dedicate oneself to being a better Jew—more kind, more willing to pursue the highest ideals of Judaism. Coming just before Christmas as it did, it gave her the chance to teach them the importance of not only being good Jews but good Christian Jews, more dedicated to Christ and his gospel as well as to the Torah, more dedicated to teaching others and living the gospel in everyday life.

But for their family it was more than that this year. Hanukkah, or the Feast of Lights as it was called for generations, came out of the revolt of the Maccabees centuries earlier in which they won back Israel and rededicated the temple to God. As they now fought to regain their homeland again, the Feast of Lights seemed to have added meaning for them, and when coupled with a belief in Christ as a Messiah who had come to this land and would come a second time, it gave them all even greater joy.

Beth pulled the menorah from her bag and put a candle in each of the nine places. The shortest was on the left end, the longest on the right. Eight nights ago they had used the ninth candle to light the first of the remaining eight which represented the eight days of Hanukkah and the eight days before Christmas. Each night they lit another until they were now ready to light all of them. Each night they read a few more verses about the events surrounding Jesus' birth and talked about the symbolism of the menorah and its lighting in the temple of Herod.

Everyone watched as Beth lit the candles, then listened as David explained to Jack and the soldiers what they meant. His explanation was brief but clear and had all of them nodding when he was finished. One by one, Brother Michael's candles were blown out, leaving the grotto to dance with the flickering light of those in the menorah.

Hannah read Psalms 113–118—the Hallel—that had been read during Hanukkah for centuries. The custom originated in temple times and was sung when the Paschal Lamb was sacrificed and then eaten during the celebration of Pesach or Passover. It seemed particularly appropriate to Hannah because she had come to see Christ as that sacrifice. More than anything else she had come to understand in her new faith, this was the most comforting—He had come, made the sacrifice, and would come again.

Ephraim pulled out his scriptures and moved closer to the candles before turning to the story in Luke. His voice echoed off the walls and ceiling, and Hannah relished the moment. Was this the place where Mary gave birth to Jesus? Perhaps, but looking into Jacob's eyes, she could feel what Mary must have felt that night. A son. A glorious, wonderful son, born in the stale, cool air of a cave lit by candles and warmed by hay. Mary had snuggled her son to her breast and looked into his dark eyes for the first time. What a peaceful, wonderful moment it must have been.

Her mind rushed ahead of Ephraim's reading, past the birth to the temple and Simeon and Anna's pronouncements, then fleeing the country to Egypt, returning only when Herod the Great was dead. She glanced toward the doorway that led to the grotto dedicated to the innocent children slain by a power-hungry, threatened, insane Herod. What had the magi who had come to honor him thought after realizing they had been responsible for those deaths? What had Mary thought when she heard of Herod's insane act? Oh, how it must have broken her heart!

She wiped away the tears from her eyes. She had read those stories so many times in the last two years, but this was the first time that it had hit her so hard.

Jacob's fussing brought her to her feet, and she rocked him so as not to detract from this special feeling in the grotto. Ephraim had everyone's attention—Beth and David sat quietly, their eyes wide with wondering awe and completely different from last year's urgent wishes to go home; Jack and his hardened soldiers, their attention total, their weapons discarded. Possibly for the first time they were feeling what happened, not just hearing it.

Ephraim finished and closed the book. There was a thick, comfortable silence in the room. No one moved, no one spoke.

In the silence Ephraim began singing "Silent Night." Beth joined in first, then David, then the others, some of whom had to clear their throats. She tried, but the lump in her throat simply wouldn't let her, the soft gentle words tugging at her heart strings with such force that she couldn't speak.

Ephraim glanced her way with a smile in his eyes, then looked away as his own voice cracked with emotion. As they finished the second verse, she was able to join in. Her cracking voice didn't allow for much harmony, but by the time they were finished, it didn't matter. Everyone was off-key.

Jack chuckled, "That was the worst rendition of that song I have ever been privileged tae hear," he said.

"And yet the best," said another.

Nods all around. As the moment gently settled over them, David pulled out a small box and handed it to Ephraim.

"For you and Mum, from Bebe and me," he said. "We wanted t-to g-give it to you here."

Ephraim gave him a smile and a thank you, then opened the box. Inside was a carving made of olivewood. It was of a man and woman standing side-by-side, their arms around one another, their eyes fixed on some distant point, as if watching for someone. The man wore a baseball cap and a pilot's jacket and Hannah immediately recognized it as Ephraim. The shortness of body and the round face of the woman revealed it must be her. Tears sprang to her eyes at the beauty of the carving, the wood selected carefully so as to accent the clothing while leaving the faces clear.

Ephraim cleared his throat. "It . . . it is the most beautiful piece I've ever seen," he said with reverence. "Thank you, David. Beth. Both of you."

"I learned t-to do it at Ben Ghehazi's shop. He c-carves, you know, and t-teaches others, b-but I had to finish it myself once the Quarter was c-cut off from his place. Beth sanded and p-polished it."

"Thank you, both," Hannah said, taking the precious item gently in her hands.

"Very nice," Jack said. The others proclaimed the work as fine as Ephraim had pronounced it, and even better. Hannah placed it carefully inside the box as Ephraim pulled two packages from his pocket and handed them to David and Beth. Beth turned the still sleeping Joseph over to Ephraim and still had hers open first. She found a beautiful gold locket on a gold chain inside and her mouth dropped open as she pressed on the small latch and it sprung open to reveal a miniature photo of her real mother and father. It was obvious she was pleased with the gift and quickly embraced Ephraim.

"This is my mother's. But how did you find it?" she quizzed. "How . . ."

"Joseph. You remember him?"

"The German who helped you in Berlin? The one who sent us the pictures of the church and the members there?"

"Yes. He is with West German intelligence now, and I asked him to find out about your mom and dad." He reached inside his jacket and withdrew an envelope. "That tells their story and how the locket was found. I am only sorry that they didn't survive."

She nodded, then stepped back and sat down, her eyes on the picture in the locket, her hand clutching the letter.

David had listened to it all and neglected to finish opening his own package. Now he quickly tore into the brown paper, removing the lid of the cardboard box. Inside he found a familiar, worn copy of the Torah.

"Papa!" he said aloud, his eyes wide. He lifted the book and opened the back cover to find the inscription he knew was there—*To Ezra Schwartz, all my love, Deborah.* Reverently he thumbed through the pages of his father's Torah. There were notations in the columns, written in Hebrew, and segments of scripture were highlighted. His father had read to his family from this book so many times, the pages were worn and a bit stained with the oil from his hands. David lifted it to his nostrils and the sweet smell of his father's cologne seemed to permeate his senses.

"Joseph also?" David asked.

"Yes. It was found in the wall of your home where your family lived before your parents were killed. Your father must have hidden it there. After the war, the house was still in tact but in bad need of restoration. During the work, this was discovered and law requires all such things be turned in to the new government. There were several other items that Aaron is getting for Christmas as well. The authorities contacted the Jewish Agency about them and Dov, the man who originally arranged for Hannah to take you out of the country, contacted her through authorities here. We had Joseph retrieve the items for you."

David closed the cover and ran his fingers over it, then he turned and hugged Hannah with all his might, tears running down his cheeks. "*Todah Rabah,*" was all he could say.

The first candle had burned out during the singing of Silent Night and the second gave its last light as David thanked Ephraim.

"I guess we had best be getting' home," Jack said looking at Hannah. "I'm glad we came. A very nice Christmas. Very nice indeed."

The other soldiers agreed as they stood and retrieved their weapons.

"One last item," Ephraim said reaching into his bag. He pulled out small military copies of the Bible for each and handed them to Jack who passed them on, keeping the last for himself. "I have marked the scriptures we read tonight in each of those. It isn't much, but I couldn't think of anything else that made better sense for a night spent in this place."

They each thanked him, and Hannah could see that the gratitude was sincere. There were more good Brits than she had thought.

"Time to go," Ephraim said. The room grew quiet as they relished the last minutes of the night, then gathered their paper, their gifts, and the two children and found their way back to the door, then upstairs. There was a mass going on and they left as quietly as they could. The black sky glittered with stars as they crossed the courtyard and returned to their truck. As the soldiers helped them into the back, then followed, Jack radioed for the escort. A few minutes later they came around the corner and pulled into formation. The fires of Arab camps greeted them along the highway, and in the distance Hannah thought she heard gunfire, but it did not concern her.

She hugged Ephraim, even more grateful for him than ever. The night had given her strength to go on.

CHAPTER 20

Aaron figured Mary would either go to the Church of the Holy Sepulcher or the Garden Tomb. The Church was well within the Arab Quarter and out of his reach; his only chance was if she decided on the Garden Tomb. Though also in East Jerusalem, the British guarded it heavily. After all, it had been discovered by a British Officer and was considered by many Anglicans to be the real burial place of their Lord. They were not about to let it be a battle ground on Christmas.

He still had his British uniform and forged British papers and used them to get through British roadblocks that seemed to be everywhere. He kept a sharp eye out for Lassiter and others who might recognize him. When he finally reached the entrance to the Garden Tomb, he found himself at the end of a line of more than a hundred pilgrims trying to get in.

After nearly half an hour, the Lord Governor arrived in a fancy car and strutted up the narrow street to bypass them all and pay his respects at the tomb. Aaron resisted the urge to confront him about his unfair trial and imprisonment and the lie he told Hannah and Ephraim. As he returned and shook hands with each soldier wishing them a Merry Christmas, Aaron bit his tongue, shook, and let the man get on with his life. No sense pushing his luck.

In another ten minutes, he arrived at the gate and was about to go inside when he saw her at the back of the line, a shawl over her head, her dark eyes and round face as beautiful as ever.

Inside he wandered about, looking for a place to sit where he could watch both the gate and the tomb, while playing with the box in his hands that Ephraim and Hannah had given him. A gift.

Ephraim had told him to find a peaceful place to open it, a place where he could think. It had piqued his curiosity, and he had nearly opened it several times over the last dozen hours, but he decided to wait until coming here, entertaining the hope that he might have Mary there when he opened it. He pulled a second, smaller package from his pocket and stared at it, wondering if it was good enough, if Mary would even take it. He shoved it back in his pocket. He would know in a few minutes.

A group of pilgrims began singing a hymn nearby. "Silent Night." He had heard it a lot around Hannah's place, one of her favorites. He listened, letting the warmth of the tune remind him of last year's Christmas with Hannah and Ephraim while he waited. It was that night that he really understood how deeply rooted Hannah's beliefs had become.

He saw Mary come through the gate and turn to the right. He followed. She reached an open area that faced a mountain with small caves that resembled a skull's eyes and nose. She sat down on part of a long, heavy wooden bench vacated by a young man and proceeded to pray, using her beads. He waited until she finished. When she glanced up, she found him standing a few feet away. At first the look gave him hope, but then it changed to anger and she quickly got to her feet and walked away.

He caught up and gently grabbed her arm. "I owe you an apology," he said.

She stopped and faced him, the crowd mingling around and between them. She stepped back out of the way and he joined her as soon as he could step between two people.

"How does one apologize for blowing up my brothers' business?" she said in a hissing whisper while folding her arms stiffly across her midsection. "Go on, I would like to hear this. It will cost Izaat two thousand British pounds to fix his shop. How does a poor boy like you replace two thousand British pounds?"

Aaron grimaced at the use of the word boy; it stung more than the amount. No matter, he had not come to apologize for blowing up the shop, but for breaking into her home.

"I came to apologize for breaking into your house, not for blowing up your brothers' shop. Your brothers had weapons in the basement, or didn't they tell you?"

She turned away from him. "You did not need to blow up the shop."

"I am a soldier. I did not know but what other weapons were hidden there, and we had no time to search. I had no choice."

She turned away, confused, angry, pleased all at once. Her heart raced and her mind kept pace with it as she tried to decide how to react, how to show him her displeasure without chasing him away. "I did not expect to see you here." It was a lame statement.

"I came to let you know I was sorry for taking liberties with you I had no right to take." He reached in his pocket to retrieve the gift he had brought her, but decided against it. Now wasn't the moment. "You said this is your favorite spot. I know you hold it sacred so I won't burden you with my presence any longer. Please, accept my apology." He started away.

"Wait," she said reactively and with mixed emotions. She couldn't bear to have him leave, though her better judgment screamed otherwise.

He turned back, waiting as people went by, whispering, smiling at what they thought must surely be a lover's spat. It wasn't an unpleasant thought. She grabbed his sleeve and pulled him out of the way. "People are watching," she said, "I don't know what to say to you. You are the most exasperating person I have ever known!" She folded her arms, her face stern with frustration. "Why do you keep insisting that our paths cross when you obviously hate my family and my people? Is this some sort of cruel punishment? A sick way of making me miserable? Why can't you just leave me alone?"

"Because I think I love you," he said without hesitation.

Her mouth dropped open in disbelief, and she was even more flabbergasted. Speechless. Paralyzed.

"I know, I know. We hardly know each other, but from the first time we met, I . . . well, I just haven't been able to stop thinking about you."

Her mouth was dry as cotton and she had to force her tongue from the roof of it. "Do you blow up buildings that belong to all the girls you profess to love?"

He couldn't help the smile. "No, you are the only one."

"You are a sick young man, do you know that?" she said, her heart banging against the inside of her chest, her face flushed.

"There is a cure," he said.

"Shooting you?"

"Well, that wasn't what I had in mind. Would you consider something a little less final, say spending a few minutes with me on this Christmas Day, here, in this place? If you do, I promise I won't blow up any more shops belonging to the Aref family."

"Is your illness contagious?"

"Which one—the insanity or the fact that I might be in love with you?"

She was flattered and blown over by his audacity and directness. It was very outlandish, and yet it made her face burn with pleasure. She turned away as if offended. "You're incorrigible. Do you think I am some teenage girl who can be swept off her feet by your good looks and wild behavior? Now go away. You have made your apology, and we have nothing else to discuss."

She felt him touch her arm and pull lightly, turning her to face him. He had a package in his hand. He opened hers and placed it against her palm. "Merry Christmas." He then touched her cheek with his fingers, his eyes revealing sincere love, before turning away and walking down the path. What foolish words she had spoken to him. What if she never saw him again? But what could she do? The anger, the hate between their people that had existed for so long—no, she mustn't stop him. She . . .

"Most Catholics don't come here," she said matter-of-factly. "We believe the real place of burial is in the Church of the Holy Sepulcher." It was the dumbest thing to say under the circumstances, but her head was empty of anything else. She had to stop him.

He turned back, smiling. "Yes, I know. I am glad that you think it was here. I don't think I could have managed the Church of the Holy Sepulcher without getting a few extra holes in my uniform."

"A British uniform."

"I . . . uh . . . sort of served with the Brigade in Italy. Open the package."

She looked down at the package as if seeing it for the first time, then pulled the pins loose and unfolded the plain white tissue paper from around a small box. Inside she found a gold brooch that depicted a tree of unique design, one she had seen before. "The Tree of Life."

"An ancient motif used in Egypt, ancient Israel, and even in Babylon. They say the idea comes from the Tree of Life in the Garden of Eden. Mum says it represents Jesus and His sacrifice. As a Jew I am a bit skeptical, but I thought . . . as a Christian . . . you . . . ah . . . might like it."

Her face had turned to putty. It was very beautiful. "I like it very much. Thank you."

She removed the brooch and handed it to him. "Will you pin it on my coat, please?" She smiled.

"I'd be honored." He took the pin, unfastened the clasp, and attempted to put the brooch in place. After some fumbling, he finally pierced the fabric well enough to hook the clasp. "There."

"Thank you."

"You're welcome. Is there a chance you'll forgive me, or must I go away brokenhearted?"

"I'll let you know. For now go with me to the tomb. I have come to pay my respects." She put her arm through his, and he felt the warmth of it burn through his jacket and shirt.

They entered the path and fell in line with others waiting to enter the tomb. Aaron had never felt so alive and yet so content, and he hoped each person before them would take forever to pay their respects.

"This cannot work you know," she said.

He didn't answer. He had never felt this way, had never had a formal date, kissed a woman, or even carried on much of a conversation with anyone other than Naomi, and he was at a loss for words to convince her they should at least try. There were barriers, but he had been overcoming barriers most of his life. If a person wanted to survive badly enough, if he wanted a woman like Mary more than he cared about life, what could stop him but death?

"Tell me Aaron Schwartz, do you believe in resurrection?"

Another question out of the blue! The woman was nearly as unpredictable as he was. The difference was his unpredictability was due to lack of social skills while hers was due to a preponderance of them. "Uh, it is hard to think in terms of a resurrection when you aren't sure about the existence of God."

"Did you believe in God before the Nazis?" she asked.

"I was young. The young believe because their parents do. As I grew older I saw no proof for a God, and I see none now."

"Then you are blind."

"What do you mean?"

"I believe, many of these people around you believe, and doesn't the woman you call Mum and her husband believe? Are not all of us proof?"

"The faith of others is not something I can grasp, Mary. It's not real."

"You want scientific proof. I'm sorry, but spiritual things stand in a different realm than science and cannot be proven or disproven thereby."

"That sounds like it's right out of a textbook," Aaron said.

"Perceptive," she smiled. "A professor from Oxford. I attended a colloquium where he spoke, but he is right. God does not dwell in the realm of science. His realm is beyond their ability to discover, at least for now." She pointed to her heart. "God is found here first, then He may appear to us in this world. But He does not need to." She saw the skeptical look on Aaron's face and smiled. "At times it does not seem like enough for me either, but then I come here and my faith is renewed."

"And where does religion work into your faith?"

She smiled. "I'm still working on that. I wish I could tell you that my faith in Catholicism was as strong as it is in the existence of God, but I can't. Not yet."

"Sorry, but I don't have either," Aaron said.

"No?" She reached for the book in his shirt pocket and pulled it out. "This Bible is not here to shield your heart from bullets." She opened it and a confused look crossed her face. "But this is not a Bible."

He grinned at her momentary confusion. "A Book of Mormon."

Recognition replaced the confusion. "The Mormons. I have heard of them—an American religion, very young. We studied them a bit in my comparative religions class. They are intriguing, but my professor called them a cult and said little else."

"The book belongs to a member of the family who thinks I lead a boring life and should read more."

They were at the entrance to the tomb. "And what do Mormons believe about this place and what happened here?" She thumbed through the pages.

"I couldn't say for sure, but Mum and Eph come here. Regardless of what their church might think, to them it seems to be one of the most sacred places on earth."

"And what do you think?" she asked.

He paused as they entered the door to the tomb. "You have to understand something about my new family. We are a conglomerate of survivors brought together by strange circumstances and the Mormon faith of Ephraim Daniels. First Hannah and he marry and she joins his church, not because they married, but because she really believes it. Then they teach my real brother, David, and another survivor Beth, whom I think of as a sister now, about the Church and they really believe it too. Now all four of them are after Naomi, another survivor and member of the family, and me to study it as well. That's why I have that book, and it is also why I am not as sure as I used to be about the nonexistence of God." He took a deep breath. "I said I was having trouble believing in God and all this," he waved his arm toward the tomb, "and that's still true. But a year ago I believed that when you're dead, you're dead. Now I am not sure."

She was amazed by his explanation, but now stood facing the rock platform where Jesus was supposed to have been laid. Now on one knee in a reverential curtsy, she crossed herself and said a quick prayer.

Aaron watched. Her sincerity was evident. She really did believe, maybe not the same as Hannah did, but the dedication was there. She and Hannah, both believers. Why couldn't that be enough proof for him? He supposed it was his skeptical nature, a need to see to believe.

She stood and the crowd moved in a half circle and back toward the door. Mary and Hannah were alike in another way. They both were able to turn a man to mush. Mum had landed Ephraim because of it. Mary deserved an Ephraim, a believer, a man who could raise children in the same faith. That was not Aaron Schwartz. He didn't have enough faith to blow a mustard seed off its branch, let alone move the mountains Mary deserved to have moved. For the first time he realized he was neither worthy of her or the man of her dreams, and it was a gut-wrenching feeling.

Walking toward the gate, he felt the warmth of her hand as it slipped back through his arm and touched the skin at his wrist.

"What is this package?" Mary asked.

Aaron had forgotten he still had it. "A gift from Eph and Hannah."

"It is Christmas. Open it."

They stood aside from the crowd as he pulled the wrapping from the box and removed the lid. Inside was something soft wrapped in tissue paper. He nearly stopped breathing when he saw it.

"My father's prayer shawl. But how is this possible? He was killed in Germany. Everything was taken from us."

Mary stooped down and retrieved a note that had fallen from the tissue. "Possibly this will give you the answer."

Aaron took the note, read it, then explained. "The authorities found it in the ruins of my family's house. They notified the Jewish Agency who sent a letter to Hannah and Ephraim and they had a friend retrieve and send it here, along with my father's Torah. David has the Torah."

There is something else," she said, looking in the bottom of the box. The object was wrapped in a white cloth which Aaron quickly removed. Inside was his father's diary. He gripped it tightly with both hands, unable to speak. His knees gave way as he sat down on a low rock ledge. Mary sat next to him, allowing him time to get control.

Aaron opened the diary and shuffled through the pages. His father hadn't written regularly, only when something important happened to them or their family. The first page of over five hundred thin, parchment pieces began with the entry of his mother and father's wedding; the last was made the night before they died together at the hands of Nazi butchers.

"Everything important to my father is written in this book," he said softly. "I . . . I don't know what to say. I never thought . . . when I saw him shot . . ."

Mary put an arm around him in a sudden desire to give him comfort. "You should stay here and read it, alone. Take care, Aaron. I hope to see you again." Impulsively she kissed him lightly on the cheek then stood and started away, turning back as he instinctively got up. "God lives, and so does your father. Not just in that book, but in another, better place. When you read those words, I think you will know it."

"Mary, I . . . I want to see you again."

"Soon," she smiled. "I left the Old City to stay with my aunt in Katamon, but I always come here when I can. I will leave word with the caretakers when I can come again."

He pulled the Book of Mormon from his pocket and extended it to her. "Take it. I want you to tell me what you think."

She hesitated.

"Please, Hannah and Ephraim have plenty, believe me."

Mary took the book, flipped through its pages, then looked at him again before smiling and turning toward the gate where she soon disappeared in the crowd.

Aaron stood there staring at the book in his hand, at the shawl that lay on the ledge next to him, then at the direction Mary had gone. His heart was full of it all, and he felt unsure of what to do, but he knew it was time to leave. As he was about to get up, a strong hand gripped his arm in a painful squeeze. Aaron looked up and into the eyes of Mary's brother. They were filled with anger and hate enough to burn the flesh from his face, but Aaron kept his eyes empty of emotion while resisting the desire to break the fingers that gripped him. Mary would never forgive him.

"You are British. My sister is Arab. If you see her again, I will cut out your tongue and feed it to the dogs."

Well at least he wasn't here because he knew Aaron was the one who blew up their store. "Rhoui Aref, isn't it?" Aaron said, faking a flawless British accent.

Rhoui's eyes widened with anxiety as they searched for how this British soldier knew of him. He let go of Aaron's arm as if it had bit him.

"Your sister does not require your protection," Aaron said.

Rhoui's face turned to stone. "You know nothing of my sister. You—"

"I," Aaron grasped Rhoui's arm as firmly as Rhoui had gripped his only a minute before, "know she is a grown woman and does not need you watchin' out for 'er like a jealous 'usband." He squeezed harder. "I also know she 'as displeased you because she refused to put 'er 'eadscarf in place at the funeral of your father, and I know this meetin' today displeases you. Because of this displeasure, you will be tempted to mistreat 'er, but I warn you, if you lay even a finger on 'er I will come for you. I and another 'undred of my men, and if we do not kill you we will lock you up in the deepest, darkest cell we 'ave and throw away the key. That is what I know." He let go of the arm.

Rhoui stood, rubbing the ache in his arm and quickly moving away without answering. The look in his frightened eyes told Aaron the hate was still there, hot and burning. Rhoui was insane with it, and Mary was in danger. Aaron quickly gathered up his father's precious items and went for the gate, his heart pounding. He could not bear the thought of what Rhoui Aref might do to his sister and must make sure she was warned. Where was it she was going? Katamon. Stuffing the diary and shawl inside his jacket and under his belt, he hurried to catch the bus.

* * *

Rhoui crossed the street heading toward the bus station. How could she do this? Her rebellion against all things important to their family was beyond reason. And this Brit! He was arrogant and had probably killed Arabs as easily as he killed chickens. How could she even be seen with such a man?

As he arrived at the bus station, he found himself one among several hundred waiting, pushing, and shoving, trying to board the late buses out of the city and back to the villages. Many had come to worship at the churches, even though the overall numbers were much less than previous years. Others were visiting friends for the holidays and now wanted to get home before worse fighting broke out, as they were sure it would.

No sign of Mary. Working his way through the crowd to the buses at the far end of the station, he found the Katamon bus just as it was about to leave. He boarded and searched for Mary but did not find her. Getting off, he turned back toward the Old City. Possibly she had decided to go back to the house for the night and return to Katamon in the morning.

He crossed Suleiman and walked along the Old City wall toward Damascus Gate. He needed to get to his own home soon. His wife and children would worry at his long absence. He had gone to his father's house to borrow some olive oil for cooking when he had seen Mary leaving the Old City. Curious about why she was here instead of in Katamon, he had followed. Her friendship with the soldier had been a complete shock.

He was about to cross the bridge into the Old City by way of Damascus Gate when he saw them. The soldier had a hand on Mary's arm, speaking to her with sincerity.

Rhoui's temper flared, the warning Aaron had given him forgotten as the red heat of anger coursed through his blood. He saw a knife lying on the table of a fruit vendor and, in a state of rage, swept it into his hand as he crossed the last two steps. He raised it above his head to drive it into the back of the British soldier. The man must die.

* * *

Mary saw Rhoui just to the left of Aaron, the knife raised ready to strike. She screamed, grabbed Aaron's arm, and thrust him away, but the knife caught his right arm and sliced a cut an inch long and nearly to the bone. Reactively he yelled out in Hebrew as he spun around to face his attacker, one hand holding the bleeding wound as he kept a wary eye on the sharp blade, Rhoui sweeping it left and right in an attempt to do further damage.

"You are a Jew!" Rhoui screamed. "I heard you! You spoke Hebrew!"

The crowd was backing away, forming a circle around the two men.

"Put the knife away before it gets one of us killed," Aaron said.

The smile broadened. "A Jew in a British uniform." He glanced at his sister. "You fool! You have sullied our name once more!" He swept with the knife and drove Aaron against the crowd who held him up and gave him balance. He sidestepped to the left and away from the stab that followed.

"Idiots! He is a Jew!" Rhoui yelled. He turned on them, threatening with the knife. They gazed on in confusion, his anger and the British uniform getting in the way of belief.

He cried in disgust. "I will finish him myself."

"No, Rhoui," Mary said in firm desperation. "It is not what you think." He threatened her with the weapon but she held her ground. "Rhoui, quit this insanity!"

Rhoui turned away from Aaron for the briefest of seconds, giving him a chance to grab the arm holding the weapon. Wrenching it, he swung Rhoui around and planted a knee in his midsection. As Rhoui bent over in pain and loss of air, Aaron twisted the arm even more and Rhoui's fingers lost their grip, allowing the knife to clatter to the stones. Releasing the arm, Aaron used his fist across the back of

Rhoui's neck and he hit the stone pavement facedown, blood streaming from mouth and nose. He struggled to get to his knees then fell back, moaning.

"Go!" Mary shoved Aaron toward the street, her eyes on the crowd as they whispered with growing animosity. Jew or Brit, they didn't like what had just happened, and she knew that within seconds they would turn on Aaron. "You must get away, now!" she said in low tones. "Go!"

Just then someone yelled "Jew!" then another and another, and the crowd began pushing toward them. Aaron grabbed her arm with his good hand and pulled her quickly after him.

"Stop him!" someone screamed. "The rotten Jew tried to kill one of us! Get him!"

Someone grabbed for Aaron's coat but he brushed the hand aside. Another man stepped in his path and Aaron sidestepped him. A fist came out of nowhere and hit him to the side of the head as the angry crowd turned into a mob. Mary screamed something in Arabic and they backed off except for two men who blocked them.

"Get out of the way!" she said with a determined, bitter tone.

"This one tried to kill an Arab and you protect him?" came the reply. The two men stepped forward menacingly and others followed their lead. Aaron braced himself as the crowd pushed in and the blows started. Both of them were pummeled with a dozen hands all at once as the mob screamed obscenities and curses. Aaron pulled Mary to him, trying to protect her with his body. He felt the blows of heavy instruments now, felt the wood of a club against his skull and arms. He saw a thousand stars as his head exploded in pain, felt he was going down, Mary screaming with fright as he tried to shelter her under him.

The sound of the whistle was loud. A gun was fired and the beating subsided as men ran in every direction. Aaron, barely conscious, allowed Mary to hold him up as she urged him to keep moving. Then strong arms grabbed him and quickly moved him away. Blood from wounds in his skull rolled into his eyes, but he could dimly see an ambulance only feet in front of him, then he was inside. Mary jumped in along with two men and the doors were slammed shut as the army ambulance siren came to life and the vehicle lurched away.

"You're a lucky one," said a British voice. "If we 'adn't been comin' by right then, you'd be beaten to a bloody pulp and thrown in the gutter." He unbuttoned Aaron's coat. "Whoa, what 'ave we 'ere?" He pulled out the shawl and book and held them up. "Souvenirs?"

Mary took them. "They belong to my father. He was carrying them."

The soldier shrugged and poked about Aaron's ribs causing a good deal of pain as a second one wrapped his cut arm in a bandage to stanch the bleeding. "No 'oles, but your skull 'as a crack or two in it."

Soft hands quickly checked the wounds in his head and face. He knew they were Mary's.

"Are you alright?" he asked.

"Yes," she said. Her face came into view above him and she used a wet cloth to clean the blood out of his eyes and from his face as someone else pushed a compress against the cuts in his head. He ached all over, dizzy and sick to his stomach.

"We'll 'ave you to 'ospital in no time," said the British voice. "Doctors can take a good look at you then, see what's broken. 'Old tight. Only the best for a fellow officer."

Aaron couldn't help the smile; the disguise was still working.

"I . . . I'm sorry," he uttered in English, both his head and stomach spinning.

"It is not your fault. Please, don't talk. Rest." Mary replied. Her soft hands caressed his forehead and her words gave warmth to his freezing flesh. He closed his eyes and did as she said, letting the distance gather between them, the sounds of the vehicle, the voices, drifting off into the darkness until he heard nothing at all.

* * *

Several hours later, Aaron found himself lying in a hospital bed, a dim light on the wall near his head. He blinked several times to focus correctly, and then remembered what had happened.

"Mary?"

There was no answer, but a nurse appeared to his left and took his arm, feeling for a pulse. "*Shalom*. Nice to have you back."

"The girl who was with me, where . . ." He tried to sit up, but she put a hand on his shoulder and gently resisted the effort.

"You have bruises, cracked ribs, and a busted skull that warrants a concussion. Somehow you avoided that, but barely. Though it did

take a couple dozen stitches to sew you up. You better take it easy."
She smiled. "The woman is in the women's ward, resting."

"Is she alright?"

"Fine, except for a few broken ribs of her own."

"Any British soldiers waiting to have me hung?"

She chuckled. "You didn't start ranting in Yiddish until after they'd
dropped you into our emergency room. Your little secret is safe with us."

"Then I am at Hadassah Hospital."

"Yes." She finished taking his temperature and giving him some
aspirin, then left. After a moment he forced himself to sit up, wincing
against the pain in his chest. He sat for a moment and noticed the
diary and shawl sitting on the table.

After several shallow breaths, he dropped his feet over the edge of
the bed. More pain hit him in the back of the head, a sledge hammer
beating at his skull that made him close his eyes tight until it
subsided. Once under control, he put his feet on the floor and started
for the door, thankful they had not removed his pants.

Aaron avoided the few nurses at the main desk and soon found
the women's ward. The place was quiet, the dim light making it hard
to see. But when his eyes adjusted, he found only half a dozen beds
with occupants. Mary lay in the third one to his left. She lifted her
head when she felt his presence and gave him a forced smile.

"*Salaam*," she said.

"*Salaam*." He smiled. He touched her hand, and she gripped his.

"How are you feeling?" she asked as she sat up, the bed covers
held tightly around her shoulders.

"Like I was run over by a bus. And you?"

"If you were hit by a bus, I suppose I could claim something in the
range of a donkey cart."

He reacted with a painful laugh. "You look as beautiful as ever."

"That is not a compliment. If this is how I look ordinarily I am a
most ugly woman." She smiled, but it disappeared quickly. "I am
sorry. Rhoui . . . He has a temper. A very bad one."

"It isn't me he will take his wrath out on, it is you," Aaron said.
"You cannot go back to your home, or to Katamon. Not now."

"He will not hurt me. Izaat would kill him if he did."

"And Izaat, will he be pleased with what has happened?"

"He understands Rhoui. I will explain what happened. You need not worry."

The nurse came in, saw the two of them and immediately took him by the arm. "Back to bed with you," she said, pulling him away.

Aaron gave a last smile, then left. A last glimpse caught her smiling at him with a look he had only hoped he would see. It would make sleep come easier.

When he awoke the next morning, he still ached from head to foot, but he was quick to get himself out of bed and to a shower, the pounding in his head erratic but bearable. As he finished, he found Ephraim waiting with fresh clothes.

"I didn't hear about your personal war with half of the Arabs of East Jerusalem until this morning. Would you like to fill me in?"

Aaron told him as he pulled on his clothes. His ribs cried out against it, but he kept on with the help of a grimace or two.

Ephraim couldn't help the smile. "So many lovely Jewish girls, and you have to fall in love with an Arab. Where is she?"

"In the women's ward. Thanks for the gifts by the way. It was an amazing surprise."

"Yes, a bit of a miracle as well. Have you read any of the diary?"

"Not yet. I was about to when all this happened." He was dressed and already limping toward the door when the doctor came through it and redirected him to the bed. "Let's look you over." He got out a light and looked into his eyes, then checked his ribs. "You're going to feel those for a few weeks. Stay away from heavy lifting, and try not to let anyone else beat on you. No concussion, though there should be."

"Thanks." He was already buttoning his shirt.

"If you're looking for the woman," the doctor said, "she was gone before the sun was up."

Aaron hesitated in his step, nodded, and went on through the door at a much slower pace. Ephraim caught up to him in the hall. "Leave it alone, Aaron. She knows what is best right now. You will only make things hard for her."

Aaron knew he was right but only nodded, his heart in his stomach. Somehow, sometime, he would find her again, and this time he would not let her go.

CHAPTER 21

January 3, 1948

Jewish intelligence work was fascinating, and Naomi loved it from the start. She had developed a quick intellect and intuitive powers surviving the camps of Nazi Germany, then the hills of Italy as she led illegal immigrants around British patrols. These made her a natural, and she was quickly accepted into SHAI, her country's new intelligence organization.

"Naomi what do you think?"

Naomi was snapped out of her thoughts with the question from SHAI leader David Sheal'tiel. During the month of December, Haj Amin's Palestinian Arab fighters had openly attempted to take territory in the cities of Jewish Palestine but had failed. Aside from the attacks on the Old City, they had also tried to take territory in Tel Aviv, Haifa, the Etzion Block, and half a dozen other settlements around the country, only to be pushed back with considerable casualties. They had taken some lives and frightened the Jews of Jerusalem particularly, but by January their efforts had foundered and then failed miserably.

She cleared her throat. "The Mufti's friends in the Arab League are unhappy with him, sir. He did not produce, and that will force them to send in their Arab Liberation Army early."

Several disagreed and finally one spoke above the others. "They aren't ready. You have seen the reports. Fawzi el Kaukji has spent the last month twiddling his thumbs. He doesn't have any coordination in his command. In fact, he doesn't really even have a command. Additionally, not one-tenth of the money promised by the League has been paid, weapons are still in short supply, and they cannot cross the border now."

"The Arab leaders don't care if they're ready," Naomi responded. "Haj Amin has failed to create even one victory for them. They are desperate and will send the ALA just to create chaos in hopes that enough lives will be lost that the world will get nervous and reverse partition."

"She's right." The man who spoke was Eleazar Bar, another analyst like Naomi. They weren't usually on the same side in an argument, but she was glad for it when it happened. Eleazar was older, wiser, and respected by everyone around the table.

"By sending the ALA, they send a message to the UN."

"What message?" one of the others asked.

"That the entire Arab world supports the Palestinians against the Jews, and if they are not given what they want, they will annihilate the Jews. They have nothing to lose by sending them in the next two weeks, and they will, whether Kaukji and his ALA are ready or not."

"And they take some of the pressure off Haj Amin's guerillas, give him a chance to regroup and do some damage. Some of the ALA will probably be sent to Khader and Salameh," said Yosef Shefi. He pushed his round, wire-rimmed glasses back up his nose even as he lowered his head to look over the top of them. "This is a move toward escalation, and it will also be an attempt to begin moving Haj Amin's generals under direct command of Damascus."

"But Haj Amin would never allow that," David Sheal'tiel said.

"He will try to prevent it, while taking what help they give him. But he must take territory now. He must show progress. It is his only chance to save face and remain influential," Naomi said.

There were understanding nods all around.

"He will hit the roads," Naomi continued. "It is what his guerillas do best—what he should have done from the beginning. It was a waste of time to attack our cities. He didn't have a chance. Now he must backtrack and do something that makes him look less impotent."

"No," Eleazar said. "He will continue to strike the settlements, but smaller ones. Concentrate his forces and overrun one or two. That will look very good in the international papers and scare a lot of politicians and Jews in the United States. Make them want to come to our aid before we get massacred."

"He doesn't need to overrun the settlements, just cut them off," Naomi countered. "Remember, most of his force are irregular village and tribal fighters. It was his weakness against the cities. They will not fight a battle they don't think they can win, and they know they can win at ambush and looting. So does Khader. It will bring more fighters."

Eleazar said nothing and the other analysts seemed agreeable. She was making headway.

"I agree," said Sheal'tiel. "I want a report showing which roads will get hit the hardest and why. Give me numbers of Arab irregulars you think can be mustered in each instance and how best to defend against them without, I repeat, without going offensive."

The room erupted in moans.

"Then Ben-Gurion is staying with this weak, defensive stance," Eleazar said with some disgust.

"We still cannot strike first," Sheal'tiel said. "Direct orders, but . . ." He waited for the murmurs to die down before finishing. "But if they hit us, we hit them back, much harder than we have heretofore. We send a clear message without looking like the aggressor."

"A thumb in the dike, eh, David?" Eleazar said. "It ends up the same. It's just slower and more painful, that's all. We have a chance to shut down Haj Amin's guerillas if we go after them. If we don't, if we let them back in this and let them get control of the main arteries—especially the Jerusalem/Tel Aviv Road—we could get beat by Haj Amin's fighters. Mark my words."

"Duly noted, Eleazar. Anyone else?"

No one seemed to want to respond to Sheal'tiel's cold stare.

"He's right," Naomi said. "I understand we aren't ready for full-scale war, and I understand that to go offensive may force the Arabs into the war or give Britain an excuse to do their fighting for them and stay around for awhile, but one or two offensive maneuvers against these guerillas and Haj Amin will be finished." She pulled a paper from a folder and handed it to the person next to her with instructions to send it around the table to Sheal'tiel.

"That's a communiqué from our friends in Lebanon. Musa Alami is holding meetings with his supporters in Palestine, especially those around Shechem and Jerusalem."

The murmur was one of surprise. She had just received the communiqué and hadn't even verified it, but she was pretty sure of the source and it needed to be aired now. Musa Alami was the one member of the opposition who could win the hearts of many Palestinians if Haj Amin fell into disfavor, and Alami would negotiate for peace. Haj Amin had run him out of the country years earlier.

"If you hit Haj Amin hard, if you give his guerillas a decisive loss, you give Alami a chance," Naomi said.

Sheal'tiel eyed the report and the room fell silent. "I'll convey this to Ben-Gurion. Excellent work. This may change things, but do not be surprised if it doesn't."

"While I am sticking my neck out here, sir, could I remind you of just one thing? Letting Haj Amin's guerillas get a foothold will be a severe blow to our morale and will cause exactly what Ben-Gurion doesn't want. If we look weak, partition will be reversed so fast Ben-Gurion will wonder what hit him."

The snickers around the table punctuated her remarks, and even Sheal'tiel smiled for a moment before he wiped it off and declared the meeting closed.

Naomi picked up her folder and started out of the room. Eleazar caught her by the arm and pulled up beside her. "Well said. Thank you for backing me up. That was good work."

He handed her several papers clipped together. "That's Yigal Yadin's latest brain child." She thumbed through the papers as they walked toward their tables, now a makeshift office.

"It, and I quote, 'discerns a tendency among the British to favor the Arabs and hinder the Jews in most areas but Haifa where the British commander is bucking the trend. This will worsen,' he says, 'if we go on the offensive before the British leave the country.'"

"That will happen anyway, and we all know it."

"But it is the main reason Ben-Gurion is dragging his feet. Yadin is afraid of the British. He's afraid the British are still looking for an excuse to stick around even though everything we tell him says otherwise."

"Then he is being a fool."

"Not exactly. As chief of operations for the Haganah, he knows *we* aren't ready, and he is buying time with Ben-Gurion by using the argument he knows will sell. Ben-Gurion has a phobia about the British, and Yadin is playing on it."

"What do you mean we aren't ready?"

"It is in the report. The general staff, it says, only recently organized, is not yet ready for directing operational activities. Transport and armaments divisions have not yet adapted, and the training corps is abysmal. Worse, Yadin says that brigades have not revamped into combat headquarters and, therefore, are not combat ready. Nor do all units have quality, combat-experienced leaders running them. Further, most Palmach units are tied to guard work and cannot prepare for offensive battle, and there are shortages of all kinds of weapons. Only fifty-five percent of the Palmach is armed, and regular units have discovered many of their weapons to be flawed due to aging. Much of the ammunition is so old that up to forty percent of those used so far have been duds. And finally, he states, settlements have not properly fortified themselves. Because the Haganah is not prepared to protect them, casualties are being taken when they should not be, while the roads, without exception, are easy to attack and they are not prepared to protect them, either. This has lead to inadequate defensive measures requiring many more armored cars, trucks, and buses, which, at present, we have few of." He smiled cynically. "Dismal, isn't it?"

"Very," she said. "Haj Amin might defeat us."

"Not if we hit them now. The only army in this area of the world that is less prepared than ours is that of Haj Amin el Husseini, but the longer we wait the more prepared he will be. If he gets his guerillas rooted in along the roads, it will take twice the force to get him out. That's why we hit them now, but we won't. Yadin, Ben-Gurion, Sheal'tiel, and anyone else within standing distance of the top leaders are scared to death we might lose." He paused. "You backed me in there and I appreciate it. I thought you might like to know why they will decide against us. It is going to be messy from here on out, Naomi, and Haj Amin is far from finished." He took a deep breath. "What is the latest on ETZEL and LEHI?"

"Since the 29th, no activity. Why?" The two semiterrorist organizations were hitting Arab targets—mostly civilian—left and right, and the Jewish Agency was constantly scrambling to disown their horrors. In the last ten days they had hit three targets, one in Jaffa and two in Jerusalem, and killed more than fifty people, most of them innocent bystanders. It was not the kind of war most Jews wanted to wage.

"They're making matters worse, that's all. Their callous killing of defenseless people will give Haj Amin a new front to open, and when he does, it will make ETZEL's attacks look small. That more than anything our Haganah will do might cost us our state." With that he walked away, retrieved his coat, and headed for the exit. She stood there in a stupor for a minute before glancing at the watch on her wrist. Nearly ten. She needed to get home too.

She put her papers away, grabbed her coat and purse, and exited the building. As she did, she saw someone step out of the shadows and stopped, then recognized the felt hat and smile of Abraham Marshak.

"Abraham!" she said with genuine feeling.

"Naomi, how are you?" He stopped in the light of the windowed door where she could see him more clearly.

"I'm fine. What are you doing in Tel Aviv?"

"I . . . uh . . . came to see you."

Her heart skipped a beat. She had thought about Abraham and had decided it could never work. Since then she had usually managed to keep him out of her mind. But now she felt guilty about it. "Well, this is a surprise."

He offered her his arm, "May I walk you home?"

She looked at the arm. She had touched him once before, and he had practically jumped into the next block. "I thought . . ."

"The world needs a good liberal for a rabbi, don't you think?"

She laughed. "Yes, I suppose it does." She put her arm through his. "How are your father and mother?"

"They are well. And Hannah and the children send their love. In fact," he handed her a package, "she sent this gift. She said there is a card inside that explains how she came by its contents."

Naomi looked at the present, then pulled the paper from the box and opened it. Inside she found a comb and brush set made of mother of pearl. "Oh," she said biting her lip. "My mother's vanity set! How . . ." She handed him the box as she opened the note and read.

Dear Naomi.

Your mother and father left these and several other items, clothing mostly, at a friend's house. When we asked our friend Joseph to look for your family, he went to Kielce and found your old house. Though others occupied it, they sent him to the house two doors down, a Herr and Frau Dremel. They gave him the box, and he sent the set to us. I hope that it brings you only fond memories. Merry Christmas.

Love, Hannah.

Naomi carefully wrapped her fingers around the handle of the mirror and rubbed it gently, tears in the corners of her eyes. "I never thought . . ." The tears flowed and Abraham could do nothing but take her in his arms and try to give comfort. It was new to him, and he felt a bit clumsy about it, but her warmth gave him courage to hold on.

After a moment she stepped back and wiped her tears with the fingers of her hand. "I'm sorry," she forced a snicker. "For a Hasid, you are quite polished at holding a woman in time of need."

He blushed. "It is something I could learn to like. I am glad for you, Naomi. To find something of your mother after this much time is a miracle."

"Yes, I suppose it is." She put the mirror back in the box and carefully closed the lid, then held it tightly to her chest before they started walking again. "I apologize for being such a baby and ruining your visit."

"Ruining? It was worth coming to see the light in your eyes. It is always remarkable to be a part of such a miracle."

She was touched by his tenderness, and while holding onto the box tightly with one hand, she put the other through his arm again. "I can think of only a few people I would want to see me cry. Thank you for being one of them." They walked in silence for a moment before she spoke again. "Tell me about the tunnels."

They were nearly home before he finished his explanations. "I think it will lead us into the quarry of Solomon, but we shall see."

"I suppose David is right there watching every shovel, every pick, eager to see what you do find."

Abraham laughed. "Yes, even I am not as excited as he is about such things. He will be an amazing archaeologist someday." They were at her apartment door and she wondered what to say. Surely he would not want to come into an apartment this late, especially with others asleep, but there was nothing open, no place to sit and talk.

"I . . . uh . . . came because I wanted to see . . . I want us to go places, spend time together. I wish to . . . uh . . . uh . . ."

"You're asking me for a date?" She could see his anguish, that he was acting contrary to everything he had ever thought right when it came to such things. This was no small sacrifice for Abraham. And to think he came all the way from Jerusalem, at a time when the roads were seldom safe. It was humbling.

"Abraham, this is not what Hasids do. Are you sure?"

"Yes, I'm sure." He smiled. "You are more important to me than tradition."

She felt both apprehension and excitement at the same time. "Your family would never forgive me if they knew what you were doing. Especially your father."

"Then it will be our secret. I am asking you for a date the next time I can come. Do you accept or not?"

She bit her lip, unsure but excited, overwhelmed but surprised.

"When do you go back to Jerusalem?"

"Tomorrow night, late. I have several archaeological items with me to deliver to professors from the United States to receive them. We will meet all day, and then I return on the last convoy."

"I will go with you next time I am in Jerusalem, but you must have your father's permission before I do. I will not do this in secret."

Abraham's face changed from a look of hope to one of despair, however momentary. This time it showed determination. "Very well. I will talk to him, but if he does not give permission, I will ask you anyway."

His conviction melted her heart, and she squeezed his arm. "Thank you for coming, and for bringing this precious gift." Knowing exactly what she was doing and casting aside all inhibitions born of tradition, she leaned forward and kissed him softly on the cheek just above his beard, then turned around and went inside. Leaning against the closed door, she listened to the sound of Abraham singing loudly as he walked away.

CHAPTER 22

Ephraim left early for work, riding out of the Old City in a British jeep with Jack Willis who was taking a convoy to Haifa via Tel Aviv. The Jerusalem/Tel Aviv Road was increasingly dangerous with attacks taking place on Jewish convoys both coming and going, and Ephraim was grateful that his British escort would offer a relatively safe ride.

As they left the Old City by way of Jaffa Gate, they found it nearly closed by a barricade, and Ephraim wondered how long even the British would be able to keep it open.

For the first time, he was afraid for his family. Late yesterday a bomb had been thrown at the Number 2 bus as it passed through Jaffa Gate to get to the Quarter. Nights in the Quarter were getting worse as well. The sniping had escalated into gun battles, and regular attempts by both sides to advance their frontlines were made almost nightly. The British, unwilling to put their men at risk by placing them in the middle of a gun battle in the dark streets and rooftops of the Quarter, kept their men out unless one side started to get a heavy advantage over the other. Then they moved in armored cars and strafed the emplacements, driving everybody back into their holes and reestablishing order. Chaos! And as soon as the British left, it would become all out war, and Hannah and the kids would be caught in the middle.

Speeding along Jaffa Road reminded Ephraim of Paris before it was declared an Allied victory. The tension then was the same; there were few people on the streets, and those who were seemed afraid, wary of even them.

Barbed wire had been placed in a number of streets by the British to keep Arabs and Jews separated. Jewish police working under the mandate now policed the Jewish sections of the city, and Arab policemen who worked under the mandate now policed only Arab sections.

"I have never seen anythin' like this," Jack said. "It is becomin' a war zone, Eph, an' ye had better get Hannah and the kids out of here pretty soon. It's ready tae explode."

Ephraim only nodded. Getting Hannah out of the Old City would not be that easy. "What's the latest on the ALA?"

"The first of them are crossin' the border as we speak, but they are a rabble lot an' yer Haganah will handle them. Yer problem is what Khader an' Salameh are doin'. They moved fighters intae villages along the Jerusalem/Tel Aviv Road an' are massin' around Bethlehem. In fightin' last night, they took more homes in Katamon an' pretty much chased all yer people out of there. Ye know what it is like in the Old City."

Katamon overlooked the southern part of Jerusalem. It was mostly Arab, and the Brits would no more drive them out than they would drive Jews out of Jewish strongholds. Gradually the city's population was dividing, adjusting to new lines of demarcation, and the British didn't care. It made their job easier when Jews lived with Jews and Arabs with Arabs—less fighting.

"We're goin' tae start withdrawin' troops in a couple weeks. Ye know about the Schneller Base."

"Yeah, we're setting it up with your contact." The Schneller Base was one of the fortified British fortresses in Jerusalem. Arrangements had been made with its commander to turn it over to the Haganah, but there were others that the Arabs were preparing to control. Bevingrad, the main troop installation in the very heart of the city, would be the one to make the difference and both sides knew it, but it was controlled by the Brits' highest officials and would be up for grabs.

The radio blared, warning them of a strong Arab presence along the Jerusalem/Tel Aviv Road.

"Any chance your army will drive them out?" Ephraim asked.

"Nae. Those are Arab villages. We won't interfere anymore than we would if Jews were movin' into Jewish settlements."

"And if we go after them?"

"Ye know the answer. We'll stop ye."

"And if they try to close the road?"

There was a pause. "We'll see."

Ephraim felt a chill. This wasn't like the war he had fought in Germany and the Pacific. There you knew the enemy, and no one was tying your hands and telling the other team to have at you. It was like playing soccer with the referees willing to throw the game but still trying to keep their collusion hidden from the crowd.

"How many of those can you get us?" Ephraim asked, pointing to the two-way radios.

Jack smiled. "I'll see what I can do. Did ye get the armored cars my friend promised?"

"Yeah, but we're keeping them out of sight for now. Your army might want them back."

"What is the latest on arms shipments?" Jack asked with a sullen look. He knew the British government was doing everything in its power to keep weapons out of Jewish hands while signing contracts to provide thousands of rifles and millions of bullets to the Arabs. It made him sick to his stomach.

"Ships are nearly impossible, but we're still working on it. The planes are still in the states, tied up in paperwork. Al Schwimmer's using a false name and airline identity out of Panama—even the Panamanians think it's real. Once we can get past the red tape and get them in Panama, we'll fly them to Europe and begin an airlift. Maybe two months."

They passed Kastel where large numbers of Arabs camped around the village.

"Two months may be too late."

Ephraim didn't respond. As he looked at the increased numbers and realized there would be at least five times this many in the villages along the Bab el Wad, he wondered how much longer the Jerusalem/Tel Aviv Road would be open. There was no airfield in Jerusalem—at least not yet—and getting to Hannah and the kids might be impossible. He made up his mind. The next time he got to Jerusalem, he and Hannah would talk. It was time to think about coming to Tel Aviv.

* * *

Hannah went to the small window and looked into the street. Deserted. Her eyes scanned the rooftops and imagined the sandbagged gun emplacements scattered on top of them, men taking aim with the intent of killing one another. They had been shooting all night, and neither she nor Ephraim had gotten much sleep. There were only about fifteen hundred people left in the Quarter now, sixty percent of normal. The anxiety and constant battles had simply worn them down. It was nerve wracking, especially when Ephraim wasn't here. She had thought of asking him for a blessing last night, then had put it off. Now she was wishing she hadn't.

Going to the kitchen, she found a note on the table. David and Beth had already gone into the tunnels to work. The tunnels were a miracle, and she wondered how many lives they had saved in the last month. She couldn't help but smile at the thought of the Arabs trying to figure out where everyone was and how they managed to move men to all the right places at the needed time. She imagined their frustration, and it made her smile.

Kneeling by a chair, Hannah said her morning prayers. It took some time to finish this morning, but it made her feel better. She saw the Torah belonging to David's father sitting on the end table, the red ribbon she had given him as a marker sticking out of its worn pages. Curious, she picked up the book and opened to the ribbon. He was reading in Exodus where Israel is saved in the wilderness by the miracles of the quail and manna. He had read a lot since Christmas, pointing out many of the passages his father had thought important enough to mark. She had marveled at how this simple little volume had drawn David closer to the father he had lost. Surely it had been a miracle to find this singular book in the ruins of Hitler's war.

There had been another miracle as well. David had nearly stopped stuttering. This renewed connection with his father seemed to have given him some sort of peace about the past that was translating into an improvement in his speech. And to think she had hesitated about giving it to him, thinking it might have just the opposite effect. Thank goodness Ephraim had talked some sense into her.

Going to the bathroom, she took a quick shower, then dressed, ate some bread and cheese, and did the few dishes. As she finished, she heard the twins playing with one another in their bed and went in to begin the morning ritual of removing rancid night diapers, bathing, dressing, and feeding them. It was nearly nine o'clock when she finished, and as the boys played on the floor in front of her, she read scriptures.

Beth and David returned around eleven and she fixed them a quick lunch as they chattered about progress in the tunnels and one of Abraham's more recent finds. When they finished she made them study both their schoolbooks and their scriptures before letting them dash off again.

After feeding the twins and putting them down for a nap, she went back to the front room window and studied the outdoors. The sky was blue, and it looked to be a warm day. Possibly when the children woke up, she would take them through the tunnels to a safe spot where they could all soak up some sun.

She saw movement from the corner of her eye and looked down into the street. It was Moddel. She was helping her husband into a small cart, her children hugging the wall in fear, their eyes darting along the distant roofline of the Arab Quarter. They were like frightened mice, looking for the predator they were sure was lurking but couldn't see. Two were fussing in fear and the other two dancing as if eager to be away, while Moddel seemed nearly beside herself with a sort of crazed nervousness of incoherent action.

Hannah opened the door and quickly descended the steps. She ran down the street and was at Moddel's side before she could think twice about the foolishness of her act.

"You cannot go by cart. It is too dangerous," she said with a calm voice. "Get the children back inside your house."

Moddel stiffened. "We are out of food! They fight all night long, and I will not stay a moment longer. I do not care what you or the Rabbi or anyone else says, do you hear me?" Moddel screamed. "We are leaving! The cart is necessary for Saul to travel, and it is only a few blocks to where the British trucks come. They will take us out!" Beyond reason with fear, she shoved Hannah aside while moving around nervously but accomplishing nothing.

Hannah grabbed her firmly by both shoulders and held her still. "And the most dangerous few blocks in the Quarter. Now get them back inside," Hannah said firmly. "I will arrange for a stretcher and men to carry it. They can take Saul through the tunnels."

Moddel hesitated, her eyes darting frantically to the roof, the street, the windows, back to the roofs, then to the children, then to Hannah.

Hannah knew that Moddel's fear was controlling her. Because of it she had stopped coming to Mithra's house for food and refused to leave the house to shop. Hannah and several others had taken them goods when they could, but unfortunately one of them had reported Moddel's condition to Rabbi Salomon. He came everyday to pray and read with her and Saul while urging them to stay. He needed them. The Arabs wouldn't hurt them—he was sure of it—and yet that is exactly what the Arabs had done. It was obvious now that her loyalty to the Rabbi and her fear were tearing her apart until she simply couldn't take it anymore. She should have left days ago.

"Moddel, get them inside!" Hannah said again while shaking her lightly.

The dazed, frightened look in Moddel's eyes seemed to fade, and Moddel nodded lightly. "Yes, inside. It . . . we . . . should go inside."

The children were indoors before she could tell them directly, Moddel joining them slowly and mumbling something. A gunshot was fired and Hannah heard the ricochet off the cobblestone pavement three feet away. They were discovered. She quickly grabbed Saul and helped him out of the cart and through the door as a second bullet planted itself in the wooden stair beam for the apartment above. Her heart raced as she lowered Saul to the couch and tried to get her fear and anger under control before turning back to Moddel.

"I'll get Mithra to stay with the twins, then go after help. It will take half an hour at most. Stay put, do you understand?" she said in Yiddish, the language Moddel spoke from childhood. Moddel nodded, her hands wringing together and her eyes staring blankly out the window. Hannah turned to Saul, afraid Moddel might still try to run. "Saul, keep her here."

Saul was weak, gritting his teeth against the pain, but nodded. Hannah turned to the door, took a deep breath, and quickly covered the distance to Mithra's apartment and found safety inside. She didn't think any shots were fired, but she wasn't sure.

Mithra was sitting in her rocker working on some knitting, but the needles had stopped in midair. "What is it?"

"It's me. I need your help," Hannah said. Mithra quickly agreed to sit with the twins and Hannah led her upstairs and got her seated in a familiar chair before she went back through Mithra's basement and into the tunnels. She found Abraham Marshak working on the new tunnel in the far end of the Cardo. When she told him of the incident, he called for help and half a dozen men went for rifles while Abraham found a stretcher. She followed.

The stretcher was quickly located, the riflemen ready, and they ran back for Mithra's basement, up the stairs, to the front door, where they caught their breath while Abraham checked the rooftops.

"Now!" he yelled.

As they darted across and down the street to Moddel and Saul's place, Hannah noticed the cart was gone and felt faint. Abraham opened the door and the three of them went inside. There was no one there.

* * *

Rhoui was ensconced in a makeshift emplacement atop a building directly overlooking the Jewish Quarter. He and a few others had advanced their position during the night, and though the Jews had tried to drive them back, they had succeeded in holding it. He sat beside Raoul and another man from the Arab Quarter Raoul had befriended, a man he idolized, a man who hated Jews even more than Raoul.

So far Rhoui hadn't seen anything but a man willing to let other people get shot while he sat about and gave orders. Unless of course there was money or looting in it.

"Jaffa Gate is closed," Rajid said. He had just arrived, and Raoul had all but bowed and licked his boots. Rhoui nodded while chewing on a piece of the bread Rajid had brought for them. The offensive to move deeper into the Jewish Quarter had been given the go ahead only after the last attack on Damascus Gate by Jewish fanatics. Because Rhoui had known two of the men who had died in that atrocious bombing, he had been hot with anger and a desire for vengeance. When they had called for volunteers to attack the Quarter and make the Jews pay with their dead children, he had jumped at the chance.

"What do you mean Jaffa Gate is closed?" asked Raoul.

"The barricade has been completed. Nothing will get through now. The British told Abou Dayieh they will not make us take it down because of the what the Kike Jews of the ETZEL did at Damascus Gate with their bombs. The Jewish Quarter is cut off." Rajid grinned, and Raoul yelped with satisfaction. Rhoui smiled his approval as well. If nothing else, they could starve them out now.

A bullet hit near Raoul and he ducked back with a curse. It was the reason Rhoui did not dance about in celebration. The Jews had proven to be good with their rifles. He had seen two dozen men killed in the last week.

"We should shoot back," said Raoul, staring angrily at Rhoui. Abou Dayieh had made Rhoui a platoon commander and put him in charge of a dozen men and this position. It was his decision, and Raoul knew it.

"How much ammunition do we have?" Rhoui asked.

"Fifty bullets at least. Plenty to kill a few Jews."

"But only enough to hold off an attack if one comes," he said with restrained authority. "If you see a good shot—one you cannot miss—take it, otherwise we keep our bullets."

Raoul peered through one of the peepholes for a minute then turned his back and lay against the bags.

"The bomb of ETZEL frightened many of your people," Rajid said. "Hundreds left in the last few days. They do not think you can protect them."

Rhoui knew it was more than that. Most people in the Old City wanted no part of the violence and did not wish to fight. Nor did they have confidence in Khader's fighters to keep them from getting killed. This was why Abou Dayieh had been ordered to attack the Quarter. A push into the Quarter would remove the danger of Jewish incursions and change Arab minds about their safety, thus stopping the flow out of the city.

"Last night we proved them wrong. When we take the Jewish Quarter, they will return and have more faith in us."

"Return? Do you think Abou Dayieh will let the cowards return?" Rajid guffawed. "Others will replace them—others who fight with us and deserve a house for their sacrifice. The fools have lost everything."

Rhoui ignored the words because he did not want to hear them and because he refused to believe them true. Instead he looked through one of the peepholes again. He could see directly into the Jewish Quarter along two streets. Nothing was moving. It seemed deserted, but he knew it wasn't. Their people had been counting those who left the Quarter and there were still at least twelve hundred people living there. Where they were and how they were surviving without food baffled him. Possibly they were so frightened they were dying of starvation. But if that were so, how could the Haganah fight with such tenacity? And how did they move their men around as they did? It seemed like there were hundreds, but for this to be they would have had to smuggle many men and weapons in under the watchful eye of the British. This would not be easy.

Raoul spat. "We should stop playing with these Jews."

"Abou Dayieh wishes to do so, but we aren't strong enough. Without the men from the Christian Quarter . . ." He let his voice trail off while glancing at Rhoui. "Your brother still refuses to fight with us."

Rhoui kept his eye to the peephole knowing his face was red with embarrassed frustration. He knew the talk, had heard the accusations. Izaat had refused to drive deeper into the Armenian Quarter from his positions along the north and west side of the Christian Quarter. Because of it, Abou Dayieh had been forced to stretch his men very thin, and they had not taken the ground they could have. In fact, along that side of the Old City, the Jews had held their ground. It had been an embarrassment to Rhoui, completely indefensible to those fighting with Khader.

"He is a coward," Rhoui said in frustrated self-defense.

"You should replace him," Rajid said. "The people would follow you. They would fight. Now they are afraid of Izaat, and they stay home."

Rhoui fidgeted. Raoul and Rajid had been pressing him to do something about Izaat and Mary, especially Raoul. "They are our enemies," Raoul said. "Izaat refuses to fight the Jews, and Mary sleeps with them."

Rhoui did not like these words but said nothing. He could not defend her actions and had disowned her, telling his wife and others to have nothing to do with her. When the time came that he could do it, he would punish her after the way of Islam. She would pay for humiliating him.

"I told you they will see Izaat as the coward he is and force him out or kill him. When they do, they will beg us to help them," Rhoui said.

"And if they don't force him out or kill him, what then?" Raoul asked.

"Then I will kill him myself." The words burned in his throat, but he meant them. His hatred for Izaat's cowardice was complete. He could not understand this foolish attempt at standing against Haj Amin. It would only lead to pain for everyone.

He saw someone come over the wall and scurry toward their emplacement, keeping low. When he was within a few feet they could see it was Izaat.

"Well, well, the coward himself," Raoul said. None of them made any extra room for him and Izaat did his best to pull his body behind cover as several bullets struck the sandbags.

"Rhoui," Izaat said in greeting.

"Izaat," Rhoui responded coldly. "What brings you here? This is a battle zone and not a place for cowards." He could see that his words pleased his two friends.

"I have come to talk to you."

"I have nothing to say to you."

"Then you will listen," Izaat said firmly. "I am sending my family to Beirut. If you wish to send yours as well, I will see that they are cared for."

Rhoui could not believe his ears. "Abou Dayieh has asked that we push the Jews back to show our people they should not flee and you send your family away?" His face was red with anger. "They are right about you, Brother. Your heart beat is that of a Jew!"

It was all Izaat could do to restrain his desire to throttle his brother, but he knew it would only make matters worse, especially with the vulture Raoul watching. "I did not come here to argue, only to offer this help to your wife and children. I know you do not have the money—"

"Only because you steal my inheritance from me. Father left me one-third of what he had, and you keep it for yourself."

"I have told you before, the money is in a bank in Beirut. As soon as it is safe to transfer money back here, I will see that it is done."

"It is safe now!"

Izaat bit his tongue. It was not safe. Most members of the Arab Higher Committee had already transferred their funds out of the local Barclay's bank to branches elsewhere, as had many others. And even if it did come, Rhoui would lose it to others. He had always been bad with money, but if that was what Rhoui wanted, if that would bring peace between them, he would do it.

"Very well. I will have it sent to your account as soon as possible."

Rhoui looked at Izaat to see if he was sincere. "Good, but my family stays with me. They would never leave."

Izaat could see that Raoul and his friend were enjoying this battle between brothers and decided not to respond to Rhoui's statement, even though it had been Rhoui's wife who had come to him, frightened and angry. Though she had been blaming Izaat for their difficulties she had come to see that this was not true, that it was Rhoui who would get them all killed. She wanted to leave, and would, one way or the other, but Rhoui would have to learn this for himself.

Raoul whispered something to the other man and gave a wry smile. "I am surprised that you consort with a man who tried to kill your sister," Izaat said to Rhoui.

Raoul stiffened as if to take action, and Izaat prepared himself. He had not finished with Raoul for what he had done and now was as good a time as any.

"I have no sister," Rhoui said, "and if you do not come to your senses, I have no brother, either." Raoul seemed content with that and eased back against the sandbags.

"I received a note from this sister you do not have," Izaat said. "She gives you her apology. The meeting at the Garden Tomb was not of her doing and your words to the Jew frightened him enough to warn her. If you had listened to her—"

"She is lying," he said in heated Arabic. "I saw the way he touched her, the way she looked at him. Under the law of Islam she should die for this humiliation!"

"We are not Islamic, Rhoui. And even if we were, that law is antiquated."

Raoul and Rajid tensed again, but Rhoui pulled a Koran from his back pocket and shook it at Izaat. "I believe this more than I believe your Bible. You know I am Muslim now. Do not offend Allah and his prophet or I will shoot you now."

"It is you who offend Allah, not I." Izaat shrugged. "If you wish to be a Judas so be it, but do not expect me to follow you. And do not expect that this family will be run by Islamic law because you follow the fanatic Haj Amin who is trying to turn Islam on its head for his own benefit." He was angry now, the stupidity of his younger brother getting to him.

"Then punish her by Christian law. But do not leave this be, Brother, or—"

"Or what, Rhoui? You will punish her yourself or let these two butchers do it? Raoul tried once, and I tell you as I told him . . ." He saw Raoul tensing again, prepared to act if Rhoui gave him any sign. The other one was just as ready, and Izaat knew he would be in trouble if they did, but he did not care. He had enough of Rhoui's foolishness and he intended to finish his words. "Lay a single finger on her and you will answer to me with your life! Do you understand?"

Rhoui flushed with anger. "You defend her? After what she has done?"

"I know Mary. I know she does not believe in this war and she does not hate the Jews as you would like her to, but that does not make her the incarnation of the devil." He kept his hand on his pistol. "Has it occurred to you she might be right about some things?"

Rhoui could not believe his ears. "Right? She is a fool, and if you think as she does, you are a fool as well!" Without thinking, he stood to accentuate his defiance, and Raoul and Rajid leaned forward to pounce. Izaat pulled the pistol as a warning, and they leaned back a little, but the foreign one fingered his rifle, ready to swing it about.

"Get your head down, Rhoui, before the Jews put a hole in it." He looked at the foreigner with cold eyes. "You will be dead before you can pull the trigger." The finger eased away.

Rhoui quickly lowered himself to his knees and looked angrily at his brother. "You had better leave us!" he said stiffly.

"Yes. I was a fool to try and talk to you with these two here. If you want your money, come to Father's office and we will talk." He started to leave. "And Rhoui, I warn you again. Do not touch Mary, ever. I will kill you if you do." With that he kept low while easing himself to the edge of the wall and the ladder he had used to access the roof.

Rhoui's anger boiled in him. He turned and looked for something to kill. Anything. He saw the Jewish woman pulling a cart quickly toward the south, her children pulling frantically while looking about, afraid. A man lay in the cart, his legs dangling out the back. Obviously they were trying to get him away. Rhoui lifted his rifle and took aim, then fired. He saw the boy collapse to the ground in a heap. He jerked the bolt of his rifle and quickly injected a second shell.

"What are you firing at?" Izaat said, turning back. He dashed for his brother and grabbed the gun, forcing it down. Rhoui shoved him aside and Raoul and Rajid jumped Izaat, wrestling him to the rooftop and pinning him while Rhoui fired again, then again.

"No!" Izaat said, busting free and planting a left hook on Raoul's chin. The foreign one jumped back, ducking away as Izaat pulled his pistol and pointed it at Rhoui's stomach. "Not women and children!"

Bullets slammed into the sandbags from a half dozen directions as Izaat faced off with Rhoui and Raoul. Izaat quickly took a look through a nearby peephole. He saw a boy and woman dead on the cobbled street. His heart ached as he felt the pain and heard the screams of other children. He looked at Rhoui with sad eyes. "You have killed a woman and a child, Rhoui! What has happened to you?"

Rhoui glared at Izaat defiantly. "And the Jews, they do not? Have you so quickly forgotten Damascus Gate?" he said.

"The killing of innocents is never justified, Rhoui, no matter who does it. God will never forgive you for this."

"I left your command and gladly! Now you can leave mine before I and my friends kill you!"

Izaat got to his knees, his gun still holding them in check, and started for the ladder, once again keeping low while bullets of retaliation danced around him until he reached the far wall and cover. He turned back to see Rhoui staring his direction in angry defiance. For the first time in his life, Izaat Aref wished he had no brother.

Raoul patted Rhoui on the shoulder. "If he comes again, I will kill him for you."

Rhoui nodded. "If he comes again, I will kill him myself."

"It is time you talked to Abou Dayieh about this coward," Rajid said. "It is time to be rid of him."

Rhoui nodded again. "Yes, it is time."

* * *

After pulling the bodies out of the line of fire while Haganah fighters gave them cover, Hannah could see that Moddel was dead. The bullet had hit her in the back and exited near her heart. She had died instantly. Her son, Shlomo, was still alive but would need to be taken to a hospital immediately. Saul had taken a second bullet in his hip and lay helplessly bleeding on the stones of the street. The other children lay huddled around him, crying, their faces pale with fright as they stared at Moddel's lifeless body.

Someone brought a blanket from the apartment where they had taken refuge from the snipers, and Hannah covered Moddel while wiping fresh tears from her dust-covered cheeks. She got to her feet and went to Saul. He was in great pain, his leg bleeding. Abraham was checking the boy's pulse.

"I should not have left them. I should have stayed and settled her down," Hannah said to no one in particular.

"We have to get them into the tunnels. I'll go for more stretchers," Abraham said. "Shlomo is still alive, and he and Saul will need a hospital." He darted across the street and through a door that would take him to the tunnels. Moddel had gotten three blocks before being hit; now they were in a different neighborhood.

Hannah ripped a piece of Saul's shirt tail off for a bandage and wrapped his leg, then went to the smallest child who was shaking uncontrollably next to her mother's covered body. She held her close in an attempt to chase away the fear that gripped the child, knowing from experience the child would have nightmares for a long time. A woman from the apartment clung closely to the wall to reach them, picking up the other daughter who stood with her face against the wall sobbing. She noticed that others had come to doors and windows but kept back, afraid the snipers might find them as a target as well. But their voices sounded out their shared misery, their mourning cries echoing off the walls of the buildings and filling the Quarter.

Abraham returned with two stretchers and half a dozen more Haganah men who joined the others returning fire as protection. Hannah finally got the little girl calmed a bit as stretchers were quickly unfolded and Saul and Shlomo put aboard, then carried in a rush across the street. Gunfire broke out again and the Haganah fired back. The sudden clap of rifles frightened the little girl again, and she screamed for Hannah who took her back and held her closer.

The rifle fire suddenly stopped.

"You have to go!" Abraham said to Hannah. "Now!"

Hannah took a deep breath, her heart in her stomach, the child screaming. She ran across the narrow street to where others waited, grabbed her by the arms and celebrated that she had arrived safely. The child was suddenly gone, and Hannah watched as she disappeared into the tunnels in another woman's arms. Abraham dashed through the door with the older girl. Two others followed with the last stretcher and the body of Moddel. Hannah felt too weak to stand any longer and collapsed to a chair as the stretcher bearers crossed the room and descended into the tunnels, Abraham and the screaming child behind them. Other Haganah men scrambled and shut the door, their faces flushed with the sweat of battle. Each glanced at her with a look of sad admiration, then went through the door after the others, leaving her with the few people who wanted to help. They all seemed to be in shock—frightened, crying, babbling incoherently. She wanted only quiet, to be left alone to try and deal with what had happened. Pushing herself out of the chair she crossed the room toward the door. As she reached it, Rabbi Salomon came to the top of the steps, his face drawn and pale. He was looking at the blood on the steps with disbelief and glanced up as if she might be able to help him understand. Then a dark cloud crossed his face. The dark cloud of guilt. If he had let Moddel go, she would be alive now, and he knew it.

Hannah pushed him to one side and went down the stairs, then turned back. "I am sorry for you. Sorry you could not see that Moddel should leave and now she is dead, but even more sorry to know that it will happen again. If you want to save your people and your city, you will have to change. You will have to at least help us fight for them. If you and others are not willing, you should leave or there will be more Moddels for us to bury."

With that she turned and stepped through the hole in the wall to the next basement where she found a corner and collapsed on the floor and cried. She knew there would be more Moddels.

CHAPTER 23

"Aaron are you with us," Zalman Mart said.

Aaron was jerked out of his thoughts. "Yes, sir, with you."

Mart smiled while the others chuckled and Aaron squirmed. He had been assigned to this detail because he couldn't go back to the Old City right now, but he knew few of these men and this was no way to start. He shoved the thoughts of Mary aside and tried to concentrate. It didn't help that he had caught a cold during the night. It felt like he had a wagon full of sheep's wool in his head and a faucet up his nose. The nasal drip was as continuous as was the sneezing.

Mart, looking annoyed, continued. "Though there are many Arabs leaving the city, there are still too many Jews doing the same. Over the last week, Abdul Khader has moved another hundred trained fighters into the Old City and two hundred in Katamon in what seems to be a new offensive on smaller targets. From Katamon he is launching raids on convoys going to the south while attacking Jewish neighborhoods of West Jerusalem. The British are doing little to stop them and more than seventy-five of our Palmach have died in the last five days.

Aaron had heard that nearly 800 Jews had been killed since the announcement of partition and more than 1000 Arabs along with 125 Brits. He hadn't believed it at first, but then Mart had shown them the report. He hadn't realized how narrow a view he had from the Old City until he left it. He was glad to hear some sort of action was being taken.

"With Ben-Gurion's approval, Mishael Shacham has been given orders to respond in an important way. We will strike directly at Abdul Khader and Abou Dayieh." Mart paused to let the chatter die down. "This falls under our policy of an aggressive defense. They have hit us hard. We will hit them back harder to teach them that their aggression will be answered with swift and deadly reprisals."

Aaron had heard the rumors about Shacham, the new commander sent to aid Amir in defending Jerusalem's Jews. Hard as nails, he had ordered the death of an Arab who had purportedly raped a Jewish girl three years earlier. The Brits had tried to arrest him for it, but he had escaped and gone underground, avoiding them. He had no love for Arabs and had already ordered empty homes on the fringes of Arab communities to be blown up, posted fliers of warning, and generally used the same tactics as the Arabs in a war of intimidation. Giving Shacham command of retaliations was sending a message that the aggression would be handled with deadly force.

Mart pointed to a spot on the map. "We have learned that the Arab headquarters are in three locations. One is here in the Old City, just inside Stephen's Gate in the Arab Quarter. Abou Dayieh directs the attacks on the Old City from here, but it is unreasonable to attack that location now. The British would stop us before we could get inside the gate because of its proximity to the Holy Mount and the Church of the Holy Sepulcher." He pointed at another spot. "There are two places here, in Katamon. We will hit one of them, the Hotel Semiramis."

Half a dozen hands went up and discussion quickly droned through the room.

"Civilians live there," said one.

"Start blowing up public places and they'll do the same," said another.

"If the Arabs decide to hide behind civilians, it is they who must take the blame for civilian casualties." Mart leaned forward, placing his palms on the table in front of him. "We believe that both Khader and Abou Dayieh meet here to make plans against our people. Should we let them do so with impunity or go after them?"

The room quieted and Mart went on, explaining that Ben-Gurion had given his blessing to do what they must do. He wasn't quite finished when a sneeze exploded from Aaron, and he reactively shoved the handkerchief over his face. "Sorry, sir, just this cold."

"Get something for it, will you? I can't have a soldier going into an operation like this with a sneeze like that. Just as well send up a flare." Everyone chuckled at Mart's unintended humor.

"I'll see what I can do," Aaron said with nasal intonation. "How do we know when Khader will be at the Semiramis, sir?"

"We have an agent in the area. As you know, Khader drives a distinctive light-colored jeep. When it is there, we will go."

"And if we don't find him?" Aaron asked.

"We won't have time for a search, sergeant. We will use explosives."

"Then there will be civilian casualties," said Aaron.

"Yes, there will be."

They were dismissed to return in twenty minutes for a briefing on their plan of attack. Aaron stayed put, his thoughts on Khader and the potential civilian casualties.

Mart turned a chair around and sat down facing him. "I hate to be the bearer of bad news, but you aren't going."

Aaron sat straight. "But sir, I . . ."

"You have a cold that will give us away. You're out this time 'round, sergeant." He stood. "Besides, I hear you already had your chance at Khader." Mart smiled.

"That's highly unlikely, sir." Aaron said. He had been told that under no circumstances was his past experience in Ramallah to be discussed—with anyone.

Mart gave a wry smile. "Good answer, Schwartz. The real reason you're staying out of this is you're still wanted by the British. If this detail gets caught and you end up back in their hands, they'll throw away the key. My orders are to keep you out of the action for awhile." He stood. "Take the night off and get something for that cold."

"Sir?"

"Yes, sergeant."

"The civilians . . . How many might pay with their lives if Khader is in that hotel?"

"At least twenty."

"It is a heavy price to pay, sir, and you will reload Haj Amin's propaganda machine, even if you get Khader. It doesn't make us any different than ETZEL."

Mart came back to his chair and sat down. "I've read your file, Schwartz. You're young, outspoken, intelligent, and you have so much moral backbone you're stiffer than most eighty-year-old trees.

Everybody says you'll be a good soldier, and when I heard you went after Khader in Ramallah, I knew you had the courage necessary to do just that. Don't screw it all up by forgetting that war is never pretty and that innocent people get hurt in order to prevent more innocent people from dying, including the men you will have to lead." He took a deep breath. "Now I'm going to tell you something you won't like to hear. The Semiramis is one of two buildings used as meeting places by Khader. The planning that takes place there has cost us lives and will cost us more. I hope we are lucky enough to get Khader, but we must send a message to him and his men. They are not safe there or anywhere else when they plot to kill our people. By sending this message to the civilians who house him, they will be less willing in the future to help him. It is ugly, but it is necessary, especially in Katamon. From there they can do significant damage to the Jewish Quarter and the New City. That cannot be allowed, and if it takes blowing up every house in Katamon we'll do it. That makes this a military operation with a military objective—the capture or death of Abdul Khader and the destruction of sites they use to foment actions against our people." He leaned forward. "If you cannot stomach such actions, you had better get out of this military or any other. You simply won't fit. Understood?"

"Perfectly," Aaron said.

Mart stood. "We have to take Katamon and push Khader out of there, or eventually we'll lose the Old City. You have family in the Old City and so do I. For me that's reason enough to hit Katamon."

Aaron grimaced, the statement hitting home.

"War is never sterile, Sergeant Schwartz, and because it isn't, innocent Jews and Arabs will suffer and lose their homes, maybe even their country. I don't intend that it be Jews this time. We didn't start this fight. We'd take peace even now. They won't. If in the end they become a homeless people, they should look back at this mistake."

He started for the door, then turned back. "And don't forget, hundreds of our people have been victims over the last month, most of them innocent victims to a war Haj Amin started. If you want to blame someone for innocent lives lost, blame him." As Mart reached the door Aaron sneezed again and Mart turned back with a grin. "Go home and find a bed and a hot cup of tea."

Aaron gave a casual salute before Mart disappeared. Some of Hannah's hot tea and a nice warm bed did sound awfully good, but getting back inside the Old City might be a problem.

He sat for a few minutes, thinking. War isn't sterile. It's like using a scattergun—you shoot and pray you're close enough to create the least amount of collateral damage. Stop Khader and you save lives. Sadistically, Aaron wondered how many more could be saved if they could get to Haj Amin.

He was mildly concerned about Mary. She was in Katamon, but the suburb was large and the chances of her being involved were small. More worrisome was how she would feel when civilians, possibly friends, died at the hands of men like him. In order to prevent the headache he was getting from something he couldn't change, he turned his thoughts to tea and a warm bed, then wondered how he could get hold of Jack Willis. He was probably the only man who could get him past the Brits and into the Old City. He would try. A night at Hannah and Ephraim's with David, Beth, and the twins could work wonders.

As he snatched his coat from the hook, he felt the weight of his father's journal in the coat pocket. Sitting down, he pulled the leather-bound volume from its resting place and stared at it. He hadn't read any yet. He had considered it several times, but as much as he wanted to, he couldn't get himself to open it. His father and mother died horribly, and he couldn't get past the deep-down, gut-wrenching feeling that it was somehow his fault, and that if he read his father's entries, they would say as much. He stuffed it back in his pocket. Now wasn't the time or place anyway. He put on the coat and walked toward the outside door. As he did he passed the men returning for their briefing. He wished them luck. One thing he knew for certain: Khader wasn't easy to kill.

CHAPTER 24

Before partition, Katamon was the home of a few well-heeled Jews who lived among hundreds of the most prosperous of the Arab community. It lay south of the new section of Jewish Jerusalem, overlooking it and the Bethlehem highway that traversed its eastern side. When Mary first arrived, she felt safe, but as more and more of Khader's men came to Katamon, they demanded more and more space, food, and loot. She watched as they systematically began stealing from Arabs just as they had done in the Old City, forcing many to give up their homes and possessions and go to other places to avoid the harassment and hard conditions placed upon them.

Despite the fighting and theft, Mary's aunt's hotel, the Semiramis, was still intact. Used by Abdul Khader and his regional commander Ibrahim Abou Dayieh for parlays with tribal and village leaders, Khader had declared the Semiramis off-limits to his thieving guerillas. Thankful for this small favor, and afraid he might change his mind, her aunt had pressed all of her still available family into the service of Khader and his men even as they planned their attacks in the dining room over Arab coffee and sweet meats. It sickened Mary.

She had never liked the Husseinis. From the time she was a small child, she had heard her father talk of them, and what he said left her little room for the admiration so many Arab Muslims seemed to give them. But she had to admit that she had been curious and even a little intrigued to meet Abdul Khader and see why someone would consider following him. She discovered that he was well-educated, charming, quick-minded, assertive, and very charismatic, though quiet—a natural-born leader. She saw why others were drawn to him and found herself listening carefully to his well-chosen words from the other side of the kitchen door. That's when she discovered he would never seek peace. His hate for Jews was deeply embedded under his love for Palestine and its people, making him unbending and merciless. He would win at all costs, and the innocent did not concern him in the least, especially since ETZEL and LEHI had made it clear that civilian targets were fair game. He had responded and was planning to respond in horrible ways, and it would only lead to further attacks on the innocent by both sides. She wished that God would strike down such men so that sensible ones could make peace, but she knew they had gone beyond that now and all the horrors of war would come to Palestine.

The matter-of-fact talk of ambushes, attacking civilian buses, and using explosives in the heart of Jerusalem in even more horrible ways than the ETZEL and their celebrating over dead civilians finally got to Mary. She told her aunt that she must leave as soon as she could get hold of Izaat. She had no money to speak of and no way of knowing how best to get to Jaffa, then Beirut. She had sent word she needed to talk to him, but until he contacted her, she had to stay. It had been nearly ten days, and she was baffled. Had he decided to disown her as Rhoui had?

Mary crossed the street to the church. She had come to pray. There didn't seem to be much else for her to do as the city slowly turned into a battleground. She was glad to be going to Beirut. At least there she could feel safe.

Once in the church, she lit a candle, bowed, crossed herself, and then knelt and tried to find peace. She had heard that the man who lived next to her in the Old City had been killed by a Jewish sniper as he opened his shop just outside the northern wall of the Muslim Quarter. He was a good Christian. She prayed for his soul and for the souls of all those who had died in that horrible way.

Then she prayed for Izaat. From what she had been told, he was trying to keep his promise to her, trying to steer their neighborhood through a dangerous time without killing or getting killed. It was like trying to sail a small ship to shore through jagged rocks and reefs in the worst of storms. She prayed long for him.

But she prayed even longer for Rhoui. His hate was more than she could bear. He had disowned her, had let it be known that he intended to punish her severely. She did not know him anymore. How could he hate so much? He had been raised Christian, just as she and Izaat had, and yet he left it all. She prayed that God would not give up on him, that somehow he would change before it was too late.

She had seen Rhoui's wife just this morning. Margaretha had fled the Old City and come to Katamon to live with her parents. At first Mary had resisted going to see her sister-in-law, unsure if Rhoui's hate had also infected Margaretha, but then she decided she must. Unfortunately it had been as Mary had expected—Margaretha had simply refused to see her and the door had been shut without Mary so much as crossing the threshold. As she had turned to leave, Margaretha's father stepped outside and closed the door behind him. They had always been friends, and he walked with her a short way. Like so many of her people, he too had aged. There was a sort of tired acceptance of things he could no longer control. It seemed strange that one month could do such a thing to so many, but there it was in the droop of his shoulders and the defeated look in his eyes.

"Forgive Margaretha. She is angry. We are all angry." He shrugged. "We take it out on those we love most."

Mary was forced to bite her lip in order to prevent an explosion of tears.

"Rhoui did not want Margaretha to leave. He was very angry with her for even proposing it, but she was living with fear day and night, and the children could not sleep, would not eat. She had to leave. So, she left without his knowledge. She is most angry at him, not at you. I think she is more afraid of you trying to talk her into going back than anything else." He sighed. "Rhoui has stopped loving, Mary. He beat Margaretha when she asked to leave, then cursed her before tearing the house apart and scaring his children nearly to death. This war, Haj Amin and his constant stream of hate, those horrible men who have come to the city ostensibly to protect us—these have made him an animal. He does not know it, but he has lost his family and may never get them back."

They had walked to where the streets crossed. "Now I must say something else. I owe it to your parents," he sighed. "I knew your father and mother since before you were born. I knew them when they fell in love and when your mother left her family to marry a

Christian. I saw the heartache that it caused your mother when her father would not even acknowledge her existence when passing her on the street."

She knew what he was getting at and quickly broke in. "I am not planning to marry—"

He raised a hand. "But I also know that your mother was happy with your father, that their marriage was a special one. Following the heart is not a bad thing, Mary. Do not let Rhoui dictate how you live your life. Even Margaretha did not let him do that."

Mary, still hurt by Margaretha's coldness, only nodded as he said his goodbyes and went back to the house. It was a full minute before she had started down the road toward her aunt's hotel again. It was strange, but she had not thought of Rhoui much as she walked home that afternoon. Instead it had been Aaron she could not push out of her mind.

She had never met anyone like Aaron Schwartz. His attempt to warn her at the risk of his own life and his rescue of Izaat in the Commercial Center had impressed her, but her feelings went much deeper than that. His carefree visit to her apartment, his kiss, then his waiting for her at the Garden Tomb and the firm determination to protect her from the mob made her love him. When he had come to the hospital bed to make sure she was all right, even though badly hurt, her heart nearly burst with a longing to let him take her in his arms and care for her.

But she had resisted. A sleepless night had led her to believe that it was foolish to believe that such a marriage would work. Any chance of them loving one another was destroyed by war and the ever-widening gap between their people. The next morning she had run.

But running had done little good. She couldn't run from his memory, and she couldn't dump it aside as easily as she had shoved his brooch into its box and put it in the back corner of the dresser in her room. His face invaded both her daytime and nighttime hours.

When dreams of Aaron first occurred, she had walked immediately to the church to confess her sin, but as the nights passed she had stopped. Even a priest could not wipe away her feelings. Only time—and prayer—could do that.

She shoved the thoughts aside again and tried to concentrate on the statue of Christ on the cross. She felt so alone sometimes, so frightened. She had drawn closer to God in the last two weeks than she had been in all the rest of her short life. She had never doubted He was there, never questioned His love and concern for her. There had been other doubts, but she had always believed in Him. He was all that kept her from going crazy.

After nearly half an hour, she crossed herself and got up to leave the church. She felt some relief as she walked down the aisle toward the doors. There were at least thirty people in pews pleading with God, and the priest had a line waiting at the confessional. It was nice to know she wasn't the only one looking for help tonight.

Once outside, she quickened her pace up the hill toward the hotel. It was very cloudy with the chill of a storm in the air. Raindrops began falling, and she ran up the path, taking the front steps to the porch by twos. It wasn't until then that she saw Izaat sitting in the swing.

"Izaat!" He stood as she ran to him. After a warm embrace, she stepped back and took a good look. He was thin, pale, and older. She had never noticed gray in his hair before.

"You don't look well, Brother," she said with a sincere wrinkle to her brow.

"You look wonderful," he replied. He glanced at the street nervously, then smiled again. "Can we go inside?"

"Of course." She sensed his nervousness and quickly pulled a key from her pocket as they walked to the door. "What is it, Izaat? Why do you keep looking at the street?"

He forced a smile as the key turned in the door and it opened. They went inside and he locked it behind them. "No reason. It just seems strange to be outside the Old City." He did not wish to worry her, but word had come to him that Rhoui had gone to Abou Dayieh, that they had talked of ways to be rid of him. In the Old City, with his men around him, he did not feel uneasy, but here, away from that protection, it was different. They went into the empty, dark sitting room as Mary removed her coat.

"I cannot stay long." He pulled an envelope with heavy contents from his pocket and extended it to her. "That is enough money to get you to Beirut or Europe. There is also an account number for Barclay's Bank. It contains your share of our inheritance. Use what you need. There is plenty."

She looked at the envelope, then at him. "Your family, are they also going to Beirut?"

"They are in Ramallah now, but they will go north when my wife's father thinks it is too dangerous to remain."

"I didn't mention leaving in my letter, only that I wanted to see you."

"I know Khader meets here. It must be uncomfortable for you."

"How are things in the Old City?" Mary asked.

He had worked his way to the window and pulled the lace curtain back, peering into the darkness. "We are at war, Mary, not just with the Jews. They do not attack us, but Khader's mercenaries do not like us shutting them out. You were right about them—they are thieves and were stealing us blind. We were more afraid of them than we were of the Jews. That has changed now, but Abou Dayieh and his men are not happy with our position."

"How many of our neighbors remain?"

"Ten dozen men. Fewer families. They stay because they do not want to lose their homes and have no place else to go."

"And because they believe in you. Have you seen Rhoui lately?"

Izaat hesitated. "Rhoui opposes me. He fights with Khader's mercenaries and commands a platoon. His hate is worse than ever." He paused. "I . . . I watched as he killed a woman and child in the Jewish Quarter."

Mary gasped, her hand going to her mouth. "No!"

"It happened so quickly," Izaat said in a miserable tone. "He is crazy, Mary. Stay away from him. He swears he will kill you for what you did."

Mary sat down, her mind spinning.

"I must go." He came over and took her in his arms and hugged her tightly. "Leave this place, Mary. I am afraid for you. The Jews know Khader comes here and they will come after him and the men he brings here. They cannot do otherwise. Katamon is a position they cannot afford to give Haj Amin."

He let her go and went to the door and unlocked it. As he reached for the knob, it was pushed toward them and Abou Dayieh stood in the opening, several others behind him.

"Izaat, I am glad we have found you. Abdul Khader wishes to see you." The tone in Abou Dayieh's voice gave her the chills, but Mary stepped to Izaat's side and grabbed his hand. If he went with these men, she would never see him again.

Abou Dayieh looked at Mary with cold eyes. "We did not realize you were family." It was said with such coldness that Mary knew that if he had known she was Izaat's sister, things would have been horribly different.

"How did you know where to find me?" Izaat asked. He gripped Mary's hand comfortably in a vain attempt to give her comfort.

Abou Dayieh turned back and the two who stood beside him stepped aside. Mary saw Rhoui standing on the steps behind them. "Your brother was kind enough to keep an eye on you. It is better this way, don't you think? Fewer people get hurt." The smile turned to a hard frown. "Take him, and the woman."

As the men stepped through the door, Izaat slammed it into them, knocking them off balance. Then he shoved it forward, driving one man's upper body through the window as the latch clicked shut. He ran for the back of the house dragging Mary with him. They were through the kitchen and out the back door as Abou Dayieh's men recovered. Izaat dashed for the back of the yard where thick shrubs grew, burst through them and into the yard of a neighbor as a gun fired. Mary clung to his hand as the bushes pulled at her clothing and flesh, ripping into both. They burst across the lawn, down the side of the house, and into the street where Izaat turned downhill and dragged her at a dead run toward the corner. More shots were fired. Mary felt something graze her leg and stumbled, but kept going, a hard sting in her calf.

Before they got to the corner, Izaat turned them across the street and between two different houses. They came to a low picket fence, and he let go long enough to jump it, then turned back, placed his hands under her arms, and lifted her over. He saw the basement steps, hesitated, then shoved her that direction.

"Go! Hide!" He started away and she took a step after him.

"You will slow me down and neither of us will escape! This way we both have a chance! When you are ready, find your way to Jaffa, then to Beirut. I love you! Go!"

She watched until he disappeared in the darkness, took the steps down two at a time, and grabbed the knob, thankful that it turned.

She closed it behind her just as several men ran past the steps. Quietly she turned the key in the lock and stepped back into the shadows, her breathing coming so hard she thought they would surely hear it and turn back.

A shadow crossed the glass of the door and didn't move. Then a man stood in front of the window trying to see inside. He had a pistol in his hand. She stopped breathing and melted further into the darkness.

Then gun shots sounded and the man suddenly bolted up the steps.

There were other shots and her shoulders jerked with each one, her mind fearing the worst. Several car doors slammed, then the squealing of tires, the chatter of people far away. What had happened? Had they found Izaat? Had they killed him?

A part of her didn't want to move, but another had to know. The two sides of her fought until she finally took a step toward the door. Reaching it, she listened. Nothing. She turned the key in the lock quietly, the click magnified in the stillness, making her cringe. Next came the knob and the door was open. Carefully she went to the top of the steps and tried to see into the thick darkness. She listened. She watched. She waited. Nothing. Finally she worked up enough courage to walk to the street. There were lights in several of the houses and their glow cascaded onto the road, allowing her to see that it was empty.

She ducked back into the shadows of the bushes and noticed it was trying to rain again. What should she do? Where should she go? Would they be waiting for her back at the house? Why did they want her? Was all of this Rhoui's doing? Did he hate them that much?

She tried to keep from crying. She could not afford the luxury of such a sound now. She stood still for some time, trying to make sense of it. She had no coat, and the cold from the icy drizzle began seeping into her bones. It was after midnight when she finally worked up enough courage to step into the street and start walking toward the church. She was at the corner when the explosion nearly knocked her over. She looked back to see the roof and upper story of her aunt's hotel come apart in the air and plummet to the ground, a thick cloud of smoke, dust, and fire shooting heavenward. The noise of it coming apart was deafening, and she put her hands to her ears as she turned and ran, never looking back.

CHAPTER 25

The attack on the Semiramis Hotel by the Haganah missed Khader by only a few hours and Abou Dayieh by even less. All twenty-six casualties were civilians—one the deputy Spanish Consul.

Aaron looked at the report Abraham Marshak had received via their radio. The Spanish government would surely cut off relations with the Jewish state. Jewish leaders were blaming it on a rogue operation or ETZEL, making apologies, trying to recover. When the truth was known it would get worse.

He handed it to Hannah and let her read. They had stayed up late the night before discussing the war and the deaths of people like Moddel and her son and the Arabs at Damascus Gate. Hannah set the paper to one side. The look on her face was one of sadness.

"It is as you said, Hannah. War is never pretty."

"When they found out Khader wasn't there, they should have let it be," she said weakly.

Aaron didn't debate with her. He felt empty inside and wasn't up to giving Zalman Mart's lecture about "hard decisions."

"Do you ever think about going to the United States?" he asked.

"Emigrating?" Hannah smiled. "Sometimes. There we would have nothing to worry about but building a home and ranching five hundred acres of land that run along the Snake River. It is a beautiful place. His father raises cows, horses, and hay, and when Ephraim and I were there, we rode horses from the farmhouse to the river. Do you know what an elk looks like? It is very big with antlers so wide I could lay in them. They are very majestic, and the trees are filled with birds, the river with fish, and you can swim in it anytime you like. The children could be very happy there."

"During the *hamsin* when it is hot enough to boil your blood and the dust chokes the roads and everything looks dry and barren, it would be particularly enticing," Aaron said.

"Many will leave Palestine during this war, Aaron, but we will not go unless they force us."

"It might get you all killed," he said fearfully. "I don't want that to happen."

"Yes, I know, and I worry very much about you too. But this is our home and always will be. Ephraim and I are bound to the land even stronger than the rest of you. Our faith runs deeper than just living on sand and stone."

"Your belief in a Messiah."

"Our belief in a people, in the need to return, and, I suppose, an inner wish—a hope that—we might see the Messiah come. But there is so much yet to be done that it is only a slim hope."

"Ephraim must dream of that river once in a while," Aaron said.

"I see it in his eyes sometimes—in his heart—but it doesn't last." She sighed.

"He is a remarkable man."

"You are very much like him. So much so that I wonder sometimes if you aren't of the same blood."

"Me and Ephraim?" He chuckled. "If I were half the man he is, I would be pleased."

"You have the same sensitive nature, you both would risk your lives for others, you both have this ability to lead that is uncanny, and you both irritate me with your stubbornness. Yes, you could be his brother, or his son." She grinned. "You even part your hair the same, have the same funny, arrogant walk and this . . . this confidence that turns the head of a lady—that is also irritating." She smiled and paused, looking thoughtfully at Aaron. "Tell me about this Arab woman you rescued."

He did, and relished it. Thinking of her without being able to talk about her had been excruciating.

"She sounds wonderful," Hannah said. "You will be careful, won't you?"

"I think she left the country. I hope she did. It isn't safe here. When this is over, we'll see." He leaned forward. "Which brings me back to you. There may come a time when it will be best to visit that ranch for awhile."

Hannah smiled. "Thank you for caring. If I ever stop believing God is in this, I might just do that. But even now, even as ugly as this foolish bombing is, I still believe he wants us here." She noticed the journal sitting on the end table. "Have you read it yet?" she asked.

He smiled. "Not yet."

"Fear of the past can only cripple you, Aaron. Read it." She stood. "I am exhausted and need sleep. Will you still be here tomorrow?"

"No, I have to get back, and Jack arranged a ride at dawn. Thanks for the tea and warm bed. They helped a lot."

She stared at him. "You have changed."

He looked surprised. "In what way?"

"More settled, less confused? I'm not certain, but it is a change I like." She kissed him on the forehead and went off to her room. Aaron picked up the journal and stared at it, then took a deep breath and opened its cover with nervous hands. He wanted to start at the back, look at the last entry his father made, what his feelings were in the few days—or even hours—before his death, but the ache and fear of having to relive those hours forced him to start at the beginning. He blinked at the first page, then rubbed his eyes before beginning.

August 4, 1922 . . .

* * *

Mary hadn't found the priest, and in fear had decided to hide in the choir at the back of the church, one floor up. She had heard several people come and go, the large front doors banging solidly to signal their entrance and exit. Each time her body tensed as she listened and waited for someone to find her.

She felt lost. Where could she go? How could she get there? She looked at the envelope she still held tightly in her hand. She had money, but no papers, everything gone with the hotel or in the house in the Old City. What could she do?

After more than an hour of anguished indecision, she thought of the convent. It was just outside the Christian Quarter near her father's house and the nuns knew him. He had taken care of them when they were ill. Surely they would take her in and keep her presence confidential until she could make other arrangements. The question was how to get there without getting shot by some sniper from one side or the other of this cursed war, or being seen by those who apparently wanted her dead. Rhoui foremost among them.

"Oh, Rhoui," she said in quiet misery, "How could you do this? What has happened to you?"

She heard one of the front hall doors open. Peering through a crack in the railing, she saw the priest entering the church from what must have been his personal quarters. He joined a lady in one of the confessionals, and Mary quickly but quietly slipped down the steps from the choir, past the low murmur of voices in the confessional, and to the door of the priest's apartment.

"Forgive me, Father," she said under her breath. Then she opened the door and went inside.

* * *

The Arab on the wall above the Soeurs Réparatrices Convent was nearly asleep in the dim morning light when the priest, dressed a bit shabbily, walked along the wall to the entrance to the convent. The knock on the door echoed in deserted Suleiman Street and snapped the guard out of his stupor. He looked down, saw the priest, and let his eyes droop again. A moment later the door of the convent opened. The discussion was whispered, inaudible to him, but he noted that the priest had apparently lost weight, his robes too large for him. But, he was Muslim—what did he know about Christian priests?

He took one last glance at the door as the priest went inside and the door closed. And all this time he thought convents were only for nuns. But then, what did he know about convents either?

He checked the buildings across the street as a matter of routine then sank back down into the sandbags he was lying on and dozed again. For him it had been an uneventful watch.

CHAPTER 26

January 31, 1948

The front page of the newspaper detailed losses by the Arab Liberation Army to Jewish forces in the north and sighted a laughable quote by Fawzi el Kaukji, who claimed it was due to "dozens of tanks, planes, and artillery" owned by the Jews. Aaron couldn't help the outright laugh. The man was getting beat even though he had superior numbers and superior armament, and he was making his only defense a lie that not even the most thick-headed could possibly believe. If Kaukji were the best the League had, the Jews would get their state.

The second article said the Haj Amin had lost considerable clout in the Arab League over the last two months but that he was determined to get it back by calling for volunteers to help him carry out the *Jihad* against the godless Jews. It was obvious things were getting desperate for Haj Amin, and the article cautioned all Jews to recognize that there were bound to be renewed efforts by Amin's generals. Aaron thought the caution was an understatement.

Khader had failed at the Etzion Block in January, but his men were still massing around Jerusalem, and the attacks on the roads were getting stiff with more vehicles and lives lost every day. Tired of licking his wounds from attempts to take more than he could with his limited forces, it seemed obvious Khader was going to try and shut down Jerusalem. It was the only move that made military sense for the struggling guerillas of Haj Amin. Keep the roads open and Haj Amin would be finished.

After reading a number of other articles, Aaron's eye was caught by another article on the Semiramis Hotel. This one finally admitted some fault on the part of Haganah command in Jerusalem and said that steps were being taken to begin a full investigation. Then there was a final list of casualties, but it was not these names that caught his immediate attention. Just to the right was a list of other people who had been living there at the time—and Mary's name was on it. Next to it were the words "still missing." He gasped. The bombing had happened more than a month ago.

His heart pounded wildly in his chest as he sat forward and stared at the words to make sure they were real. He had thought of Mary often over the last month, wondered where she was, what she was doing, and even tried to think of some way to contact her. To see her name in the paper as one that was still missing made him ache all over. What could it mean? Surely if she had gone to Beirut . . .

He got to his feet and went immediately to the offices of the *Jerusalem Post*, greeted former fellow workers, then found the man whose name appeared as the writer of the article. After exchanging as few pleasantries as possible without giving offense, he learned that Mary Aref was the niece of the hotel owners who had been killed in the blast, but that nothing had been heard or seen of her since.

"Did you contact her family?" Aaron asked. "She has two brothers who live in the Christian Quarter."

"We have no contact there anymore, you know that. But I did talk to a source who says that Izaat Aref disappeared the same night. They may have been taken by Abou Dayieh's people prior to our men even attacking the hotel. It seems Izaat refused to cooperate with Dayieh." He shrugged. "But it's all hearsay. I have no sure information."

Aaron left the newspaper offices afraid and wondering what might have happened to her. Izaat? Refusing to go along with Dayieh? And where was the other brother, Rhoui? Had Dayieh decided the entire family was to be jailed or shot? *Where was she?*

He was near panic when he thought of Dr. Messerman. He knew Mary and had many friends in the Arab Quarter. Possibly he had heard news of her. Aaron searched his memory for what Hannah had told him about the doctor. He had healed well enough to leave the hospital several weeks ago, had a house in Katamon and an office in the Jewish Quarter. Since the bombing of the Semiramis Hotel, fighting in Katamon had become worse than in the Old City, making it a no-man's-land, especially for Jews. The chances were more likely the good doctor would be found in the Quarter.

That created a problem. The Old City was still under siege, the British even more unwilling to force Jaffa Gate open since the bombing of the Semiramis. The Haganah still tried to smuggle men and weapons in by using false floors in supply trucks, bribing British soldiers, or smuggling them over the rooftops, but their successes were far fewer than their failures. The Quarter was cut off except for the British, and it seemed that both they and the Arabs wanted it kept that way. Once again Jack was his only hope.

He located Jack at his apartment getting a bite to eat before going on duty. Jack said he would make arrangements to get him in, but it would be tomorrow. Aaron was to be ready at the staging point at eight and ask for a Major Duflin.

After a sleepless night, Aaron showed up in his street clothes—just another worker ready to load and unload trucks—found the major, and caught his ride. When he arrived, he found the central plaza a beehive of activity as people came to receive goods brought in by the British a few times a week. Otherwise the streets were nearly empty.

"You must return in two hours," Duflin told him. Aaron nodded, then headed for the nearest side street. Using the tunnels and a few sections of open street, Aaron went to Ladah Hospital where he found the new Haganah commander giving instructions to several men. It was Avraham Halperin. He and Aaron would need no introduction; they had spent time together in another unit.

"Avraham, good to see you," Aaron said.

"And you. When I was sent back here they said you had been hassled and sent to Acco but escaped on the way. I was glad to hear it," Avraham said. "You probably already know it, but Lassiter bragged about what he did to you. Pulled a couple more stunts that showed his true colors as well, and your friend Jack Willis went to his commander. He's been reassigned."

"Maybe there is justice," Aaron smiled. "How are things?"

"Heating up again." He tossed several radio messages on the small table. "They tried to move in on us a few weeks ago, about the time of the bombing of the Semiramis. We pushed them back, and now they're trying again. Nightly sniping to soften us up before they make their move." He paused. "Are you here to stay? I heard about your work in the Arab sector. We could use you."

"Don't believe everything you hear, but I have asked to come back. With Lassiter gone and papers reversing my conviction on the Lord Governor's desk, it's a possibility."

Halperin sat down and leaned his chair back on two legs. "Frankly, I'm surprised you're here without those papers. Lassiter's replacement— Faulkner—will arrest you if he or his men find you here. A couple of Brits were killed in your escape, and even if you didn't do the killing, Faulkner doesn't stop to split hairs. His brother was killed at the King David when ETZEL blew it up. Watch your step. I suppose you have come to check on Hannah and the kids?"

"I'll look in on them, but I came to find a Dr. Messerman. Is he still practicing in the Quarter?"

"The only doctor who stayed." He gave Aaron the address.

They spent a few minutes more discussing everything from Rabbi Salomon's continued stubbornness to Abraham's work in the tunnels before Aaron decided it was time to get moving. "I hear you've put a lot of the Orthodox to work," Aaron said.

Halperin chuckled. "I trained to be a rabbi. I know how they feel about fighting and respect the decision of those who won't. I pay them to pray for the rest of us. They appreciate it and are more cooperative, even friendly. It is another thorn in Salomon's hide." He sighed. "Things will come to a head between me and the Quarter's Chief Rabbi sooner or later, and one of us will be leaving the Quarter."

They shook hands and parted. Aaron knew his way through the tunnels but decided to try and stay above ground. It was a fairly warm day with a bright sun, and most of the streets he would traverse weren't in the areas of Arab strength. Still he moved cautiously, finally arriving in the narrow street where he found Dr. Messerman's office some five minutes later.

He received a warm welcome from the man whose life he had helped save at the Commercial Center. After a brief discussion of the Quarter's condition, Aaron asked him if he had heard anything about Mary.

"I have not. What has happened?"

Aaron filled him in on what he knew about Mary's disappearance, and the doctor's eyebrow wrinkled with concern. "Your feelings for her are obvious, but do you think to pursue this wise?"

"I wish only to know if she is alright."

"Very well. I still have some friends in the Arab part of town, though many have fled to Beirut and other places outside the country. Such a crime," he said. "Return here in an hour."

"Only an hour? But how will you . . ." Dr. Messerman gave him a mournful, 'why do you ask this question' look, as he carefully patted the mongrel by his side. "Very well. One hour," Aaron relented.

Messerman smiled. "You can get to the tunnels through my basement. I use them all the time."

Rather than tempt fate again, Aaron nodded, crossed the outer room to the basement door, and went down the narrow, steep stairs. There were holes in the walls to his right and left and a few kerosene lamps placed intermittently along the tunnel lit the way. As he walked through the tunnels, he heard the rather eerie sounds of shutting doors from time to time while shadowy figures moved ahead of him, but none came his direction until he reached a crossroads and bumped into Rabbi Marshak. They greeted. The rabbi was on his way to Hurva Synagogue but did not look well.

"How is Abraham?" Aaron asked.

"Busy, but if you follow me you might visit with him. There was another battle last night on the roofs and several of our men were wounded. They have established a makeshift first-aid room in the basement of the Hurva."

"I didn't get a chance to thank you for trying to help me the day I was taken prisoner."

The rabbi raised a hand. "It is quite alright." He gave a wan smile, too tired to hold it longer.

"*Atah Beseder?*"

"*Ken, ken,* just a little tired. War is not what makes a rabbi thrive, I am afraid. Peace, quiet, these I miss."

"And the new Haganah leader, Halperin?"

"Excellent. He is very orthodox. Studied once to be a rabbi. I must go. Come and see Abraham before you leave." He pointed.

"The Hurva is straight on this way. *Hi shomer.*" With that he shuffled quickly into the dusty dim light.

"*Lahitraot.*" Aaron watched him for a moment. He had aged a good deal. Aaron found the basement to Mithra's apartment, bounded up the steps and knocked, heard Mithra's quiet response and let himself in.

"Hello, Mithra. It is me, Aaron Schwartz."

"Aaron? It is good to hear your voice again. Are you back to stay?"

"Not yet, but soon I hope. How are you?"

She chuckled lightly. "Old, blind, and ornery. Now get on with you."

Aaron slipped out the door, checked both ways and took the stairs two at a time. Hannah greeted him with a hug and kisses on both cheeks. It had been nearly a month since they had talked. When she asked if he had come for a visit or to stay, he told her the reason he had taken the chance.

"I see," she said, then paused a moment, obviously choosing her words. "I have thought about you and Mary a lot since we last talked." She stopped folding the babies' diapers, leaned forward, her elbows on her legs. "It is hard enough to make a marriage work without coming into it from such different backgrounds."

"We'll cross that bridge if it ever comes. Right now, I just want to know she's alive." Joseph started giggling, his arms and hands extended and his fingers opening and closing toward Aaron.

"You have always been his favorite," Hannah said as Aaron gathered Joseph from off the couch. "What do they have you doing now?"

"I start commanding a platoon of Palmach defending the convoys in a few days, but I have asked for reassignment back here."

"That would be nice. Be careful. I understand the roads are very dangerous now. Do you hear anything about Rachel? It has been so long since I last saw her."

"All I can tell you is general stuff coming through the grapevine. She is still at the kibbutz, but there is talk of moving some of them to Etzion to reinforce it after Khader's last attack there. She may be one of them, though I think it would be hard to get her out of the Negev."

"But it is much more dangerous at Kfar Etzion, isn't it?"

"Not as dangerous as it is here. I still think you should go to Tel Aviv."

"Ephraim and I have talked, but I cannot do it. Not yet. Have you heard from Naomi?"

"We talked by phone the other day." The phones in the New City still worked most of the time, though the Arabs had cut the wires between there and Tel Aviv twice. Now the Brits patrol them because they need them open. That wasn't the case in the Quarter. "She is trying to come for a visit in the next few days."

"Abraham will be glad to know she is coming back. Did you know he went and saw her a month and a half ago?"

"Yeah, he told me last time I was here." He laughed a little. "I didn't think he would do it. Hasids don't usually court a woman."

"He says Naomi promised him a date next time she came home, but meetings with Haganah leaders did not leave her time. He asks after her often and confided in me that Naomi told him he must get his father's permission for this date before she will go."

"And has he asked the rabbi?"

"Not that I know of. I suppose he'll put it off until he knows it's absolutely necessary. Rabbi Marshak is a good man, and he is liberal for the Hasids, but this would be going too far, I think." She had a wrinkle to her brow that showed worry.

He chuckled again. "One of us wants to marry an Arab and another has a Hasidic Jew on her trail. Cause for worry, I'd say."

She wiped Jacob's nose with a handkerchief. "Maybe I should lock you both up."

"Rabbi Marshak does not seem well," he put in.

"Dr. Messerman says he should go to Hadassah Hospital for tests. He has problems in his stomach, but the rabbi refuses to go. I think he is afraid they will keep him, and his people need him right now."

They talked of trivial matters, both avoiding any direct discussion of the war. He was amazed at her calmness, though she looked tired and he could tell she wasn't eating well. But who in Jerusalem was, especially in the Old City? He thought of pressing her about leaving again but decided it would do no good. He glanced at his watch and stood.

"Where are you staying?" she asked.

"At the Hotel Himmelfarb across from the *Jerusalem Post* building. It's where most of the convoy troops stay now. How is Ephraim?"

"He makes the usual flights and is coming home in the next couple of days for a short stay if Jack can get him past the barricades." Her countenance brightened considerably.

Aaron stood, kissed the twins on both cheeks, then got Jacob to laugh by throwing him up in the air a couple of times. Leaning down, he kissed Hannah on the forehead. "I have to get back to Dr. Messerman then meet my ride. *Hi Shomer.*"

She nodded, biting her lip. As always, she hated to see him go, to see any of them go. She always felt better when they were here, in view, healthy and safe. When he was at the door she gained enough control to talk.

"You know that if you choose Mary, Ephraim and I will love her just as we do you," she said.

"Yeah, I know."

Hurrying down the steps and back the way he had come, he entered the office as the doctor was removing something from his mongrel's ear. It was a small, folded piece of paper. Messerman looked up at him over the rims of his glasses and smiled. "My secret is out."

"This dog is how you get word from the Arab Quarter?"

He chuckled. "An old friend of mine and I bought this one together. We lived next door to one another then, but when I moved to Katamon, I left the dog with him. The next thing I know the little beast shows up on my doorstep for a day or two then disappears. This continues for a month. And then my friend and I go to lunch. We find he is going back and forth, between the Christian Quarter and Katamon to be with us both. So we train him to carry a little message from time to time. Now he keeps me informed."

"Uh, and you keep him informed?"

Messerman saw the concern. "Only about matters involving friends. We never talk of military matters. Never."

He unrolled the paper, donned his heavy glasses to read the very small print as Aaron pulled up a straight-backed, wooden chair.

"You are right. Izaat Aref has disappeared. It is rumored that Abou Dayieh's men took him from the Hotel Semiramis on the very night of its destruction. His refusal to take orders from Khader's men is the reason, and his brother Rhoui was the traitor."

Aaron felt sick. "Then they may have taken her as well. Rhoui hated her for what he considered humiliations to the family."

"You mean because she was seeing you," Messerman smiled. "According to this there is the rumor of a Jew in her life, but no one knows the name. I only assumed . . ."

"You assume correctly," he said softly. "I have gotten her killed for sure."

"Izaat Aref used to be a supporter of Haj Amin's forces. It is interesting to hear he changed his heart. But then his father never did have any love for the Husseinis." He sighed, "Rhoui has taken over that portion of the Old City Izaat controlled, and the mercenaries are moving in just as they have everywhere else. As a result more people are moving out. Rhoui always was an ill-tempered, impetuous fool."

"Did your friend say anything else?"

The doctor smiled. "Yes, it seems that Rhoui has asked people around Dr. Aref's home to notify him if his sister returns. If that is the case, she must still be alive."

"But no one has seen her," Aaron said with relieved concern.

"No, no one has seen her. I suspect that Mary is afraid of her brother and she now hides where she knows he will not look. Possibly she has arranged to leave the country, but at least you can calm your heart. I am sure she is alright."

"And Izaat?"

"They say he is either dead or in prison. Khader has locked up a number of his political enemies if it would be detrimental to his cause to kill them."

"And where does he imprison them?"

"He would have been taken to the headquarters building just inside Stephen's Gate for interrogation. After that he was either shot or sent to a long-term prison Haj Amin used in the 1936–39 riots. It is in Bethlehem."

"If you hear whether or not he is alive, will you let me know?"

Dr. Messerman nodded. "And if I hear of Mary, I will let you know as well." He tore the note into many small pieces and put them in an ashtray, then burned them. As they smoldered, he sat down and looked at Aaron with his old and wise eyes. "You have changed since we last spoke."

"I am not as sure of things as I once was. I wish . . . I wish we could end this senseless killing and agree to live together, but I also see why it will never be."

"And this reason?" Messerman asked.

"I see things from their perspective more than I did two months ago. I am beginning to see what was happening to me in Germany happening to them, and I hate it."

"Good, then maybe, when the bad ones are gone, you and others who have learned this lesson, on both sides, can bring peace. It is a good start."

Aaron got up to leave. "Do you live here now, in the Old City?"

"In this room. The small couch is my bed. I left Katamon weeks ago. Khader's mercenaries murdered my neighbor as he walked up his front steps. I decided I am not ready to die so easily." He smiled.

Aaron nodded. "To a long life then."

"And long life to you, young Jew."

Aaron went back into the tunnels. He would have to hurry to catch his ride.

* * *

Mary was perfectly content in the convent. The outside world seemed distant after the first few days, the sound of gunfire dim, the solid walls a protection to her. She started wearing the habit of a novice after the first week and seriously considered training and taking vows by the third, but thoughts of Aaron kept her from doing so. By the first of February, she had given up on the whole idea and was thinking more often about using some of her money to get out of the city. But she didn't know how to get papers, nor did she know how she would make the journey. She expressed her concerns to the Mother Superior who understood nothing of such things either, but said she would discreetly ask the priest about it the next time he came to check on their needs. When Mary asked how long that would be and was told six months, she began trying to think of other ways to find out what she needed to know.

Fear of the outside kept her from pursuing any of them. She was sure that Izaat had been murdered, sure that Rhoui hunted her and was using Abou Dayieh's men to do so. To take chance on discovery and face Izaat's fate overwhelmed her.

She had been very concerned about what had happened at the hotel, but because the nuns had no newspaper—would not even allow one in the convent—she made opportunity to visit with one of the men who brought groceries. His details had horrified her, and she mourned for nearly a week over her aunt and uncle and the others who had died. She had talked with most of them, become friends with many. It was very difficult to accept that most were gone, that another act of terrorism had cost so many innocent lives. Then she felt guilty for having survived. Had Izaat not come, had they not escaped from the hotel, she would have been in her bed on the third floor of the building. Why did God take so many and leave so few?

The Mother Superior had helped her through those weeks as best as she could, but Mary's greatest ally was still prayer, and after a month, the nightmares went away, and she began to accept what had happened as just the way it was. All those who had died would expect her to go on with her life, and she could not disappoint them.

But a few days ago it had all come back to haunt her again. The Jews had finally admitted that it was not ETZEL but Haganah, that they had been after Abdul Khader. Had her aunt and uncle not catered to him, let him plan his bloody attacks in their dining room, they might be alive today, along with more than twenty others. What they had thought such a blessing had proven to be a horrible curse.

She had spent one sleepless night wondering if Aaron had been involved. He was Haganah. He was fighting for his people and against Khader. He might have been involved, and it made her ache all over. Blowing up an empty shop was one thing, but to kill the innocent was another. She could never forgive him for that. Never.

For the last two days she had tried to get her mind off it again by reading from the convent's small library. Until the hotel was destroyed, she had been reading from the copy of the Book of Mormon Aaron had given her. She had finished it once and was working on Third Nephi again. In some ways it was like reading a novel, and yet it was so packed with new doctrine that she had reread parts to try and understand them. She had never read any scripture that centered on Christ so much, and His visit to the Nephite people especially intrigued her. She missed the book and had even considered writing a letter to America to ask for another, but had neglected it, her life too transient right now. Instead she was teaching herself Latin by reading from an antiquated Bible and using a Latin to English dictionary to do it. So far she had managed the first three verses of Genesis.

She arose at five o'clock as usual, dressed, and went to the small chapel to join the other sisters in prayer. They were halfway through when the front door knocker echoed through the building and the Mother Superior rose to answer it. There had been numerous visitors lately, mostly people with possessions they hoped the sisters would safeguard while they were away to some city or other to wait out the war. The convent had finally set aside a large room for such things, but only because they could use the donations given them. Food had become extremely expensive and the extra funds were needed to keep it on the table. But doing it concerned them as well. Eventually someone would learn of the growing treasure and could bring trouble to them.

The Mother Superior returned a few moments later with a letter and an anxious look on her face. She called Mary aside and gave it to her.

"Who delivered it?" Mary asked. She was shocked that anyone had discovered she was here, and it frightened her to think who might have found out.

"An Arab boy. He did not say whom it was from. Mary, he knew your full name. I could not lie. I . . ."

Mary thanked her and said she understood, then went quickly to her room, her heart pounding. She looked at the envelope for a long moment. There was no writing on the outside. Finally she crossed herself and said a quick prayer before ripping it open and removing the single sheet of paper. It had only one sentence and a signature.

I know you are there. Rhoui.

She sank to the bed, the words in her hand ominous and threatening. What would he do? When would he come? How could a brother have so much hate? The answers were frightening to contemplate, but they all led her to the same conclusion.

She must leave the convent, and she must leave soon.

* * *

Naomi saw the wire just before leaving Haganah headquarters for her apartment. The wire came out of the north from the commander of the

3^(rd) Palmach Division stationed near Safed and indicated that a pair of explosives experts, brought in from Germany in January, were training Arabs in their art. One of the men was described as a blond Arab.

She went immediately to Eleazar and showed him the wire. They had been working together on similar reports for nearly a week. Eleazar read it, then removed his glasses and rubbed his eyes.

"Do you think it's Kutub?"

"The description fits, and we know he was in Damascus two weeks ago."

"It says here that they left Safed for Jerusalem. If the information is reliable, that means Kutub is planning to answer our mistake at the Semiramis."

The blond-headed, blue-eyed Kutub, who looked more like a German than an Arab, had fought with Abdul Khader in the rebellion of 1936–39. He had loved explosives then, but his real expertise had come when he followed Haj Amin and others to Hitler's Germany where he had been trained by the best the Nazis had to offer.

"Too bad this devil didn't die in the camps," Eleazar said.

"He'll strike civilians targets," Naomi said. "The bombing of the Semiramis may have been a mistake, but it did cause a lot of Arabs to desert the city. Khader will want to match that and more."

Eleazar handed her a flier. "We received that yesterday. Khader started distributing them early in January."

Naomi saw that it was a recruitment flier aimed at disgruntled British soldiers and policemen. It recounted acts of anti-British terror committed by the Jews over the last few years, mostly by ETZEL and LEHI. Covering an entire page were the names of Brits slain by Jewish "terrorists" using explosives and calling for them to join the Arab effort to answer "blow for blow." On the edge of the pamphlet, Eleazar had written some dates and places.

"What are these?" she asked.

"Instances of deserters helping the Arabs buy and steal weapons and explosives over the last few weeks. It looks to me like Khader was making these plans even before the explosion of the Semiramis, and as near as I can calculate, he has enough explosives to blow half of Jewish Jerusalem.

She pondered the dates and names in front of her. Haj Amin's attempt to reverse partition in December had failed, and January hadn't been a banner month for him either. He was desperate, frustrated, and needed something more, something that could turn things around.

"Time is slipping away from him," she mumbled.

"He needs something big. You had better contact our people in Jerusalem. Tell them what we've found and warn them about trusting any British. Those deserters I've noted would like nothing better than getting a little revenge."

She went back to the radio room and began pacing. Something was missing. Sitting down, she scanned through all the latest communiqués, reports, and rumors they had received over the last few days. Stolen vehicles, firefights, the Quarter still under siege, road blocks, checkpoints, reduced food supplies. So many things, but nothing stuck out, nothing indicated any immediate danger. But it was there; she could feel it in the pit of her stomach.

Finally she prepared the message. Kutub was in Jerusalem. The city should be on full alert. There could be an attempt at retaliation for the Semiramis. All Arab trucks and cars should be suspect and, with more Brits deserting to the Arabs and selling them explosives, caution should be used in dealing with Brits trying to get to Jewish centers of population. At the very least their cargo should be checked and their identity verified. When finished she had it coded, then sent to Jerusalem. She only hoped they would take it seriously.

* * *

Aaron looked at his watch by the light of a window. It was 9:50. It had been a long day.

On his return to the New City, he had gone to the Jewish Agency and Haganah headquarters to check on the orders for his new assignment and to remind Amir or Shacham, whomever he saw first, that he still wanted back in the Quarter. The place had been abuzz with the fact that David Sheal'tiel had replaced Amir and Shacham. Rumor had it that Shacham had been passed over because of his decision to blow up the Semiramis even if Khader weren't in the place. It had caused more of a furor than they had expected, and Shacham was taking the fall. Even though Aaron had agreed with some of Mart's arguments that night, the end result had sickened him, and he hoped it would be a lesson learned in the Haganah. In the same second he doubted it. War couldn't be that easily manipulated.

He hung around the office for an hour discussing the pros and cons before going with others for something to eat along Ben Yehuda Street. Then he went to the Himmelfarb Hotel to get some sleep. His first convoy assignment would take place before sunrise.

He was worried about tomorrow's run. He and his platoon had trained well together, and though he had some good men, they were inexperienced. The Jerusalem/Tel Aviv Road was a focal point of Arab attacks now, and no convoy got through without being hit, some worse than others. It all depended on the size of the convoy and the Brits' willingness to fight the growing hoard covering the mountainside. People were dying, especially Palmach people. He had seen two of his men die in the Old City. He wasn't looking forward to seeing more.

Crossing the street, he entered the hotel, walked through the lobby saying hello to a few of the men lounging about, then went to his room on the top floor.

After closing the door, he removed his jacket and opened the window. The weather had been warmer that day, heating up the stale room. Taking a minute for some fresh air, he sat on the window sill and listened to the city.

It was quiet—no shots being fired, no traffic hustling about the streets. Just quiet. He closed his eyes thinking of where Mary might be. He felt more comfortable since his talk with Dr. Messerman, but he still worried. Hate like that of Rhoui Aref made devils of men.

He noticed the British army truck turn into the street a block away. It moved slowly his direction, and a military staff car fell in behind. He wondered what they were doing here this late, but he knew they couldn't have come without passing at least two Jewish police checkpoints. Letting it go, he climbed back inside and lowered the window within a few inches of the sill then glanced at his watch: 10:10. He was tired. He'd better get to bed. In the bathroom, he removed his outer shirt, brushed his teeth, and washed.

Turning off the light over the sink he closed the bathroom door behind him. He was just sitting on the bed when the explosion ripped the front of his room off and deposited it in the street below. When he revived, he was looking up at a splintered ceiling hanging down at all angles. He blinked in disbelief then tried to get up but someone prevented it. Just as well—he couldn't muster it anyway as a painful numbness took his strength. He felt himself being put on a stretcher, heard voices, smelled smoke and dust that choked him. His head ached and his ears were ringing, making everything distant. He tried to stay conscious but couldn't. His body seemed to be rolling up on him, his life a door someone was forcing shut against his will. His vision blurred, darkened, then went out altogether.

CHAPTER 27

The next morning, the news of the explosion at the *Jerusalem Post* building spread like wildfire through the Jewish Quarter of the Old City. Fear came back with a vengeance as rumors flew about the cause. The Arabs had artillery. They had the city surrounded and the British were gone. The Egyptians had sent their bombers.

It was an explosion they all heard during the night, and yet it quickly became much more. By noon, twenty-five more men asked Rabbi Salomon to make arrangements with the British for them to leave, another forty asking in the afternoon. Hannah couldn't help but wonder what was happening in the New City, how many hundred would be packing their bags to move to Tel Aviv. She knew it would not be a small number.

When the single-sheet edition of the *Jerusalem Post* arrived in the Old City a day late, it explained it all.

The *Post* first apologized for the single sheet of paper. They had been hit by a car bomb, everything destroyed, building all but gone. Some who had been working late were wounded, one dead. Under the circumstances, Hannah thought it amazing that they had put out a paper at all.

Then she saw that the Himmelfarb Hotel, located directly across the street from the *Post*, had been hit as well. She had to sit down, her eyes quickly scanning the words. It also had been partially destroyed and some of its inhabitants critically injured—no names. She could only guess at Aaron's condition. For her it was a day of endless prayers to overcome the feeling of doom. Finally she went to Avraham Halperin and asked if anything had come by radio. It hadn't, but he was very understanding of her concern. He promised to let her know if he heard anything.

David read the paper while Hannah was in her room on her knees. Afraid for Aaron, he slipped away and into the tunnels where he pressed Abraham Marshak for news.

"There is nothing new. It is still very confusing, and they're just getting the fires put out so they can search through the rubble. Maybe tonight, maybe tomorrow, it is hard to say." He put a hand on David's shoulder. "Aaron is a survivor. He is okay." Inside Abraham wasn't so sure. How many lives does God allow one man?

It wasn't good enough for David. He walked to the square where the Brits were taking those too scared to remain in the Old City any longer. Though he had heard the Brits weren't good about letting people back in, he also knew Jack could always find a way. He got lost in the crowd as they started loading on trucks, but then thought of telling Mum. She would worry. No, it would be all right. He would be back with information about Aaron before nightfall. That would make everything okay; she would forgive him. Besides, he had to know, and she might not let him find out. He couldn't stand the thought of not knowing his brother was okay. Worse, she might try to go herself. She was hurting. He had heard her prayers through the door, but the babies needed her, not him. He told himself that if he went, she wouldn't have to.

Keeping his face half-hidden by his hat, he got in the truck with a family as if they were his own. The Brits didn't question anyone anyway, so he wasn't worried much. He slipped down in the bottom of the fully loaded vehicle, out of the way and out of sight of anyone standing outside the truck. He didn't relax until it moved and started toward Jaffa Gate, British armored vehicles with machine guns falling in behind.

It was then he saw Beth.

"Bebe! What are you d-doing here?" he hissed.

She looked over at him, surprised, but put her finger to her lips to shush him. "Be quiet!"

He pushed past a couple of other children to get next to her, his face red with frustrated anger. "This is too dangerous! You have to get out. Go back!" he said angrily.

"It's too late. We're at Jaffa Gate. Do you want me to get off in the middle of this Arab mob?"

He looked through the wooden slats of the truck and saw she was right.

"But why? What are you doing?"

"Don't be silly. I'm doing exactly what you're doing. Going to find out about Aaron. I saw the paper, and he's my brother too, you know."

"He isn't, not for real, and—"

"Same as, and I love him just as much as you do. Now hush up before someone we know notices and tells the British."

David bit his tongue, the frustration showing in his face, but he kept quiet until they reached the drop-off point and began unloading. Beth got out first and was walking quickly away when he jumped to the ground and ran after her, grabbing her arm and towing her back toward the truck.

"You're going back with them," he said firmly. She was strong for her age, and it took all his effort to keep her moving.

"If you say anything to them, I'll make them take you as well," she threatened, while trying to pull her arm away.

He let go and she strutted away. David caught up and fell in stride with her. "Bebe, p-please, it only takes one of us, and it should be me. Mum needs you and—"

"She needs you more. You're the man of the house when Pop isn't around, and now here you are, where you can't protect her at all. Go back, David. Take care of her. I'll be fine."

"Not on your life. Mum would throttle me if I left you here by yourself."

She stopped, her eyes rolling to the back of her head. "Alright then, let's stay together, and we'll go back together. Did you find out when the Brits are going back?"

"No, but . . ."

She pushed him on the shoulder. "Go find out, but don't let them know we just got off one of their trucks." David stumbled away with a hard stare at Beth. Sometimes she could be so stubborn. And rude.

He asked the first soldier he saw. "S-sir, I would like to go into the Old City. When d-do you go again?" He hadn't stuttered much lately, but when under pressure, it seemed to get worse.

The Brit laughed at him. "Return? This is a one-way trip, lad. Even if we were goin' back today—which we aren't—we don't take anybody in. That's our orders."

"But . . ."

"If you don't like 'em, see the commander at Bevingrad, but that's our orders. They want you troublemakers outta the Old City before you all get yourselves killed. Nobody goes back, especially kids. Now, get lost."

David felt fear grip him between his shoulders as he walked back to Beth, but he quickly decided he wouldn't tell her. No need to get her all excited and mad. They would work it out later. Besides, Aaron would take care of it once they found him, and they could still find Jack Willis.

"Well?" Beth asked.

"Tonight, maybe t-tomorrow morning," he said. "Come on, we have to hurry."

They ran down Jaffa Road to the side street where the Hotel Himmelfarb and the *Post* building had been. What they saw was awful and stunned them both. They walked slowly toward the ruins, some people standing about, others searching the rubble with anxious but pained movements. Few spoke, the shock causing silent awe. It gave David the willies.

Seeing a man standing near the hotel, a look of importance about him, David grabbed Beth's coat and pulled her that direction. "Come on."

"Are you Haganah?" he asked directly.

The man looked at them and smiled. "What can I do for you?"

"My—" Beth jerked on his sleeve. "*Our* brother was staying in this hotel. We need to know if he's alright."

"What was his name?" the man replied, his face turning serious.

"Aaron Schwartz."

The man scanned a piece of paper in his hand. "He's in the hospital," the man replied in obvious relief. "I'm sorry, but I don't know his condition."

Beth's face brightened with relief but not David's. People died in hospitals just as easily as outside of them. He pulled Beth away.

"Hey, wait a minute. Where—" the man said.

"To the hospital," David answered over his shoulder.

David didn't hear the retort. He was already halfway down the street, Beth running to keep to his side.

When they ran up to where the buses loaded, David looked for the number they wanted. When they found it they climbed aboard, but the driver stopped them at the top of the steps.

"Sorry, children, this bus isn't going today, maybe not tomorrow. The road through Sheik Jarrah is closed. The Arabs are rioting all over the city. Celebrating all this," he said angrily. "Only emergency vehicles with wounded are getting through, and then only because they're accompanied by armored vehicles."

David and Beth couldn't believe their ears and questioned the driver again.

"I'm telling you there is no way up there. Not now. Not for days unless you own an armored car."

They got off the bus and walked quietly away, both a bit defeated.

"Maybe this wasn't such a good idea after all," Beth said weakly.

"Don't worry, I'll think of something." They were walking past Bevingrad and David glanced over at the truckload of soldiers just passing through the gate.

"Jack Willis can get us up there. And home."

Beth brightened, then the look changed to doubt. "But how do we find him? We don't know where he lives, we don't know—"

"They'll know," he said pointing at the compound. "Wait here." He crossed the street and asked the guard at the gate if he knew Jack Willis. The guard nodded.

"Do you know where he lives?"

"No, sorry kid, but it wouldn't matter anyway. Jack left for 'Aifa yesterday. Took a convoy, and I don't know when 'e'll be back."

He thanked the soldier and went slowly back to Beth, then explained what he had learned. They sat down on the curb to think. It was getting dark, and they were quickly running out of options.

"I heard Ephraim tell Mum that there's a curfew. If the British catch us on the streets after dark, they'll send us to jail," Beth said.

"They don't put kids in jail. Maybe an orphanage or something, but not jail."

"Jail. Yup, they'll put you in jail," said someone from behind them. David turned to see a man sitting with his back against the wall eating some dried dates, or gumming them at least, a half-empty gin bottle in his other hand. His head swayed side-to-side and he seemed unable to see, his eyes looking up into his head most of the time.

"They don't," David said. He turned back. "Never mind him. He's crazy and half-drunk to boot."

"Jail. They throw us in jail. Been there. Jail. It's not so bad." He popped another date in the general direction of his mouth, missed, but didn't notice.

"David. If he's right . . . This was really stupid. I want to go home."

David put an arm around Beth's shoulder to calm her. "It will be alright, Beth. I'll figure it out."

"Brits don't like the Jews. Jail. That's what they do with us! They say it's our fault, put us in jail! Like the Nazis. No different. Don't like Jews."

The man was talking fast, his hands shaking as he put another date in his mouth then took a swig from the bottle. Between sentences he seemed to be mumbling. He was making David both nervous and angry.

"Come on. I've got an idea. Never mind him—he's crazy."

"Crazy. Yup. Crazy," the man said, his head darting from left to right and back again. "Can't fight the British. They have all the guns. All the guns."

David guided Beth up the street, then across.

"I wonder what happened to him. Why is he that way?"

David only shrugged. "The war, the camps, maybe both. I saw guys like that in Berlin, don't you remember?"

"Not like that, but there was this woman in the camps . . . I . . . don't want to think about that though. This was really stupid, David. We have to try and get back to Mum. I thought I'd just come and see Aaron, then go back, so I didn't tell her. Did you?"

"No."

"She'll be worried sick. We have to get back. Tonight! We should go back to where the convoys start."

"They aren't going back today," he said. "And they don't take anyone with them anyway. It's the rules."

"But you said . . ."

"Don't worry. I'll get us back." They walked toward Ben Yehuda Street, David mulling over the possibilities. Somehow he would find a way. He had too.

* * *

Hannah had looked everywhere. No one had seen them, no one knew where they were. What had happened to them? She reached the basement of their apartment complex and went up the stairs. They had better be home, waiting.

She opened the door to Mithra's apartment to see the babies still asleep on the blankets on the floor. Mithra sat in the chair, but Abraham Marshak was on the couch and both had concerned looks on their faces.

Hannah felt fear go up her spine. "What is it? Mithra, what has happened? Abraham?" She immediately went to the babies.

"They're fine, Hannah," Abraham said. "It's Beth and David. They're gone."

"Gone? Gone where? What do you mean?"

"They went out of the Quarter in the British trucks. Rabbi Marshak's wife saw them board separately, but on the same truck. She thought surely you were aboard, but when she heard you were searching for them . . . Anyway, they are gone," Mithra said.

"Aaron!" Hannah said. "They went to find out about Aaron." What if they find that he didn't survive? How would they handle it alone? "Have we heard about survivors of the explosion yet?" She asked the question as calmly as she could, but her hands were shaking.

"Yes," Abraham said, glad he could give her some good news for a change. "Aaron is in the hospital."

Hannah put a hand to her mouth to stop the sob of joy. "Is . . . is he hurt bad?"

"We don't know his condition." He took a deep breath. More bad news. "The children can't get to him. There are fights all over the city, and the Arabs of Sheik Jarrah have shut off the road to Hadassah Hospital. They won't reach there, and they can't get back, at least not tonight. The Brits aren't coming back for at least another day, and you know their policy about bringing people in."

"Do they have any place to go?" Mithra asked Hannah.

"No. Jack Willis is gone. That's why Ephraim didn't come home from Tel Aviv last night," she said frantically, "They can't even get to Ephraim." She stood. "I have to go and find them."

"There is no way out of the Old City, Hannah. You will only get yourself shot, and the twins need you." Mithra said.

Drained, Hannah nodded again. She was right. "Can you get word to Ephraim?"

Abraham couldn't respond as positively as he would have liked. "Yes." Abraham got up to leave. "Do not worry. David is a smart boy—one of the best on the roofs. A survivor. He will take care of them, and I have the Haganah watching for them. If they're found, they'll be cared for until we can work something out."

Hannah nodded one more time, but he had already closed the door. It was the first time since she had been given charge of them in Germany that she and the children had been separated, and she was completely helpless to do anything about it. She paced, both angry and frightened. First Aaron, now this? How could they do this?

"They are just children, Hannah," Mithra said, reading her young friend's mind. "Do not think too harshly of them." Mithra rocked the chair back and forth. There had been many times when she had quietly wished she were not blind but this was the most poignant of all. She had come to love Hannah and her children. They were the family she lost to the war, and it made her ache to be so helpless when they had such a great need. But none of them could help. They had no way out of the city. They must trust God—and the children. She reached over and took Hannah's hand. It was going to be a hard night.

* * *

David purchased a round loaf of bread from a market in Ben Yehuda Street with the few coins he had in his pocket.

"Where did you get money?" Beth asked as she devoured a handful of bread.

"Working for the butcher. When meat comes, I carry it to the butcher's shop for him, but I haven't made much lately. Not with the price of what little meat comes in, and I have been busy running messages."

Beth knew about his work at night for the Haganah. He was the youngest of the boys to do it, but they all said he was the quickest. As the fighting escalated, the Brits tried to enforce a curfew, and the messengers were the only ones who had the ability to move around the streets. "You should stop doing that stuff. It's too dangerous."

David only shrugged while noting that things weren't much better here than in the Quarter anymore. Though people were trying to go about their business, they did it with a nervous anxiety that didn't allow them to take time for others or to even say a kind word. Their faces were filled with tension, and they seemed to be watching everyone else with a wary eye—as if they were wondering if those around them might be an enemy. It was a horrible way to live but he understood it. It was the way he and Aaron lived in Germany during the war. It was the kind of fear that eventually led you not to trust anyone and even to turn away from them.

"Come on," he said to Beth, taking her hand. "I have an idea."

"Where are we going?" she asked.

"Do you remember the woman Mum used to buy clothes from? The Arab woman with the sewing shop?"

"Yes, she made this dress," Beth said.

"Well, she's Mum's friend. Maybe she can help."

They walked along Jaffa Road until the walled compound of Bevingrad came to an end and a street joined to the right. Turning, they walked nearly to St. George Road to a group of small Jewish and Arab shops. Further on, at the intersection to St. George Road they could see a barricade set up and sandbagged emplacements in which men warily eyed the Arab section on the other side of the street. It was the beginning of the no-man's-land between Arabs and Jews.

"Those are Jews aren't they?" Beth asked. "Why do the Brits allow them to have weapons in the open when they don't allow our soldiers to do it in the Old City?"

"They're policemen, and they worked for the British before this mess. Now the Brits let them guard our part of the city. The Arab policemen do the same in their part of the city. See, over there." He pointed at barricades on the far side of St. George. "Those are Arabs. It used to all be one police force, but now it is two."

"But if that is the case, why don't they let our men have weapons, let us have police?" Beth asked.

"We've never had police in the Quarter, either Jewish or Arab. It's controlled by the British army. They do things sort of different and don't want us messing with their authority. Here they watch the police on both sides, make sure they act only as police not soldiers. As long as they do, they let them keep their weapons. If they misuse them, they take them. Neither side wants to lose their policemen to a British prison because of fighting, so they just police and stay calm. We will need a police force when the Brits are gone, so will the Arabs. It's complicated."

"I'll say. Look," Beth pointed at a far rooftop where Arab heads covered with kafiyehs could be seen just above sandbags. "They could shoot us from there." She ducked into a doorway and pulled him with her. "We shouldn't be here, David."

"They won't shoot, not here. This is one street the British wouldn't put up with it. They need it open to get their troops in and out of the city. Besides, this is the shop we want anyway." He tried the knob and the door opened. Inside they found the shop a mess, a few pieces of clothing strewn about on the floor, furniture broken, and the sewing equipment ruined.

Beth gasped, and David only nodded as he stared at the room. Beth leaned down and picked up a headscarf, feeling its texture. It had been torn and was dirty but still usable. She walked slowly around the room picking things up, putting them back in place as if doing so would restore things to the way they had been. "This is awful, David. Who could have done this?"

"It is an Arab shop, Beth. Who else but Jews?"

"But why? She wouldn't hurt a fly."

A bit exasperated, he picked up a chair and sat it down rather hard. "Do you think it is any better in the parts of the city the Arabs control? The Jewish shops there are just like this! This is war, Beth, just like in Germany!"

She seemed ready to cry as they stared at each other across the room.

"I'm sorry. I didn't mean to yell. It is this way on both sides now. We drive each other out of our share of the city. It will be this way forever." He stepped past her to the small room at the back. Boxes were scattered about, the precious cloth and other items they used to contain gone. He rummaged through the piles of garbage and found two more head scarves and a torn dress, along with several pieces of unused material. It gave him an idea. It would be a bit dangerous, but he could do it. He knew he could.

"Can you fix this?" he asked Beth as he brought the pieces back into the main shop.

She looked at the dress. "Yes, if I can find needle and thread. Why?"

"I have an idea." He searched along the shelves and in the refuse strewn about the room. He found thread still attached to the battered sewing machine. Beth found a small package of needles on the floor. She was soon repairing the dress while David watched out the window.

"The shop next door is Jewish. I wonder . . ." He turned to her. "Keep working. I'll be right back." He slipped from the shop before she could respond and went next door. It was locked and the windows boarded. He looked at the next shop and the next—all Jewish, all boarded up, locked. The fourth was an Arab shop and closest to St. George Road. It had been boarded but still broken into. He slipped through the hole that had been made and went inside. A souvenir shop that sold goods made of olive wood, much of its inventory lay smashed on the floor. The carver's tools were strewn about the floor, their handles broken off, their blades bent so they couldn't be used. He found nothing else that would help his plan and returned to Beth just as she was finishing the repairs on the dress. She threw it at him in anger, fire in her eyes.

"I hate you sometimes," she said.

David gave her a puzzled look. "What . . . what did I do?"

"You left me alone, without even so much as . . . as a word about what you were going to do! Don't ever do it again!"

She was near tears, her lower lip quivering slightly.

"I . . . I'm sorry, Beth, I didn't realize . . ."

She broke down. "I'm scared, David. This was so stupid. I wanted to believe everything was all right out here, in the New City, but it's just as bad, maybe worse. We really don't have any place to run, to hide from all this. When we got out of Germany, I started to believe it was all over, that we had finally found peace and a good life. But now everything is in danger again. Everything! We could lose Mum and Dad, and I could lose you and the twins. I can't do it again! I just can't!"

David put his arms around her, his heart aching. She was so small, so fragile, and he wanted to ease her fear, but his own was eating at his gut like acid. He had to get her back to Mum quick. No more games and dangerous plans. Just home.

But how? What would Ephraim want him to do? Swallow his pride and do the safe thing, that's what.

"We need to get help, Beth. The only Brit I trust is Jack, so that leaves the Haganah. We'll go to their headquarters. They can get hold of Mum with the radio and let her know we're all right. Somehow they'll get us back in the Old City, or we'll wait until Jack gets back from Haifa."

She nodded as she backed away and wondered why they hadn't thought of it before. As he turned to go to the door she grabbed his hand and held on. They were just outside the door when a British armored vehicle pulled to the curb and two soldiers got out, their guns pointed at David and Beth.

"This is out of bounds territory for civilians. You will 'ave to come with us."

Beth stepped closer to David, her eyes on the gun. All David could think to do was squeeze her hand. It hardly seemed enough.

* * *

They found themselves in a building a few blocks away from the Bevingrad compound. Across from them sat a very thin, plain, but uniformed lady with pince-nez glasses hanging on the end of a long nose as she read the report of the two soldiers who brought them in. When finished, she peered at them over the top of her glasses.

"Full names?"

"David Schwartz and Elizabeth Schneider."

The woman glanced back at the report. "The soldiers state that you are brother and sister, but you don't 'ave the same last name."

David tried to explain. "Ephraim Daniels is our father now, but we kept our old names until a bunch of paperwork is done in the states."

"And you say you came out of the Quarter and your mother is there, is that correct?"

"Yes, can you get us back in? She will be so worried," said Beth.

"You didn't tell 'er you were leavin'?"

David and Beth looked at each other sheepishly. "No ma'am," David said.

She snorted. "It is a little late to recognize your mistake, isn't it?" They both nodded.

"Can you get us back in?" David asked.

"Well, certainly not tonight, and maybe not tomorrow. Command is not pleased about you Jews stayin' in the Quarter. But, I'll do what I can." The tone was one of condescending frustration.

"Can you get word to Mum somehow? The Haganah . . ." He was about to say they had a radio but then wasn't sure if he should. Did the Brits know they had one? He decided it would be better to leave it out.

"We'll contact your 'Aganah," she said looking at him over her glasses. "We know they 'ave ways of getting' word in." She sat back, her thin fingers rhythmically beating the top of the desk. "The question is what to do with you until this mess is all worked out." She had been given these chores a lot lately, and they annoyed her. Too much paperwork in dealing with orphanages and lost kids. "The orphanage would be put out if we took you there. They don't like overnighters. Come with me," she said, waving her hand back and forth to hurry them along.

"Where are we going?"

"To the convent. The sisters of Souers Réparatrices will take you in for the night. We'll work this out tomorrow."

"B-but that is in the Christian Quarter, and they are mostly Arabs," David said.

"The Arabs 'old the convent as sacred and won't 'arm you. And the sisters are good about this, lately at least. And most aren't Arabs. The only question will be about you bein' Jews."

"We're Jews by birth, but we're Christians by religion," Beth said.

The woman looked back at her as they walked down the hall. "That's even better. They aren't likely to turn two of their own faith out, are they?"

"But why there?" David said.

She stopped, folded her arms across her stomach and gave him an annoyed stare. "Because we don't take in children 'ere." She turned and started walking again, expecting them to follow. "Besides," she mumbled to herself, "you'll be out of my 'air for twenty-four hours."

"I say we take off, run, get out that door before she can stop us. I told you, I don't trust 'em," David responded.

"And those soldiers at the door, can we get past them too? We're stuck David, but at least we're safe. She'll let the Haganah know where we are, and they'll tell Mum and Dad, and they can get Jack to come and get us. I say we go."

The woman stopped at a far door and gave her irritated wave again, telling them to come along. David took a deep breath. He didn't like it, but Beth was right. They'd never get past the soldiers at the end of the hall, and an attempt would only irritate Miss Stiff Britches even more. Besides, they were tired, hungry, and the convent wasn't a bad idea. He'd delivered a package there for Mum once at Christmas, and they had invited him to their kitchen for some hot bread. The thought of it made his mouth water.

"Alright, come on," he said. They caught up to the worker who led them to another desk. She ordered an armored car and some soldiers for an hour. He nodded and barked an order for the vehicle to be brought around immediately. They waited a few minutes, then two armed soldiers joined them.

"Time to go," she said while forcing a smile. As she walked away, the soldiers waited for Beth and David to fall in behind, then they brought up the rear. David felt like he was being marched to a firing squad or something but relaxed a little. They were soon outside, where an armored car was idling. The woman received a battle helmet then got in the vehicle, and with that annoying little wave told them to do the same. A moment later the door was closed and they were off.

"If it's so safe, why are all of you wearing helmets and such?" David said stiffly.

"Because your Jewish fanatics 'ave been shootin' British soldiers. Sixteen in the last few days. They blame us for the bombing of the *Post*."

"From what I hear, they're probably right. They were B-british vehicles and B-british soldiers driving them."

"Those were stolen vehicles and deserters. Your ETZEL ought to stop poppin' off our men. Not exactly winnin' friends," she said it with anger. "Your people are to blame. The Arabs are only retaliatin' for that miserable bombin' of the Semiramis 'Otel and what you did at Damascus and Jaffa Gates. You've asked for it, and now you're gettin' it, simple as that." She breathed deeply to regain her composure.

David was beginning to understand why this woman was so irritated with them. He sat back and kept his mouth shut.

"Why are you going with us to the convent?" Beth asked.

"Because they won't take you unless I ask them."

The armored car stopped and the soldiers unlatched the door and got out. Once they were positioned, the woman followed, telling Beth and David to keep close.

David looked around as he got out of the car. There were Arabs all along the wall of the Old City above them, their guns visible. Their demeanor showed annoyance that the British were there, but they did nothing.

The entrance to the convent was on Suleiman Street, which had become another dividing line between Arab and Jew. David could see more barricades and barbed wire along the street, but no people. It was usually crowded. It was obvious this was also quickly becoming a war zone, a critical juncture for whoever controlled the city. He wondered how long the Arabs would let the nuns stay in their home, how long before they took it as the fortress necessary to control this important city block.

The woman rapped firmly with the metal knocker, then waited, her eyes on the small, closed window in it. A moment later the metal was slid from the window and a face appeared.

"Who is it?" said a voice.

The woman gave her name and position, the window closed, and David heard the sound of a heavy key in the door's lock. A moment later it swung open and a nun stood in front of them. The British woman spoke to her in French, and the Mother Superior was obviously concerned at her request, her worried eyes going to them and back to the woman several times as she explained their situation. Finally the nun seemed to shrug agreement and stepped back for them to enter.

"You can stay. I will return for you as soon as I know you can be reunited with your parents. Behave yourselves. They'll take good care of you." She gave them a forced smile then walked to the waiting armored vehicle, got in and they all left.

"I don't think she liked us much," Beth said.

"Witches never have liked children. Don't you remember Hansel and Gretel?" David said.

"Come in quickly," the nun said, nervously eyeing the ramparts along the top of the Old City wall.

Beth went in first, and David followed. The Mother Superior locked the door behind them. David watched her as she turned to look at them. Tall, thin, gaunt face and aquiline nose set between two blue eyes, her lips forming a natural frown.

"We don't understand French. What did the British woman tell you about us?" David asked in English.

"That you had been foolish enough to get yourselves separated from your parents and needed a place to stay until things could be worked out," she spoke with a heavy French accent.

"Did she tell you we are Jews?" he asked. The look on her face told him she had not.

Beth gave David a hard look. "We *are* Jews, but we are Christians as well. Our father baptized us two years ago in the Jordan," Beth said.

"A Father baptized you? Then you are Catholic?"

David winced a little. He had tried to explain his faith so many times he had lost count. Neither Jew nor Christian, no matter the denomination, knew what a Latter-day Saint was, and when he used the word Mormon, the response was usually negative.

"We're Mormons," Beth said. David rolled his eyes.

The nun's left eyebrow raised, but a slight smile creased the left side of her mouth. "I know of the Mormons. Utah, in the United States, as I recall." Then the smile disappeared. "Your faith is an abomination, but that is not your fault," she sighed. "Very well, follow me." She started down a narrow hallway, then hesitated and turned back. Beth nearly ran into her, but the nun was agile enough to skirt her and return to check and lock the door, then put a solid bar of heavy oak into the metal irons at each side of it. "Follow me."

They fell in behind her as she took them from one narrow hall to another. Rooms joined on each side, and there was a small chapel to their right where several nuns knelt, praying before a statue of the crucified Christ. She reached the end of the hall and opened a small door, revealing a tiny room with one bed. "You can stay here." She hesitated. "You are a boy. You must not leave this room unless I or one of our sisters is with you, is that understood?"

David only smiled, but Beth said they understood while giving him another hard look.

"I delivered a package here once. There was a backdoor that opened into the Christian Quarter. Is it still used?" David asked just before she turned to leave.

She nodded. "But the Arabs on the wall can see there as clearly as they can the front of the convent, and there are gangs of ruffians wandering the streets, especially since a new commander directs this part of the Christian Quarter." She paused, her eyebrows raising slightly. "If you are thinking of going home that way, it would be very dangerous. The British woman will return for you. Until then—"

"Thanks for your help," David cut her off as he pushed Beth into the room and closed the small door. He bolted it shut and then listened as Beth collapsed on the side of the bed and lay down slowly. The day had exhausted her. She curled up. "Take the blanket if you want. It will make the stone floor a bit more comfortable." Her eyes closed. A moment later they opened again. "David?"

"Yes."

"Thank you."

"You're welcome."

She turned over and closed her eyes again while he pulled the blanket from where it lay under her feet and spread it on the floor next to the bed. Beth was asleep before he was finished.

Blowing out the candle on the small table, David let the darkness envelop him.

He thought about that backdoor. He could get over the roofs from here, get them home, at least get them help. But if gangs roamed the street . . . Maybe he should go and take a look. Maybe . . . he felt so tired . . . he would sleep only a few minutes . . . then he would . . . go . . . and look . . .

CHAPTER 28

Ephraim's face clouded as he read the brief message. Beth and David were outside the Old City and alone. They had gone to find out about Aaron. He crumpled up the paper and tossed it aside. He had tried to find out Aaron's condition himself, but in the chaos nobody seemed to have answers. Naomi was still trying, but so far, she knew nothing but that he was in Hadassah Hospital.

He turned to Remez. "The landing strip in Jerusalem, what are the chances I could land there without doing a face plant?"

"None. You know we only started work yesterday. Why, what's happened?"

He told him. The brow wrinkled deeper. Remez liked Ephraim Daniels. He was a talented flyer who could handle the stick of about any kind of plane they could buy. He certainly didn't want to lose him to some foolhardy attempt at landing in the field of olive trees and stone they were trying to make into an airfield.

"And, thanks to British unwillingness to force the Arabs to break the siege, Hannah can't get to them without extreme risk." Both of them knew that over the last month requests to the British to force a lift of the siege had fallen on deaf ears, the Brits continuing to use the argument that the Arabs were only protecting themselves from bombings. Ludicrous—but useable if you favored the Arabs.

"What about Jack Willis, or Harry Philbin? They'd help in a heartbeat," Remez said.

"Jack's in Haifa, and Harry already left for England, part of the advance resettlement team. That leaves me."

"David's a smart kid, so is Beth. They're probably okay," Remez said weakly.

"Yeah," Ephraim paused. "But would you take the chance if they were your kids?"

Remez took a deep breath. "Then you only have one option. There's a convoy leaving for Jerusalem in half an hour."

Ephraim was already headed for the door when he thanked Remez.

"Hey, Eph!" Remez shouted.

Ephraim turned around in time to see Remez hold up his .45. He walked back for it and a box of shells. "I would let you take the .30-caliber machine gun Jack gave us, but the British are still searching our convoy vehicles for weapons most of the time. We can't afford to lose it."

"I understand," Ephraim said, cutting him off. "Thanks for the gun." He left the building.

Jerusalem was an important religious center to most of the world, and the British were supposed to keep the road open for travel. The only problem had been their definition of "open." To them it meant the ability of their vehicles to travel it without getting shot at, but they went back and forth to Jerusalem only twice a day at a pace too fast for any convoy. That left the Jews to form their own and protect them. The trouble was the Brits randomly searched them for weapons, confiscated them, and left the convoys without proper armament. Finally, through wrangling over issues that should have been obvious, the Lord Governor had issued an order to have searches stopped. British Army leaders didn't like the decision and opted to show their discontent by letting the Arab presence grow in the Bab el Wad, rescuing convoys only if it looked like it might be a massacre. As a result, the attacks were growing fierce, trucks destroyed, their goods pillaged, and more and more often their drivers and Palmach defenders were dying. Just another case of so-called British neutrality running amok.

Outside, Ephraim intended to grab one of the mechanics to take him to the convoy staging area when a horn honked. He turned to see Naomi in the passenger seat of a beat-up Italian model convertible waving at him. As it pulled up, she gave him a smile and asked if he wanted a ride. He jumped over the side of the car into the backseat, and they were on their way.

She introduced her driver friend as a fellow SHAI worker name Eleazar who had offered her a ride, then she handed Ephraim several grenades. "We'll need these," she said.

"We?"

"Abraham sent his message to me as well as you, Ephraim. I'm going along. I have connections with SHAI agents in Jerusalem and have already got them looking. They may even have them found by the time we get there."

"No need for you to go, Naomi. The road is dangerous and—"

"They're my family, too, Eph." She handed him a piece of paper. "That finally came through. Aaron's alive, and he has no injuries that are life threatening."

Ephraim was relieved and shoved the message in his pocket. "Does Hannah know he's okay?"

"I don't know. As for the road to Jerusalem, reports indicate that it's been relatively quiet the last two days, due in large part to a phone call from the Lord Governor's office to one of the few remaining representatives of the Arab Higher Committee still in Jerusalem. The governor actually threatened the Arabs to stop these infernal attacks."

"You still have a wire tap," Ephraim smiled. "If the governor really threatened them, it's nothing short of a miracle, but Haj Amin doesn't take kindly to threats, and neither do his generals. We both know it."

"Just the same, I'm going. And don't forget—I am a better shot than you." She smiled.

"You had just as well give up," Eleazar said. "She is stubborn as any donkey my family ever owned."

Ephraim chuckled as Naomi punched her friend in the arm.

He was grateful but worried. He had come to love Naomi like his own sister, just as he had Rachel. To see them in harm's way made his gut churn. In his American way of thinking, women didn't fight on the front lines. That was the job of men—protect the home fires and all that. It just didn't feel right to have her and others sitting next to him when shooting broke out. Even the Jewish government hadn't fully committed to women in the trenches, but there were some, and they often performed better than men.

It was getting dark as they approached the staging area. From the number of vehicles parked along the road, Ephraim could see every money-hungry merchant in Tel Aviv had learned that things had quieted down along the Road and were attempting to send supplies into the city. It would be a very large convoy.

He looked around for British soldiers carrying out searches and was relieved to find none. Maybe this wouldn't be such a bad trip after all.

He hopped out of the convertible and thanked Eleazar for the ride, then made one last attempt at changing Naomi's mind as she pulled her army surplus duffel bag from the back of the jeep.

"You might not get back for a few days. Won't your new boss be a bit upset? I mean you're his best," he said weakly. When David Sheal'tiel had been assigned as regional commander of the Jerusalem region, Isser Be'eri had replaced him as head of SHAI.

"Nice try, Eph, but Be'eri gave me the okay. In fact he wants me to meet with Yitzhak Levi about the information we have on the bombing that wounded Aaron and the possibility of more. It's important."

Ephraim could see the bag was heavy and reached for the straps. She let him do it, and the weight nearly took his elbow out of joint.

"What's in this thing, a cannon?"

"That would be nice." She gave him a wry smile. "Just a few rifles, bullets, a couple of grenades for myself, and a change of clothing."

"Then you knew the British wouldn't be coming to do a search."

"They're busy right now. A possible riot in the no-man's-land between Jaffa and Tel Aviv. It was something Be'eri came up with. Keep the Brits busy enough they won't have the time to bother with us. We won't use it often. Even a nitwit catches on sooner or later."

"Why tonight?"

"Well it isn't for me, that's for sure. I'm just a small cog in a big wheel, Eph, but my guess is that the Haganah is sending weapons and ammunition on some of these trucks. Not many—a test run—to see if a diversion like this will really work."

They walked along the line of vehicles looking for a familiar face. The truck cabs were covered in various kinds of makeshift armor, their drivers standing about, waiting for things to get moving. He noted that several of the trucks were overloaded, their owners trying to get everything they could to Jerusalem. A Haganah sergeant was arguing with a driver, telling him to unload some of it. When the driver refused the soldier ordered several of his men to board the truck and lighten the load, at gunpoint. They were throwing off crates as Ephraim and Naomi walked past.

It was necessary. Overloading the trucks slowed them down and endangered both their drivers and the entire convoy as they crawled up the Bab el Wad. More than once, lives had been lost to such greed, and Ephraim was glad to see the Haganah had been instructed to put an end to it.

One of the disappointments for Ephraim about the war so far was the fact that Jewish businessmen were taking advantage of Jerusalem's increasing lack of food. Prices had soared for everything from flour to shoes, and the businessmen were the cause. They ought to force the merchantmen to ride a convoy into Jerusalem. Maybe fear would help them overcome their gouging of helpless civilians.

He saw the armored cars sitting near by. There were six of them and three were new. They weren't like the British cars, their armor makeshift—two slabs of metal with wood sandwiched in between—but, though cumbersome, slow, and underarmed, they would have to do.

"*Shalom*," a young man said to Ephraim as he and Naomi approached the lead armored car. He carried a rifle, an ammo belt slung over one shoulder, but it was his smile that made him stand out. He couldn't be more than eighteen, though fighting the Arabs made him look much older.

"*Shalom*," Ephraim responded. The first time Ephraim had come to Tel Aviv with the Furmanim as escorts, he had been a bit nervous about their ability, but he learned quickly that what they lacked in age they made up for in maturity and courage. Over the last month the convoys had been shot at constantly, some of this boy's comrades getting killed, but they stuck to it like glue to paper.

"We need a ride to Jerusalem. Any available space?"

The smile grew wider as he gave them both the once over, then looked at the heavy bag. "On the bus, unless you would like to ride with us in this." He nodded at the armored car.

"I'm not particular. How about you, Naomi?"

"Where do you need us?" Naomi asked.

"We're shorthanded on the bus." He pointed back down the line. "It will be at the other end of the convoy, just in front of the last of our armored cars. Tell them Yehuda sends you."

Ephraim nodded and they started back along the convoy. When they were only two vehicles from the bus, his nose caught the strong smell of oranges and he glanced into the back of one of the trucks to find it completely filled with the fruit, a man nestled in a heavy box in their midst, rifle in hand.

Naomi picked up one and squeezed it—hard, green, still growing and ripped off the trees prematurely. She looked around to see if there were any ripe ones and found half a dozen that might be edible.

"You're sending this a bit soon, aren't you?" Ephraim said.

"Depends on what you think we're sending," the man said. He dug a small hole and revealed several boxes. The guns Naomi had heard about. He pushed the oranges back in place.

"How much for some oranges?" Naomi asked.

"Take what you like, but there aren't many ready to eat."

Ephraim lay his rifle aside and starting searching for a few good oranges. He was hungry.

"Have you been in the city lately?" Ephraim asked the guard.

"This morning." They were both glad to hear he had been across the Road once today and survived. It was a good sign.

"How are things along the road?" Naomi questioned.

"I fought in Germany with the Jewish Brigade. Got caught in a crossfire once and nearly killed. Though today was quiet, it's usually like that. You feel like you just walked into a shooting gallery only to find you're on the wrong end. The guard looked at an orange, tossed it back on the pile and searched for a better one and tossed it to Ephraim.

"When I came down a few days ago, there were more Arabs moving into Latrun and Kastel. Are they still there?" Ephraim asked.

"Yeah, still there. We see them when we come out of Jerusalem, sitting around, eating the food they looted off us in the morning. Then when they know we're coming back with more, they line up and take potshots at us." He paused. "Today, most of them were sitting there both when we came out of the city and when we went in.

Not much action, and we didn't lose a single truck last run. Nobody killed either. I get the impression they're waiting for something—going to hit us hard. Maybe tonight. Maybe they found out about what I have under these oranges."

"They don't know about those?" Naomi said.

The man shrugged. "Maybe."

"Are the Brits around if you need them?"

"Sometimes, but they don't do much but shoot above the Arabs and hope they'll get the message. Sometimes they do, sometimes they don't. The Arabs are here for the loot, pure and simple. Nothing more than thieves and murderers, and they're good at both."

"I hear the Arabs are having trouble getting goods into the city as well. Is that true?" Ephraim asked, as he peeled a less than ripe orange.

"They send stuff through Ramallah, but our boys hit them hard today," the guard said. "A little payback for what they're doing to us here I guess. Arab goods still come from Transjordan though. Expensive from what I hear." He lifted another orange, but peeled this one for himself. "In Jerusalem, they'll charge you a pound for a bag of these. An Arab will charge a British pound for just one. Worse crooks than our merchants, and that's saying a lot."

"If our merchants are such crooks, why does anyone drive for them?" Naomi asked. "It seems a pretty high risk so the merchant can get rich," Naomi said.

"This truck belongs to a friend of mine. He pays for it by hauling goods. If he doesn't haul, the merchants ask someone else, and he goes out of business. The merchants get it their way all around. This time I got my brother to carry for the Haganah. He gets paid and does his duty at the same time." He looked at Ephraim. "You look like you're military, but you're an American. How come you're in this fight?"

"I married a Jew. We live here and want to stay."

"If you have any influence with the big boys, you tell them to stop fooling around. This is war, and the Haganah sits on its thumbs while the Arabs take potshots at us."

"Thanks for the oranges." They started for the bus again. "It is hard to justify, isn't it?" Ephraim said.

"What?"

"Why a guy like that has to put up with a constant fight up the Bab el Wad. If we put a brigade in here and took this road, he could forget worrying about whether or not he'd see his family tonight," he needled.

"Try and convince the politicians. Try and convince Ben-Gurion."

"Maybe they ought to take this ride sometime," Ephraim said.

"I'll suggest it," Naomi smiled. She finished her last orange segment—a little bitter, but edible.

They found the bus, armored with similar plating as the armored cars and rows of slits down each side for firing weapons. The bus driver stood at the door helping others board. Ephraim handed him a fairly decent orange. "Yehuda sent us," he said in Hebrew. "He said you might need a hand."

The man looked them over and nodded toward the steps. "See the Furman leader inside. "Why do you go to Jerusalem? It's a war zone and foreigners—" He had already peeled his orange.

"We live there." Ephraim smiled. "We Israelites have to stick together now, don't we?"

The bus driver only nodded, his mouth biting down on the first section of fruit. His face winced at the tartness, but he kept eating.

They got on the bus, and in the dim light, Ephraim eyed the few passengers. Half a dozen, most of them civilians but two soldiers busy loading rifles and not looking up from their task.

"Need some help?"

The offer caught their attention and both sets of eyes came up, a broad grin on their faces. "It's always nice to have an extra rifle or two." The Furman who spoke glanced at their bag. "You brought your own equipment, I see. You better get it ready. We'll be leaving soon."

Ephraim put down the bag and Naomi opened it, pulling out the weapons. One of the two men whistled at the small arsenal. "Oy, the lady is magic. The newest British rifles, plenty of ammo and grenades." He looked at the other man. "Our chances suddenly improve, my friend." He looked at Naomi. "You must have connections most of us only dream about."

"Just in the right place at the right time," she answered. "Where do you want us?"

"We'll be up front, you two can take the middle, each side. How's that?"

"Good enough," Ephraim answered.

The evening chill suddenly filled with the rumble of starting motors, and their bus driver boarded and started the engine. Then he shut and barred the door and the interior darkened until the driver lit a kerosene lamp he hung from a hook.

"No search. How nice," the driver remarked with a cynical smile.

"The Brits are busy elsewhere tonight," Naomi said.

"A rare thing, but nice when it comes 'round," said one of the furmanim. "This is Benjamin. My name is Eli. Our fifteenth trip. They call us seasoned experts," he said through a smile. He spoke in a stiff British accent, and Ephraim knew he was an import. A Jew from England was his guess. If he were British, Ephraim couldn't help but wonder what he thought about his country's army these days.

"Abdul Khader 'as it down to a fine science, 'e does," Eli continued. "'As 'is spies let 'im know when we're on our way, then puts 'is men in place and waits for us to get to the Bab el Wad. Blocks our rear so we can't get back, then blocks our front so we can't get up." He smiled, but there was an empty fear in his eyes. "Then the fun begins."

Ephraim had seen that fear before—in the mirror just before climbing aboard his fighter to escort bombers over Germany. He understood the turmoil Eli felt inside. Understood it perfectly. It was beginning to stick its ugly head into his own gut again.

Ephraim took the rifle Naomi handed him and sat down. Taking shells from an open box, he loaded while wondering if he'd live long enough to be of any help to Beth and David.

"They'll manage, Ephraim," Naomi said, forcing a smile and touching his arm with her hand.

"You read minds now?" He smiled back.

"Excellent skill to have when you work for SHAI, don't you think?"

"SHAI," Benjamin said. "That explains the weapons. Why don't you folks get a few more of those in here. These old British bolt actions are slow, and their bullets are so old only about half of them fire."

Naomi held her gun out to Benjamin. "Try this one. Tell me what you think before I put in an order."

He hesitated, thinking she was joking, but when she still offered it, he took the gun and examined it with an envious eye. "You're on, love," he said.

"Not me," said Eli. "I've learned the sights on this old friend, 'ow the action works, which bullets might be duds. Goin' into a fight is no time to change."

They finished loading their guns. Ephraim checked the .45 before sticking it back in his belt. "How are things at SHAI, new boss and all?"

"Good. Be'eri is different than Sheal'tiel. It will be interesting to see if he can work out the kinks in our organization, and there are a lot of them." She paused. "Commanders don't pay attention to what we send like they should. I gave them a warning about the explosives expert behind the bombing of the *Post,* but they didn't do much."

"That's no good," said an attentive Benjamin in a caustic tone.

"It gets worse. We know they'll strike again, but no one is trying to figure out where and when. Sheal'tiel assigned a couple of us, but they're so swamped with other things that it's not getting the attention it needs. Finally I went to Be'eri and told him something needed to be done. That's one reason I'm on this bus."

"Kind of shot yourself in the foot, didn't you," said Benjamin.

"Kind of," Naomi smiled.

"Any sign of Arab buildup in the south?" Ephraim asked. His early flight that morning had revealed a lot of movement there. He wanted more information.

"Not much. Attacks on small settlements by clans, but the Egyptians haven't appeared on the horizon. Not yet at least. Kaukji and his ALA are more worrisome than the south. He's hitting the roads like Khader is down here. They're making progress where they didn't before, forcing us to send more men up there."

"Leaving us here to roast in these hot cars and die defending roads they should have taken a month ago," Benjamin said sarcastically. "When is Ben-Gurion going to figure out that we are at war and we better start fighting like it?"

The bus lurched forward, putting off further discussion. Naomi was grateful as each got up and found a place they liked. She was no longer in any mood to talk.

Ephraim noticed that the passengers were women and children and would be of little use in a battle. He wondered why each of them was going to Jerusalem. Their reasons could be anything from emergencies like his to a notion that these relatively calm days along the road suggested they could return in safety. They'd soon know if that notion were premature.

He watched as Naomi worked the bolt on the rifle, getting used to its feel and any problems it might have, then replaced the bullets in the clip and snapped it back in place. She reached for the grenades and hooked them to her belt. As Ephraim watched, she smiled while holding up one of the grenades.

"These won't be much use in here, but if we get stopped, have to change vehicles or something, who knows?"

He nodded, a bit awed by her ability and calm. He knew she had been well-trained in Italy, knew of some of her hair-raising experiences there, but he had never seen her in this setting before. A sudden feeling of guilt passed through him as he realized he was grateful she was here, and that quickly mingled with his fear that she might get hurt, making him sick to his stomach. It reminded him of the feelings he had for some of his buddies when they went into battle, the fear they might not come back. But this would be worse. He concentrated on watching through one of the slits. The convoy was moving very slowly with the weight of the vehicles. At this rate it would be at least an hour before they reached the steep ravine of the Bab el Wad.

Sitting down, he pulled his baseball cap down over his eyes and lay his head against the seat, trying to relax and keep his shakes under control. Battle had never bothered him before, but now he had people he cared for, a family.

Not that death frightened him. There was no doubt in his mind about a life after death; it was leaving Hannah and the kids behind that scared him. Just the thought raised the hair on the back of his neck, made him more cautious, less willing to put himself in the line of fire. That might cost someone else their life, and that was nearly as frightening as losing his own. He could never live with himself if he failed under fire. Never.

Sitting forward, he placed his forehead on the seat in front of him and closed his eyes. He said a silent prayer that the Arabs would continue their lull in activity along the road, for whatever reason, and, if the devil did get into them, that God would help him to be honorable. The only thing that calmed his nerves was prayer.

Now was no exception.

* * *

As they began climbing through the canyon, the young Furmanim in the convoy started singing, but as they entered Bab el Wad the only sound you could hear was the loud echo of motors bouncing off the trees, soil, and rocks of the deep ravine. Ephraim moved to the back of the bus and peered through the slit. Three armored vehicles should be behind them, but he could see only the dark outline of the first. They had turned off their lights when they first entered the canyon, relying on experience to guide them along the narrow road while hoping the darkness would make them less vulnerable. He turned back and blew out the lamp. The light would illuminate each slit in the armored skin and give the Arabs a target. No sense giving them more advantage than they already had.

The plink of a bullet hitting armor filled the interior, then another and another. The shooting gallery had begun. He readied his rifle and peered out a slit in the side of the bus, sweat pouring down his face. So much for a lull in the fighting.

Even on this cool January night, the interior of the bus was stagnant and hot. He saw nothing but darkness at first, then a brief flash of light accompanied by a loud boom. It lit up the night for a brief second, and Ephraim caught a glimpse of half a dozen riflemen taking aim at various vehicles. He fired, injected a second shell, and waited for another visual.

The steady sound of bullets against their armor continued as four more flashes of light exploded, the last near the front of their bus and hitting with enough force that it knocked Ephraim off his feet. He scrambled to get up as the bus came to a halt.

"Barricade buster is clearing the road," the driver yelled loudly. The loud clap of Naomi, Benjamin, and Eli's rifles echoed through the bus as Ephraim got back to his position, shoved his rifle through one of the slits, and looked for targets.

He saw movement in the dim light of the small fires created by the explosions, took aim and fired, reloaded and fired again. Sweat poured down his cheeks as the rush of battle filled his veins and he prayed the barricade buster would succeed. If it didn't, they would be trapped.

"Wait!" Eli said. "Our men will fire a flare above the convoy in a moment. You will be able to see them on the 'ills. Then you will 'ave better targets."

Ephraim and Naomi stopped firing. "Are you okay?" Naomi asked from across the bus.

"Peachy. You?"

She chuckled at his term. "So much for an easy trip to the big city."

"Yeah, makes you wonder if they aren't after our load of tart oranges, doesn't it?"

The flare ignited in the sky, and Ephraim peered through the slit. What he saw were hundreds of Arabs on the hillside, some openly shaking their fists, others dancing about in defiance. One of these was hit, fell, and rolled down the mountainside. The others took cover.

"Fool," Ephraim said under his breath. "What did he think we'd do, applaud his creativity?"

The light of the flare disappeared after a moment and only the fires gave them anything to see. Then they started moving again.

"They had their chance. Why didn't they come?" Naomi yelled at Eli.

"When they think they 'ave us trapped, they will come, not before. It's then you'll see the light of more flares. For now, try to make good use of your ammunition. Shoot only when you know you can kill them."

Ephraim could feel both hate and anxiety in Eli's words, words tinged with the fear that comes to the trapped. He was feeling it himself with second thoughts about coming, but then he thought of Beth and David. It was the right thing to do.

The plinking noise doubled in volume, a bullet piercing the thin top of the bus and hitting the seat next to him.

Another came through farther forward, and he heard someone cry out. With the lamp out he couldn't see who it was or how badly they were hurt.

"Eli, Benjamin, are you alright?" Naomi asked.

"Yes, that was the old woman. She's dead." There was anguish in Benjamin's voice, and Ephraim felt it pierce his own heart. An old woman! It made him angry, his blood boiling hotter.

Suddenly the slit lit up with light as a flare was fired. He quickly looked out and saw half a dozen Arabs jump for cover only a hundred feet away. They were coming closer. He raised his rifle and added his shot to those of dozens of others in the vehicles before and after them. Then the light was gone and the firing stopped. He rejected the shell and heard it hit against the metal of the wall of the bus, then the floor. There wasn't another to replace it. He quickly removed a box of shells and reloaded. He squinted through the slit and saw what he thought must be a man racing down the hill screaming *"Allah Akbar! Allah Akbar!"* over and over again. As he got close Ephraim realized the crazy fool had something in his hand and was about to throw it. Guns fired, but he kept coming. Ephraim aimed. Fired. Missed. He reloaded. Aimed at the darting figure again. Fired. The man spun around but kept coming, then heaved his package. It went to the left, in front of the bus, and exploded in flame—a Molotov cocktail.

"They hit the truck in front of us," the driver yelled, his voice full of desperation. "If it burns, we won't be able to get around it!"

But they were still moving. Another Arab came running toward them. This one didn't get as far, his makeshift bomb exploding ten feet short of its target. Another followed, darting right and left. Ephraim fired as he sensed Naomi join him on his side of the bus.

"Nothing happening over there," she said. She poked her rifle out the window and fired. Her bullet hit the bottle the man carried and it exploded in his hand. He screamed as the flame covered him. Ephraim grimaced and turned away as the dance of horror was enacted in front of them. The reality of such a death nauseated him, but he choked it down, while appreciating the determination of the man who died. It was then he noticed they were stopped again.

"The driver is dead!" Eli yelled. "American, come! Drive!"

Ephraim quickly moved to the front of the bus. Eli was already lugging the body out of the seat and Ephraim slid into it, sweat pouring down his face. He handed his rifle to Eli and turned the key on the stalled bus. It churned but didn't turn over. He could hear weapons being fired from all directions and the constant plinking of bullets on armor meant they were concentrating on them and the truck in front of them, like hens in a coop pecking at a couple of sick chickens. He squinted through the slit and was horrified to see the entire truck ahead engulfed in flames along with its occupants.

"You will 'ave to move it," Eli said. "If you don't, we'll be next. Go!"

Ephraim turned the key again, pumping the gas feed. As the engine roared, he slammed the gearshift forward and let out on the clutch, driving the vehicle ahead with a lurch. It hit the back of the truck and he kept pushing, the flames so hot against the slit that he had to avert his eyes.

They kept moving. He pushed harder on the gas feed, forcing himself to look through the opening. The truck was moving off the side of the road to the left. He jerked the wheel right and then left again, forcing the bus to push harder. The truck began to roll down the slight embankment and out of the way. They were clear. He shifted, forcing the vehicle to its greatest speed while saying a silent prayer for those inside the truck. They would not survive.

Though they were only crawling, he could see the rear of another truck a hundred feet away. It leaned to the right, both tires flat on that side. Rifles were poked from the slits and shooting at the enemy along the hillside, many trying to get close enough to torch them. Worse, they blocked part of the road and Ephraim wondered if he could get his bus past the crippled truck.

"We have to take them with us! They don't have a chance if we leave them here!"

Eli agreed as he fired his weapon. "If you move alongside, they might get to us before the Arabs can shoot them."

"Naomi!" Ephraim yelled.

"Here!"

"What's happening to the armored vehicles behind us?"

Naomi bolted to rear of the bus and peered out. "They're still with us."

"Tell them we're going to stop for the survivors in this truck. Tell them to let any Arab have it who pokes his head up. We need to buy these men time to get to us."

In Yiddish she yelled the instructions and an answer quickly came that they understood. She ran back to her post.

They lumbered their way to the side of the truck and Eli yelled to those trapped inside.

"We'll be ready. Just give us the word," came the reply.

Ephraim looked up the road to witness another truck catch fire. They were far from being out of danger.

He also noticed the buster was in the ditch to his left. It might have cleared the barricade, but it had been wrecked in the process. If the Arabs had any more blockades, they were in trouble.

"Any chance there are survivors in the barricade buster?" Ephraim asked Eli. He felt guilty that he hoped the answer would be no.

Eli looked through a front slit. He saw no weapons, heard no calls for help, but it wasn't burning, and there were no Arabs close enough to have finished them off. "Yes, but they may be unconscious."

Ephraim only nodded as he maneuvered the bus closer to the truck.

"Look out!" Eli shouted and ducked at the same time. The explosion rocked the bus and moved it to the left at least a foot. Ephraim was knocked out of his seat, momentarily stunned. Shaking his head against the ringing in his ears, he struggled to get back into the seat. Eli was lying unconscious on the floor, and most of the others were as well. It was then he saw the gaping hole near the front door. Had he hit a mine or had someone thrown explosives? It didn't matter, they had been hit. The front door was mangled, and there was fire in the stairway.

"Naomi!"

No answer.

Fear struck at his heart nearly stopping its beat. "Naomi!"

"I . . . I'm . . ." she groaned. In the light of the dying fire and through the rearview mirror he saw her hand appear above the seat, saw several others begin to move. He grabbed the driver's gallon bottle of drinking water and quickly put out the remainder of the flames with a stream of liquid, bullets hitting near the hole. They had to get moving!

Turning the key, the bus roared to life, and he rammed the shift handle into gear. He moved them a few feet farther forward so that the hole was hidden behind the truck. Looking through the slit he saw a rifle sticking out of a similar one in the truck.

"Now!" he yelled.

The door flew open and two men quickly jumped to the ground. A heartbeat later the first was wriggling through the hole and into the bus. The second didn't follow.

Ephraim looked out the slit again. The second man had run to the plow and was trying to open the door. Bullets were striking around him and he ducked down, curling up to get his body out of view. Luckily the truck blocked the way of the opposite hillside or he wouldn't have had a chance.

Ephraim saw several Arabs trying to get closer. He picked up his rifle and fired. The closest fell. He fired again, pinning the second behind a boulder. The rescuer from the truck got up and worked at the door, then spun around and went to the ground. He'd been hit, but not mortally. He crawled behind the plow for protection.

Ephraim knew someone would have to go after him.

He looked at the first man from the truck. He was in shock, bleeding badly. He couldn't send Naomi, and Eli was either dead or unconscious. He tried to find Benjamin and saw him sitting in one of the seats, his head against the wall as if asleep, his rifle still stuck in the slit. He wouldn't be going either. That left him.

He was exhausted, more afraid than he could ever remember, even when shot down over the Pacific. He couldn't go out there! Hannah, the kids! He put his head down, praying. He had to. There was no other choice.

He removed his revolver and quickly injected a bullet into the chamber, then pulled the grenade from his pants pocket.

"Naomi!"

"Yeah." The reply was a weak one and he turned to see her standing, trying to shake the cobwebs out of her head. "I'm going after a guy trapped out front here. If I don't get back, you'll have to take this bus on up the hill. You up to it?"

She had reached the front of the bus. "That's suicide, Ephraim," she said.

He handed her his rifle. "Keep them off my back will you?" He forced a smile, then quickly crouched down and went through the hole.

The sound was different out here, the ringing in his ears less intense. He looked left and right, then ran for the plow. Bullets hit to the side of him and one grazed his thigh but he kept going, diving for the cover of the plow. The man lifted his head as Ephraim rolled in next to him to get out of sight.

"Crazy fool," he said. "No sense another of us getting killed over this!"

"Anyone inside?" Ephraim yelled at the cab of the overturned plow.

"Yes," came the weak reply.

"My sister," the wounded man said, then he grimaced against the pain. "Just a kid."

Ephraim looked at the man. He wasn't more than twenty himself. "Can you open the door?" he shouted.

He heard the movement and the removal of the protective bar, then the door swung up but fell back in place with a bang.

Ephraim looked for the armored cars but couldn't see them, his bus completely blocking the road. He looked up at the slit of the bus, Naomi's eyes staring back at him. "There's someone inside. I'm going to lift the door. Give me cover!"

Naomi's rifle came through the slit as Ephraim stood, lifted the door, and looked inside. A bullet hit the metal door, then another as he grabbed the girl by the arm and lifted her out in one motion. He dropped her behind the plow and followed, the door slamming down on the side of the vehicle. A barrage of bullets planted themselves in the dirt next to them as he pulled himself into a tight ball.

"Anyone else in there?" he asked.

"Not alive," the girl answered. "I had to run the plow and . . . and . . ." she started to cry, then bit her lip. She was shaking, nearly crazy with fear.

"Take it easy. We'll be safe in no time." Under the circumstances, it sounded ridiculous.

He looked at her wound—a bullet through the side that was draining her blood too quickly. He turned to her brother and checked his wound. His bleeding had stopped. "I'll come back for you," he said to him. There was no answer.

"Hey!" he said, shaking the man gently. He felt for a pulse but there was none.

"No!" she cried out. "No, he can't be dead!" She grabbed his collar and shook him with what little strength she had. Then she passed out.

Ephraim felt sick, too weak to move, as exhaustion set in. He looked at the bus and knew the armored cars behind them depended on him getting it moving. They were probably running out of ammunition, exhausted, wounded, some dead or dying. He had to go, or they'd all die right here.

"Time to go," he told himself. He moved his foot an inch and a barrage of bullets honed in on it.

Naomi and the armored car followed with a volley of their own, but it would never be enough.

"If you move, you're dead for sure," Naomi yelled.

"Yeah, well if I don't, it'll end the same. I'd rather die running."

He crouched, keeping his back down behind the plow. As he did, he saw movement to his side and turned, his pistol already reacting in his hand. The Arab was hit in the chest and knocked backward into a companion. Ephraim fired again but the enemy was already behind the truck. They were coming. He pulled the clip on the grenade, waited for a body to show, then threw it. Picking up the girl and flinging her over a shoulder as the explosion rocked the truck, a sudden thought prompted him to wait. He started to ignore it, then heard it like a shout in his head. He settled back, the warning heeded. He slipped the girl from his shoulder and lay her down as Naomi yelled from the bus.

"Look! Up the road!"

He positioned himself to see without getting shot and saw two armored cars coming their way. They were British. He could only wonder what had taken them so long.

He felt the warm liquid on his shirt and looked down to see too much of it. Had he been hit? He searched his flesh but found nothing. The girl!

He pulled up her shirttail and looked at the wound in her side. It was ragged and the size of a silver dollar, probably shrapnel of some kind. And it was bleeding badly. Tearing a piece of cloth from his shirt as she moaned to consciousness he shoved it directly into the hole to stanch the bleeding. She screamed with pain.

"How old are you?" he asked, attempting to distract her pain while keeping his eyes on the wound.

She moaned. "Not old enough for you."

He laughed lightly. "I'm married. Have a bunch of kids."

The pain subsided. "I'm sixteen. This is my first trip." Her words were becoming slurred. Blood loss. He had to get her moving or he'd be packing dead weight.

"Let's hope it isn't your last." He looked up at the armored cars. They were in position. "I'll carry you, but when we get to the bus, you'll have to crawl through the opening in the side. A bomb put it there and sealed the door shut at the same time. Got it?"

She nodded her head, flopping slightly to the left.

Ephraim looked up at the slit and saw Naomi looking back. He nodded and she yelled a warning for those in the armored vehicles.

Suddenly half a dozen Arabs skulked around the truck and fired, but the British gun on the armored car drove them back. Ephraim slid his arms under the girl and stumbled to the bus. Slipping between the two vehicles he did the best he could to put her inside, then let go. Naomi pulled her in, and he scrambled after her. As he collapsed to the floor, Naomi shoved the bus in gear and rammed on the accelerator. The heavy vehicle lurched forward and slowly began the climb to freedom.

Ephraim took several deep breaths then pulled himself to his feet, the plinking of bullets echoing through the bus. He looked through the slit and saw the fire was dimming, but movement across the top of the hill had increased as hundreds raced along its rim to get in their last shots. He stumbled to the back of the bus and peered out to find one of the armored vehicles practically against them. A second was lurching up behind and the third close to it. They passed the two British armored cars and Ephraim saw that the gunner was Jack Willis. He had returned from Haifa. He bowed his head in exhaustion and thanks, wondering what might have happened if he hadn't been warned. It was nice to know that God did care.

He heard another explosion and looked out again. They had come around a bend in the road where more vehicles had been attacked and were burning. He squinted, looking for survivors, but saw only Arabs, half-hidden behind rocks and taunting the inhabitants of the vehicles to come out. He grabbed a rifle and began firing. Shot followed shot until he was empty. He saw men hit—saw them fall—but didn't care. They wanted a war, now they would pay the price of that war. It was the only thing they would understand.

As he emptied his clip, they reached another bend in the road and the scene disappeared behind them. He had counted the burning trucks—fifteen in all, plus the plow and at least one armored vehicle. From the look of the flames and the vultures waiting to claim what was left, there would be no survivors. He hoped each had saved one last bullet for themselves. If not, the Arabs would skin them alive.

The plinking suddenly stopped. He turned and looked at the interior of the bus. The wounded girl from the plow lay on the floor next to Eli and the dead driver. He heard moans and tried to find their source. A child under one of the seats clung desperately to her mother who wasn't breathing. It broke his heart, but he didn't have the strength to help her understand. He checked the old lady near the front. Gone.

Slowly the others climbed back into their seats, shaking, pale, some violently ill from fear. The place reeked of death and heartache as he stumbled back to the front and knelt by the girl from the buster. She was unconscious but breathing. He felt the bandage in the dim light. The blood had stopped flowing. She would probably make it. Then he checked Eli for a pulse. Nothing. The survivor from the truck was sitting in one of the seats, his head down, his hand gripping a wound in his arm. He would live.

Ephraim fell into the seat behind Naomi and put his head in his hands. He felt numb to the bone.

Naomi's fear finally hit her. She broke into sobs as he stood and put a hand on her shoulder, trying to calm her. She couldn't stop. She ducked out of the seat and he quickly replaced her.

One of the other survivors finally pulled the child free from her dead mother's body. She was screaming, filling the bus with her heartache. All because they wanted to get to Jerusalem. They hadn't really understood what the cost might be. He hadn't understood. The highway was no place for civilians. There should be no more buses, and the Haganah should clear the Bab el Wad of its murderous infestation.

His hands stopped shaking by the time they got to the outskirts of the city. People lined the streets. Some were waiting for the food, some for family. Many would be disappointed. He pulled the bus over and turned off the key but didn't have the strength to move. Someone came to the door and began pounding, prying, trying to get in. Then a head appeared in the hole. It was a young man not much older than Eli, another young Furman.

"How many dead?" he asked matter-of-factly.

"Four, maybe more," Ephraim answered in Hebrew.

He nodded slightly. "Hold on. We'll get some pry bars and get you out."

Ephraim sat back, his mind a blank. He could hear people yelling outside, hear the cries of awful discovery as relatives learned that they had lost someone.

A head appeared in the hole again—an older man this time, with gray hair that shined even in the darkness. "Excuse me," he said in Hebrew. "My wife. She was coming from Tel Aviv. Her name is Dinah, Dinah Melman."

Ephraim looked at the old woman. She was lying in the first seat next to Naomi. He looked at the old man with sad eyes.

"She is dead," he moaned. "My Dinah is dead." The head disappeared.

They banged on the door, jimmied a dozen different directions, and finally pried it open. The old man immediately came aboard and took his wife's head in his hands, then slid under her, saying a prayer in mournful Hebrew for her soul. When there was an opening, Ephraim helped Naomi and they slipped from the bus and walked away. Neither wanted to hear more.

The scene was surreal. Wounded were being taken from the other vehicles, loved ones grasping at them as they were put on stretchers and the damage attended to. If the drivers couldn't go on, they were replaced by others, and the trucks were immediately driven away. It embittered him to think of what the price had been and how the merchants would use it for profit. He made up his mind that he would do what he could to change that. He noticed the truck with the oranges. The weapons had made it. At least they would save lives.

Ephraim found a spot out of the flow of rushing bodies and the two of them sat down.

"How are you doing?" he asked.

She lay her head back against the wall and closed her eyes. There was pain, but she couldn't say it was in just one place. Instead it ran through her body in a steady, pulsing ache. "Fine. You?"

"You always were a poor liar." He looked down at his leg. There was an extra sting there and the pants blood stained, but it was all relative. He could walk, and under the circumstances he counted himself truly blessed. "I wish I had a Band-aid or two, but other than that I'm ready to go dancing."

She laughed lightly, then both fell silent, watching the mass of humanity in front of them. Ephraim saw Jack pull up in his armored car and get out, then look around. Another man walked up to him and they talked. Ephraim recognized him as Dov Joseph, the man responsible for supplying the city. Jack's words were probably hitting him right between the shoulder blades. Ephraim watched as they both crossed the street and came their way.

"Ephraim, laddie, good tae see ye made it," Jack grinned. "We were just talkin' about ye."

"No swearing I hope."

"Naomi," Jack said.

"How many did we lose, Dov," Naomi asked, after smiling at Jack.

"Twenty, but two others may not live through the night."

"If Jack hadn't shown up, you would be adding another dozen," Naomi said. She looked at him. "I thought you were in Haifa."

"Finished up early." Jack stooped down, pulled up Ephraim's pant leg and looked at the wound. A bullet had nipped a chunk of flesh out of his calf. "Ye need a bandage." He called to a nurse carrying a case and she quickly came over. Pulling items from the case, she began working on Ephraim's wound.

"How about ye, lassie?" he asked Naomi.

"A new wardrobe would be nice," Naomi said with a tired voice. "Too many died tonight, Dov," she said coldly.

Dov looked down, biting his lip, then he looked her straight in the eye. "It takes thirty truck loads a day to feed our people. Two thirds of that have been getting through until tonight. Now we're at half. If they shut down the road completely, we'll be rationing within two weeks and starving in two months. A hundred thousand people will die, Jerusalem will fall, and the Arabs will shove us into the sea. We have no other choice than to keep trying."

"They need tae attack the Arab positions, Dov, drive them out of there," Jack said.

"They're working on it, believe me. But don't forget your people have to be circumvented as well, and do you think any other Brits would have done what you did tonight? They don't, not often," Dov said. "Get them to change, to send more of your troops along or have them clear out the rabble along the rim. Until you do, more will die."

Obviously upset, Dov excused himself and walked away. Jack watched him leave, his shoulders slumped with the weight of more than most men would carry in a lifetime.

"'Tis times like these that make me ashamed I was British-born."

"You saved our necks, Jack. Thanks."

"When I got back, I delivered an item to Haganah HQ an' heard about yer kids an' that ye were comin'. When we learned the convoy was in trouble, I decided tae go on patrol an' just happened tae come yer way," he grinned.

"They'll hang you out to dry, Jack."

"They willnae know. All these boys are wi' me when it comes tae sides, laddie. Anyway, most of 'em enjoy a good brawl and would nae have missed it."

Jack had been watching the girl treat Ephraim, and as she finished, he thanked her and she went off to help others. He helped Ephraim to his feet.

"Come on. Let's see what we can do about David an' Beth."

Ephraim forced himself to his feet while Jack gave Naomi a hand.

They walked across the street to the armored car. A moment later they were on their way.

* * *

Hannah couldn't sleep, Abraham's message that the convoy from Tel Aviv had been attacked heightening her anxiety. To travel the Jerusalem/Tel Aviv Road when it wasn't needed was foolish.

She had alternately cursed and worried about Beth and David. Their foolishness had put themselves and now Ephraim at risk, and yet they had only good intentions. Wherever they were, she could only pray they were safe.

The loud clapping of rifle fire jolted her thoughts and she snuggled against the twins in the cold night. She was grateful the walls were of stone and that the twins could sleep through about anything, but she was beginning to think like so many others—it was foolish to stay, to protect something that could not be protected. There were so many odds against them. And with Beth and David outside the walls—if Ephraim could not get to them, or if something happened to him, or . . .

A wave of fear collapsed around her like a heavy blanket, giving her a sudden urge to pick up the children and run. It was the same feeling she had when they had lived in Poland and the Nazis had come. Run! That was what she felt then, and had she heeded it, had her family heeded it . . . Oh, how the memory hurt. But worse still was the nagging feeling she was repeating it.

She got up carefully, wrapped a blanket around herself and went into the living room. Wasn't this the same feeling, the same voice, warning her? If she didn't heed it would they be imprisoned again, or slaughtered? She moaned in anguish, the fear nearly overwhelming. She fell to her knees as the tears came to her eyes and sobs started from her throat.

"Dear Father! Please don't let this happen to us again! Please! I . . . I couldn't stand to lose my family. I just couldn't!"

Hannah poured out her feelings, her fears, and pleaded for solace, comfort, anything but this overpowering feeling to run and hide. She had survived Germany, had found happiness, a husband, children, everything good that life had to offer. The pain of losing so much had healed, and now the chance of having it all happen again tore at her heart mercilessly, and it took all her strength to fight it.

Finally, after nearly an hour of anguish, her head in the chair where she had knelt, exhaustion overcame her and she fell into a listless sleep.

She awoke in a cold sweat, her eyes staring into the blackness of the room as her mind tried to see. Who was it? Who was there? Was that a knock?

Getting to her feet, she went to the door. "Who is it?"

"Just us strangers."

Her breath caught in her chest as she struggled to unlock the door. "Ephraim!"

The next moment she was in his arms. After a long kiss she lay her head on his shoulder and held him tight. Then she saw Naomi and grabbed her as well, pulling them both inside as the tears flowed. They were home.

CHAPTER 29

David woke with a start and sat up in the thick but cool darkness of the small room. He could hear Beth breathing gently in the bed and it all came flooding back. They were in the convent.

He got to his feet. How long had he slept?

His eyes adjusted, and he could see a small window in the very top of the wall. The light was dim, but it was morning. He had slept too long!

Feeling his way to the door, he listened. Silence.

Opening it slightly, he looked into the dimly lit hall. No one. Slipping out, he closed it behind him slowly, the old iron hinges screeching lightly as he did, making him grimace.

No one came.

Down the hall, he found a chapel where several nuns were involved in morning prayer. He continued to where he thought the kitchen must be.

He listened at the door but heard nothing. It was early. Entering, he looked around, two apples and the backdoor catching his attention at the same time. Shoving the apples in his pocket, he went to the door, opened the small, iron-grated window and peered into the street. Looking left and right as far as he could, there didn't seem to be anything out of the ordinary. Shutting the grate, he lifted the wooden bar from its iron moorings and quietly set it to one side before pushing on the latch and opening the door. Cautiously he looked about, saw nothing, then stepped into the street. It was quiet, even peaceful. He saw no one. They might make it if they could get . . . He saw the man appear out of a dark shadow and quickly ducked back, then shut the door behind him and put the wooden bar back in place, his heart racing and hands shaking. He peered out the small window again and saw the man walk past, yawning. Just one, probably going to spell another guard. But to stop him and Beth, it would only take one guard.

He heard someone behind him and turned to find a nun standing near the door, her dark eyes watching him. She was young, with a round face and skin color that looked Arabic. Nor did she wear the regular habit of the nuns.

"You are trapped," she said. "They watch the street carefully, and to try and escape would be foolish." She spoke good Hebrew, but the accent was definitely Arab.

David gulped but tried not to let it be too obvious. "We want to go home, that's all. And I can—" he stopped himself. Revealing his plans to an Arab could be dangerous, even if she were a nun.

"And you think you can get home that way," she smiled. She had a pleasant smile, and it eased his anxiety some. He didn't answer, just the same.

She looked at his bulging pockets. "You're hungry," she said.

He glanced down, his face turning red at the thought that he was stealing food from nuns.

"Don't worry. We do not consider your need stealing, but that will not be enough for both of you, will it? Bring your sister and let me fix you something."

"You know about us?"

"Everyone in the convent knows. Having Jewish Mormons for guests is a rarity. Now wake your sister and bring her here."

He was at the door when she spoke again. "Do you have a brother named Aaron?"

He stopped moving, then turned quickly around, his eyes narrowing in question.

"And your mother and father, also Mormons, live in the Old City. Ephraim and Hannah, I believe."

"How do you know this?" he asked softly.

She folded her arms and looked at him with a gentle smile. "Because Aaron and I have met, and he has talked about you."

"You, a nun, know Aaron? Aaron is not a Christian. He is not even a very good Jew. Why would he come here and talk with you?"

"It's a long story. One your sister might want to hear. Fetch her, and be quick about it." She turned away and busied herself with work. David hesitated a moment, then left the kitchen and hurried back to their room. Beth had to hear this.

* * *

Jack looked at his two friends, his brow wrinkled with frustration. He had spent the morning following up a lead he thought would find the kids, and it had ended up a dead end.

"Your soldiers took them to the Administration for Children's Services, but they can't find them?" Hannah said incredulously.

"The people on duty last night left afore I got there, an' no one else kens what happened. Any report is either lost on someone's desk or filed in the wrong place. But they dinnae even know if the kids arrived, let alone what happened tae them."

"What about the people on duty last evening? Have they been contacted?"

"There are at least a dozen, and the head man of the department insists we must wait until they come on duty again this afternoon rather than make half his office spend hours chasin' them down all over the city. He says he hasnae the time. Between the war and tryin' tae get packed an' off to England, he's just too busy." He took a deep breath, "But Naomi is there, waitin' an' doin' a little investigatin' of her own. She has also been tae the Haganah tae find out if they know anythin'. If anyone can get information, she can."

"We have to wait because they're incompetent and need to pack their boxes?" Hannah did not raise her voice often, but this time she couldn't control it. Beth and David were at risk here, and she needed answers. "What if they put them in an Arab orphanage or sent them to the ones we operate in Tel Aviv or Netanya? No, we have to find them now."

Ephraim stood and took her in his arms, trying to calm her pacing and her fear. "They wouldn't send them to Tel Aviv after what happened on the roads last night. And they aren't so stupid they would put them in an Arab orphanage, are they, Jack?"

"Let's hope nae," he said.

Ephraim gave him a hard look.

"Uh, nae, of course nae. Children's services are one of the best things we do. They would have put them with Jews, maybe even a rabbi or one of yer Yeshivas or somethin'. Naomi will find out."

Hannah stepped away from Ephraim and gave him a determined look. "I trust Naomi, but I will not wait here. I will have the babies fed in half an hour and ready to leave shortly after. Jack, I want you to take us to this office of children's services. I want to talk to them. They must have places they use regularly. We can check each of them."

Jack only nodded, feeling foolish for not having thought of it himself.

"And what of Aaron?" she asked.

"He is well enough to leave, maybe today, or tomorrow," Ephraim said.

"I want to see him. Can you get us through Sheik Jarrah?" she asked Jack.

He nodded. "It's dangerous, but it can be done."

"Then we will do it." Hannah disappeared in the bedroom and Jack and Ephraim sat down. Both had been up all night and were exhausted.

"She's determined," Ephraim said.

"She should be. I willnae take the kids through Sheik Jarrah, laddie. We leave them here."

Ephraim nodded. "We better get some sleep while we can. Ten British pounds says I beat you to it."

Jack was already stretching out on the floor. "Ye're on."

Ephraim won.

* * *

They sat at the table where David devoured the rice and vegetables Mary had prepared while Beth played with hers and listened to Mary's story. She thought it was as romantic as anything she had heard. "When Rhoui turned on Izaat and me, I knew it was time to find a place to hide. As a Christian who lives just a few blocks away from this place, it came to mind. I've been here a month now."

"Then you don't know Aaron was hurt in the bombing of the *Post*," David said.

Mary stiffened. "How bad is it?"

"We don't know. We left the Quarter to find out but can't get to the hospital, and no one seems to know anything."

Mary felt weak but tried not to let it show. "I am sure he's alright. When he saved me, I learned he is a very tough man. Most men would have been killed by that beating."

"How long can you stay here?" Beth asked.

"I must leave soon. I received word that Rhoui knows I am here. The devil has him by the thumbs, and I'm afraid he will come soon."

"Then go with us when the British come to take us home," David said.

Mary leaned forward and touched David's hand. "Thank you, but I don't think—"

"Why not? We don't hate Arabs, and Aaron wouldn't forgive me if I left you here." David licked his fingers and pushed the plate aside with a grin.

Mary looked at her hands, thinking. She had put off leaving out of fear, hoping the reality would change while convincing herself that Rhoui would not desecrate the convent even if he wasn't a Christian any longer, but those efforts at denial didn't make it easy to sleep at night. What he had done to Izaat, his betrayal of them, had bred a fear in her that was nearly paralyzing. Could this be the answer? Could she just walk out the front door with Aaron's family, or would his hate overflow and endanger them as well? Would Aaron forgive her if that happened? Would she ever forgive herself?

"It's God's doing," Beth said. "He wants you to leave with us."

"You are kind. Let me think about it. For now, we'll clean up the dishes, then you can earn your keep and this poor excuse for a breakfast by doing a few chores, alright?"

They nodded and all stood and began gathering the dishes and washing them. As they finished, several other nuns greeted them as they came in to prepare breakfast for everyone else. The Mother Superior was with them and asked Mary to see that the other children in the convent were awakened and dressed. Mary said she would do it, and Beth and David went with her. It was something to keep them busy until someone came for them.

* * *

Rhoui walked from his house to the command post, glancing over his shoulder several times. For the last few days he was sure someone was watching him, but he saw no one. He had alternately blamed the feeling on lack of sleep, the desertion of his wife and children, battle fatigue, and the nagging feeling Izaat would make him pay for his treachery, even though Izaat was locked deep inside a prison in Bethlehem.

He had not wanted to betray Izaat and Mary; they had forced it upon him. Rajid and Raoul had been right to take it to Abou Dayieh in forcing the issue. His brother and sister were traitors, and had to be dealt with. Abou Dayieh had made it clear—it was either Izaat or a bloody massacre of the entire section of the Christian Quarter. But they were tired of Izaat's being in the way. It had been best for everyone.

He reached the command post. After looking both directions, he went inside, the nagging feeling of being watched still irritating him. Three of his men sat about drinking dark Arab coffee and visiting with a fourth, the mercenary assigned by Abdul Khader to be Rhoui's "advisor."

"Good morning," Mohammed Rajid said with a wan smile. Rajid still didn't like the fact that Rhoui was in charge, and Rhoui knew it was only a matter of time before the mercenary tried to get him removed as he had Izaat. And he would have Raoul to help him.

Most of the people had left this portion of the Old City, and the few who remained had little or nothing to do with him after they learned how Izaat had disappeared. Theo, Sami, and most of the others had slipped out of the city when Izaat hadn't returned from Katamon, and most of the others spoke to him only if forced. He didn't care as long as they did what they were told. What he did was necessary to protect the Old City from the Jews and to support Khader's plans to take the rest of the city. Popularity was not an issue. When they city was theirs, they would change and thank him for what he'd done. It was the way it would be.

"*Salaam*, Rhoui," Raoul said.

"*Salaam*. Any problems during the night?"

Before answering, Raoul glanced at Rajid who gave him a slight shrug. It amazed Rhoui how much control the mercenary had over his one-time friend. It was why Rhoui knew he would have to watch both of them if he wanted to survive. They were like vultures who had devoured one corpse and were waiting for the second to stop kicking, but this time they would find that their intended victim would outlast them.

"Nothing of importance. Only another delivery at the convent last night. More children. The British woman brought them," Raoul said.

"Was there any other activity at the convent?"

Raoul smiled. "If you mean did Mary try to leave, the answer is no. She *thinks* she is safe. Why should she run?"

Rhoui nodded. He did not wish to hurt Mary as he once had, but he would punish her if she left the convent. He was Muslim now and Islamic law required that a woman's family be responsible for the immoral behavior of its wives and daughters. He intended to carry out his every duty as a new Muslim.

He had learned of Mary's whereabouts from Raoul. Under orders directly from Abou Dayieh, Rhoui had assigned Raoul to keep track of goods being deposited for safe keeping at the convent. The reasons were obvious. For fortification purposes, Abou Dayieh had already made plans to possess the convent as soon as the British left and couldn't stop him. Further, as the Christians of the Old City left, storing the best possessions at the convent, Abou Dayieh had seen a possible treasure trove of wealth that might help finance his depleted war chest, and he had asked for a daily accounting.

A few weeks earlier, shortly after Rhoui had replaced Izaat, an unusually large truckload of goods had shown up at the convent's front door accompanied by an old couple who needed help in unloading their possessions for storage before leaving the country. The initiates had been enlisted, and as Raoul watched them through a pair of field glasses, he had caught sight of a nervous Mary darting between truck and door. Raoul had come to Rhoui with the information, but Rhoui decided to leave it be. If she really were a num, she could stay and he would not interfere. If she were only hiding and had not taken vows, eventually she would feel safe enough to come out, and they would be waiting. He felt no rush.

"I'm going to the wall," he said.

"Don't you want to hear about the great victory at Bab el Wad last night?" Raoul asked.

Rhoui was already outside the door and in the street. He had heard the story when stopping for coffee this morning. He did not wish to hear it again, especially from Raoul.

The street had a few early morning shoppers, but it was not as it used to be. With the Quarter mostly deserted, there were not half as many people as there might have been, nor was there the excited, happy feeling that had been normal for the souks. Everyone was fearful, irritated, even angry, and a lot of it was not because of the Jews. The mercenaries were back to stealing, and he was letting them.

For Rhoui these men were the necessary evil. They would lose to the Jews without them, and when it came time to fight, his decision to let them come would be vindicated, he was sure of it.

He found the steps and climbed to the top of the wall. Keeping low, he went to the first sandbagged emplacement and found the men asleep. Kicking them back to consciousness, he moved to the second, then the third where he could see into Suleiman Street and the front of the convent. He found a place to sit and asked for the field glasses kept by the guards at this spot.

Carefully he checked the other side of the street. The hospice directly across from them was of great concern. Though now in the Arab section of the city, it fronted Bevingrad, the British compound for military and police forces, and if the Jews captured Bevingrad, they would take the hospice and from its upper floors they would be able to look down into these very emplacements and pick off anyone in them. The day he spotted a Jewish sniper in one of those windows would be a turning point for the fortunes of Arabs in the Old City.

He looked to the west. Barbed wire and barricades had been put up in the intersection of Jaffa and Suleiman. The Jews controlled the buildings on the other side of Jaffa Road and he could see that they had more emplacements today than they did yesterday. Since the bombing of the *Post,* Jewish killing of British soldiers in that part of the city had escalated and the Brits had finally withdrawn altogether. Now the Jews were making serious preparations for war. The day the

British walked out of Bevingrad, the battle for these streets would begin. And it would be a most bloody one.

Lastly, he peered at the door of the convent as if the glasses would somehow allow him to see inside. They did not, and he gave it up, returned the glasses, and headed back down to the street. His men had orders to notify him or Raoul immediately if anyone tried to leave the convent and then prevent them until their arrival. They were also under orders to kill any Jew who tried to enter. Mary would not leave and her Jewish friend could not come to her rescue without Rhoui knowing. He trusted that and let it go. Going down the steps and back into the street, he went to the next corner and turned left. It was time to check the emplacements on the rooftops.

* * *

Naomi glared at the woman while biting her tongue to get control. "Let me see if I understand this correctly. Two children were brought in here last night, and instead of seeing that they got home to the Old City, you put them in a convent, is that right?"

"Those are our orders. Traffic in and out of the Quarter is limited to convoys under the direction of Jerusalem command and no other traffic is authorized." She could have been reading it from a book.

"Did they tell you they were American citizens?"

"They said it, but I could not verify it. The consulate was closed at that hour, and our orders are that any such statement must be verified before being acted upon. I intended to do it, and to contact their parents, as soon as I returned to duty today," she said stiffly.

Naomi had done her homework and discovered that this woman had put more than a few children in the convent and little had been done to place them with their families. "Just as you intended to see that the other children you put there were reunited with their families." The papers Naomi had in her hand and gave to the woman had been pulled from the files with the help of a young British file clerk enamored by her smile. The woman turned a bit pale when she realized what they were.

"'Ow did you get these? This is confidential information from our files. 'Ow—"

"I am about three seconds away from walking into your commanding officer and registering a complaint against your dereliction of duty. Don't push your luck."

The woman glared back. She would not be cowed easily. "These children 'ave no family, they—"

"Have you looked? Those reports show no indication you have." She grabbed the papers back and quickly pulled one from the stack. "I had time on my hands while waiting for your friend over there to get a hold of you and get you back here. I called half a dozen people in the phone book with this boy's last name. His father is worried sick about his son. They got separated more than a week ago on an overloaded bus, and the boy got off with the wrong people at the wrong stop. He has been in the convent ever since."

The woman turned a shade paler and sat down. Naomi was finally getting through.

"Now I don't know what your problem is, if you're pro-Arab or just lazy, but I want a couple of armored cars and a few British soldiers to accompany me to the convent and get those children—all of them—and when we get back here I am gong to take David and Beth back to their parents under your continued protection while you sit down with the others and do your job. And I warn you, if I return here the next day and find any of those children haven't been taken care of, I will have those stripes you so proudly wear on your arm ripped off and given to someone else. Do we understand each other?"

The British woman looked up at the young Jewish girl leaning over her desk and knew there was only one answer to be given. "We can leave in fifteen minutes."

* * *

Raoul was on the wall when the small convoy of British vehicles pulled up to the front door of the French convent and unloaded a dozen soldiers while training their machine guns on Arab emplacements along the top of the wall, then cocking them to leave no doubt as to their intent if they met any resistance.

Two women got out of one of the armored cars and Raoul saw

immediately why the soldiers had been so direct. One of the women was a Jew in military khakis and she was going into the convent.

"Halt!" he yelled from his position. The British woman hesitated but the Jew grabbed her arm and they disappeared inside. Raoul immediately sent a message to Rajid. He needed reinforcements.

* * *

Anne, the British clerk, was breathing hard and had to sit down once inside. She was sure the Arab would shoot them when they ignored his command.

"Relax, Sergeant. You're in the convent. It's safe, remember?" Naomi said it with an edge to her voice then turned to the Mother Superior. "We have come for the children. All of them. Can you gather them up quickly?"

The Mother Superior nodded, a thankful but curious look on her face as she turned and gave the order in French to several other sisters who peered around corners down the hallway. They scurried away to do as ordered.

"What has happened?"

"Nothing to alarm you," Naomi said with a smile. "The children will be found homes today—tomorrow at the latest—and the sergeant thought now would be a good time to bring them back to where their families could find them without trouble." Naomi was beginning to realize what kind of position the convent held in any future battle. "Sister, do you realize the danger you are in here? When—if—a war really begins, both sides are going to want this place and . . ."

"Yes, yes, we know. But we rely on God's protection. We will be fine."

"Do you mind if I get a drink of water?" Naomi asked.

"Not at all. The kitchen is that way," she pointed down the hall to the right. "But please, do not interrupt the sisters in their prayers, and their rooms are, of course, off limits."

"Yes, I understand. Thank you. Would you like a drink, Sergeant?"

Anne shook her head. "Don't be long is all I ask. The children will surely be ready any minute and—"

"I'll be back by the time they're ready," Naomi was already halfway down the hall, her eyes scanning the place and her brain making mental notes of everything she saw. She arrived at the kitchen only after opening a few doors and taking a quick trip into the basement, then walking through the areas around the small chapel. When she pumped herself some water from the convent's old-fashioned well in the kitchen, she made note of the door and even took a quick look through its steel grated window. She could see into the street where Arab men were gathering. It looked like the man on the wall they had ignored was calling for reinforcements. She returned to the front hall and saw Beth and David standing next to a young Arab woman near the door. They didn't see her until she called Beth's name, then both ran to her, broad grins on their faces.

"You know these children?" the Mother Superior asked.

"My brother and sister, and the real reason I came."

Beth turned to the sergeant and thanked her. The sergeant gave a wan smile while glancing at Naomi who didn't return it.

"Mary has to go with us," Beth said. She went back and took the Arab woman's hand pulling her toward them.

"I am not sure . . ." the sergeant started to say.

"You may come if you like, Mary, but we need to go now. I noticed while in the kitchen that the Arabs on the wall have called for reinforcements."

Mary stepped back, her face suddenly clouded. "Then I should not go. It will endanger all of you."

"You think they are after you?" Naomi asked.

"Her brother hates her because of Aaron," Beth said.

Naomi was confused and it showed, but this was no time to get the details. "If they are after you, this is your one chance at freedom. We will not come back, and the Arabs will not kill the British over one Arab woman, no matter what she has done. I think you should come."

Mary hesitated only a moment then nodded. "You are Naomi, Aaron's uh . . . sister."

Naomi flinched a bit at the appellation. One time it had been more than that, but she supposed that now it was probably the right one. "Yes, come on. Let's go."

The sergeant held back, but Naomi grabbed her arm and moved forward. "You first, Sergeant. A safe place, remember?"

Anne didn't smile, her knees a bit shaky, but she went to the door and grabbed the handle, took a deep breath, then opened it.

Stepping into the light, she blinked again and again before her eyes adjusted. The soldier in charge of the troops was standing a few feet away, a concerned look on his face as he peered up at the wall.

"Is everythin' alright, Lieutenant?" she asked.

"Depends on your definition of all right. If you mean are we ready, the answer is yes. But if you mean do I think we might have a bit of trouble gettin' out of 'ere with our 'eads, the answer is still yes. Take a look."

She stepped next to him and looked up at the wall. It was lined with armed Arabs, the guns pointed this direction. She felt the bile in her stomach churn. "What do they want?"

"I 'aven't asked, and I don't intend to. I've radioed for more soldiers, and if they want a fight, we'll give it to 'em." As he finished, several other armored cars roared up to the barricade and were let through, then positioned themselves alongside the others, their machine guns at the ready. A distinct murmur rose from the Arabs on the wall and several appeared to be ready to back off, but a tall, good-looking one with a scar on his face told them to hold their position. They hunkered down again.

"They seem determined," Anne said.

The lieutenant heard footsteps behind him and turned to see Jack Willis coming from one of the armored cars, another man with him.

"Lieutenant," Jack said with a smile. "How is it?"

"A standoff, sir," he looked at the other man. "Ephraim Daniels, isn't it?"

"That's correct, Lieutenant. Two of my children are in there."

"Hey, British," the tall Arab said. "You took a Jew inside and now you bring another. You offend Raoul and all the Arabs of the Old City."

"This man is the father of two of the children. The woman came only to retrieve them for him. They are no danger to you."

"The woman has seen the convent and knows its strengths and weaknesses. She is a spy, and we will not let her leave."

"May I, Lieutenant?" Jack asked.

The lieutenant nodded. "Be my guest, Colonel."

Jack looked up at the tall Arab on the wall. "Ye have five minutes tae take yer men off this wall. If ye dinnae, mine will fire on ye, an' yer families will bury ye afore mornin'. This is a French convent, the people inside are French, American, an' British citizens, along wi' citizens of Palestine, an' until we leave this country, we are sworn tae defend them wi' our lives. I intend tae do so. Is that understood?"

Another man appeared. Jack knew this one. Mohammed Rajid was one of Khader's men. These were not just Old City residents defending their homes. That changed things a bit, but not his position, and Rajid was smart enough to know that.

"You drive a hard bargain, British," Rajid said.

"I drive nae bargain. These people are nae threat tae ye, an' if ye dinnae back off, ye will start a battle that ye cannae afford, Rajid."

"This may be so, but you offend our honor now. Surely, you who have fought with us do not expect that we leave without some sign of your willingness to restore it." The tall one argued with him, but Rajid put him in his place with a few choice words, and the tall Arab left the wall.

"Rajid has nae intention tae fight, but he wants somethin' tae save his honor for leavin' the field of battle," Jack said quietly. "An' what would it take tae restore yer honor?" Jack asked Rajid.

"You have many weapons. Our honor could be salvaged for a dozen rifles, and a thousand bullets for them, of course."

"Ye know I cannae do that an' wouldnae if I could. Yer rifles often find British targets, an' givin' ye more would only add more of my friends tae the list of the dead. I will deliver tae New Gate a car for yer use, nothin' more."

Rajid thought a minute. He knew it was a good offer, but he could not look too eager.

"And fifty gallons of gasoline for its motor," Rajid said.

The other Arabs along the wall were pleased with their leader's negotiations. A car for a woman who was obviously incapable of being any kind of Jewish spy and for this man's children was more than could be expected.

"Ye have my word," Jack said.

The lieutenant was about to protest, but Jack put a hand on his arm. "Relax, Lieutenant. I know what I do."

Rajid ordered his men off the wall and they began leaving. Jack motioned Ephraim to get the kids loaded into the back of the waiting truck. Ephraim quickly entered the convent and told them to get moving while he hugged Beth and David, then gave them both a hard look.

"I'm glad you're alright, but we will have a long talk about this when we get home. Now get moving!"

"Mary has to come," David said.

Ephraim looked up at the Arab woman standing next to Naomi.

"She's Aaron's friend," Naomi said.

An astonished smile crossed Ephraim's face. "Mary, nice to meet you. Aaron wanted to introduce me at the hospital the last time the two of you were there, but you checked out early."

"This is *that* Mary?" Naomi asked.

"Come on, we'll talk about this later." He clasped Beth and David by the hand and headed out the door. Naomi and Mary followed.

* * *

Rhoui was just coming back from his inspections of the emplacements on the rooftops when he saw the men coming down from the wall, praising Rajid's prowess at outsmarting the British. When they were finally down and the steps empty, he climbed to the top to see Rajid still standing on the wall, two of his most trusted men with him. They were watching something at the convent and Rhoui joined. It was then he saw Raoul. He was in the second emplacement, a rifle to his eye, its barrel in front of a peephole in the stack of sandbags placed on the wall. Rhoui ran to where he could get a view of Raoul's target just in time to see a man with two children leaving the convent and the appearance of two women. One of them was Mary. Sensing Raoul's intent, Rhoui removed his revolver and aimed.

* * *

The gunshot sent everyone ducking for cover. Jack saw Rajid dive off the wall into a sandbag emplacement as the British soldiers in one

of the armored cars fired their machine gun. Realizing that only one
shot had been fired, Jack yelled for a cease fire three times in rapid
succession as Ephraim ducked behind the truck and Naomi pushed
Mary back into the convent.

The street went silent as Jack scanned the wall for the person who
had fired the shot. He saw Rajid's head pop up, look both directions
and then curse someone in Arabic before smiling down at Jack and
giving his explanation.

"An unfortunate incident. One of my men tripped on the steps
and his gun fired. Accept our most humble apologies."

"Apology accepted," Jack said. "Get movin', Eph. Let's get out of
here afore another idiot trips over somethin', shall we?"

Ephraim was already lifting Beth and David into the back of the
truck and Naomi and Mary joined them. He helped Mary up while
Naomi grabbed hold of the side of the truck and hoisted herself in,
then Ephraim closed the tailgate.

Mary looked up at the wall to see Rhoui, a pistol in his hand. He
had a puzzled look on his face and was staring down at someone she
couldn't see.

"Rhoui!" she said.

He looked directly at her, blinked away the confusion and
turned away.

Ephraim pushed her into the truck, closing the tarp behind her.
"Get going!" he yelled to the driver. "Come on, Jack. Let's get out of
here," Ephraim said as he walked past his friend. Jack joined him as
the lieutenant ordered his men to get their vehicles into formation.
About to slide into his own armored car, Jack turned back to the wall
where Rajid was yelling something.

"This does not affect our bargain, Colonel. I expect the car to be
at New Gate by tonight." he shouted.

Jack only smiled as he closed the door and told his driver to get
moving.

"A car? That's quite an offer," Ephraim said.

"Wait until ye see the car," Jack said with a grin. "They used it tae
blow up the *Post* the other night. A bit air conditioned now, but suit-
able fer a man like Rajid, nae? I'll have it towed in tae place after
dark. Nae man can say Jack Willis doesnae keep his bargains."

"Don't forget the fifty gallons of gasoline," Ephraim said.

Jack laughed. "Nae, I willnae forget."

They passed through the barricade and quickly drove to meet Hannah and the kids.

"I don't know how we'll survive without you, Jack," Ephraim said softly.

Jack didn't speak for a minute. "Did I ever tell ye I lost a brother durin' the war?"

"Can't say that you did."

"Good man. He an' I buried our parents after one of Hitler's bombin' attacks on London, then he joined up an' went into air corps trainin'. Flew fighter planes just like ye. I never thought I would find anyone quite like him, then I ran into ye." He looked at Ephraim. "Ye are all the family I have now, Eph, an' I intend tae see that ye live a long life."

Ephraim was too choked up to respond before they pulled into the compound of Children's Services. As Jack got out, Ephraim finally said the only thing he could think of.

"Jack, you should stay in Palestine."

Jack smiled. "I intend tae, laddie. I intend tae."

SEE CHAPTER NOTES

CHAPTER 30

Mary waited outside the children's services building where Jack told her to be. She had purchased some new clothing, a suitcase, and a room at the St. George Hotel for the night. There had been hot water and a tub, and she had spent hours soaking before passing out in the soft bed and sleeping like a baby until nearly five, but the closer she got to leaving the city, the more sadness filled her heart.

She could see a corner of the Old City wall from where she waited, and it brought tears to her eyes to think she might never see it and the homes and shops that lay beyond ever again.

The roar of motors broke the morning air and she saw the line of British vehicles coming up the street toward her. She picked up her suitcase and stepped to the curb as the first of them came to a stop in front of her. A door opened and she nearly dropped her suitcase when she saw Aaron get out, his arm in a sling, an American pilot's flight jacket over his shoulders.

"*Salaam*," he said with a grin.

She saw the bruises on his face and took a step and touched them. "Another truck?"

"He took her hand and kissed her fingers gently. "The side of a building."

"What are you doing here? You should be in a hospital."

"I'm leaving the country for a few weeks. How about you?"

"What are you talking about? How can you leave now with this awful war going on? Your family, everything you love and want are here."

"Recuperation, rest, a new assignment in Europe, but mostly, you."

Mary was distracted by all the grinning faces in the armored vehicle, and the 'you' in his answer didn't hit her at first. "We have an audience."

"Bodyguards." He put an arm around her and they started walking. She stopped in her tracks. "What did you say?"

"Bodyguards."

"Before that."

"Recuperation, rest, a new assignment." He grinned. "And you."

"What does that mean?"

"Ephraim has managed to get me an assignment in Europe for a few weeks while I heal. I fly out of here this afternoon. Jack offered a ride to the airport." He pulled out a piece of paper and handed it to her.

"What's this?"

"A second ticket. Paris."

"Paris?" she asked, a questioning look on her face. "What are you talking about?"

Aaron took a deep breath, putting his good hand on her shoulder. "I love you, Mary Aref, and I want to marry you. Today."

"Marry you?" she said, a bit dazed. "Now? Today?"

"Yes. I want you to come to Paris with me. A honeymoon away from this madness! Just you and me. We'll make it work, Mary, in spite of the odds. We'll make it work."

She looked into his eyes as if to find some clue that he wasn't really serious, that this was some sort of joke or . . . or something. But all she saw was love, the kind of love she had searched for all her life and wanted more than she wanted to live. She wrapped her arms around him and they held each other as thoughts raced through her mind. Could an Arab and Jew have happiness? Would their people allow it? And what of her family? Would they ever forgive her, ever accept her again?

Thoughts of her mother and the words of Rhoui's father-in-law days ago ran through her mind. Her parents had a good marriage, filled with love and caring for one another, but there was also her mother's loneliness and alienation from her family. Could she give up everything for Aaron that her mother had given up for her father?

"I know we will have our challenges, Mary. I know it won't be easy, but I love you, and it would be worse not to try, to give up and walk away. I can't live without you. I can't." He lifted her chin with his fingers and found tears running down her cheeks, her lip quivering slightly, her eyes filled with such love he thought he would melt away. "Marry me?" he said gently. "Make my miserable life worth living," he smiled.

She couldn't help the slight laugh and finally nodded. "It must be a Christian marriage, Aaron, I—"

He shouted a 'yahoo' so loud she thought surely he would wake all Jerusalem. Then he turned, grinned, and shouted toward the vehicle, "She said yes! She said yes!"

The celebration and grins erupted from the armored car and suddenly they were on the street surrounding her and Aaron and celebrating with them. Mary had never been so happy, so wonderfully contented and yet exultant as Aaron hugged her so tight she thought she might burst. Then as quickly as the laughter and celebration had started, it stopped, and she found herself being moved toward the armored car. Just as she slid into a spot on the floor and Aaron was sliding in next to her, he saw her luggage and ran back for it. He threw it up to the soldier standing behind the machine gun, then slid in next to her, putting an arm around her shoulder and pulling her close.

"I love you, Mary Aref," he whispered softly in her ear. "I promise you happiness," he smiled, "*and* a Christian wedding."

She took his hand and held on tight as the vehicle did a sharp turn and headed back the way it had come. She heard Jack Willis give orders over a radio phone for the rest of the convoy to go on to Tel Aviv. They would follow shortly. For now they had a wedding to attend.

* * *

That night, after the surprise wedding for Mary and Aaron, Abraham took Naomi's hand and guided her into the new section of the tunnels, then to the new dig that would connect to Solomon's quarry. The incline was steep, and Naomi took off her shoes so she wouldn't slip and fall. When they reached the bottom, he flashed the light on a table set for two. He pulled her chair out for her, and she sat down, thanking him. With nervous fingers, he placed food—the best the Old City had to offer in the way of a kosher meal—on the plates. He lit the candle, turned off the flashlight, and sat down himself. Searching her eyes, he waited for approval. Naomi gave him her best smile, grasped his hand, and bowed her head.

A comfortable air settled around them as they ate their candle-lit picnic. They were surrounded by the work and struggles of their ancestors in a place where they were trying to carve out a future for themselves. It was the perfect place to have that promised picnic.

CHAPTER 31

Aaron read the letter of reassignment with a furrowed brow. He had been called back to Jerusalem. He looked at Mary working in the kitchen to put together something to eat. Their time together was about to end, and he wasn't ready.

But things were getting worse back home. Only this morning he had read the most recent report from SHAI sent by courier to their offices in Paris. Abdul Khader had continued tightening his grip on Jerusalem. After the convoy on which Ephraim and Naomi had nearly been trapped, no supply trucks had come through unmolested, and many were lost while dozens then hundreds of men died on both sides of the firing line. Though the Arabs were taking the most casualties, they were winning the war for Jerusalem's roads, slowing to a trickle the life-giving supply of food needed for Jewish survival in the Holy City. Palmach units guarding convoys were taking the greatest number of casualties and that weighed on his conscience, despite how happy he was with his new bride. One of those units had been his to lead. He couldn't help but wonder if others had died because he was having a good time in Paris.

Things had been happening elsewhere too, things that he had known would come. He had felt it the night Mart had tried to justify the attack on the Semiramis Hotel. Khader had used that act to order more bombings of his own. The first took place February 22, a couple weeks after he and Mary had left Palestine. It destroyed much of Ben Yehuda Street, killing 52 and injuring 38 others, of whom six died later. Once again it was British soldiers using British equipment, uniforms, and passes to get around Jewish checkpoints who placed the bomb and lit the fuse.

And the Arab bombings hadn't ended with Ben Yehuda Street. With Jewish morale plummeting, Abdul Khader had sent his bomb specialist back to Jerusalem on March 11. The report indicated that members of SHAI, including Naomi, had gone by special convoy to Jerusalem for meetings with David Sheal'tiel and his struggling command at the Jewish Agency building. As they gave a brief analysis of what might come next, including warnings that the very building in which they sat might be a target, a bomb exploded next to the building, destroying most of one wing. Fortunately for the SHAI contingent and most of the leaders of the Jerusalem command, the explosion had taken place at the other end of the building. Naomi had barely escaped.

From the explosion at the *Post* to the bomb at the Jewish Agency, a single month had passed and all had hit in the heart of Jewish New Jerusalem, destroying Jewish morale in the city and giving the Arabs much needed victories. But from what Aaron could tell, the bombings were a sideshow—the real targets for the Arabs continued to be the roads.

Mary wiped her hands on an apron and came into the small living area of their apartment with two glasses of fresh juice in her hands. She gave him one, sat down on the couch next to him, and took a sip of her own.

He thought about the time they had spent together. He had seen more castles, museums, palaces, and landmark tourist sites like the Eiffel Tower than he had hoped to see in a lifetime, and he had enjoyed every minute of it. They both had a love for such things, and to see them together made them unforgettable. How could he ever forget the excitement in her eyes as they stepped onto the top plat-form of the Eiffel Tower and the way she clung to him, her warm body and beautiful scent making his heart pound with joy? Though Paris was still recovering from the war, the stained glass windows of Notre Dame and San Chapelle didn't seem to notice, their beauty timeless. They went to mass, had long walks along the Seine, and sat in the evening in one of the endless parks around historic monuments where they read and discussed the Book of Mormon and his father's journal, drawing their hearts closer, entangling him in a love for her he never thought possible. Now he must leave her. The thought made him ache.

The wedding had taken place in the Old City at Hannah and Ephraim's apartment. Jack had used his influence with several people in the mandatory government to get them a wedding license, and Ephraim, given authority to perform baptisms, weddings, and funerals by leaders of his church in Salt Lake City, had performed the ceremony. It had been short, sweet, and quietly impressive. Ephraim had given them good counsel and, though Aaron knew that both Ephraim and Hannah were worried about how he and Mary would deal with the future, Ephraim expressed confidence that they would make it work. Aaron had no doubts.

"When must you leave?" she asked, eyeing the letter he had placed facedown on his lap. They had discussed the letter the moment he had walked through their apartment door, and to keep herself from showing her torn feelings, Mary had busied herself with dinner. Aaron knew she was struggling with tears, had even seen her wipe them away a couple times with her apron.

He fingered the cool glass of liquid without drinking. "Monday, the early flight. My boss here already knows, and I've cleaned out what few things I accumulated at the office. I'm yours for the weekend."

Mary knew things had worsened. Though Aaron said little, the French newspapers carried stories almost daily, and a kindly neighbor, an old man who had been a professor of history at one of the city's universities and knew a half dozen languages, had translated them for her. Things were getting ugly in Jerusalem, Haj Amin's generals defeating the Jews and reversing what some thought was a sure defeat for Haj Amin's irregulars. It scared her. She wanted happiness for her people and knew it would never come under Haj Amin. She prayed continuously that other Arab leaders in Palestine would see that peace with the Jews was the only way, but her confidence in such a thing waned each day as news of the Arab League's position hardened and the Arab Higher Committee in Palestine continued to declare its support for the Mufti of Jerusalem.

She lay her head on Aaron's shoulder while touching gingerly the bandage on his arm. Due to a late infection, it wasn't fully healed, but it wouldn't give him any problem either. He took her hand and lifted it to his lips, kissing it gently. She set her drink to one side and leaned into him as he took her in his arms.

"I'm frightened," she said blinking back the tears.

"Don't be. I'm like the cat—I have nine lives."

She leaned back and looked at him in dismay. "Three of which you've already used."

There was silence between them as both dealt with their feelings. Aaron had never had much to live for before, and death had given him little pause. Now he found himself afraid—not of fighting, but of losing her. It was something that kept him awake more often lately.

"I wish to go to Beirut while you are away. I must tell my family and ask for their blessing. If they do not give it, at least I know that I tried."

"Rhoui is not in Beirut and neither is Izaat. Does anyone else really matter?"

"We do not know this for sure. Rhoui's family is there. He may have followed. Though he would not admit it, he loved them and could not live without trying to make things right. As for Izaat, if he survived, was released, or escaped, he is in Beirut with his own wife and children. And, yes, the others matter. They also must know from me, not from rumor or the voice of others. I must go."

He had a knot in the pit of his stomach the size of his fist. "Wait until I can go with you."

"You can never go to Beirut, and we both know it. They would kill you the moment you stepped off the plane. Right now they would do this to any Jew."

"Not a Jew carrying a British passport and claiming British citizenship. To do so—"

"And when they discover your little deception, they will shoot you as a spy. No, I go alone. Then I come to Palestine. This is the way it has to be."

He had discovered over the last few weeks that Mary was strong-willed, even stubborn, about things important to her. It was a quality he admired about her while being frustrated by it at the same time. She shouldn't go, and yet he knew he could never stop her. He took a deep breath. "Alright, but it is foolish. They will never accept me, Mary, none of them. I am the enemy, and if you tell them you've married a Jew, they might kill you, or at least prevent you from coming back to me. I don't want you taking such a chance and—"

"These are Christians, mon ami, and my family. They will not harm me."

"Don't forget, love, Christians have been butchering other Christians for at least a thousand years." He sighed. "I can't change your mind?"

"No, I must go," she said softly, her head against his shoulder and neck.

He didn't respond for a long few seconds, thinking about what she had told him about her parents, especially her mother. Mary had never known her grandparents because of their bitterness toward her decision to marry outside Islam, and though she wouldn't admit it, Aaron knew that the thought of walking down Jerusalem's streets and being shunned by her brothers, especially Izaat, haunted her. Though her mother had never said she would ever have changed her decision to marry her father, Mary had seen what grief that decision caused her mother. Mary had possibly made the same sacrifice for him. How could he deny her this chance to make things right, to at least clear her own conscience?

"Will you promise not to stay more than a few days? If they're not there—"

"I will come to Palestine as quickly as I can. I promise." She kissed him lightly. "Thank you for understanding."

He forced a smile. "Will I ever be able to say no to you?"

She returned the smile then kissed him again. "Where will I find you when it is time to come to Palestine?"

"Stay at the Park Hotel. I will find you."

She thought of something she had wanted to ask him since he had come home. "Did you finish it?"

"Last night."

"And?"

"And did you?"

"You know that I have read it several times and that I believe it."

"Hannah and Ephraim would be pleased," he paused. "Give me time. I'm more of a skeptic than you."

"What about your father's journal?"

He pulled it from his pocket. "I could have saved myself a lot of grief if I would have read the last entry first."

"What does it say?"

He opened the book and read.

Aaron left this morning. I sent him after David who is staying at his uncle's house. The Nazis will come for us today, and we don't want the boys taken. I know Aaron would fight them, and in the process, they would kill him. He must survive. David must survive. This way they have a chance and our family will continue. If this book is ever found, if the boys ever have a chance to read it, I want them to know that we love them. And Aaron, do not feel guilty for not being here. It was the way I wanted it. Nothing that happens to us is your fault. Take care of David. Love, Abba.

He closed the book and stared at the horizon. "For years I blamed myself for not being there. After all, I could have saved them, or at least gone to the camps with them, helped them survive. Father knew what would happen and gave us a chance. He was right, but I still wish—I still wonder—if I shouldn't have been there."

"Your father would be proud of what you have done with your life, Aaron. He lives through you. They both do, in your eyes, in your laugh, in your determination and goodness. They would not have it any other way. Let it be." She turned his face toward her. "They're alive, waiting for you."

A pot boiled over in the kitchen, and she quickly got to her feet and dashed in. He watched her as she deftly pulled the boiling potatoes from the hot plate and got things under control again, all business, but beautiful business. Two days before he had to leave. It would be the shortest two days of his entire life.

CHAPTER 32

April 1, 1948

As March turned to April, Jewish morale was fading to dangerous levels, and Naomi wondered how they would ever turn things around. They were losing the roads, both in the north and the south, and Jewish settlements, towns, and villages were either starving, under siege, beaten, or abandoned. A convoy sent to relieve the Etzion Block, so critical to Jerusalem's defense from the south, had been ambushed, beaten, and destroyed. Only British intervention, late as it was, had saved them from a massacre. Even then it had cost them every last truck, armored car, and weapon they had been carrying. It was a disaster.

But that wasn't all. A second convoy that had tried to get to Yehiam in the north, another critical position for defense from Transjordan and Syria, had also been destroyed. The Arabs had returned to what they did best—guerilla warfare—and used it to control the roads. For the first time, Naomi was beginning to wonder if they could win. Khader's guerillas were winning decisive victories, and if they could do it, the Arab armies would surely keep their promise to drive every last Jew into the sea.

She met Ephraim for lunch at noon. He had just come from the airport where he had listened to military reports that another convoy had been stopped at Hulda, way before it ever reached the Bab el Wad with relief for Jews in Jerusalem. Absolutely no vehicles had gotten through for the second day in a row. The Holy City was completely cut off.

"Plenty of food here," Ephraim said.

"Plenty of everything," Naomi responded. "Not everyone is into sacrifice. Black marketers, opportunists, a criminal element. All seem to be springing up as a part of this mess. I was glad to hear Dov Joseph stopped most of it in Jerusalem, but here it is rampant and makes me sick to my stomach."

"The government should do more," Ephraim responded.

"It is hard when it takes all they have to fight a few thousand Arabs. We're losing, Ephraim. Two months ago we had them on the run, and now we're losing. Whereas Haj Amin was all but shunned in the Arab centers of power, he has new life, and we gave it to him because of our unwillingness to take the fight to the Arabs. The defensive policy is ruining us."

"That's one thing I have noted about you people from Judah. You never do things the easy way." He forced a smile.

They ate their boiled eggs and vegetables in silence, both hungry, both feeling guilty. Hannah, the kids, and a hundred thousand other Jews were on simple rations in Jerusalem, and here they ate like pigs at a trough. They both shoved their plates away at the same time, sitting back.

"How are you going to get back to Hannah?" Naomi said.

"The airfield southwest of the city is nearly finished. It's dangerous, even for a small plane, but at least it's a place to land. The trouble is getting into the Old City. With Jack out of the British army and most of his friends already shipped off to England, I haven't got an easy way in. Dov Joseph promised he would try to make arrangements," he shrugged, "but who knows. Somehow I'll get in."

"Jack quit the Brits?"

"Got fed up and resigned. He's been given a commission in the Haganah and is training a new battalion of recent illegal immigrants, students, draftees, and volunteers."

"A potpourri of the best we have to offer," she said cynically. "I wish him luck."

"You're in a bad mood. What's up?"

"I'm scared. I see too much, hear too much. We're losing the roads, morale is low—too low—and if something isn't done soon, the Americans will reverse their position and so will the United Nations. And look at these people. They go around doing business like nothing is happening, and yet we are a hair's breadth away from losing everything."

"They say ignorance is bliss."

"Then I wish I were ignorant."

"I read your report. So did everyone else."

"My report?"

"Be'eri said it was yours, mostly."

"You mean the one I burned the politicians with? The one in which I questioned their sanity for continuing this ridiculous defensive policy?"

"That's the one."

"And?"

"It's got people hopping mad, right from Ben-Gurion on down. Everybody tried to defend their position, then Ben-Gurion told them you were right. It was time for a change."

Her chin dropped to her chest. "You're lying."

"I'm a good Mormon boy. I don't lie, but lest you get a swollen head, he also told Be'eri that whoever wrote the report needed to learn diplomacy, and he recommended that it begin with a stint in an obscure embassy where you could learn your manners. After we become a state of course."

She chuckled. "*That* sounds like Ben-Gurion. So now what?"

"They considered, for the first time, evacuating settlements," Ephraim said. "But you know Ben-Gurion thinks we'll lose everything if we give up even an inch of land without a fight, so he put them off on that issue."

"He's probably right."

"His solution is to open the Jerusalem/Tel Aviv Road. Full offensive."

"Full offensive? How . . . how do you know this?" she said sitting straight. "And when will they begin?"

"Remez was in the meeting remember, and it has already begun. Ben-Gurion told our arms shippers to get some weapons here. They're coming in the next few days by ship and plane." He leaned across the table. "You're doing a whale of a job, Naomi. Don't give it up, ever."

"Thanks. I'll try to remember that. Now will you take a little advice from a SHAI operative who doesn't mind sticking her nose into other people's business?"

"If you don't mind if I ignore it," he smiled.

"You should get Hannah and the kids out of the Old City. Those who live there are much worse off than everyone else, and even though I know you and Hannah put away food for just this occasion, it is far too dangerous to let them stay."

"I told Remez if she didn't come out pretty soon, I would have to go back and stay."

"What did he say to that?"

Ephraim smiled. "He told me to get her out even if I had to carry her." He watched the street. So little was changing here. It was a stark and very bothersome contrast to Jerusalem. "No snipers. Not even gunfire."

"It will come. Bombs, too." Naomi said. "Information out of Egypt says they have purchased more than a million dollars worth of the big ones the Russians had left from the war. They'll end up here, in these streets, before June. Then these people will understand what you and I have seen in the Holy City."

Another silence as the waiter came and Ephraim paid the bill then stood to go. "I have a plane to meet." He looked at Naomi. "One other thing. Aaron's coming home. He's being reassigned due to this push to take the Bab el Wad. We need leaders with at least some fighting experience."

"And Mary?"

"His wire said she would join him later. Something about finding her family in Beirut."

Naomi had to admit that, at first, seeing Aaron marry had hurt. But when she saw how happy he was—how happy both of them were—she had finally let go. Her growing feelings for Abraham had helped, even though she still couldn't see herself married to a rabbi. Regardless she had finally been able to let go. He was a brother now, nothing more.

"When will he be here?" she asked.

"Tomorrow or the next day. Did I tell you he ran into Wally?"

"Your old friend from Berlin? The one who brought us the chocolate bars the day we left with Hannah and Rachel?" She smiled. "I was very rude to him,"

"He's flying with a small one-plane company contracted to bring a load of arms in tonight. He sent me a wire and says he'll be aboard when they get here."

"Don't the Brits still control the airport?"

"We're going to open a new one." He kissed Naomi on the forehead and said goodbye. She watched him disappear through the door. She always felt better when Ephraim was around. His strength gave her the ability to go on. Abraham was a lot like him—spiritual without being obstinately pious, confident in God without being haughty. The difference was Abraham was Jewish, the son of a rabbi and a rabbi to be. She couldn't marry a rabbi.

Glancing at her watch, she got up and started toward her office building. It was time to go back to work. As she walked the distance, she couldn't help but think of Abraham. The date in the tunnel, how comfortable she felt when she was with him, and even the desire she had to hold him and feel his touch. It gave her goose bumps, and she rubbed her arms against them. A rabbi's wife. Could it be that difficult? Would she have to change that much? And did he have to be the rabbi? Surely others . . . but, no, it would kill Abraham's father to have his son turn away from his flock. Wouldn't it?

She pushed the thoughts aside as she reached her office. They would talk next time she saw him. They had to. She either had to come to some understanding with him about the future, or she had to leave him behind. It would only hurt them both if she lost her heart to a man she could never live with. They must talk.

And she must decide.

CHAPTER 33

The shipment of arms Ephraim anxiously awaited was the first sign the Jewish arms procurement program was finally bearing fruit in actual weapons. Though they had started making some weapons in secret factories in the country, the industry was small, borderline efficient, and unable to produce enough weapons for the quickly growing conflict. With the Arabs now having success on the roads, and with the British only a month away from total departure, they needed many more arms and they needed them quickly. That was especially true now as they tried to retake the roads around Jerusalem and free the city from the partial siege it was under.

Most weapons had been purchased in Europe and were now waiting on docks or aboard ships in ports in Italy and France until the British were gone. Only one, the *Nora,* had set to sea with weapons buried in a sea of rotting onions and potatoes. The cargo had been selected especially to discourage British inspectors once the ship arrived. Hopefully the guns in *Nora's* load would get here for the new offensive. But just in case the rancid cargo did not sufficiently discourage inspectors, plans had been made to bring another load of weapons in by air, fresh out of Czechoslovakia. Ephraim knew it was insufficient in itself, but its 5000 rifles, 200 machine guns, and five million bullets were a beginning—actual manna from heaven.

Ephraim looked up at the night sky, his ears attuned for the sound of engines. Nothing.

He stood at the end of Beit Darras Airport in the darkness, grateful for a moonless night. They had come in trucks only a few hours earlier. When Ehud Avriel had sent a coded wire indicating

SHAI had found a company that had accepted the challenge to fly them some weapons, they faced a dilemma. The main airport at Lydda was still controlled by the British. They would search the plane and take the weapons if it landed there, and there were no other airports with long enough runways to handle the *Constellation* Wally's company was flying in. Then Remez had thought of Beit Darras.

Beit Darras was in Arab territory, but the rundown airport had little to offer, and the Arabs had no interest in it. Knowing it would not be watched, Remez had loaded a half-dozen trucks with shovels, picks, and men enough to fill the holes and remove the clumps of grass and weeds that littered the field. The Haganah's head of operations, Yigal Yadin, had sent enough soldiers to put in a perimeter for defense should the Arabs take a sudden interest in what they were doing. Ephraim's job had been to see that a row of electric lights was strung along each side of the airfield and plugged into a generator. When the plane made radio contact, he would switch them on for the first time and pray they worked. This was not a place for practice runs.

"Hassida," the radio operator said. "Come in, do you read me?" He repeated it over and over with no reply. Ephraim couldn't see Remez in the dark, but he knew he would have that wrinkle to his brow that gave away the fact that he was worrying. The flight was late. Very late.

Hassida meant *Stork* in English—an appropriate name. It would bring them new weapons and give them new life, but if the stork didn't deliver, the Haganah would once again go into battle under-armed, and failure would surely follow. Ephraim wasn't sure how many more failures they could stand but knew it wasn't many.

"What do you think?" Remez said.

"They'll be here. From what we know, the owners need the money desperately, and this will solve their problem."

"I hear an old friend of yours works for them."

"Yeah. We flew together against the Nazis." He couldn't help the smile. Wally had been his best friend at the end of the fighting in Germany. He had been there when Hannah was still in the hospital, had fallen in love with one of her friends, but had lost her to injuries she had received in the camps. Wally had taken it hard. He was Jewish. He figured he'd found the perfect Jewish girl to take home to mother. It hadn't worked out.

Since then Wally had been kicking around from place to place, trying to find a cockpit he could call his own. The American airline companies hadn't hired Jews, catering to an anti-Semitic element that hadn't seemed to die even after the Holocaust and was excused by the fact that pilots needing work were a dime a dozen. Wally had finally started working for Ocean Trade Airways, a charter airline incorporated in Panama. They lived on the edge by flying contraband into France and Germany. It was while taking American goods into Paris that Ocean Trade's owners had been offered a deal they couldn't refuse. Flying weapons into Israel. Being Jewish, Wally had agreed to work the flight.

Now Ephraim wasn't sure if his old friend was going to make it.

Do you think *Nachshon* is going to work," Remez asked, trying to keep his mind off the lateness of the hour.

Nachshon was the operational name given to the attempt to take back the Jerusalem/Tel Aviv Road. It would be the first real offensive using full brigades to pull it off. The trouble was that most of them still weren't ready, the more seasoned troops in the north. These were immigrants recently smuggled into the country, volunteers, and one or two battalions that had some experienced fighters. Worse, they weren't properly armed nor properly outfitted. They didn't have radios for command and control and few experienced leaders. It was like pouring wet cement into a crack in a dam and expecting it to hold, but Ephraim was sure they would win. Somehow. This was the time for the Jews to return, the time for Orson Hyde's words given so many years ago to begin to be fulfilled. It was not a time for failure.

"If it doesn't, I'll hire you to brand cattle on my father's ranch back in Idaho."

"Thanks. I may just take you up on it."

Ephraim listened again. Still nothing. "Wally, where are you?"

* * *

Wally didn't know where he was. The sky was partly cloudy, the night lit by a half-moon, but their radio was so weak they weren't hearing much. The navigator had done his best in the intermittent clouds of the night sky to give them some celestial navigation, but so far no sign of land.

Then Wally, sitting behind the pilot, saw something out the left side of the plane. Lights, and from the look of them, they were along the ocean. "Hey! That must be it. That must be Tel Aviv!"

The pilot grabbed a map and studied it for verification. "Uh oh!" he said. "That's not Tel Aviv—that's Port Said. We're headed straight into Egypt."

"You've got to be kidding!" Wally said, grabbing the map. He looked at it, saw the curvature of the land and knew his buddy, who was already banking the plane hard to his left, was right. When the *Constellation* was flat and headed north again, the pilot checked the gas gauges, then flipped them with a fingernail.

"Well boys, say your prayers. If the Egyptians don't get us, the sea will."

Wally felt his belly jump. Maybe coming along wasn't such a good idea after all.

* * *

The radio operator heard the answer to his call when they had all but given up on the plane. Ephraim moved closer and identified the voice of the plane's pilot.

"Nice to hear your voice, Hassida," the radio operator said. "Where have you been?"

"We thought we'd take the scenic route, see a little of Egypt. We're south of you about ten miles, and we're low on fuel, so let's try to do this on one run, shall we? Give me some coordinates, and when you hear my engines turn on some lights."

Ephraim ran for the generator. If the pilot said he was low on fuel, he was running on fumes. They would have only one chance.

* * *

Wally saw the lights come on just as the plane's left engine sputtered for the first time. He gripped his seat as the pilot put down the landing gear and clipped the top of a few trees before turning on his landing lights and hitting the runway. As his plane came to a halt at the far end of what he thought must be a pasture for goats, several men appeared with flashlights and guided him to the waiting trucks where the locals were already celebrating their arrival. As he stopped the engines and they came to a halt, celebrators started climbing all over the plane, greeting them like heroes. Wally went to the rear and opened the door. Once the workers started hefting crates out the exit, Wally and the others removed their flight gear and left the plane to be unloaded. As Wally jumped clear he heard a familiar voice.

"Ugliest plane I think I've ever seen."

"Yeah? Reminds me of a friend I knew in Germany," Wally responded.

The two men hugged and took a good look at one another before Ephraim pulled him to a jeep where Wally's two buddies were waiting. "We'll take you to town, let you get a little food and shut-eye before we send you out again."

"Fine welcome," Wally said as the jeep bumped over the rough surface to the road. "What's going on?"

Ephraim told him what he could.

"The news back home is filled with the demise of the Jewish state. It's a mess in the States, but the president finally put Henderson and Forrestal in their place—at least for now. But you folks better get a victory or he might change his mind."

They were on the narrow highway, several rather unique armored cars in front and behind. Wally could tell this was a ragtag army in need of a lot more than a few machine guns and bullets. "How are Hannah and the kids?" he said, diverting his mind.

"Cut off in the Old City, but other than that, healthy enough. Are you going back for another load?"

"Maybe. How old are the twins now?"

"Just over six months. Stick around and you'll get a chance to see 'em."

Wally turned to his friend. "Are you kidding me? You tell me Jerusalem is cut off, and that the Old City is in worse shape, and you talk like it's a calm summer's day. Holy smokes, Ephraim! Your family is living in a war zone!"

"Things can only get better," Ephraim said, forcing a smile. "When you were in Czechoslovakia, did you see any fighter planes waiting to be sent here?"

"Yeah but half of 'em are junk. Copies of the German Messerschmitt made by the Hungarians or somebody. If you live to fly one of those babies, watch yourself. They turn real bad, shut down in a hard dive, and handle like your daddy's old Plymouth."

Ephraim laughed. "You should see what I fly now."

"And what would that be?"

"A Piper Cub with extra metal plating under the seat. I drop Molotov cocktails while they take potshots at me. These Messerschmitt's sound like a great improvement."

"Yeah, a dream. What have you gotten yourself into, Eph?"

"War, my friend, and we need all the help we can get. Bring me a Messerschmitt next trip. Save my life will you?"

Wally looked over at his friend. They hadn't seen each other for more than two years, and here they were right back in the same soup. "Just like old times, huh Eph?"

"Yeah, with one big difference. I've got a wife and four kids, three new sisters, and a Jewish brother or son or something who just married an Arab whose brother hates Jews like dogs hate cats."

Wally laughed. "You've aged like no one I know. Who are all these people?"

"The kids Hannah brought out of Berlin. You remember?"

Wally remembered the sad, miserable bunch he had waved good-bye to. "Only you and Hannah could make such a bunch family. The brother/son must be Aaron, the one I ran into in Paris. He was the most belligerent of all when they left Berlin. You've done wonders for him, *Dad.*"

They pulled up to the hotel and went inside to a hot meal with plenty of food. They ate, and Wally's buddies went off to find a drink while he and Ephraim sat on the small veranda and talked about old times. Then Ephraim told him about his burgeoning family.

"What ever happened to Rachel and . . . what's the other one's name?"

"Zohar. Rachel is living and fighting on a kibbutz near the Egyptian border. Zohar was on one of the *Pans* and was interred on Cyprus."

"Have you heard from the couple who married in Berlin while we were there—the pianist and the conductor?"

"Still in Berlin. Fighting for survival against the Russians: Ike made a mistake by letting them take Berlin, didn't he? Should have beat them to it."

"I suppose it seemed the right thing to do at the time." He glanced at his watch as he heard Wally's two friends come into the hotel lobby. "Time to get you back to the airport." As Ephraim started to rise, Wally put a hand on his shoulder. "I'll come back, Eph, and I'll bring you that Messerschmitt."

"What about Ocean Trade Airways?"

"They can replace me easy enough."

"I won't lie to you, Wally. We could lose this war. Fact is, we're losing it now. But with a few more planeloads like you brought tonight and a government who holds to this new offensive stance, we might turn things around. We could use you and a hundred more just like you, but it won't be a picnic."

"Yeah, that figures." They headed back into the lobby, then to the jeep. At the airfield Wally shook Ephraim's hand. "Stay alive, buddy," Wally said. "I'll see you on the next trip." He ran to his plane and got in, waved, then closed the door as the other pilot started the engines. Five minutes later they flipped on the field lights, and Wally disappeared into the night. Ephraim could only hope he would see him again.

CHAPTER 34

Aaron arrived from Paris the next morning by regular airline. After a thorough inspection by the British, he caught a ride from the airport to the highway, then hitchhiked to the staging area at Yonah just north of Tel Aviv. He handed his letter to a clerk who didn't know what to do with it, shrugged his shoulders, and ushered Aaron into a tent where another looked for his name on lists that seemed endless, out of order, and chaotic. His name was finally discovered on what looked like a crumpled sheet of brown bagging paper. He was told he would serve in the Har-el brigade and should report to its commander.

"And where would that be?" he asked.

"Don't know. Ask around."

"Do we have weapons? Where do I get a rifle, ammunition—you know, things to fight with?" he asked, a bit irritated at the lack of any real order to things.

"Your commander will tell you. If you're lucky you'll have some of the weapons from the *Nora,* If not, you might have to throw rocks." The clerk turned to help someone else.

"Has the *Nora* docked?" he asked the clerk when he finished with another young soldier whose primary language was Russian but spoke enough English Aaron could understand him.

"Yeah, in Tel Aviv. The Brits boarded her but didn't go into the hold. The shipment of potatoes and onions were rotten. I guess they didn't want to get their uniforms mussed up. Thank the one God for little favors. Our people will unload the weapons tonight and deliver them to the different brigades."

"Do you know if Jack Willis is assigned to the Har-el Brigade?"

The clerk rummaged through his lists again and nodded. "British liaison. He's trying to train you poor souls before we send you off to die."

"Thanks." He left the tent with the horrible feeling they weren't ready for something this big.

He began asking for directions, got few he could understand, and decided he'd just have to look while wondering if he should have stayed in Paris. Over the last few weeks, he had worked with the underground to buy and send more weapons into Palestine and learned just how difficult the British and even the Americans were making it. His contact with Ocean Trade Airways and Wally Markin had made it less so.

Aaron had been with SHAI agents when they found the owners of Ocean Trade at the Paris airport with a fuselage full of American nylons and other goodies, and offered the deal they had been authorized to give the fledging airline. Wally had been there and had added his two bits when asked by the owners. After business was finished, Aaron had reintroduced himself as the ornery kid an American pilot had thrown boxes of chocolate bars to in Berlin. It had been a good reunion.

He hung around Paris for two more days, acting as liaison with Wally's airline and getting them off to Czechoslovakia with all the right paperwork. Finally Aaron had boarded a plane to Palestine, arriving this morning.

He hadn't heard from Mary. Nor had he expected to. Hopefully, he would find a letter floating around somewhere in Tel Aviv, but he didn't hold much hope. Neither of them knew where to write or even if they should, especially him. Getting a letter from a Jew might not be a good thing in Lebanon, and getting one from her in the chaos he was seeing all around him would be a miracle equal to the parting of the Red Sea. Instead, he just checked at the Park Hotel to make sure she hadn't shown up, then thought about her every minute he wasn't swamped with other matters.

After nearly half an hour he found the Har-El brigade headquarters and was just getting his assignment when Jack walked in.

"Hello, laddie. Good tae see ye," Jack said, grabbing a hand and nearly squashing it. "How's the bride?"

"Well, uh . . . still in Paris." He forced a smile. No sense mentioning Beirut, mostly because he wasn't sure how to explain it. There were some things that couldn't be expressed in the middle of a crowd with a war boiling all around.

Jack looked at the clerk. "This one should be assigned tae my company. A platoon leader, got it?"

The clerk looked through his papers quickly, then nodded and made a check mark next to Aaron's name. Jack put an arm around Aaron and guided him outside where his face lost its smile. "We have a mess here, Aaron. If we dinnae get slaughtered it will be a miracle that rivals Jesus raisin' Lazarus."

"Sounds encouraging," Aaron said flatly.

"We've still got men with nae rifles, radios, or packs tae carry ammo, food, an' water. Nae even rags tae clean the grease off the few new guns we just received. I told the men tae take off their shorts an' use them." He threw his hands in the air. "We got some MG-34 machine guns. Great, I thought. We finally have some weapons that can make a difference. Only trouble is nobody knows how to fire them, an' when I pull an expert in here tae show them, he finds they shoot only one bullet at a time. Some machine gun! Had tae send one of the men fer an ordnance expert tae file down the firin' pins. Who kens if they'll actually work when we go into action? It's a mess! Never seen anythin' like it."

"I thought the Haganah was training, preparing for this. What have they been doing the last three months while the Palmach has been carrying the load of battle?" Aaron asked a bit irritated.

"We've got trained men, but they're all up north. I havenae got a single platoon leader in this company that has been in actual combat. Nae one. Most of the men dinnae even speak the same language. Just off the boat, an' we've got them from Russia an' Poland, Ukraine an' Germany . . . some of that Yiddish, too. It's a bloomin' joke."

"Well, you just picked me for one of those platoons, and that doesn't make you any better off than you were."

"Ye speak German an' some Russian, along wi' Yiddish an' Hebrew. At least that's what Eph told me. Besides, ye can take an order, an' that's half the battle in this business. We'll tell ye what tae do, an' ye go do it. Some of these greenies argue every time I give them a command."

"So what are your orders, sir? What's going on?" Aaron tried to smile.

He took a deep breath. "We're tryin' tae get a convoy through tae Jerusalem. Big one. If we dinnae, it could be catastrophic—UN reversal, Arab morale soars, yer people lose their state. That's what yer leaders say anyway, an' I believe all of it. We have tae get this done."

"Then they are going on the offensive."

Jack nodded. "That's right. They should have done it a month ago, an' now they get in over their heads an' want tae pull off a miracle. Frankly, they arenae plannin' tae do enough. I tried tae get Yadin tae see he needed tae take more time, but Ben-Gurion wants the city relieved now. So they say we move in, do the job, an' get out." He pulled a map from his back pocket, unfolded it, and laid it on the hood of a jeep. "Here is the worst part." He took a deep breath. "I cannae get it through anyone's head that Kastel is the key. We have tae take it an' hold it, laddie. It rules the upper portion of the road, an' if they want the road tae stay open, we have tae control it. They say it is nae a problem—that most of the Arabs left over the last two weeks after one of our platoons raided the place two weeks ago. We can waltz right in an' take it. Maybe, but it willnae last. Khader isnae stupid. He knows he will have tae get it back an' he'll put a major force in there tae do it. If he does, they'll stop us cold an' we'll lose."

Aaron looked at the map, noting the circles and lines Jack had drawn. Kastel sat on the rim of the peak Nebi Samuel where according to tradition, Moses had sat in judgement on Israel, where the Maccabees had launched their attack on Jerusalem, and where Richard the Lionheart had first seen the Holy City before attempting to take it away from the Arabs of his day. At the foot of Kastel and Nebi Samuel lay the road, exposed and vulnerable.

"And you want my platoon to take and hold it," Aaron said.

"Alex Sela will take it. I'll recommend that yer platoon, along wi' another commanded by a fellow named Gish, reinforce them an' hold the village." He paused, his eyes searching Aaron's. "If things go the way I think they will, it willnae be easy. The Arabs will hit ye wi' their best, an' ye will only have sixty to seventy men tae fight them off. Less if Gish doesnae make it an' Sela takes all his people off the mountain wi' him."

"How long do we hold?"

"Until those knuckleheads in central command see the importance of the place an' send reinforcements."

Aaron felt his stomach tie into knots. He had never led a platoon. He was absolutely sure he couldn't pull it off. "I appreciate your confidence, Jack, but I can't do this. I haven't got the experience or the training."

"Ye've been through platoon-leader training, right? Ye used some of those skills in Italy circumventin' the British an' the Italians, an' ye led twenty men tae do it. Then there's that raid in the Old City an' the attempt tae kill Khader in Ramallah. I dinnae doubt yer skill as a leader or yer courage. I just wish I had the time tae let ye practice, get tae know yer men, let them see ye can do it. Yer disadvantage is nae yer ability tae lead. It's that ye havenae led *them*. Ye might have tae kick a few tails tae get them up that hill an' then keep them there, but I trust ye have a big enough foot tae get it done."

"They must already have a leader. Surely he would be better prepared to get them to do what's needed."

Jack shook his head adamantly. "Just off the boats, like I told ye. I spent the last week wi' them workin' on standard signalin' procedures, discipline issues, weapons trainin', an' half a dozen other things. Frankly, they're better trained than eighty percent of the men we're usin'."

Aaron shook his head in disbelief. "Is our army this bad off?"

"All armies are bad off until they see action. Nobody has experience. As near as I can tell though, the Arabs are worse off than we are, an' by the time we get a few of these under our belts, we'll be ready fer the armies yet tae come. Right now, we're green. Real green. That's just the way it is."

"What about the men who served in the Jewish brigade against Germany?"

"There are some crack units fightin' the ALA up north. Cannae be spared. Some are company commanders or brigade leaders in General command down here. The rest that are worth a grain of salt are platoon leaders like ye but in other brigades that may see hotter action. Frankly, ye have as much ability as most of them. Come on. I'll introduce ye tae yer men." They started walking across the camp and Jack put an arm around his shoulder. "I won't leave ye out there wi' nae help, laddie, but ye an' Gish have got tae hold Kastel as long as ye can an' still survive. Are we clear on that?"

Aaron nodded. He understood, and the prospect scared him to death.

* * *

Ephraim dipped the nose of the Piper Cub over the top of the hill and it plummeted onto the short landing strip with a bump that made the plane bounce several times before settling down permanently. He taxied the Piper to the end of the field where several men waited jubilantly for his motor to shut off. It was the first landing on the new airstrip in west Jerusalem.

When he opened the door, Dov Joseph was waiting. "What do you think? Can we get bigger planes in here? Can we airlift?"

"I hate to disappoint you, Dov, but the winds coming over that ridge would pancake a big bird. You need another hundred feet, no less. That way they can come in higher and the wind won't be such a factor."

Dov, dejected, forced a smile and a nod then turned to the men behind him and gave the instructions to keep digging. With slumped shoulders, the men went toward the end of the strip and called to dozens of others to get busy.

"The convoy comes tomorrow," Dov said as they walked toward the nearby narrow road on the outskirts of the city.

"Yeah, I know. I have to fly reconnaissance. How are things in the Quarter?"

"Hannah has helped us take inventory of food stocks. They're better than we thought, but once the British stop taking in the marginal supplies they now provide, what is left will last only a few weeks. As for the military condition, it seems to be a standoff. They attack, we attack. They snipe, we snipe. But neither side has taken any real initiative to conquer the other with the British standing squarely in the middle." He sighed. "But the day the British leave, the Quarter will be a battleground, Ephraim."

"Did you bribe the British truck driver? Do I have a ride in?"

Dov smiled. "You have your ride." He gave him a sad look. "But, please bring your family out when you come." Dov stopped on the edge of the road as Ephraim started walking into town. "*Shalom,* my friend."

Ephraim waved, then broke into a jog. With only a few hours before he had to fly back to Tel Aviv he didn't want to miss his ride to the Quarter.

* * *

Hannah and Ephraim walked down a street in an area of the Old City where snipers couldn't reach. These brief minutes alone were so precious to them both, and yet this time Hannah found herself concerned about her husband's quiet, even depressed spirit. After playing with the twins and putting them down for naps, he had spent a little time with Beth and David before they had gone for their walk. She had noticed that in all of this, he wasn't his usual talkative—even cheerful—self but had talked about serious things and the future. It unnerved her.

"You've been awfully quiet," she said, clinging to his arm with both of hers while looking up at him. "Is there something wrong?"

He didn't speak immediately, just patted the top of one of her hands. "You have to come out of the Old City, Hannah. It's time."

Hannah felt her stomach jump and her mouth go dry. Ephraim didn't dictate to her, and when he spoke in such humble and direct terms, she had learned that he was feeling something beyond fear or expediency. "Are you sure?" she said softly.

"Sure."

"When?"

He gave a relieved smile. "No arguments?"

"I have learned that when you speak in that tone, there is more to what you say than meets the eye. Now answer me, when?"

"I'll arrange for a house in Tel Aviv, then come and get you. Three days at most."

There was silence as she felt the impact of it. She was glad now that she had not belittled others for leaving, regardless of their reasons but it would still be difficult leaving others behind while she fled to Tel Aviv. "I trust you, Ephraim. I always have."

"Then it's settled." Ephraim breathed easier. He saw the jeep pull up across and down the street. He stood and pulled her into his arms.

"I am beginning to realize that the return of Israel to this place may take a miracle," she said, a bit of depression in her voice.

"If that's what it takes, that's what we'll get." He kissed her, then smiled down at her. "It must be time to return or we wouldn't be here, would we?"

"No, I don't suppose we would. We have been a bit driven, haven't we?" she responded.

He pulled back and touched her nose lightly with the end of his finger. "You are an amazing woman, Hannah Daniels, and I love you more than I can say." He lifted her chin. "Stay safe. No chances, okay? I'll get word to you as soon as I have a place for you and the kids."

She nodded as he stepped away, then stepped back to kiss her one more time. The car was already started when Ephraim got in his seat. She watched them turn the corner and head for the gate then walked home. She always felt stronger when he was here and absolutely lost when he wasn't. Three days, maybe four, and they would move to Tel Aviv. Then they'd be together more. It seemed like an eternity.

* * *

Aaron arose just after midnight and walked to the top of a small hill just east of camp. He sat down in the sand and desert grass and thought about the day ahead. They weren't ready. Though the *Nora* had been unloaded and her new weapons distributed, few had been sent to his brigade and none to his platoon. Jack was trying to get them at least one machine gun, more rifles, and some hand grenades, but so far he hadn't been successful.

But that wasn't the worst of it. Half the men in his platoon of 30 had been thrown into this without choice and would prefer not to fight. They had wanted to come to Israel, but they figured the Jewish brigade or some other illusory organization would step forward and do their fighting for them. When they walked off their ship and into the hands of the Haganah, it had been a shock for most, though half a dozen did have some training in DP camps before being smuggled out of Europe. After working with them half the night, Aaron figured at least one, maybe two, would desert him before they ever got to

Kastel. Maybe half the others would freeze under fire, but then he wasn't even sure about himself in that arena.

He remembered the conversation he had had with Avner Gershon the night the two of them had driven to the Negev to tell Ben-Gurion that partition had passed. He had pleaded for a command then. Now here it was, and he found himself wishing it hadn't come. It had all seemed so heroic then, so important. And it was important, but the heroism was for the American movies, his need to be a hero swallowed up in the last three months of discovering war is horrible—and in finding Mary.

At only twenty years of age, he felt small and inadequate, and he was asked to lead a group of men who were even less ready for this than he was. How would they ever survive? How would he react? How would they? When bullets started hitting around them, when others started dying, what would they do? What would he do? It was these uncertainties that scared him the most and left sleep out of the question.

Pulling the letter from his pocket, he lifted it to his nostrils and smelled the sweet scent of Mary's perfume. It had been waiting for him after today's training exercises. He opened it again and scanned the clearly written words.

Dearest Aaron,

There are no words to express how much I love and miss you. My dreams are filled with you, and sleepless nights seem to be my lot in life. As you can understand, everyone here is very upset with recent developments in Palestine and call for the Arab countries to send their armies to destroy the Jews. It is such a horrid feeling, and I find peace only in scripture and prayer and in thinking of you.

I cannot get out of the country. The government confiscates all British passports issued in Palestine and interrogates those who carry them. Though I have nothing to hide, I am afraid. They fear Jewish spies, and if they started asking questions, I would surely say something stupid, or it would be discovered that you and I are married. Better for me to stay here for now though I dream of our reunion.

Izaat has not come, nor have I told others about us. When I arrived, things were very different than I expected. But I had to come and see for myself. The hate is so strong, especially among the Palestinian refugees whose numbers grow by the hundreds everyday. The Lebanese government is very concerned because there are so many and most have no way to support themselves. They have opened camps in the south of the country and force them to go there, and there is talk of shutting off the border to prevent any further migration that will upset the delicate balance of power between Christian and Muslim that exists here. Some even advocate sending refugees back to force the British or the United Nations to deal with them. They say it would make the world look at partition differently. It is horrible that people are becoming pawns in this. It is another reason I wish to stay out of view. I am afraid they will make me go to one of these camps, and I will never be able to come to you.

I must close. I love you with all my heart, and I miss you horribly. I pray for peace even though wicked men like Haj Amin insist on war, and I pray for your safety. Do not worry about me. I am safe and well.

All my love, Mary

P.S. Though I cry for a letter from you, such a thing from a Jew in Palestine would be the death of me. I will write when I can, deliver it to the American consulate and have them send it as I did this one. I have finished Hannah and Ephraim's book again. I wish to talk to them about these beautiful things!

Kisses. Mary

He put the letter back in a pocket, his soul one big ache mixed with a profound love. He had never felt so helpless in all his life, but at least she was safe. More and more he wished he had never let her go, and for the first time he was afraid, very afraid, he might never see her again.

He got out Beth's small book and opened to one of the pages where he had turned down the corner. It was in Alma chapter 60 and promised that those who died fighting for others would see God again. He had read it a lot lately, but it seemed particularly appropriate now. Faces he would see today would be gone tomorrow. He wanted to believe they had a future—that he had a future. That somehow death would not separate him and Mary. He supposed that more than anything else, the last few months had given him the longing for an afterlife. Especially now, now that he had Mary, now that he had to go to war and death might separate them. Were the words of Beth's book true? Was there really a resurrection, an afterlife? His heart wanted to believe, but his mind and his experience fought it.

He and Mary had read it together. When he did, he felt peace, a quiet calm about God that he hadn't felt even before Hitler's war. But did that mean what it spoke of was real, or was it just his own desire to have it be so that was making him believe it?

He wasn't certain about life after death, but right now he wanted to believe. It gave him hope for a future no matter what happened to him today, tomorrow, or next week. It kept him from panic, from running back to Paris a coward, his fear of losing Mary overcoming his desire to do what was right.

The camp came to life and trucks began loading. Time to go. Bowing his head he said a quick prayer, one his father taught him when he was a boy. "Behold, God is my salvation; I will trust, and will not be afraid, for God, the Lord, is my strength and song, and He is become my salvation. Therefore . . . salvation belongeth unto the Lord; thy blessing be upon Thy people. The Lord of hosts is with us; the God of Jacob is our refuge." Then he added. "Father, give me courage. Help me lead. And bring me back to Mary in one piece. That's all I ask."

Taking a deep breath he got to his feet, the first rays of the sun striking above the Bab el Wad. "God go with us," he said softly. "You above of all must know we can't do this alone."

CHAPTER 35

Aaron's platoon was ordered to the Tzuba Quarry post. It wasn't an easy assignment. The quarry was on the upper end of the Jerusalem/Tel Aviv Road, which meant they must either go round or straight through the majority of Arab emplacements. Aaron led out with 30 men in two squads, most moaning about going at all. He'd let them complain up to a point. They were nervous, and complaining about something helped them vent and keep things under control. But if it began affecting morale, he'd shut it down no matter the cost.

Along the way, they encountered the enemy on two occasions. On the first they had engaged them in fire. It had probably been unnecessary, but Aaron saw a chance to bolster their confidence—help them get over their jitters and face their fear. The Arab group was smaller, scattered, and seemed even less prepared for battle than they did. They had no automatic weapons, no machine guns. Much to his surprise, his group was better armed.

He ordered four of his more trusted men, two from each squad, to get to higher ground and use their better marksmanship to hone in on the enemy while the rest kept them busy. Soon the four were in position, and at Aaron's signal, the remaining platoon lay down a fire that scattered the Arabs and drove them into the four awaiting marksmen. With men suddenly under fire and taking hits, the Arabs panicked and left the area.

The victory had worked, giving them all a layer of confidence, though one fearful recruit, a boy by the name of Beni, was too busy keeping his head down to fire a single shot. Instead of chastising him openly, Aaron pulled Beni aside for a little heart-to-heart reassurance that might help him get under control. But it didn't seem to help much, and Aaron, afraid he would endanger everyone else under circumstances that would surely get worse for them, ordered Beni back to the nearest settlement to await the platoon's return. The boy refused to go.

Embarrassed and humiliated for his cowardice, Beni begged to stay. Aaron finally agreed, demanding that Beni stay close and promising him that if he buckled again, he'd shoot him. Beni got the message.

The second encounter was too close to an Arab village to do battle without bringing a hundred others that would surely wipe them out. Aaron kept them out of sight until the Arabs were at a safe distance he felt confident they could move on. His men responded well. At least no one panicked with a potshot that would have ruined everything. For Aaron, the self-control was encouraging.

They arrived at Tzuba Quarry an hour later, tired and eager for a rest. As they dropped to the ground in helter-skelter fashion, Aaron ordered them to find cover in case of attack. At the same moment, the sound of gunfire nearby put an exclamation mark to his order. They all hustled for a safer place to wait.

The headquarters was in a building at the Quarry, and Aaron filtered through other platoons digging in to get there. Inside he found Mordechai Gish, a lieutenant and the commander of the other platoon that was to go to Kastel. Gish demanded a reason for their delay and when satisfied, told Aaron that plans had changed. Only Aaron's platoon would replace Sela at Kastel.

"I thought both platoons were to replace Sela," Aaron said. He knew that trying to hold Kastel very long with only his 30 men would be difficult if not impossible.

"We will, but in stages." Gish pulled out a map. "Arabs are coming from Ein Kerem to the south and from Tzuba itself to try and retake Kastel from Sela. We'll go together and intercept them here and drive them back. Then I and my men will retreat to Tzuba Quarry and hold it while you go on to Kastel and replace Sela's men."

Aaron knew they had to hold the quarry if they could. It was an even more important position than Kastel. "But with the number of platoons here already, why do you have to return to defend it?"

"The men you see here now are all going elsewhere because other platoons have run into stiff opposition. There's no one else but my platoon. Sela is already behind schedule in securing the positions above this narrow spot in the canyon," he pointed at the map, "and that leaves you."

"When will you reinforce us?"

"As soon as another company comes in here and takes charge of the quarry."

"You're holding something back. Let's hear it."

Gish folded the map. "The Arabs now seem to think Kastel is worth something. SHAI intercepted a communiqué this morning indicating they will pay a heavy price to get it back. If my men get stuck here—if we can't reinforce you—you'll be on your own at horrible odds."

"Then I'd better see your pretty brown eyes coming along the main street before sunup."

"Yeah, I'll try. But if we're not reinforced by then . . . well, we have to stay, or we'll lose the quarry and then you won't have a prayer and neither will anyone else along this ridge."

Aaron nodded, his mouth too dry to speak. What Gish was telling him was Tzuba Quarry was more important than Kastel to the Haganah, while Kastel was more important to the Arabs, and Kastel wouldn't get reinforced if others along the ridge needed men. He would be last on command's list.

"I'll give you two machine guns, grenades, plenty of bullets, and Sela will leave the mortar. Have you had any experience with one?"

"Yeah, fire them regularly for evening entertainment."

"Don't get cute, Sergeant. If you haven't, Sela will take it. Otherwise you'll blow somebody's head off trying, and we'll just lose it to the Arabs."

"Yeah, I can fire it, and so can my second-in-command."

"Alright, get them moving."

Aaron found his men catching some shut-eye, rousted them, and explained their orders. Pointing directly at Uri Shomari, he told him that when they got to Kastel, he would be in charge of the mortar.

"Never fired one, sir," Uri answered.

"Then pretend like you have. I don't want it leaving the hill with Sela's men, got it?"

"Yes, sir."

"Pack everything you can. I noticed extra water containers over by those stones. Snatch one if you can, and be sure your weapons are fully loaded and ready." Each nodded as they began gathering up their gear.

"Where's Shmu'el?" Everyone looked around, shrugged, and went back to work. "Alright then. Let's get moving. Beni, stay close."

Beni nodded, clutching his rifle with two sweaty hands. "Shmu'el deserted, didn't he?"

"It looks that way, but who knows? Maybe he's just doing a little recon of his own," he said cynically. As they started toward Gish and his men, Aaron wondered how many would still be with him when the platoon reached Kastel. And if their leader would fail them.

CHAPTER 36

Aaron watched the last rays of the sun flee as if frightened by something it had seen in the coming darkness. Tonight, fear of the dark would hit a lot of men just as hard.

They had reached Kastel and replaced Sela's men who had immediately left the area, taking the mortar with them. Sela had also questioned their delay, but had said no more when Aaron told them he had just lost two men in a battle to keep half-a-hundred men off his platoon's back. When Sela then refused to give up the mortar, Aaron, tired and unwilling to debate with him, pulled his pistol and pointed it at Sela's stomach. "Gish says it stays. That is a direct order. Take it up with him if you don't like it, but don't expect me to let you walk out of here with the one weapon that may keep us alive."

Sela could see he meant business, shrugged, and told his man to put the mortar down along with the pack of shells.

"You and I will have words about this later, Sergeant," Sela said firmly.

"If we're both alive when this is over I'll be glad to discuss it in any way you wish. For now, the discussion is over. Be on your way."

Sela led his men from the area without looking back, and Aaron ordered Uri to take possession of the weapon. His men had doubted that Sela would give it up and were impressed by their leader's willingness to fight for them. They set it up on the mukhtar's roof in the middle of the village just captured that morning, and Aaron showed both Uri and two others how to operate it. One of them was Beni.

"Beni, you said you do well with math, geometry, and that sort of thing. Figuring trajectory and where your shell will land relies on those principles. Of all of us, you should be the best at hitting a target." He continued to explain the operation, while telling them they would have no shells for practice, but if they wanted to be alive in the morning they had better be accurate.

"Who are we up against, Sergeant?" Uri asked.

"Arabs, Uri, who else?"

The others laughed and Uri's face turned a bit red. "I mean, which commander will bring his men in here to force us out?"

"Abdul Khader runs this sector, but SHAI says he's in Damascus. That leaves Kemal Erekat or Hassan Salameh," Aaron said. "Whoever it is, we can beat them." He set his rifle down next to him, leaning the barrel against the wall of the house. "I'm going to be honest with you. Haganah command doesn't think the Arabs will want Kastel. Jack Willis and a few others believe they're wrong. Because command doesn't believe as they do, they won't send reinforcements up here any time soon. But if we let Kahder's men take this position, the Nachshon convoy will fail, and Jerusalem will go hungry." He stood, pointing at the winding road below them. "It doesn't take much in the way of intelligence to see that this holds a commanding position that will allow the Arabs to stop anything coming through the Bab el Wad, although it seems to elude Haganah operations."

There was snickering, and Aaron couldn't help but smile himself. "The Arabs will try to take it back, and they'll do it soon. We have to stop them. We might be on our own doing it." That put an end to any snickering and several stood to look at the road.

"There aren't enough of us to hold off Arab regulars very long, Sergeant," Beni said weakly.

"Numbers aren't important. Position is. You and the mortar are here, and we'll put in a perimeter with our machine guns there and there. The rest of you will dig in where you can move from position to position, reinforce where the Arabs hit the hardest." He pointed. "If we have to retreat, we do it in increments, each time collapsing on the center. But we don't back off a single position unless we're about to be overrun. We have to make the Arabs pay a heavy price at every point." They nodded. "Beni, if you and Uri hit us with that mortar, you'll wipe us out. So if you're going to miss the Arabs, miss them long."

Beni nodded as the others gave wan smiles. Aaron could see they weren't confident in his choice to run the mortar, but Beni would come through. He had to.

Aaron assigned each man a place to fight. "The mukhtar's house will be our command center. Build fortifications, pill boxes that give you an advantage and enable you to cover each other's positions. Remember, you want open spaces around, and if that means blowing up a few houses, get it done. Judah has the explosives. Finally, work out some paths for retreat and so you can get messages or ammo or help. If we plan well now, we'll beat them. Uri, you, Judah, and I will map out a retreat strategy just in case it's needed." Judah was the other squad leader, an older man with a round face and steel cold eyes who said little. But he had the strength of an ox and didn't flinch like the others had when learning hand-to-hand combat. His only problem was he didn't speak very much Hebrew or English and no Yiddish. But he seemed to understand them all and got the job done.

"Judah, Uri, select a man from each of your platoons to get to high ground and watch for Arab troop movements while we dig in." He looked at all of them. "Any questions?"

"What about food?"

"There are a hundred homes here, but most of the food might already be gone. After you're dug in and ready for battle, see what you can find and stockpile it in your digs. The main thing you want is water. The well is outside the village and down the ravine toward Tzuba, so get what you need now and be conservative."

Judah and Uri selected the two lookouts and everyone began scrambling to their positions. As Aaron watched and directed them, he thought that for the first time they all understood this was no game, it was survival. Would some of these twenty-eight men still run? Maybe, but he didn't think so. Would he get them all killed? A good chance. Though he remembered a lot of his training, troop placement was critical and learned only in the field. He had never been in the field. He knew the rudiments. He would try. But the doubt was there just the same.

Three hours later, everyone was dug in, but there were no Arabs. Aaron walked to the outer perimeter where several houses had been blown up to give them a view of the entire quarter of the village. They could see the lights of a village on the next hill over and one of them asked him what village it was.

"Deir Yassin."

"Will they come?"

"Our leaders aren't sure. They haven't been involved up to now. In fact, they made a pact with the nearby Jewish village to stay out of it. Just in case, the Haganah is sending in someone to keep an eye on them."

"I hear ETZEL is assigned that duty," one of them said.

Aaron was surprised. "Where did you hear that?"

"From Gish's men back at Tzuba Quarry. Because we're spread so thin, the Haganah made a deal with the ETZEL and they invited LEHI. Just a rumor probably."

"Yeah, probably," Aaron said. He didn't like the sound of it. He had come to despise the fanatics of ETZEL and LEHI.

He went to the next group of soldiers and checked their placement, then went back to the mukhtar's house where Beni was eating some flat bread. He had a small fire going inside the house and had stirred up some bread and fried it over the round hot plate left by the villagers. He handed Aaron a piece.

"Thanks." He devoured it, hungry to the core. "Who is on the roof?" He asked.

"Uri and two others. I thought we took Kastel two weeks ago," said Beni in his rapid Yiddish.

"We did," Aaron said as he cleared his mouth of food. "SHAI found out Khader intended to take Tzuba Quarry from Kastel, so the Haganah sent in a unit of the Palmach the middle of March. They drove out most of the people, but the British told the unit they couldn't stay."

"The Brits," Beni spat to his side. "Their refusal to keep this road open has cost me many friends. I spit on British graves."

"Well, this time the Brits didn't let the Arabs back in—not right away. But Khader started moving men and supplies in two days ago. Fortunately the force was still small enough when Sela hit them this morning that they left with hardly a fight."

"That's why we have no dead to bury," Beni shrugged. "Too bad it wasn't us who came first, replaced by Sela. It will be tougher to keep the Arabs out," Uri said.

Aaron was handed another piece of hot bread. "Do you have enough for the others?" he asked.

"Plenty."

One of the men came in. He had smelled the bread. Beni sent some back with him and fried up more. As he left they heard a shot fired, then another, then the sound of Brens. Aaron and Beni had their guns in hand and were up the steps to the roof in seconds. It was starting.

* * *

Over the next twenty-four hours the Arabs attacked a half-dozen times, and Aaron's men drove them back. Though none of his men were killed, he had several badly wounded, and as they had no real medical treatment and little morphine, they were suffering. If they didn't get them to a hospital soon, they would become casualties. He learned one of the men had helped in a camp infirmary after the war and assigned him to do what he could, then had the wounded brought to the mukhtar's house where his new medic could do his best.

Aaron was pleased with the courage of all his men but was especially proud of Beni. He had calculated his mortar fire well, making it instrumental in driving back the larger numbers of guerillas at times when they were about to overrun one or the other of his perimeter positions. Because of it, they hadn't had to retreat from any ground.

They were also aware that the entire mountain was a series of battles. Tzuba Quarry was being hit especially hard during the night but was quiet in the morning. He wasn't sure who had won. No Arabs climbed toward them from that direction, but there had been no reinforcements from Gish either. Would they come? He didn't know, but as another day and night passed, he knew he had to find out. His men were exhausted, falling asleep at their posts, shaking from lack of strength, mentally stretched to the limit—and it was showing in their use of ammo as they fired at anything that moved, their fear strong and their thought processes erratic. Now they were nearly out of ammunition and had two casualties. He decided it was time to act.

After sunset, Aaron sent Uri and Judah through enemy lines to deliver a message to the highest ranking officer they could find. They needed more ammunition and reinforcements. Now. As he watched the two men skulk away in the darkness, he wondered if they would ever return, and he listened intently for gunfire in that direction. None came.

It was a long, grueling wait, but his two squad leaders returned near sunup. They had as much ammunition as they and two other men could carry. The two men were the extent of their reinforcements. Gish was trying to hold the quarry, and things were even worse further down the Bab el Wad where villages held the Haganah at bay, delaying the convoy's efforts to leave Tel Aviv. Gish told Uri and Judah that with things the way they were, it might be another twenty-four hours.

"The lieutenant told us to hang on if we can. It's helping everybody else," Uri said. With that he and Judah immediately lay down on the bare floor and fell into a quick, exhausted sleep.

Aaron felt sick inside but kept it to himself. He was sure the Arabs would be here in force by morning. They didn't have twenty-four hours.

He was right. The Arabs came an hour later in such numbers that Aaron was forced for the first time to withdraw some positions. The Arabs were in the outer village now and fighting hard to push Aaron's men back farther. One gun emplacement in the outer perimeter was cut off, and only Judah's quick response kept them from being massacred. He took half a dozen men and rushed the Arab positions with such tenacity that they fled long enough that Judah could pull the men in the emplacement out. Judah was the stuff heroes were made of.

It was mid-afternoon during a lull in the fighting that Aaron awoke from a listless sleep to hear the sound of motors and soon found three armored cars pulled into the street just in front. A squad joined the fight and brought with them food, more ammunition, and a few mortar shells. The commanding officer had a note from Jack.

We have taken most of the villages down below and cleared the canyon. The convoy is on the way. Hold out for another few hours and we'll reinforce. Keep the road open at all costs. We're finally winning. Jack.

The armored cars took the wounded and went back down the road while Aaron did a quick count and found that he was back to twenty-eight men. Unfortunately, the reinforcements had been fighting in other places and were nearly as exhausted as his own men. Most found a corner to fall asleep in as soon as they were assigned an emplacement. Aaron feared that some of them would not awaken even with a battle raging around them and told Uri and Judah to be prepared to make the rounds to roust them when the Arabs came again.

The Arabs fired on the armored cars as they left with no effect, then seemed to filter away, content to get some much-needed rest of their own.

Aaron was too tired to stay awake and dozed a little as the warmth of mid-afternoon turned to a cooler evening. He jerked back to consciousness as he heard the sounds of dozens of motors coming up the road. Running to his most forward emplacement, he looked down on the largest convoy he had ever seen. As the first vehicles reached the road just below them, the Arabs started firing from positions on the opposite hill. Aaron ordered his men to reposition their largest machine gun and strafe the Arabs as the convoy pushed past them toward Jerusalem. He then ran to the mukhtar's house and told Beni to use his mortar to blast the emplacements the Arabs had taken from them earlier, believing that the sight of so many Jewish trucks and armored cars, along with the shelling, would drive the enemy back. By the time the last of the trucks successfully topped the hill and shifted gears for the last dash to Jerusalem, Aaron had retaken nearly all the emplacements and the Arabs were on the run. What they had been fighting for was finally getting through to Jerusalem.

As night slipped once more over the hills, heavy clouds streamed in from the west and settled over them like a thick blanket. It began to rain. Aaron felt relieved—the weather and the darkness would discourage another attack, at least for awhile. Returning to the warmth of a fire in the mukhtar's house, he ate some dates and bread. Half a dozen men were fast asleep on the floor and he was sure those in emplacements around Kastel were mostly doing the same. He just prayed the Arabs needed it as badly as his men did.

* * *

Jack was appalled. Khader had heavily reinforced his command at Kastel, had taken half a dozen other villages, including Tzuba Quarry, and was now preparing for the overthow of Kastel. If Aaron didn't get more help immediately, Khader would seize the village, and Aaron and his platoon would be slaughtered.

The boy had done what Jack had asked. Against overwhelming odds, he had held Kastel until command saw its importance. Now they wanted him to stay, fight longer, without reinforcements, even though the odds had increased considerably and Khader was directly involved. Jack was regretting asking the boy, afraid he had dug a grave for Aaron that Khader was going to fill in and pack down.

He had gone to Yadin and Avidan, operations commanders for Nachshon, and asked for reinforcements. Far too little had been done, and the radio had allowed Jack to hear the two men argue and debate about what must be done next. As a result of each man's unwillingness to accept responsibility, a single convoy with eight men had been sent to reinforce, but no replacement forces were in the works.

Their misunderstanding of what was happening at Kastel, and what seemed like their indifference to the lives of Aaron and his men, made Jack realize that it had come down to him keeping his promise to Aaron personally. He got in his jeep and went to find Ephraim. They were Aaron's only chance.

CHAPTER 37

Khader's men attacked as the mist from the rain lifted against the heat of a rising but invisible sun. It was a brutal attack with hundreds of Arabs hitting Kastel from all four sides, but the constant stream of fire Aaron's men laid down drove the enemy back, once, twice, and then a third time.

With each attack, the situation worsened for Aaron's men, and he began pulling back toward the command center. The enemy was quickly moving into grenade-throwing distance when Aaron heard the sound of a plane overhead. He looked up to see that familiar Piper Cub shaking its wings at him then watched as Ephraim's plane dropped three 45-pound bombs and four 18-pounders on the Arabs, shells recently received via the *Nora*. It wasn't an American B-17 bomber, and it wasn't pretty, but it was effective. Arabs scattered for safety as a second plane followed with more of the same. As both planes swung around for a strafing run, the Arabs were running down the side of the hill in chaotic disarray. The retreat was beautiful to see, but Aaron didn't let his men celebrate. He gave immediate orders to move back into the forward emplacements, and though tired beyond reason, the fifteen men still standing moved out and quickly took the positions.

Aaron, exhausted, had waved weakly as Ephraim had flown over to drop a crate full of food to a grateful platoon. Israel's new airforce had saved their lives.

* * *

Abdul Khader was depressed. He had lost nearly eighty men in the last attack, more than a hundred during the day. Morale was low, and several tribes had slipped away after the last defeat, taking their dead with them. Drenched to the skin and shivering, he turned to Kemal Erekat and told him to prepare the men for a final assault—one he would lead.

"But General, this is a very dangerous situation. You cannot . . ."

Khader put his arm around his deputy's shoulder. "Do you know what it will mean if we lose control of this road? Do you understand that all will be lost? Our men are already losing faith in us, Kemal. More will leave during the night unless we have a victory. I would rather die trying to retake this hill than lose them. Now get your men up and prepared to fight. We attack as soon as you are ready."

* * *

Judah was at the command post, while Aaron, Uri, and Beni were near the sheik's tomb on the outskirts of the city when the attack came. Then, as quickly as it had begun, the attack stopped.

"Why did they stop so soon?" Beni asked, stifling a yawn.

"Do not be disappointed, my friend. They will come back and give you more," Uri said in a tired voice. He wiped the sweat from his dusty face, then began reloading. "This is my last box of shells."

"Now would be a good time to get some more," Aaron said. "I need to check on the others. Beni, how many mortar shells do you have left?"

Beni didn't answer. His head lay against the wall, his mouth sagging, his eyes shut in an exhausted sleep.

Aaron quickly checked. Two mortars left. "Keep your head down. I'll get ammo and be back as soon as I can."

Leaving an exhausted Uri giving orders to one of the fresher recruits, Aaron slipped out and worked his way back through the renewed gloom of another storm. Nearing the command post, his eyes caught sight of what he thought must be three men carefully placing boxes of something against the wall of the mukhtar's house. The rain was thick, and he couldn't see clearly, but a fearful warning buzzed around his mind. He melted into the shadows and readied his rifle. Were they Judah's men? If so, what were they doing? He tried to shake the cobwebs out of his brain. He had been awake so long every-thing seemed to drift together in a jumble. If they were Judah's men and he fired on them . . . No, they were Arabs. They must have slipped them through on the last attack. That was why they withdrew so quickly. They were buying time to get these men past our outposts.

He heard footsteps and tried to push himself even further into the darkness as the three men rushed passed him at a dead run. Two of them wore British uniforms; one was an Arab wearing a kaffiyeh. He stepped into the road behind them and fired. The Arab went down while the two British collaborators dashed into a side street. Aaron heard shouts from Judah at the command post and turned quickly to identify himself.

"It's me, Judah. Aaron. The containers at the front of the house," Aaron yelled to Judah. "Arab bombs!"

Judah cursed, but Aaron didn't see him bend over the boxes—he was already chasing the two others. Aaron approached the corner cautiously, saw nothing around it, and stepped into the shadows of a building, working his way farther along the rubble and half-standing houses. He was sweating as he cautiously moved forward. Reaching a path that went between the sheik's tomb and the mukhtar's house, he heard someone speaking in Arabic. It stopped him in his tracks. He had heard the voice before, but where? He remained motionless, waiting, squinting into the bleak gloom of the storm for the slightest sign of movement.

He heard something fall in the house across the street, then saw someone step through the doorway, followed by two others. Then there were more voices, more Arabic, more shadows farther up the street. The Arabs had found a way through their defenses. He tried not to breathe, not to move and reveal his location, while frantically trying to figure a way he could escape. Suddenly he heard someone else come around the corner behind him and froze completely.

"What the . . ."

It was Uri and a few others, and before he could finish his sentence, Aaron yelled. "They're Arabs, Uri! Run!"

Uri and the men with him saw the danger, lifted their weapons and fired with Aaron. The shortest man of the three down the street fell as Aaron injected another shell and fired again. Suddenly the street was a chaos of battle, but it quickly subsided as the Arabs retreated at a dead run and the street cleared. Uri and the others jumped to their feet and went after them as Aaron went cautiously forward to check the man who lay facedown in the dirt. His heart pounding from the sudden action, Aaron knelt down and rolled the man over. Abdul Khader Husseini stared back at him.

"Water," he rasped.

Aaron pulled a flask from his belt and gave Khader a drink. He coughed and spit most of it up as Aaron checked his wound. It was in the chest, and Aaron didn't have a bandage.

"You have killed me, Jew," Khader said with a wry smile. Then there was a gurgle in his chest and his head fell to the side, his eyes fixed on some distant point.

Aaron lay his rifle down and searched Khader for his identity card. Snatching half a dozen items, he put them in his pocket, then dragged the body into a deserted house and left it before going for the much needed ammo. When he entered the command post, Judah queried him on what had happened. Aaron handed him the personal items of Abdul Khader.

"Khader? You shot him?" Judah said in confused English.

"Someone did. It was a battle. Who knows who hit him, but he's dead. When the Arabs hear we've killed their leader, they'll come like mad dogs to make us pay for it. I need a messenger, Judah. Can you do it?"

Judah, nodded, his brow wrinkled with worry. "Get to Gish," Aaron said. "Give him those papers and tell him what happened. Then get on the radio and contact Jack Willis. If he isn't at headquarters, have them hunt him down and tell him to get some armored cars up here by morning or this will be our graveyard. Do you understand? Jack Willis, no one else. Jack will come. I'm not sure about the others."

Judah nodded, then went out the door. Aaron could only pray he'd get through. Though he felt they could retreat on their own, they couldn't take the eight wounded and survive. They needed those cars.

* * *

The Arabs heard Khader was missing and the word went out to find him. Erekat, wounded by Uri as he tried to escape, was sent back to Jerusalem to a doctor. He spread the word that Khader had not come out of Kastel, and it flew through every souk in East Jerusalem.

By the time the storm had cleared and the afternoon sun was warming the trees, the mountain and forest of Nebi Samwil was crawling with Arabs. Some were the well-armed regulars from Iraq and Syria that made up the core of Khader's command, but most were the villagers who lived around Jerusalem and were loyal to Haj Amin and Khader. Most were armed with rifles, but the Jews defending Kastel could see many with scythes, rakes, and shovels ready to hack them to pieces once they overran their position. Aaron made a mental note to save a bullet for himself when they came.

But they had no leader and weren't sure how and when to attack. Until someone finally decided they should stop mourning and start shooting, they would keep their distance, filling the air with the shrill sound of Arab tongues that made Aaron's skin crawl. He glanced at his watch. Judah had been gone several hours and no sign of help. Aaron was beginning to think that his second squad leader had been ambushed.

"They look lost," Beni said.

"Stunned is more like it," responded Uri. "Or maybe they're just waiting for more help. Though why they think they need it is beyond me. There are enough men out there that we would run out of bullets and still only kill half of them."

Aaron heard the motor of a vehicle and lifted himself as high as he dared to see what it was.

"Armored cars," he said with some excitement. He saw the large frame of Jack Willis in the turret of the one real armored car they had—the British one Jack had arranged to get them weeks ago. They had a chance.

The shrill sound of Arab trilling reached a fevered pitch, then it stopped and they began chanting the name of Abdul Khader in angry Arabic.

"Here they come!" Aaron said as he braced his arms on the ledge and prepared to fire. "Beni, use up your mortars protecting those cars. If they don't get here, we're dead men!"

A few seconds later the attack came in all its fury, and Aaron found his battle-worn platoon in a last desperate fight to live. Aaron was in the middle of lobbing a grenade when Beni was hit and killed. He watched as two more men died before his eyes, one of them a machine gunner. He grabbed the gun and kept firing while ordering Uri to get ready to retreat to where the occupants of the armored cars were fighting for their own lives. Uri lobbed the last of the grenades, driving a group of Arabs back beyond the building next door, and helped one of the wounded stand then put his arm around his shoulder. The other two men stood at the door of the house in which they had taken refuge only minutes earlier. Aaron picked up the smaller of the two machine guns and handed it to one of them. He then picked up the larger one and went to the door.

He turned to the man with the smaller machine gun. "Give me cover. When I'm in place, you guys can make a dash for my position while I cover for you. Then we'll do it again and again until we reach the armored cars."

The man nodded, fear the only thing keeping him conscious. Aaron heard a cry from the Arabs and knew it was now or never.

He zigzagged from the house and up the narrow street, bullets striking around him. He hurdled a short wall and fell, the weight of the machine gun too much for his worn-out muscles. With shaking hands, he turned back, placed the gun on the wall, and put a belt of bullets in the chamber. They were his last. He saw several Arabs trying to get to the house where Uri and the others waited. Aaron fired, driving them back.

Uri appeared and helped the wounded men run as fast as they could up the street. When an Arab appeared at a window or door or rooftop, Aaron fired. Uri stepped to one side when the wounded man was hit. He dropped him to the ground and checked for a pulse. Finding none, he came across the rubble and jumped behind the wall with Aaron as the rest of the men ran after him.

Aaron kept up fire as he shouted for the others to keep going. Uri called to one for his rifle and it was immediately tossed to him. He injected a shell and joined in as the others disappeared up the street. Aaron glanced over his shoulder to see if the man with the other machine gun was setting up to cover them. He was nowhere in sight. They were on their own.

* * *

Ephraim looked down at the mass of Arabs and wondered how the fighters at Kastel had held on so long. The odds must be fifty to one. As he flew low over the village, a thousand rifles aimed up at him and fired. He heard the bullets hit against the iron plating under his seat; heard them pass through the metal of the fuselage. He swung hard left. Making a big circle in the direction of Jerusalem, he noted that Jack's convoy was nearly inside the village.

More than ten times in the last twenty-four hours Kastel had required help, and nothing beyond a few men had been sent. As Jack and Ephraim had begged for more, they had been told there were none or they were needed elsewhere or the men at Kastel would have to hold on. The command leadership argued, debated, and blamed, but ultimately did nothing. Finally Jack had been contacted by one of Aaron's men via the headquarters radio at Tzuba Quarry telling them Kastel needed immediate evacuation. Jack had stomped into Avidan's office and yelled until he got the armored cars and a dozen men to go after them. From the looks of it, they had nearly come too late.

He swung to the right and flew back toward the village. As he came in low over the trees, he saw that the armored vehicles had reached their position, but the mass of Arab humanity kept those trying to get to them at bay. He wrestled with the 18-pound bomb on the floor and dropped it on the Arabs, then a second, and a third. They ran for cover and he banked right to avoid the merciless fire aimed at his plane. A second pass saw the Arabs concentrating on the armored vehicles, but Jack was fighting them off and finally taking on passengers. Ephraim banked left for his last run.

* * *

Aaron saw the armored cars from his position, saw them take fire, the Arabs rush to cut them off. He told Uri to get to the command post and tell the others it was time to leave. Uri ran, dodging bullets as Aaron used the last of his ammunition to protect him. He saw the plane come over for a second run, heard the explosions, saw it bank left for another run. He knew it was Ephraim. He offered a silent prayer of thanks to God while also praying that it wouldn't cost Eph his life.

He saw Uri getting everyone to the armored cars, saw them boarding. He was the only one left. Taking a deep breath, he picked up the machine gun to keep it out of enemy hands and ran. He took deadly fire and had to throw himself to the ground to keep from getting cut down. He heard Ephraim coming for another pass and struggled to his knees with the machine gun. It was this time or never.

* * *

Jack threw open the turret and tossed several grenades at Arabs in houses close by. He heard the plane coming low, then saw it through the trees. The bombs started an Arab scramble for cover. He glanced up and saw his friend at the stick, saw him hanging another bomb out the window, watched it fall and scatter more of the enemy. Suddenly black smoke exploded from the front of the Piper Cub, and the engine stuttered as Ephraim banked it left. Jack's breath caught in his throat as he realized the plane was going down in the rocky, tree-covered hills to the north of them. It was in the heart of Arab-held territory and difficult to get to. He cursed as he aimed the machine gun and tried to concentrate on saving the men still in the camp. Then he would go after Ephraim.

* * *

Ephraim tried to control the stick as smoke and oil blinded him through the bullet-riddled and broken windshield of the Piper Cub. He was flying blind when he hit the tops of the trees, then crashed through them, his plane literally ripped apart as it plummeted to the ground. He was thrown forward against the steering column with such force he thought he would break in half as the plane hit a large tree, careened to the right and slid down the side of the mountain into the canyon below. When it came to an abrupt halt, his seat broke free and he was thrown into what was left of the windshield. Pain exploded in his head in a wave of darkness that entirely engulfed him. When the plane came to a stop, Ephraim Daniels didn't move.

SEE CHAPTER NOTES

CHAPTER 38

Aaron was the last one aboard Jack's armored cars, and they were quickly on their way out of Kastel as the Arabs overran the village. Jack watched through a peephole as they celebrated their victory and hunted for any men left behind. There were less than a dozen aboard the armored vehicles, but there were no living left to the vengeance of the mob behind them. Jack called that a success.

"Just in time," Aaron said.

"Ephraim's plane went down. I heard it crash." Jack's voice was filled with pain but determination. "We are goin' after him."

"Where?" Aaron asked with stunned disbelief.

"In the hills just north of us."

Aaron pushed his aching, bloodied body to its feet and asked for ammo.

"In the box over there." Jack pointed as he looked over the exhausted kid, the cuts and scrapes leaving their mark in blood that stained his clothes and skin. But there were no life-threatening holes. "Alright. Anyone here that doesnae want tae go after the pilot who just saved ye from certain death?"

Aaron looked at the faces of his men. Uri, Judah, and two who had come as replacements he didn't even know. None balked.

"We go," said Judah in broken English.

"He's right," Uri added. "The guy saved our necks. We don't leave him."

Jack gave the order to the driver and they turned onto a side road and headed into the hills. They had to get to Ephraim before the Arabs did.

After finding a path along the ridge that separated one hill from another, they saw the smoke of the wreckage and left the armored car with the two replacements and the driver of the car, took the machine gun Aaron had salvaged, now reloaded with ammo, and went down the ravine. The defeat at Kastel proved a blessing for the moment, all Arabs hustling there to celebrate the victory. They reached the plane without incident. Jack and Aaron were together when they saw the wreckage, and Jack immediately made the comment that no one could have survived such a crash. Aaron was already sliding down the hill, his heart pumping at a rate that would kill most men, his mind filled with what he could possibly say to Hannah and the children. When he reached the wreckage, he found the doors ripped away and Ephraim gone, a trail of blood headed in the general direction of the valley below. He followed and found Ephraim propped up against a tree fifty yards farther on, his .45 in his hand, but his eyes closed and head lowered to his chest. With his heart in his mouth, Aaron quickly knelt down and checked for a pulse. Ephraim's head jerked back to consciousness, the gun coming up ready to fire.

"Easy, Eph. It's me, Aaron."

Ephraim's eyes frantically searched Aaron's face, then recognition replaced the fear. "Glad to see you made it. From the look of things back there . . ." A sudden wave of pain hit him, and he gritted his teeth against it.

Aaron felt the blood and ripped aside Ephraim's shirt. There was a hole the size of his fist in Ephraim's side, and he grimaced against what it might mean. As Jack fell to his knees beside them, he pulled a bandage from a pocket and quickly began wrapping it around his friend.

"He'll survive." Jack said it with calm coolness that belied his own fear. Ephraim could bleed to death before they got him out of here if they weren't quick about it.

"Come on. We have to get him back to the armored car and to a hospital. Can you walk?" he asked Ephraim.

"No. I can't feel my legs."

Uri and Judah joined them and watched for the enemy as Aaron and Jack tried to pick up their friend. When they got him up, Jack saw why Ephraim didn't feel anything. The bullet had exited

Ephraim's back at his backbone, and at least part of it was missing. Aaron held him up while he used another bandage to quickly stanch the flow of blood and cover the wound.

"We have company," Uri said.

The first bullet struck nearby, and Uri and Judah returned fire as Jack and Aaron picked up their friend and started up the hill. Suddenly Arabs were firing from a dozen directions and they had to take cover. Jack yelled at the car to move farther west to where a small canyon would give them some protection as they climbed up. When the car was in place, they stood and started up the ravine and Uri, Judah, and the machine gunner on the armored car tried to give them cover. They were nearly there when a barrage of fire came from three directions, forcing them to take cover again. Aaron looked back and saw Uri lying in the path holding his arm, his weapon at his side.

"Take him to the car, Jack. I'll cover for you and then bring Uri." Without waiting for an answer, he darted the few steps, picked up the rifle, and grabbed Uri's collar, dragging him to better cover. Telling Uri to get moving, Aaron injected a shell into the rifle and began firing as Jack shouldered Ephraim and all of them headed up the hill. Aaron did his best to keep Arab heads down, injecting and firing shell after shell until the magazine was empty. Then he yelled at Judah who was also out of ammo, and they started up the path twenty feet apart. As they reached the armored car, he saw Jack laying Ephraim on the floor of the vehicle and shoving him in. As he was about to finish, a bullet struck Jack in the back and threw him forward on top of Ephraim. The two replacements worked feverishly to get both men inside as Aaron and Judah took momentary cover against a barrage of shells.

"I do not think I can make it," Judah said.

Aaron looked at him and saw blood on his stomach, his hands trying to cover it. He crawled to Judah and checked the wound. It was pumping blood, and Aaron couldn't see how serious the damage was. "You're going back, my friend," Aaron said. He picked him up and put him over a shoulder and started for the armored car. The first bullet grazed Aaron's leg; the second took off a bit of ear. But as he tossed Judah into the waiting arms of the replacements, a third struck him directly in the back. He reeled left from the blow and lost all strength, going to his knees, his hands sliding down the side of the vehicle. He never knew when he hit the ground.

One of the replacements started out of the car to retrieve him, but the hail of bullets stopped him, then Uri shoved him aside, dove out of the vehicle and crawled to Aaron. Rushed by the bullets striking around him, he quickly felt for a pulse. There was none. A bullet creased his arm, another hit near his forehead. As he scrambled back to the vehicle his heart ached with the revelation that his leader was dead.

"Go!" he yelled. "He's dead. We can't help him now. Go!"

As the vehicle worked back to the road, another armored car greeted them, then covered their backtrail while they sped toward Tel Aviv. When they arrived at the staging area, the vehicle came to a halt in front of a field hospital, and Judah quickly yelled for a doctor. One ran from a tent and helped Judah pull Ephraim, then Jack, from the vehicle and carry them into the tent, laying them on tables next to each other.

As Uri was helped to a chair, other doctors gathered around and began working to save the two men's lives, realizing only one would survive.

CHAPTER 39

Rhoui was near the door when the plain pine box was lifted through it and above the heads of the men waiting silently to honor their leader. A gun was fired, igniting a cacophony of the same all over the Old City, then all East Jerusalem. Rhoui, like everyone else, was screaming, crying for vengeance as the body of Abdul Khader passed overhead along the road of wall-to-wall humanity. Rhoui pushed himself through the crowd, taking the shortcut through the Old City's narrow streets to the Holy Mount and the Dome of the Rock mosque. He had to fight crowds as men pushed and shoved to get there, to see one more time the remains of their great leader. The coffin was just coming onto the square and thousands welcomed it with a roar of mourning. He had never heard such noise! It was as it should be. In the minds of Nationalist Palestinian Arabs, there had been no greater fighter for their freedom than Abdul Khader, and now he was gone. Their hearts, their spirits, were broken.

But they would rise again. He would rise again. When tears for his leader washed the stones of the mount, when the time of mourning was over, he would fight! They must not give up Khader's dream. He would never give up. Never.

As the body passed inside the Dome of the Rock mosque, the determination of these thousands of fighters resounded off the walls and stones of the temple mount, tears on every cheek, anger in every eye. They would die as martyrs as he had done, fight for Palestine as he had fought, their will and determination solid as iron. But who would lead them? Who could help them carry out their promises?

There was Khader's brother, taking hold of the coffin to carry it inside, next to him Emile Ghoury and Kemal Erakat. Hasan Salameh stood farther off as did others who had fought with Khader in half a dozen places for fifteen long years. But none of them were like the man they loved and admired more than any other. Though most would not admit it, though Rhoui Aref refused to see it, the Palestinian army would die with Abdul Khader Husseini. They would fight, they would try, but the military machine of the Arab League was preparing to swallow them up.

Rhoui returned to his battlements later that day, stunned and fighting the fear that comes with great loss. Finally, he left another in charge and returned to the streets of the Old City. He wandered aimlessly, eventually looking up to find he was standing in front of their shop. Theo's work was left unfinished, the windows and doors boarded shut. He thought of the days when he and Izaat had sat here discussing how they would have many shops and be wealthy men, selling goods from far away places and dreaming the dreams of the young and free.

But those days were over. Izaat was gone. So was Mary and their father, his wife and children. As he stood there, an overwhelming feeling of utter emptiness nearly knocked him to his knees, and he had to lean against the rough-sawn timbers of his burned out store to keep his feet.

What had happened to them? How long had it been since the day Mary had walked into the shop and found them talking so brashly about war and killing? He remembered Izaat's words. *And you, Rhoui. You have a family. Are you willing to lose them?* The reality of his life hit him in the stomach like a man's fist. His family—gone. The cost had been higher than he had imagined.

He pushed himself away from the wall and forced himself back up the street. He must get away from here. There was no turning back now. His family would come back when this was finished, and Mary with them. Though he could do nothing about his father's death and Izaat's imprisonment and possible execution, most things would return to normal again once the Jews were gone, the war won. He steeled himself against the emptiness and picked up his pace. The Brits would be leaving the Old City soon, then they could finish with the Jews in the Quarter. After that he would go to Katamon and bring his wife and children home, find Mary and work things out between them. Surely she had seen what he had done for her that day at the wall. Surely she understood that he really did care for her. She would understand. But first he must fight a war. It was all that was left to him.

SEE CHAPTER NOTES

CHAPTER 40

May 14, 1948

The battle for the Jerusalem/Tel Aviv Road went on several more days, even though most of the Arabs had followed the body of Abdul Khader back to Jerusalem. ETZEL and LEHI, desperate to get into the picture of success that the Haganah had drawn, attacked the village of Deir Yassin with Haganah consent and once more assaulted Kastel. Because most of the thousands of fighters that had come to avenge Khader's death had gone back to the city for his burial the Jewish soldiers entered what was left of Kastel nearly unopposed. In Deir Yassin the fanatic members of ETZEL and LEHI went crazy with blood lust and massacred almost an entire innocent village of mostly Arab women and children. It would be one of the biggest blunders of the war, giving the Arabs something even greater than the death of Abdul Khader and the bombing of the Semiramis Hotel to rally their lagging spirits and once more ignite their desire for vengeance.

With Kastel and most of the road back in Jewish hands, the *Nachshon* convoy could finally return to the coast and did, 86 hours and 49 minutes after leaving for Jerusalem. It quickly loaded for another run and over the next few days, the dwindling supplies of the Jewish portion of the Holy City would be replenished.

Ephraim didn't return to consciousness for nearly two weeks. When he did, he saw Hannah standing above him with tears in her eyes, her hand tightly gripping his. She leaned over and kissed him on the cheeks, crying, telling him how much she loved him. Then he floated off into dark space again.

It was another two weeks before he recovered enough to be told that Aaron's death had been no dream and that Jack had died of his wounds. His body had been sent back to England. Ephraim cried out in anguish of soul, and he and Hannah shed enough tears to water the dusty plains of the Negev before he could get control again.

"Did they find Aaron's body?" Ephraim asked.

"The Arabs control that part of hills. We couldn't get to him."

Ephraim bit his lip against the tears. "How . . . how is David?" he asked when he could finally talk.

"Both he and Beth are okay." She paused for a long moment before speaking again. "David has stronger faith than I realized, Ephraim. So does Beth. They have been a great strength to me over the last month." She was so very tired. Aaron—gone. She still couldn't believe it, still expected him to walk into the apartment and sit down to talk. She couldn't believe that such talks would never happen again. She took a deep breath. There was only one person she knew it would hurt more. "We haven't been able to find Mary to let her know," she said sadly. "We contacted the American consulate in Beirut. They say she was taken to one of the refugee camps in the south of Lebanon. They will try to reach her. I sent them a letter to give to her. I . . . I wish we could go . . . that we could help her. It will be horrible for her."

"We can try." He wanted to sit up but knew he couldn't, his strength still not sufficient. "As soon as I get out of here, we'll find her, Hannah."

Hannah rubbed his cheek with her fingers. "There is something else, darling. Something important."

He could see the concern in her eyes and felt it in the tightening of her hand around his. "We have to take you to the United States."

He lifted his head, a questioning look in his eyes. "To the States? But why? I can . . ."

"You won't walk again without the right kind of surgery. Even . . . even then . . ." her voice trailed off as her throat and mouth dried up. "You have a spinal injury. They can't help you here. We leave for the States as soon as you are able to travel. No arguments."

Ephraim felt the sick feeling in his stomach grow, the words bouncing around in his head like a ping-pong ball. "No, I . . . I'll be fine. We can't leave. This is our home, Hannah. We—"

"Can return as soon as you are able. For now we have to get you the right kind of help or you may never walk again." She said it firmly this time. "No arguments."

"But what about David. And Beth. They . . ."

"We can take care of them." The voice came from the doorway, and Ephraim lifted his head enough to see Naomi standing in the doorway. She quickly came to stand on the opposite side of the bed, Abraham at her side.

"Hi," Naomi said, gripping his hand. Ephraim could see the tears in her eyes and that she was doing her best to keep them back.

"Aaron will be alright, Naomi. Death isn't the end, I promise." Ephraim said it weakly but squeezed her hand.

Hannah choked back the tears and several dropped from Naomi's eyes onto the bed sheets. She sniffed to get control as Abraham spoke.

"Perhaps this isn't the best time, but if I don't speak now . . . well . . . I . . . I may never get the courage again. I . . . uh . . . I've waited nearly a month, and I can't sleep or eat. I have to do it now." He stiffened his backbone. "Ephraim, you aren't Naomi's father, but she says you are as close as any man could be to one, so I must ask you." He took a deep breath as Ephraim wiped away a tear. "Ordinarily my father would ask this, but Naomi says she expects me to do it, and if I can't, to forget it altogether." He glanced at Naomi who was smiling. "She says many things will have to change, but—"

"Never mind that. Just ask him," Naomi said.

Another deep breath. "I want to marry Naomi. Will you give your permission?"

Ephraim looked at Naomi, their conversation sticking in his mind. "Are you sure you are ready to be a rabbi's wife?"

"I am sure I want to be Abraham's wife. We haven't decided on the rabbi part yet." She looked at Abraham. "Who knows what a good woman can do to change the mind of a good man." She gripped his arm and held him close. Abraham began to sweat a little, and Ephraim couldn't help but smile.

"Of course you have my permission. What about you, Hannah? Is this a good match?"

"Yes, I think it is. Congratulations," Hannah said, coming around the bed to hug them both. Ephraim watched them as his heart ached with happiness and with grief. Oh, how he wished Aaron were here to see this. How he wished the boy had not left him.

Naomi leaned down and kissed Ephraim on the cheek. "Thank you, Pops." She said it with a grin. "I want you at the wedding."

"I wouldn't miss it," he said, gripping her hand and kissing it lightly. Suddenly he felt very tired, and Hannah could see that he was worn out.

"Off with you," she said to Abraham and Naomi. "We'll talk more later."

"Wait," Ephraim said in a weak voice. "Abraham."

"Yes," Abraham turned back, a questioning look on his face.

Ephraim reached for his military copy of the Book of Mormon that sat on the end table and extended it toward Abraham. "I have only one requirement. Read this. Both of you. Together."

"But I . . . I am a Jew and . . ."

"It is about Jews."

Naomi understood. "We will read it, Ephraim. For you and for Hannah."

With that they were gone, and Hannah gripped his hand once more. They sat quietly, both dealing with their elation and their grief until Ephraim dropped off to sleep. When she knew it was a sound one, Hannah slipped her hand free of his and walked to the dresser near the door where she had put their radio. Almost midnight. Almost time. She turned it on and adjusted the volume to a whisper, then sat close, waiting.

A lot had happened in the last month. They had lost the Jerusalem/Tel Aviv Road again, but they had gained many victories in other places, and she was confident they were finally ready to fight for a country. American support had finally come with President Truman telling his cabinet that once a state was declared, they would recognize it. After that, they would have only a war to win. It would not be easy, but she had never lost the feeling that it was worth it—even when she had been told about Jack, Aaron, and Ephraim. The cost of freedom was a heavy cost, and the cost of Judah's freedom would be no different. Oh, how she had prayed that all her family would be protected, even as she knew the chances of losing some of them were great. As she had grieved those first few nights over Aaron, and for

Mary, she had come to realize that his blood, like the blood of many others, would be the price. No family in Israel would go untouched. No family! Not even hers.

She heard the announcer and knew the time had come. David Ben-Gurion and other Yishuv leaders had gathered at the Tel Aviv Museum for the reading of her country's Declaration of Independence. The announcer faded away and the strong, raspy voice of David Ben-Gurion replaced it. He read the words of their new declaration and she listened intently to each one.

"The State of Israel has arisen!" Ben-Gurion's voice was confident, determined—the example of all Judah. "This meeting is over." There was no applause, no celebration, as there had been that night months earlier as Hannah and Naomi had stood in a Tel Aviv yard and heard the announcement of partition. Everyone now knew what the price of their freedom would be. It was nothing to celebrate about.

Hannah reached over and switched off the radio, then leaned back in the chair and closed her eyes. Soon she, Ephraim, and their children would go to the United States. She only hoped their new country could survive until they returned.

* * *

Mary stared at the letter in her hand. It was from Hannah. The shock roiled over her like a desert sandstorm. Through her tears she reread the words. *I am so sorry to tell you that Aaron was killed at the battle for Kastel. We grieve with you—for you—and want you to know we pray for you and love you.*

The letter then mentioned Ephraim's wounds and the need to take him to the States. It ended with the words: *Please, if you come back to Israel, and if we are here, find us. May God grant that our paths will cross again. Eternally, Hannah and Ephraim.*

She watched blankly as the line of Palestinian refugees walked past her, hardly noticing her shaking shoulders as her heart broke and the rush of anguish beat on her mercilessly. "No," she whispered. Then she screamed it, her face to the heavens and her fists pounding her chest. An old man stopped to help as two of the Lebanese soldiers came over, their faces stern. Knowing they might use force, the old man waved them back as he tried to coax Mary to her feet and get her moving. She got up, her shoulders sagging with grief. She stumbled for more than a mile before she exhausted her tears, the old man still helping her struggle toward the camp to which they and other refugees had been sent.

"Stop!" yelled one of the soldiers. "Time for rest. Ten minutes."

Mindlessly she sat down. The letter was crumpled, but she slowly unfolded it and read it again. It was not a dream. Aaron was gone. She lay her head back against the large rock by which she sat, closing her eyes, her hand going automatically to her stomach. They had spent a month of their lives together. Only a month, and yet it was the most wonderful month of her life. The weeks since then seemed like an eternity. How could he be gone? How could she endure without him? How could it be that their child would never know him? Frantically she rummaged through the small bag with her belongings and found the Book of Mormon Hannah had given her. With more tears flowing, she shuffled through the pages. She read, she shuffled more pages. She read more, trying to find some comfort, some reason, some escape from the horror that gripped her heart. How could she survive without him? How could she go on? How?

Then a peaceful but powerful thought came to her. The baby. Boy or girl, it was Aaron's child. It would never know his father except from her. She must live for the child. The child must bear his name, his face, his laugh, his love.

"Time to go," the soldier yelled. The long line of people got to their feet. Mary stood and fell in line. She dried her tears, stiffened her back and her resolve. Somehow she would return to Palestine and raise their baby. Jew and Arab, the child would live to carry its father's dreams into the future, and somehow the two of them would survive. It was enough to go on.

SEE CHAPTER NOTES

CHAPTER NOTES

PROLOGUE

Elder Orson Hyde, like all members of his day, had heard the Prophet Joseph talk of the gathering of Israel and the return of the Jews. The prophecies were clear, Joseph said, and the Jews must begin to gather to their homeland. The Spirit had been moving upon Elder Hyde as well. In March 1840, he had been given a vision that outlined his mission to the Holy Land. Each major city he would travel through was shown him, along with many things about Jerusalem. Upon revealing this sacred dream to the Prophet, Joseph assured him it was of God and he must make plans to go. He then assigned him officially to dedicate the land for the return of the Jews.

Following Elder Hyde's dedication of the Holy Land, the spirit of the Lord began to brood upon the Jews. Out of the political, economic, and religious turmoil of Europe and Russia, men such as Moses Hess, Joseph Salvador, Moses Montefiore, Leo Pinsker, and Theodor Herzl were touched by the spirit of gathering. They wrote a number of tracts appealing to the religious communities of Jews to flee to Jerusalem. Then, with the advent of political Zionism in the late 1800s, even those who considered themselves Jewish by blood only began to return to the land of Israel, then known as Palestine. But it took the unfortunate events of the Nazi holocaust to move them in much greater numbers. Out of this furnace of affliction came the greater physical return of the Jews, and from it would grow the insatiable desire to make for themselves a home, a desire that would lead them to continued conflict and persecution.

The future of Palestine after Elder Hyde's dedicatory prayer would, unfortunately, be as bloody as its past. The tribulation heaped upon the Jews did not end with the beginning of their return to Palestine. It will continue until the day they are finally turned to God, as the scriptures do not say the return of the Jews would be a totally righteous endeavor. They are in an apostate condition, and with rare exceptions, it is the furnace of affliction that drives them back to Palestine, not faith. Jews may live on the land politically and militarily, but their spiritual gathering is yet future. This greater return, the return to the God of Israel both as Jehovah and Messiah, will take place only after more persecution. God will separate himself a people prepared to receive him as their God and their Messiah. Up to the very last war we know as Armageddon, this purging of Judah will continue, but Judah will survive as a people. As Wilford Woodruff said on one occasion to Edmond Rothschild, a prominent Jewish Leader who was instrumental in providing funds for Jewish settlements in the beginning of the physical return: "But when this affliction comes, the living God, that led Moses through the wilderness, will deliver you, and your Shiloh will come and stand in your midst and will fight your battles; and you will know him, and the afflictions of the Jews will be at an end" (Matthias F. Cowley, *Wilford Woodruff: History of His Life and Labors,* [Salt Lake City, UT: Bookcraft, 1964], 509).

CHAPTER ONE

Haj Amin El Husseini is one of the most controversial characters of his day. As Grand Mufti of Jerusalem, he had great influence in the Arab Muslim World and used it effectively against the Jews and in favor of his nationalistic goals. "The mufti was the key nationalist figure among Muslims in Palestine. Fearful that increased Jewish immigration to Palestine would damage Arab standing in the area, the mufti engineered the bloody riots against Jewish settlements in 1929 and 1936" ("Haj Amin el Husseini," *Jewish Virtual Library,* par. 1). During World War II the Germans welcomed Haj Amin with open arms and a chance to continue his fight against the Jews. He organized The Research Institute on the Jewish Problem in the Moslem World and a Muslim clerical academy in Dresden. The graduates of the Academy were destined to spearhead Nazi rule in Muslim lands as they were conquered. When the war was over, the Allies considered including him in the Nuremberg trials, but he escaped before they made a final decision.

The Balfour Declaration was issued in 1917 by Arthur James Balfour, the British foreign secretary. It pledged British support for the Zionist movement and stated:

"His Majesty's Government views with favour the establishment in Palestine of a national home for the Jewish people, and will use their best endeavours to facilitate the achievement of this object, it being clearly understood that nothing shall be done which may prejudice the civil and religious rights of existing non-Jewish communities in Palestine, or the rights and political status enjoyed by Jews in any other country" (Schroeter, 74).

Of course, the Arab and Jewish interpretations of this letter are vastly different, and the Arabs call it a betrayal to previous promises given to them whereby Palestine was to become a part of the greater Arab states. Because of the unrest in Palestine from 1936–39, the British issued the Churchill White Paper, which offered a new interpretation of the Balfour Declaration. He stated,

"Unauthorized statements have been made to the effect that the purpose in view is to create a wholly Jewish Palestine. . . . His Majesty's Government regards any such expectation as impracticable and have no such aim in view. Nor have they at any time contemplated as appears to be feared by the Arab Delegation, the disappearance or the subordination of the Arabic population, language, or culture in Palestine" (83).

The White Paper also affirmed that Jewish emigration to Palestine would be regulated to prevent there being "a burden upon the people of Palestine as a whole" (83). It is interesting that the Jewish leaders, although they viewed it as a serious whittling down of the Balfour Declaration, signed it, whereas the Arab leaders, who should have been glad for it, refused.

The British Mandate was given by the League of Nations after World War I and ran from 1922–1948.

The British found themselves, because of their contradictory promises [to Arab and Jew], in a most difficult and untenable situation— but one primarily of their own making. On one hand the Zionists anticipated large numbers of Jews immigrating to Palestine and even began to speak of the establishment of a Jewish state. On the other hand, the Palestinians feared dispossession at the hands of the Zionists and naturally rejected British promises to deliver their country into the hands of what were, by virtually any definition, outsiders.

Despite British policy and its back-and-forth nature, first supporting one side and then the other, Jewish immigration did in fact increase. Indeed, after the Nazi victory in Germany in 1933, immigration rose sharply and in 1935 over 60,000 Jews came into Palestine. ("The British Mandate," *Palestine,* www.arab.net, article, par. 6,8)

However, at its most critical juncture from 1936–39, the British seriously curtailed immigration, causing the Jews to revolt and organizations like ETZEL and LEHI to flourish as they determined to drive out the British and force war with the Arabs.

CHAPTER TWO

With the British willing to confiscate every weapon they could find both aboard incoming ships and in hidden caches around the country, getting guns and ammunition, fighter planes, and armor to Eretz Israel would be nearly impossible without transport planes. The very life of the Jewish state depended on getting an air force. One of the planners of the Israeli Air Force was Aaron Remez, Israeli pilot who had flown for the British for four years during World War II. Remez and a half-dozen others began the process of building an air force with four private pleasure planes, an air taxi, and twenty pilots with varying degrees of ability. They set up office under the guise of the Palestine Flying Club.

Their first task had been to train pilots and build crude airfields without British clearance. Eventually they would try and occupy the British airfields. Under the guise of fields being readied for planting, they cleared ten strips at settlements that might be cut off in a war. Ben-Gurion had told the Haganah that no settlements were to be given up, that if they were to hold on to the land they had been given, they could not let the Arabs drive them from one inch of it. The airfields were one way of trying to ensure supplies if the Arabs controlled the roads.

CHAPTER FOUR

The Mufti Haj Amin el Husseini wished to establish Muslim superiority in Palestine, and though he needed Christian Arab cooperation, Christians had every reason to be wary, and most refused to support both him and his methods because of his historical treatment of Christians.

> In the early 1900s, sporadic attacks on Christians by bands of Muslims occurred in many Palestinian towns (just as they were against Jews) . . . : and "during the Palestinian Arab revolt in the late 1930s, which involved very few Christians, if Christian villagers refused to supply the terrorist bands with weapons and provisions, their vines were uprooted and their women raped . . . In 1936 [the rebellion led by the Mufti and his fanatic followers] marched through the Christian village of Bier Zeit near Ramallah chanting: 'We are going to kill the Christians.'" (Yehoshua Porath, *The Palestinian–Arab National Movement, 1929–1939: From Riots to Rebellion*, [London: Frank Cass, 1977], 268–70 as quoted in David Raab, *IMRA Report: The Beleaguered Christians of the Palestinian Controlled Area*, 15)

Many Christians stayed neutral or left the country, whereas others decided that Amin was their only alternative.

CHAPTER FIVE

Shoshanna Farhi is a real person who was killed aboard the bus. This and the attack on the Goldman boy, also mentioned, were the first in several that day, and they are considered the first Jewish casualties of the War of Independence.

CHAPTER SIX

ETZEL and LEHI were two semiterrorist military organizations that did not agree with the leaders of the Jewish Agency and decided to take a more violent approach to getting a state. Though the

Haganah had used violence against repression and unfair tactics by the British on occasion, their intent was to force the British to be evenhanded while sending them a message that they had the ability to fight back as a people. For ETZEL and LEHI, the greatest danger to the Jewish people was the British. They had become single-minded in that belief, making the destruction of everything British their first priority. They attacked and kidnapped soldiers, blew up warehouses and railroads, and generally carried on a terrorist war against the British. Even when it seemed apparent that the British were going to leave and the Arabs were the growing threat, ETZEL and LEHI continued to put the pressure on the British. None of it helped Jewish-British relationships. In fact, their terrorism had turned many British against the Jews as a people and were continuing to do so when it was needed the least.

CHAPTER ELEVEN

In A.D. 66–72, the Jews tried to throw off the Roman yoke at a time when the Empire was in chaos. The Romans responded by sending their legions. The final battles took place in Jerusalem as Titus put it under siege.

To breach the walls, Titus began building earthworks and siege engines for the assault. While this was being done, the Jews dug tunnels underneath the walls of the city, supporting the ceiling with wooden beams. When the Romans pushed their machines over the tunnels, the Jews set fire to the beams and retreated back inside the city. The tunnels collapsed under the heavy weight of the machines, toppling the machines and saving the Jews for at least a few more weeks. Portions of those tunnels remained for centuries. The Cardo was built later when the Romans rebuilt a portion of the city and called it Aelia Capitolina. In the centuries that followed, it was buried under ruins and other buildings.

Avraham Halperin was the one who "rediscovered" the tunnels and opened them for use by the Old City's residents. The British learned of the tunnels late in the war and tried to get the Jews to allow them access, but the Jews refused. The British, knowing it would cause a bloody battle if they forced their way in, decided to leave it be. The tunnels proved to be extremely important to the defense of the Jewish Quarter until that part of the city was captured by the Arab army of Transjordan.

The scrolls referred to are the Dead Sea Scrolls that were actually found at this same time. Sukenik discovered a portion of the scrolls, but others were found as well. Scholars with the American School of Oriental Research in Jerusalem viewed several belonging to Metropolitan Samuel. The existence of these was announced on April 11, 1948, and Sukenik announced his two weeks later. So secretive had been the dealings surrounding both sets of scrolls that neither group knew of the existence of the other. During the war, Metropolitan moved his to Lebanon, then on to the United States where he put them up for sale. Yigal Yadin, head of Haganah operations (1947–48), was also an archaeologist and the son of Eleazar Sukenik. He was in the United States when Metropolitan was trying to sell his scrolls. Through a series of cloak-and-dagger negotiations, Eleazar purchased the scrolls and returned them to Israel where they have become one of the most important finds of the twentieth century.

CHAPTER FIFTEEN
The Arab Liberation Army (ALA) was made up of volunteers from the Arab world, and though it sounded awesome on the radio and in the papers, it was an untrained and undisciplined group. Because it had commanders and fighters from all the League nations, it was fragmented and ineffective, each commander more loyal to his own country than to Kaukji. Furthermore, because the ALA was concentrating on larger scale operations for which they were not trained or prepared, the guerillas were pushed back by smaller, better-trained Haganah forces.

CHAPTER EIGHTEEN
The Druze are another religious community that has inhabited the the Middle East for the past 1000 years. Their roots are in Islam, but they aren't Islamic. Their religion is an interpretation of Islam, Christianity, and Judaism, and they follow prophets from all three, including Salaman the Persian and Mohammed, John the Baptist and

Jesus of Nazareth, Moses and Jethro. They don't adhere to the rituals of any of these faiths, which has separated them from all three, though Muslims have attempted to keep them in the fold for centuries, mostly for political reasons.

During the Arab-Israeli conflict of this time, some Druze villages aligned themselves with the Jews, others with the Arabs. Many attempted to remain neutral. By the end of 1948, however, most villages had signed agreements with the Jews, anticipating better treatment under a Jewish government than under an Arab one.

CHAPTER TWENTY-NINE

The Jerusalem/Tel Aviv Road was a significant lifeline for the Jews who were living in Jerusalem. Abdul Kahder initially planned to cut this lifeline with a semipermanent roadblock. This would be easily defensible with a small number of his fighters. Two things, however, prevented him from implementing this plan.

First, the British, he realized, would be compelled to break the roadblock. Second, Abdul Khader wanted to draw the villagers in the communities along the road into his campaign. And so he decided to launch individual attacks on each passing convoy and to allow the villagers who had aided the attack to join in looting the convoys afterward. Knowing well the mentality of his people, he knew that each success and its spoils would provide a spur to draw into his ambushes an even larger number of village fighters. Their growing numbers would give him a steadily expanding strength to match the certain growth in the size of the convoys' escorts. . . .

His offensive caused the British little concern. For the British Army, the Jerusalem/Tel Aviv road had assumed a secondary importance to their main evacuation routes, in the north to Haifa, in the south to the Suez Canal. . . . [They] ran a two-car patrol twice daily down the road. The patrol was called a "swan." "You'd boom down in the morning and boom back," recalled the squadron's commander. "Then you'd do the same thing again just before nightfall." The safe passage of those patrols was sufficient, in the eyes of the British command, to constitute an open road. Abdul Khader's men were careful to interfere with them as little as possible.

For the Jews, each convoy to Jerusalem was an ordeal, a brutal, desperate struggle to claw one more load of goods past Abdul Khader's increasingly effective ambushes" (Collins and Lapierre, 143–145).

CHAPTER THIRTY-SEVEN

Abdul Khader was in Damascus on April 3 when he heard of the Jews' attempt to gain control of the road to Jerusalem and that Kastel had fallen. He immediately went to the League's chairman and pleaded for artillery to support his attempt to recapture the road but was denied. Safwat Pasha, head of military operations, told him Kaukji needed the artillery in the north and it couldn't be sent to Jerusalem. Khader angrily declared the chairman a traitor. He left Damascus determined he would never return, never beg for another rifle, bullet, or grenade.

He arrived at Ramallah and Beir Zeit on April 4 and immediately took control of command of the battle. As Khader's forces began to lose more and more villages along the ridges overlooking the road, he realized that retaking Kastel might be their last hope.

After consultation with his aides and commanders, they decided that an all-out assault from four directions was necessary. To accomplish such a feat, they must first retake several villages occupied by the Jews. Khader called for more men from Jerusalem, then left for the battlefield. By the time he reach Nebi Samwil, 220 men joined him, bringing with them enough mortars to blow up half the mountain.

When Khader reached his destination near Tzuba village, the rain that had been pummeling them most of the night stopped. Under cover of darkness, he deployed his men and prepared for battle against the villages he needed. Before dawn, they had taken Tzuba Quarry and were moving toward Kastel.

CHAPTER THIRTY-NINE

Abdul Khader's body was "wrapped with flowers and the flag of his Palestine movement and exposed in a plain pine box in the sitting room of his brother's house. . . . Since Moslem tradition demanded swift burial, neither his wife nor his children would reach Jerusalem in time for his interment" (Collins and Lapierre, 276–77). As his body left the house, a shot was fired as "the signal for the wildest outburst of gunfire Jerusalem had yet heard. From every corner of the Arab city, Abdul Khader's followers sent a noisy barrage skyward, snapping telephone cables and electric wires and killing two bystanders. . . . Thus began the most grandiose funeral Jerusalem had witnessed in generations" (277). He was interred in the octagonal Dome of the Rock Mosque—a rare privilege.

CHAPTER FORTY

Like the Haganah's bombing of the Semiramis Hotel, the massacre at Deir Yassin by ETZEL and LEHI forces was a blotch on the record of the Jewish dream of a state. ETZEL and LEHI captured the peaceful village and then methodically murdered more than a hundred men, women, and children—with apparent tacit complicity by some Haganah leaders. It was several days before word got out of what had happened, and then rumors began to fly. The truth would not be known for years, and even today there are serious differences of opinion on what happened and how it affected the war. However, one author states the opinion of most:

"Deir Yassin had a profound political and demographic effect. Despite a formal Jewish Agency Executive letter of apology and explanation to King Abdullah [the one Arab who seemed to want to make peace with the Jews], the incident seemed to push Jordan into the arms . . . of the Arab states. . . . Certainly the news enraged Arab fighting men, and "Deir Yassin!" became a rallying cry for combatants bent on revenge" (Morris, 209).

A few days later, Khader's supporters would reap vengeance by attacking a convoy of doctors, patients, and nurses going to Hadassah hospital. They would butcher 77 men and women who were unarmed. A few weeks later they would participate in the attack on the Etzion block by Transjordan's Arab legion. When the block was forced to surrender, they would round up the survivors in the central settlement and mow them down. Another 120 were killed. The cry was "Deir Yassin!"

"The battle for Kastel wasn't the only effort put forth by the Haganah as they turned offensive. The Arabs initiated two battles in the north, and the Jews answered them effectively. The ALA, with the cooperation of numerous villages, attacked the kibbutz of Mishmar Ha Amek and nearly overran it, but the Jews took the offensive and leveled ten villages surrounding the kibbutz, and all the inhabitants either fled or were expelled. The ALA was driven into the mountains west of Galilee to lick its wounds. It was the same at kibbutz Yohanan where a Druze unit of the ALA—all Druze had not committed to the Haganah by this time—attacked. Driven back on April 16, the Druze sued for peace, then allied themselves with the Jews. It was another defeat for the ALA.

With more victories over villages around Jaffa, and with Arab militiamen looting Arab houses and abusing their occupants in Jaffa itself, the population fled. By the time Ben-Gurion declared statehood on May 15, only five thousand of the eighty thousand Arab inhabitants remained.

This would no longer be a Palestinian war, but an Arab one. The big losers in Haj Amin's greed to have it all, and in the unwillingness of so many Arabs to negotiate a peace with the Jews in those early months, were the Palestinian people. Encouraged by both the violence and the promise of the Arab nations to return them to their homes soon, hundreds of thousands left the country, foolishly trusting their destiny to Arab leaders who had only their own interests at heart and who would do as much damage to Palestinian sovereignty as the Jews ever dreamed of.

When David Ben-Gurion stood on a podium and declared the Jewish state of Israel on May 15, 1948, it was the darkest day in the history of the Arabs of Palestine. In my opinion, that is not just because of the state of Israel, but because they had lost the chance to have a state of their own.

SELECTED BIBLIOGRAPHY

Armstrong, Karen. *Islam: A Short History*. New York: Modern Library, 2000.

Collins, Larry, and Dominique Lapierre. *O Jerusalem!* New York: Simon and Schuster, 1988.

Galbraith, David B., D. Kelly Ogden, and Andrew C. Skinner. *Jerusalem: The Eternal City.* Salt Lake City, UT: Deseret Book, 1996.

Gilbert, Martin. *Israel: A History.* New York: William Morrow, 1998.

Glassé, Cyril. *The Concise Encyclopedia of Islam.* New York: Harper Collins, 1991.

Heckelman, A. Joseph. *American Volunteers and Israel's War of Independence.* New York: Ktav Publishing, 1974.

Hiro, Dilip. *Sharing the Promised Land: A Tale of Israelis and Palestinians.* New York: Olive Branch, 1996.

Kagan, Benjamin. *The Secret Battle for Israel.* Translated by Patsy Southgate. Cleveland, OH: World Publishing Co., 1966.

Milstein, Uri. *History of Israel's War of Independence.* 4 vols. Translated and edited by Alan Sacks. Lanham, MD: Univ. Press of America, 1996–98.

Morris, Benny. *Righteous Victims: A History of the Zionist-Arab Conflict, 1881–1999.* New York: Vintage Books, 2001.

Murphy-O'Conner, Jerome. *The Holy Land: An Oxford Archaelogical Guide.* 4th ed. New York: Oxford Univ. Press, 1998.

Schroeter, Daniel J. *Israel: An Illustrated History.* New York: Oxford Univ. Press, 1998.

Weiss, Jeffrey, and Craig Weiss. *I Am My Brother's Keeper: American Volunteers in Israel's War of Independence, 1947–49.* Atglen, PA: Schiffer Military History, 1998.

Excerpt from Faith of Our Fathers
Volume Three

2 July 1863
Gettysburg, Pennsylvania
Little Round Top

"We're supposed to hold them off for how long?" Luke Birmingham stared at Colonel Joshua Chamberlain's assistant as the shots continued to pop all around them.

"As long as we must. If they take this hill, they'll infiltrate the whole Union line."

Luke stared at the man for a moment and finally nodded once and gripped his weapon, crouching low beside the other men of the 20th Maine. Luke and his cousin, Ben Birmingham, had been sent with a few others of the 1st Massachusetts Cavalry to reinforce the troops fighting on the outskirts of a small town called Gettysburg, Pennsylvania.

Luke and Ben had been separated, as had Luke and his horse. The horses were in the care of his commanding officer of the 1st Massachusetts, and Luke and Ben both had received an extremely hasty education in foot soldiering. They were fighting as infantrymen for the first time since their enlistment, and although being without the animal caused Luke no small amount of anxiety, his separation from Ben affected him much more strongly. It galled him to admit that as a man of twenty-eight he was nervous to be without his cousin, but in the year since their enlistment, he and Ben had spent every waking and sleeping moment together, side by side. To now be under such ferocious fire without him was unsettling.

The Confederates had reportedly entered the town of Gettysburg looking for shoes. As Ben watched them swarm the hills and fight on the fields below his vantage point, he wondered how they managed to go onward, marching barefoot for miles up and down the eastern seaboard. Luke was exhausted much of the time, and he usually had a horse to ride, let alone shoes on his feet.

Now, as he tried to focus on the task at hand, time stretched ahead, punctuated by the continual pop of gunshot and boom of cannon. His head ached horribly from the noise, and fear lodged in his throat, choking him. He had swallowed his own bile time after time when watching men around him fall—sometimes dismembered, disembow-eled, or beheaded—to the ground. The thought that he was inflicting the same on the men who charged the hill made him all the more sick, but self-preservation was a powerful motivator, and Luke forced himself to remember that it was better that the enemy fall than him, shoeless or not.

In his mind was a prayer that repeated itself over and over again. *Please, Father, please let this be over soon.* Could it have been only scant weeks before that Ben had baptized him so peacefully in the river? Luke had felt such calm then, such joy. A feeling of love unlike any he had experienced had enveloped him that day, and he had basked in it. Such a simple prayer it was too, yet poignant in its spiritual beauty. *I baptize you in the name of the Father, and of the Son, and of the Holy Ghost . . .* He had wanted to fly to the very heavens that day and proclaim glory to the Father for the entire world to hear.

And now he was in purgatory. How could two such events occur so closely together in time? How could one experience the glory of God one day and be thrust into the fiery depths so soon after? *Father, there are so many things I haven't done! I want to share Thy goodness with the world. I want to serve Thee, to love Thee. I long to see my sweet family again, my Abigail . . .*

For one brief moment, it was as if he were far away from the horror of the battlefield, and he felt silence, peace, and an arm about his shoulders, buoying him up and bidding him, without words, to be strong. Then, as quickly as the impression had come, it vanished with a loud crash and the acrid smell of death and gun smoke.

Luke looked quickly about him as Chamberlain shouted to his men, who now numbered less than five hundred. Their ammunition was nearly gone, and still the rebels pushed upward. The Union soldiers would surely be overtaken in a matter of minutes unless something drastic happened. Colonel Chamberlain was outlining that something drastic to the men as Luke strained to hear.

"What did he say?" he asked the man next to him.

"We're charging down the side of the hill."

"With *what?*"

"Our bayonets."

Luke looked toward Chamberlain in disbelief but found comfort in the grim determination on the man's face. Chamberlain was a college professor by trade. He was a gentle man who loved learning and loved his country. Luke took a deep breath and fell into place beside the others as they prepared to stampede down the hill.

And then they were running. Luke screamed with the rest of the Union blue as they charged toward the advancing gray-clad men. He was bracing himself for the worst when, to his complete surprise, the Confederate soldiers, who apparently assumed there were more to the 20th Maine's meager number than reality proved, turned and ran.

They ran! Luke stared ahead as the rebels ran back the way they had come only to be confronted and attacked from the rear as well by Chamberlain's Company B, whom Chamberlain had assumed had long since been demolished. As Luke and the others scrambled back into a defensive position atop the hill, he shook his head in disbelief. A passing man in blue slapped him on the arm and said, "Looks like we're not going to die today, eh, soldier?"

Luke released a shaky breath. "Not today."

* * *

3 July 1863

The shells came from nowhere and were suddenly everywhere. Ben stared in dumb shock as men around him dropped to the ground, some with food still clutched in their fingers. Many had been napping, only to rise up in surprise at the sound—a movement that had been their last.

Ben scrambled to the side and took cover behind the guns that were now answering with return fire. He looked around in vain for his commanding officer and shifted his attention instead on finding his cousin. After being separated for a day and a night, they had found each other in the early hours of the morning, and he had been loathe to leave Luke's side for even a moment. When he finally spotted the man who was the mirror image of himself, he saw that Luke was crawling along the ground, favoring one leg.

Ben rushed over to him and pulled him to relative safety far behind the guns. The sun was unmercifully hot overhead, the sky a beautiful blue. On more than one occasion, it had struck Ben as completely ironic that sometimes the ugliest, fiercest battles were fought on the most beautiful of days, in the most beautiful of places. He had seen more of the United States countryside than he ever imagined he would, and he wished it might have been under different conditions.

What had begun for him as a quest to right a wrong, to free the slaves, had grown from there and evolved into a fierce desire to put the country to rights, to unite it as it never had been before. But where the countryside itself was beautiful, the people who inhabited it hated each other with a virulence that drove men to slaughter each other like dogs.

The cousins now served as reinforcements for the men who held the ground at Cemetery Ridge. The first day's fighting had ended with both sides warily withdrawing to assess damage and plan for the next day's maneuvers. Some were saying the rebs had won the day, but only those who dared give voice to truth. The bulk of the soldiers Ben questioned insisted that the Union had emerged ahead at the end of the day despite the fact that they had been driven back into the town of Gettysburg itself, fighting in hand-to-hand combat before finally retreating to Baltimore Pike, southeast of the town.

He could only imagine what the citizens of the town thought as they watched the war being played out on their streets and yards, in front of their churches and places of business. Ben had seen women and children huddled behind their windows, viewing the drama that unfolded before their very eyes.

The second day of fighting saw losses on both sides, but by evening the Union still held advantageous, high-ground positions. Now, as the relentless barrage of Confederate cannon fire continued, answered in kind by the Union guns, Ben pulled Luke toward a ledge of ground that provided shelter for many men who were already gathered there, lying low in the oppressive heat and waiting with their rifles to rise up and fire.

The shells smashed into the ground well behind the small ledge, as well as in front, but the area just behind the rise of earth remained blissfully safe. "Are you hit?" Ben finally asked Luke, having to repeat himself to be heard above the noise of the shell exchange.

Luke looked at his cousin, his expression pained but sheepish. "Not with a shell, no. A man fell on me back there and landed hard on my ankle."

Ben laughed with relief, feeling slightly giddy. Fear had made him insane and lightheaded. "A broken ankle is easily enough fixed," he said, although they both knew that to trust a doctor was to take one's life in one's hands, even if it was an issue of only a small bone. If he weren't careful, a man having entered on complaint of a cough would leave without a limb.

The time Ben and Luke spent in the shelter of the ledge stretched interminably, shells exploding around them and the roar of answering cannon screaming as though it would never cease. Luke checked his pocket watch, wiping away sweat that dripped into his eyes. "Two hours this has been going on," he said. "Don't think I've ever heard of such a thing before."

Ben nodded his head in agreement. "I haven't either." He paused as one brave soldier next to them rose slightly above the line of the earth behind which they hid. The man's gasp was audible, even over the noise of the cannons.

"They're marching across that open field," the soldier shouted to them. "It's hard to see because of all the smoke, but they can't be more than a half mile away by now, marching shoulder to shoulder in perfect formation."

Ben stared at the young man. "Are they mad?"

"Their memories of Fredericksburg must be awfully short," Luke added. "*They* whipped *us* when we tried that."

The soldier shrugged and raked a hand through his hair, which was sodden with sweat. He replaced his cap, his attention turning to the Union artillerymen who were planning a different assault on the advancing Confederate lines. The artillerymen changed their shot to canister, which, according to the soldier who again raised his head to watch, rained shrapnel and balls upon the enemy, exploding on impact and taking large chunks from the rebel ranks as they continued marching across the open field. Each time a hole opened in the lines of gray, the men closed ranks and continued their forward assault.

The soldier sank back down onto the ground with a shake of his head and imparted his information to those crouched low with him. "They must know they're marching straight to their own deaths," the man said. "I think old man Lee has taken leave of his senses."

Ben leaned back against the earth, his thoughts spinning. From the direction of the advancing enemy, they had obviously been occupying Seminary Ridge, a position of high ground. Why on earth would the rebels abandon it for a foolhardy advance that could surely come to no good? Perhaps they assumed their two-hour cannon assault would have sufficiently weakened the Union advantage of high ground on Cemetery Ridge.

Ben looked around to assess the damage behind the wall and saw that while many had fallen, the majority remained unharmed and at the ready. He touched his own weapon for reassurance and readied himself for the command that was sure to come. He didn't have long to wait, for the shout to rise up and open fire rang out, and he and Luke, side by side and surrounded by a sea of blue, lifted their guns to their shoulders and took aim on the enemy.

The soldiers in gray were stopped up behind a fence along a road as they tried to cross, and they fell like toys knocked down in a child's game. Still, the men climbed over one another and marched forward, shoulder to shoulder, arm to arm, holding their fire and their customary rebel yell. They must have been instructed to do so until they were close enough for the effects to be fully felt, and Ben could attest to the chill that crept down the spine of a Union soldier at that awful scream. But the great majority of these men were never going to make it that far. They fell like flies, and Ben could only stare in wonder at their continued advance. How could they keep marching forward like that, knowing, *knowing*, they couldn't possibly escape with their lives? *I would never have believed this if I hadn't seen it with my own two eyes*, he thought as he emptied his gun.

He blinked repeatedly, grateful for small gaps in the smoke that gave him a quick glimpse of the enemy. It was like firing into a fog. He reloaded his weapon and took careful aim, knowing full well that if he didn't fire upon the men in gray, he would be killed himself. It was the only thought that kept him sane in battle; when he examined the matter too closely, his stomach turned and he wondered if God would forgive him.

To his surprise, in his mind flashed images of scripture—verses from the Book of Mormon and thoughts of Captain Moroni and Nephi. There were things that God understood fully that man did not, things that men did to each other that perhaps only God would be able to sift through when the dust settled. Ben knew he would never comprehend the whole of it. All he knew was that he had come to fight for a cause. He had never imagined the toll on both the body and the mind.

Ben gritted his teeth together and continued at the task before him, taking no joy in it but somehow not feeling estranged from his Eternal Father as he had on other occasions. It was for a greater good, a worthier cause than most would comprehend, and Ben could only pray to live out the day with Luke, healthy and well, by his side.

* * *

4 July 1863
Gettysburg, Pennsylvania

The gore of the aftermath was unimaginable. Nine brigades of Confederate manpower had marched on the hill in what was quickly being termed as "Pickett's Charge," and except for one quick break in the Union line, which was summarily stemmed, the brigades had fallen to their doom. It was estimated amongst the men in blue that only half of the rebels who had begun the charge returned to their former position on Seminary Ridge. Some said less than half. Luke overheard a man describing the aftermath as "ghastly heaps of dead men," and another claimed that "the dead to the front of us were so thick that it reminded me of harvest, like huge sheaves of wheat."

Luke had to agree—the piles of spent humanity were almost beyond comprehension. After a while, his conscious mind shut off, and he moved about mechanically, barely noticing the limbs and torn flesh visible on all sides.

The charge up the hill could only be called bravery; the Union men knew full well that as a soldier, one was meant to follow orders. There wasn't a man among them who didn't know how much fear must have settled into the hearts and minds of those who had continued marching while those around them fell to the ground, broken into pieces that could never be fixed.

Luke hobbled on an ankle secured with a makeshift splint and leaned heavily on a long, sturdy stick he had found to use as a cane. "This one's alive," he said to a pair of medics at his side who were walking the ground with stretchers. He knelt down at the side of a young boy in a gray uniform whose shallow breathing was visible in the subtle rise and fall of his chest.

The medics reached under the boy's shoulders and feet and hoisted him on the stretcher. Luke winced at the groan sounding from the soldier's throat and watched as the medics carried him off the field, slipping in puddles of blood and stepping over the dismembered bodies and limbs that littered the ground. More than once he saw those with him, searching for survivors, losing their lunches or heaving from stomachs that had been empty. Luke fell into the latter category; he and Ben both had been unable to eat that morning, the sights and sounds precluding any attempt at appetite their protesting stomachs might have made.

The Confederate army now marched away from the Potomac, slow and arduous the process. Someone had told Luke earlier that morning that the train of retreating soldiers was seventeen miles long. Ben had muttered that it would be wise to rally their forces and go after the rebels, ending the war once and for all, but General Meade had other ideas. The Union had sustained heavy casualties of its own; they needed to rest and regroup, according to the new Union commander.

Luke had agreed with his cousin's assessment—as would Lincoln, they were sure—that although difficult, it would be sound indeed to pursue the rebels while they were weak and put an end to the war. The Union soldiers were exhausted, however, and while in theory it would have been wise to finish Lee's army, Luke wondered how the men would have reacted had Meade given such an order.

Lincoln was far away, not present to give the order himself. There was nothing to be done for it now except to gather their own dead and wounded and try to help the doctors and medics handle the seven thousand Confederate wounded who had been left behind. The small, quaint town of Gettysburg had added to its constituency by thousands when the addition of wounded soldiers from both sides of the conflict were taken into account.

Nearly every available building, including homes, was transformed into a makeshift hospital. Carpets were soaked with blood and ruined beyond repair. Stacks of books, used as pillows, were sticky with blood that flowed from head wounds and severed limbs. As Luke looked around himself at the open fields of battle, he wondered if he would ever be able to banish the awful sight of ruined humanity that surrounded him on all sides. Rarely had he ever considered the fragile state of the human body, nor had he ever imagined he would see so many bodies mangled, destroyed, or ghoulishly bloated from the oppressive heat. Almost as an answer from heaven, the skies eventually opened and rained down a shower that washed away the puddles of blood that had collected on rocks and stone ledges.

Luke raised his face to the sky and closed his eyes as the rain pelted his face and cleaned some of his own grime. It soon was raining so hard that he was forced to duck his head as the pounding hurt his face. Blinding sheets of the moisture fell to the earth in a torrent the likes of which he didn't think he'd ever seen.

Luke didn't envy the retreating Confederate army their task of marching along in the mud, the wounded jarred at every bump or rock in the road as they sat listless in their wagons. He imagined them returning home to their families, who had since faced poverty in most quarters because of the cost of the war, trying to resume their lives and reclaim some sense of normalcy amidst missing limbs, broken bodies, and broken spirits. He felt a stab of pity and compassion that he didn't usually allow himself.

As for the military command, General Meade was pleased that the Union soldiers had kept themselves between the Confederates and Washington. Another attack on Union soil had been a brave attempt on the part of Lee and his men. If the Union had been defeated on their own ground, morale amongst the citizenry of the country would undoubtedly have plunged. As it was, according to the newspapers, cities across the North were celebrating the Fourth of July with renewed vigor and excitement. A major battle had just been won, and politically for Lincoln, it was crucial. If the rebels had been victorious in their assaults, they might even now be marching to the Union capital city, demanding a truce and recognition of the Confederacy. Then all hopes for reuniting the Union with her errant sisters would be destroyed.

The thought of sisters brought to mind an image of Luke's own sister, Anne. The crazy girl had enlisted and been fighting for the past year with a regiment from Ohio, and only just recently had she been discovered and returned home under a flag of truce. She had been wounded, his father wrote, and was ill and weak from time spent in a Confederate prison camp, but otherwise her wound was on the mend.

What had she been thinking? He had asked her as much in his last letter home, but had yet to receive a reply. She was brave and reckless, and he would wager his military pay that she had done it to provide fodder for her writing. Underneath his shock and worry, however, was a deep sense of pride. She had the bravery—or perhaps the foolishness—of ten men.

The rain ran across Luke's neck and shoulders in rivulets, and he leaned heavily on his cane for balance, thankful that he was standing and not lying prostrate, as were the men groaning around him on all sides. He envisioned his family, the people he loved back home in Boston, and wondered how long it would be until he would see them again.